BEYOND
THE NOT SO
IRON CURTAIN

BEYOND
THE NOT SO
IRON CURTAIN

HENRY PETTIT

First paperback edition 2023

978-1-80541-005-8 (paperback)
978-1-80541-004-1 (ebook)

CHAPTER 1

When I was still a schoolboy, I was a bit of a fan of France: French holidays, French language, French food, people with French accents, and so on. I enjoyed learning French at school, too, and along with history and politics, I sat it for A-level in 1989. During my last few months at school I thought that I would probably choose to go to university and study French there. But in a moment of clarity, I realised that there would be nothing unique about me leaving university being able to speak French along with maybe five thousand other job-seeking graduates of French.

Russia was somewhat of a mysterious place to me, a vast country with a rich history and locked behind the Iron Curtain for most of the last century. So, I decided to find a course in Russian instead. I liked learning languages and about other cultures, too, so I quickly got excited about learning all things Russian.

From studying history, I was also familiar with Winston Churchill's quote that Russia was "a riddle, wrapped inside a mystery, inside an enigma". I'd learned all about the Bolshevik Revolution, which led to Russia leaving World War One early in 1917. Then, how Lenin had led the country into the communist era, how Stalin then moved it into a rather terrifying, closed-off place, and about the Cold War years since the end of the Second World War.

It was quite a frightening prospect to *actually* go there, as I would have to do as part of most university courses. Indeed, my first idea after cooling on French had been to study Czech at university or *Czechoslovakian*, as that made it sound even more exotic. I thought that speaking the language of a country with a name as long and complicated as that would be impressive, but there were no courses on offer for Czech. So, the idea of Russian loomed larger, and I settled on a Russian studies and Politics joint honours degree at Bristol University.

The film *A Fish Called Wanda* had just come out in 1988, and the character played by Jamie Lee Curtis got majorly turned on by John Cleese's character when he spoke in Russian. While *A Fish Called Wanda* was perhaps a significant contributing factor for me choosing Russian, I still found the place alluring. It would still be cool to be able to speak Russian, I thought. I also managed to back the decision up with the realisation that as a major world power and a vast country, there could be job opportunities if Russia carried on with its opening-up and rebuilding that Mikhail Gorbachev had begun. Or, to put that another way, *glasnost* and *perestroika*. At Bristol, it turns out that they offered a short mid-course option of learning Czech anyway, so I picked up (and forgot) some Czech, too.

Having achieved the required grades to be accepted by Bristol university, rather than going there straight away in September 1989, I took the option of a year out first, to earn a bit of money and see some of the world. I would spend six months living in Paris, from October to April, having found myself a job there, and then three summer months travelling around America on the Amtrak trains with my best friend from school, Steve.

The stay in Paris would allow me to sign off on my first love, French, and get it as good as possible before throwing myself into the Russian language from scratch when the next year rolled around. The trip around America was purely for some backpacking, sightseeing and fun.

I got sorted with an office job in Paris at a nationwide carpet tile company called Heuga, starting in October 1989. It was nothing more than work experience and came about via a bit of nepotism, as Steve's dad worked for the company's UK arm and pulled a favour for me. I was a general dogsbody carrying out various duties, mostly photocopying, filing, and office clerical work. I also gave a weekly English lesson to some employees using textbooks someone had provided to me. Everyone was amiable, and it was a valuable bit of independence for me. I had my nineteenth birthday while working in

Paris and away from home for the first time.

To begin with, I rented a room at the house of one of the company managers, in the western suburb of Nanterre. It was OK but in a tranquil neighbourhood. After a few weeks, I had made a few friends who were third-year international students at the Sorbonne university, and often I would find myself crashing with them. One of them had a sofa bed in a studio apartment more centrally located, in the 5th arrondissement on Rue St Jacques. But I kept my Nanterre room as my official digs.

Meeting the students who became my friends came about because a schoolmate of mine had just spent the summer working in Paris. As my time overlapped his stay by a few weeks, I managed to fast-track into the social circle he had developed. For most of my six months in Paris, I was best friends with two Swedish students who were both called Anders, and an American Greek student from New York University called Pete. They were all doing their 3rd year in France as part of their degrees in their home countries. It was in Pete's studio apartment where *my* sofa was situated. By day, I was experiencing a grown-up office job, but by night I was getting a foretaste of student life and partying, in advance of my own university life still yet to begin.

We had our own local, a cool student bar called Le Piano Vache, on Rue Laplace, a small street behind the *Pantheon*, which an Irish bartender called Sean managed. We almost lived in that bar, staying until the very small hours, way too many nights per week. Sean had to implore us to go home most nights, poor guy. I was burning the candle at both ends, immersing myself in Parisian nightlife, and smoking like a proper Gaul, too. I liked the Gauloises Blondes cigarettes in the gallic blue packet. I would also favour the blood-red Winston brand, developing a habit that would, unfortunately, stay with me for about twenty years.

I managed to succeed with the primary aim of getting my French to a high level. Until this point in my life, I had not been what you would call an overconfident person; I was rather shy, not speaking out in class too much or craving attention. One night, a French person I had been chatting to for a few minutes thought I was French, although admittedly it was late, a bit noisy, and some beverages had been consumed. Nonetheless, as a nineteen-year-old English guy from the southeast of England, I was happy about it. And I was always a bit too skinny for my liking, although I was 6ft 2ins. But since leaving school, I had become more outgoing; this time in Paris gave me independence and more self-confidence. Earning my own money, paying rent, and making new friends helped me grow up a bit, although I did still demonstrate plenty of childishness and naivety, too, no doubt.

After this, the three months of travelling around

America with Steve improved my physical and body confidence. It sounds cliché, but it was a year of self-discovery. We lugged our rucksacks around the country, camped, hiked, and got good suntans from the sunshine of Florida, Louisiana, Texas, and California. I also managed to meet up with one of the Anders and Pete in New York for a few days, where I was briefly smitten by Anders' sister, Mia, on whom I practised some newly acquired Swedish phrases learned from Professor Anders. By the time I finally entered university in September 1990, I was undoubtedly a degree or so more confident than I would otherwise have been.

I had to commute to work, just to the south of Paris, on the overland train, and after the first couple of months, I decided it could save me time and money if I bought a car. I picked up an old banger of a white Renault 4 for a couple of hundred pounds. Getting my "Certificat d'Immatriculation", which permitted me to drive it around, was a bit of a painful process. Nonetheless, it was fun to drive that old French car around, with its gear stick coming straight out of the dashboard. But sadly, the car didn't last very long.

As well as to work and back, I used to drive it from Nanterre to Pete's studio on Rue St Jacques, which required me to go around the tricky Arc de Triomphe, taking my life in my hands a little bit. The car was no end of trouble, though, and I was constantly having to replace a spark plug here, or fix a leaky tube there, learning new French vocabulary along the way. In the end, it failed to start one day. The car was parked right outside Pete's place, and we could see it from the window, so I just left it there. A couple of days of being stationery soon turned into a week, then two weeks. It was mid-winter, and as his studio was limited on space, it became a kind of temporary fridge for a while for keeping drinks cold in the boot. The tickets eventually racked up, and then it was towed away to the pound eventually, never to be seen again, though we rescued our beers from it just in time.

During the winter of 1989, we occasionally watched the television news, in Pete's studio apartment on Rue St Jacques, between the vital business of spending all our money in the bars. As the political tensions around the eastern Bloc began playing out, we watched.

Then, on November 9th, images played on the TV of East Germans finally breaching and smashing down the Berlin Wall with sledgehammers. It was amazing to see it and watch the East German police just standing by, letting it all happen. The week before, the same police would have closely monitored anyone getting too close to the wall and perhaps shot at those trying to get over.

"That is history happening right there." Anders (from Stockholm) said as we all watched the TV in Pete's place, after a night out.

"We should go!" said the other Anders (from Malmo),

"How long does it take to drive to Berlin from Paris?"

"Come on guys, are you serious?" said Pete "…ten or eleven hours maybe."

Malmo Anders was a very outgoing guy, good-looking, successful with the opposite sex, and the pack leader in many respects. He was also the one, with the lovely sister, that I would also meet up with in New York a few months later. Anders was also persuasive. He had a very Swedish, boxy, blue Volvo estate car in Paris, which he had driven there from Sweden. It was beaten up and abused, but very trusty. So that night, we hatched a plan to drive to Germany as soon as possible to see history first hand and the Berlin Wall being pushed over by the revolutionaries.

I had tried to resist joining, as I was supposed to be going to work full time, and I didn't have annual leave as such. To be honest, I was also still a bit risk-averse as a person.

I didn't feel too comfortable joining the revolution, and besides, there was some important filing to be done in the exciting carpet tile firm.

They wouldn't take no for an answer, so a couple of days later, I found myself telling the boss of the company that I'd had some bad news from England; my uncle was seriously ill in hospital, and I wanted to go over to see him for a few days in case these were his last.

I don't know why teenagers, like me then, must

make up such ridiculous yarns. It would have probably been fine if I had just asked for some time off. I wasn't performing a critical role for the business at all. In fact, you could perhaps say that my contribution was minimal.

Late next morning, myself, the two Swedes and the American Greek, set off in the big blue Volvo estate car with sangria stains on its bonnet, from a previous trip to Spain apparently, heading for Berlin. We prepared very little for the journey and had no accommodation booked, but at least each took a small bag with a change of underwear in…I think. We drove all day, with occasional stops for more snacks and to use facilities, and the journey seemed to go on forever. As we approached Berlin, it was after midnight, and we were tired and unsure where to go. We decided to find a quiet place to park up to get a few hours' sleep in the car, so on the outskirts of the city, somewhere between Brandenburg and Potsdam, we pulled over and found a spot beside a lake and snoozed until dawn.

At daybreak, we were not really in the mood anymore, and calculating already when we needed to leave to get back to Paris again. We drove around a ring road but couldn't see where we might witness this *history*. We kept finding diversions and road closures.

Hungry and irritable, we found a café for some breakfast, which included beers for all of us except Malmo Anders, who was driving. He was content with his *Snus* machine, which was a pen-like contraption that popped measured amounts of damp, dark tobacco paste inside his mouth onto his gums where he would keep it for an hour or so. It released nicotine straight into this bloodstream for all the stimulation he wanted.

Through the café window, we saw some street hawkers drumming up a bit of business on the opposite pavement. We ambled over after we finished, and to our astonishment, there was one guy at a table selling bags of "genuine" Berlin Wall fragments. There were five or six fragments of concrete per bag, selling for ten US dollars each.

This would have been unthinkable only a few weeks before. We bought two bags to share and felt pleased with our unverified souvenirs.

We could now jump back in the car and bomb it all the way back to Paris and hopefully make it back to our favourite bar, Le Piano Vache, before closing time. The simple gratification of our silly social lives was momentarily more appealing than the profound historical significance of standing atop the Berlin wall. Fortunately, or perhaps because Anders did have some clue where he was, after all, a few turns later, he declared we were close to Potsdamer Platz, which was the scene of one of the wall breaches we had seen on the TV. We couldn't see anywhere obvious to park the car. As Anders was wary of leaving it unattended during a revolution, as he said, we drove on, circulating slowly around west Berlin, taking it all in. There were more tables, with people selling more bits of wall, and crowds of people on the streets soaking up the atmosphere. We went round and round, driving very slowly, feasting our eyes on jubilant Berliners. We drove parallel with sections of the wall at many points and could see people around it and even sitting on it, with German flags draped around them. We felt we were now succeeding in witnessing something important. The excitement was palpable. In retrospect, we ought to have dumped the car, got out, and spent more time there that day. In our defence, I suppose the present-day rarely feels like history, yet history was precisely what was being made right then. But we were just big kids, so having had our quick fix, we left with our pieces of history in bags. Unbelievably and regretfully now, we ticked off seeing the fall of the Berlin wall in one morning. By midday, we left the city, heading west, back towards home.

Two days later, I was back at my desk at work in the carpet tile company. My boss came over and welcomed me back, asked how my trip to London was, and most of all, how my uncle was. I sheepishly lied that he was probably going to be OK now, but that it had seemed very serious at the time, hence why I had to travel to London.

Even at the time, I didn't think he believed my story, but he compassionately told me that these things happen and that it's important to put family first. I thanked him but felt like a naughty schoolboy.

CHAPTER 2

Paris was also the scene of my first experiences of being mugged. I was mugged twice, but each time by comedically inept muggers. The first time was after I had been there for around two months. I was travelling back to Nanterre on the Metro late one Sunday night. My carriage was almost empty, and two guys who looked to be in their late twenties presented themselves by plopping down in the two seats facing me, in a pod of four. At first, I didn't pay them much attention, avoiding eye contact, until I realised they were leaning forward conspiratorially, trying to get my eye.

"Hey, mate, come here," said the one that did most of the talking.

I leaned in and gave a look to invite him to say whatever it was he wanted to say. He opened his coat pocket a little as if he wanted to show me something. At first, I thought he was trying to sell me something, a knocked-off watch or a plastic Eiffel Tower. Now I was looking; they seemed like they could be hawkers, selling cheap goods around the station entrances. He held a razor blade in his hand, the type you see in a Stanley knife. I couldn't see the point in trying to sell those independently, though.

"You see this blade?" he went on, "Very sharp. Can easily cut you from here to here!" he said, motioning with his finger around his neck under his chin.

I suddenly went cold, my legs froze, this was a mugging, and it was new to me. This guy was also threatening to spill my blood. I looked around and realised we were alone on the train as it pulled into my station.

"OK, what do you want?" I asked.

"You come with us off the train at this station," the main man said. As I wanted to get off at that stop, I was happier to get off in a familiar place rather than elsewhere, at least.

"And you give us, you know, some money?" This time it was the second guy talking, but it didn't feel well delivered; almost like it was a suggestion rather than an order. For some reason, I began to relax just a little. The way the second guy had asked for money made me think he was hopeful, rather than confident, of pulling this off.

We all got off and walked the white-tiled corridors towards the exit. "We go outside," said man one, as they flanked me. I figured they probably wanted to do the robbing away from the station's premises. I made a quick inventory of everything I had on me. My wallet, keys, a prepaid *carte orange* (a monthly travel card for the trains and buses), and a phone card with a bit of credit.

They weren't going to win the lottery, but I hoped

they wouldn't turn violent nonetheless.

As we neared the exit, they seemed almost cheerful, then bizarrely, one of them asked me if I was OK. I didn't know how to take that. I supposed that he didn't want to draw any undue attention, and make it look like three blokes just walking along, nothing sinister.

But nobody looking at us would have mistaken us for friends; while I was dressed in black 501s and a pale blue denim shirt, these guys were both wearing a shell suit cum shiny tracksuit number, and without putting too fine a point on it, did not look like my mates. But, I was still unsure what was going to happen.

"What do you mean *am I OK?*" I objected to their question, "of course I am *not* OK; you're mugging me!"

They ignored my complaint, and we pressed on towards the door. When we got out in the dark, cold night, they asked me to empty my pockets. They turned over my wallet in their hands and fished through it. I only had about eighty French francs in there, and they pocketed it fast. It wasn't much, only about ten pounds sterling.

They then took out my phone card and asked if it had much credit. I replied that there was probably a little bit of talk time. I used that card for phoning home from the phone boxes, but I could quickly get another. He took that, too. Next, man one took my Barclays bank card out. It was a debit card, and it was what I used to get cash from the machine as my salary was paid into my UK Barclays account. I was nervous they'd march me to the ATM and force me to withdraw cash.

"What's this? Any good?" he asked.

"No, it's only for England, no good here," I ventured, not expecting him to buy it, but to my surprise, he tutted and put it back in my wallet. They hadn't frisked me, so my travel card, the *carte orange*, which was of more value, perhaps, than the francs he'd had, was still safe in my back pocket where I had put it after we went through the turnstiles.

Looking dejected maybe by their measly winnings, he handed me back my empty wallet, including my bank card. "But I am keeping the cash, mate."

They both then offered me their hand to shake as if we'd just finished a business meeting. I took the hand, as it's human nature to do that, maybe, but I was shaking my head.

"What's wrong, are you angry with us?" said man one.

"Yes. Definitely." I replied.

"Why? We're not friends now?" he asked. He looked as if he'd just been accused of eating peas with a knife. Maybe he thought I should be happy they'd been easy on me.

"Friends? Of course not, you just took my money. And now I don't have enough for the bus from here to Nanterre!"

Why I said that I don't know, any other person would have quit while they were ahead, and in any case, I didn't need money for the bus as I had the *carte orange*.

After I said this, rather than launching back at me with their point of view, fists, or even their razor blade, they just looked at each other. I worried in case I had offended them. Perhaps my big mouth had gone a step too far.

"How much is the bus?" man one asked of man two. Man two just shrugged.

"It's seven francs to where I am going," I interjected, incredibly relieved inside.

Unexpectedly, they then started looking in their pockets for some change. They had only taken notes from my wallet, so they were now looking for coins from between them. Man one had nearly enough, and man two made up the rest, and I was duly handed seven francs *in change* after being robbed.

"Listen, mate, no hard feelings. We French are not all that bad, OK?" said man one, as we shook hands again before they turned and walked away into the cold night.

As I boarded the bus a few minutes later, I kind of wished they were out there in the dark somewhere and could see me flash my *carte orange* at the driver, not using any of the money they gave me for the bus.

The second time I was mugged was around three weeks before the end of my six months in Paris. It was in the city centre as I was jogging back to Pete's studio at about three in the morning in the pouring rain, after a night out on the tiles. I had been trying to keep out of the worst of the rain by skirting the buildings with overhanging structures and using underpasses as it was hammering it down. To be fair, I was probably quite tipsy and had lost my inhibitions, so when the mugger stepped out, I was calm.

Out stepped a man with his arms outstretched like the police trying to slow down a speeding car. It was very dark, and I couldn't make him out well, but again a youngish guy, probably late twenties. I stopped to see what he wanted, not thinking it was a mugging, maybe someone that was lost.

"Give me your wallet, man!" he said, both arms raised as if to calm a horse.

"Oh, OK," I said, assessing it as best I could. I took it out and passed it over.

"But I have to say, I am *really* not happy about this!" I added, thinking back to the first time. Emboldened by the drink, or could you say stupefied by it, I went on: "I don't believe this is happening to me again".

"What do you mean, *again*?" He asked, still holding and looking at my wallet.

"Well, I'm only here in France for a two-week holiday, and this is the second time this has happened to me. I am not getting a good impression of this place," I said.

"Really? What did they get last time?" he asked.

"Nothing much, about eighty francs, I think. I don't have very much anyway," I replied.

It went on like that for a bit longer, and in the end, he just handed me my whole wallet back, apologised, and didn't take anything from me at all. So, as I say, some of the worst muggers you will ever get, or could that be the kindest or most conscientious muggers? Either way, I got off very lightly.

CHAPTER 3

Three years later, after completing the first two years at university, it was an exciting moment to finally be arriving at Moscow's Sheremetyevo airport in September 1992 to begin my time in Russia.

In my childhood, I had been fascinated by the vastness of the lands that stretched beyond the iron curtain. It went almost halfway around the geography classroom globe. These lands seemed full of intrigue, romance, and place names that were impossible to pronounce. The USSR was a superpower, the land of the Red Square tank parades and the Kremlin. It had a deep history full of Tsars and Tsarinas, Tolstoy and Dostoyevsky, Doctor Zhivago, the Bolshevik revolution, and the gulags. Characters like Lenin, Trotsky and Stalin had intrigued and scared me in equal measure. It was a land of communism, contradiction, and vast, snow-covered tundra.

Growing up in the 1980s I had witnessed the frenzy of the nuclear arms race, the cold war, and the ever-present threat that either president Reagan or Brezhnev could press the big red button at any moment. Rather than slugging it out in the boxing ring as in Frankie

Goes to Hollywood's Two Tribes music video, an actual conflict could have led to a nuclear catastrophe to wipe us all out. From the literature of twentieth-century authors such as Alexander Solzhenitsyn, I understood how the population had been firmly controlled, monitored, and spied upon by the authorities, the KGB, and the citizens themselves. Comrades informed on comrades, sometimes with brutal consequences. It was a fascinating and slightly scary place to me.

In 1985, Mikhail Gorbachev had come into the top job, General Secretary of the Communist party, hence leader of the Soviet Union, and he had started reforms and liberalisations. He introduced glasnost (or "openness" to give it its English translation), under which he tried to introduce more transparency, both with the general population and with foreign countries. There was also perestroika ("rebuilding"), which I understood would restructure the country's running, including the economy. He became the first president of the Soviet Union, and one result of his constitutional changes had meant the communist party was no longer necessarily in charge by default. Elections would follow. This democratic nod perhaps inadvertently brought about the end of the Soviet Union and the creation of the Russian Federation.

There was a dramatic coup d'état in August 1991, which played out on televisions worldwide. I watched as Gorbachev was arrested in his summer dacha and brought back to Moscow. Soviet hardliners were unhappy with the loss of control of various Eastern European states and were generally dissatisfied with how they perceived the communist party's grip was loosening everywhere. They tried to take back control of the country. Tanks shelled the Duma (Russia's parliament) from the other side of the Moscow River, and there was a tense stand-off and power struggle. I remember this ending with Boris Yeltsin, something of a people's hero at that time, climbing atop an army tank, appealing to the insurgents for calm, and managing to diffuse the situation. Although Gorbachev was restored to power, he was effectively politically finished after this, as Boris Yeltsin's stock continued to rise.

Shortly after that Yeltsin pressured Gorbachev to resign for the good of the nation. Despite his reforming and progressive intentions, Gorbachev was still seen as one of the *old guard*. Of course, I had no idea at the time, but I would shake hands with Gorbachev myself some three years later when he visited Oxford University to give a speech.

Yeltsin himself signed agreements in 1991, officially ending the Soviet Union, and he then became President of the newly formed Russian Federation.

I watched for news from Russia, knowing that I was soon to go and live there for nine months, and the place was falling apart. Seventy years of communist rule was ending, and the Soviet Union was collapsing. It was exciting but daunting. The dissolution of the Soviet Union was not the only world event of note. Yugoslavia also began to break up. Croatia and Slovenia declared their independence, which was just the start of a series of events in the Balkans leading to a few years of terrible conflict and war in that region. Estonia, Latvia and Lithuania also became independent states. A serial killer called Jeffrey Dahmer was arrested for multiple murders in the USA, boxing sensation Mike Tyson was arrested for rape, and a guy named Tim Berners-Lee invented something called the World Wide Web. The world was going through interesting times, although it also seemed normal, of course, just the times we were living in. I was equally as interested in Steffi Graf and Michael Stich winning Wimbledon for a German clean sweep at the tennis, as I was to see news of the United States and the Soviet Union signing nuclear treaties to reduce the number of warheads between them.

In September 1991, I returned for the second year at Bristol University. Although there were still twelve months before I travelled to Russia, I was keen to see how seven decades of dictatorship would be dismantled. Any progress towards a more democratic and fair society was of particular interest to me. A stable democracy would be a massive ask and would not be easy. Russia's so-called *wild west* years were about to commence, and I was going to ride that bucking bronco for at least a little bit of it. As the time for my trip beyond the *not-so-iron-any-more-curtain* grew ever closer, world politics kept on ringing the changes, too.

Having been released from prison a year earlier after his twenty-seven years' incarceration, Nelson Mandela became the leader of the African National Congress in March 1992, and apartheid came to an end. Margaret Thatcher's eleven years in power came to an end, and Neil Kinnock contrived to snatch defeat from the jaws of election victory and allowed John Major to become the next UK Prime Minister. In February 1992, George W Bush met with Boris Yeltsin in Camp David and signed a deal officially ending the cold war, which was nice to see, and some comfort to me personally.

By September of 1992, after my second year of studies, it was safe to say I was not top of the class. In fact, in April, I failed my Russian language first-year exams and had to re-sit them. If you didn't pass the re-sit, you can't continue. Fortunately, I passed at the second attempt, but I found learning Russian from scratch quite hard. Russian was still a rare subject to study at university at the time; there were fewer than twenty students on our course and little more than one hundred in universities across the rest of the UK.

My first and second years had their fair share of socialising and parties for me, which should be no surprise, as we were students. I also embarked on an eighteen-month relationship with a fantastic girl called Lucy in the first term of Year 1. I think it was our first serious relationship for both of us, and we valued each other greatly.

They say you always look back fondly on your first love, and I am no exception. But student living is quite erratic, and I was also swept up in having fun. The relationship with Lucy suffered and unfortunately did not last until the end of year 2, spoiled as it was by my immaturity, as I prioritised exploring my social circle and partying more than my relationship with her.

But now, at the start of the third year, I was finally here, facing the serious business of living in Russia; immersion therapy, which would dramatically improve my ability to speak and understand Russian. At Moscow airport, approaching passport control, I was about to talk to my very first live Russian person. My inner excitement was off the scale.

I was in a group of about twenty-five British students from around the UK who had been signed up to a programme run by a study abroad company called Russian Language Universities Scheme (RLUS).

The RLUS had agreements with various Russian universities to place UK students in Russia for the academic year. My choices had been to split the year between Moscow and St Petersburg, or Moscow and

Pyatigorsk in the south, or stay the whole nine months in one place, Voronezh, a medium-sized city 400 miles south of Moscow. I had opted for the latter, so I could get settled in real Russia for the whole time and not have to relocate midway through the year. Six of us from my university course made this choice: Becky, Jane, Tom, Connor, Gwyn and myself. Others from Bristol had opted for other locations in Russia or another country for the first half if they were doing another language as part of their degree. We had just met the rest of the group that day for the first time at Heathrow before boarding the plane.

As we shuffled forward towards the passport booth, I was impressed by how surly the Russian customs officers looked with their military-style oversized caps with a red star in the top band.

It already felt like a film set or a John le Carré book. Although Russia was now opening itself up to the rest of the world under the glasnost initiative, it was still a shady, closed-off country to most people.

It was only five years previously that the nuclear power plant in Chernobyl had blown up in 1986, and the state had kept news of the catastrophic event from its own public and the rest of the world. Official news channels reported nothing, and questions were asked only after we experienced acid rain falling on our sheep in places like East Yorkshire. With similar stories coming out of

Scandinavia, and various countries pressing the Russian government on the causes, they finally admitted nearly a month later that there had been an *incident* and then the true nature of the terrible disaster. The media was under complete government control back then, via the official news agency, Tass, and via the official broadcasting radio station, Radio Moscow. There were no privately owned or independent media outlets in 1986, although a little later, the first independent news agency, called Interfax, was founded in 1989.

Interfax was a bold new enterprise founded by ex-Radio Moscow journalists. Interfax's original business model had been to report general news about the country, but mainly political, or nationally important news, daily. Its first customers were the foreign embassies in Moscow, who had only had Tass to rely upon before that, which was of course relatively worthless as it only reported what the government wanted it to. The *fax* part of their name derived from their early business model, too. The company did not have the traditional means of getting the news to their customers in the foreign embassies via TV or radio broadcasts; access to the airwaves was not an option. So they leased fax machines to their first customers for sixteen dollars per month and then sent their daily general news digest via the fax machine they just provided them with. Interfax had a tricky first couple of years, and in fact, the owners were arrested and detained temporarily during the August '91 coup attempt to prevent news reporting.

Eventually, Interfax became the largest independent news agency in the country, producing up to three thousand news stories per day. It was readily subscribed to by foreign governments, media, and businesses looking for something more reliable in terms of real news from the region. As I shuffled to the front of the line in passport control in September 1992, I had absolutely no idea I would one day become the director of the Interfax news agency's UK office and run things for them in London; I had never heard of them at that point. At this point, I still knew little about what I would do when I *grew up*.

When I got to the window, and fed my passport through the hatch, I tried to look the officer in the eye, but he had a disconcerting expression as if he was looking straight through me. I thought it must be their mysterious inscrutability. But I later found out he was probably just checking my height against the height marks incised on the glass booth window to see if it matched my stated height in my visa paperwork.

I took a second, trying not to be put off by him, and said "zdrastvootie" in my best Russian, trying to look friendly.

He did not smile but returned my gaze finally and said "zdrastvootie" back, and I think I detected an eye smile.

It was a real buzz; I had entered the former Soviet Union.

"I just spoke to my first Russian person, and he understood me!" I said to my fellow adventurer as we headed for the luggage carousel.

"I know, me too; I can't quite believe what we're letting ourselves in for!"

This was Alastair Stone, known as just Al for short, a brown-haired Scot from Edinburgh, studying at Manchester University, who would become a good friend over the next few months.

CHAPTER 4

Our destination, the city of Voronezh, has a population of about one million and lies about five hundred kilometres south of Moscow, about halfway to the Black Sea. A historically significant town founded by the Cossacks, so I read in my handout from the RLUS, built on fertile earth on the banks of the Voronezh River, just upstream of the mighty River Don. Voronezh also had a big university where we would enrol for our exchange programme for the year. In my first year at university, I had been quite taken by the epic Sholokov novel, *And Quietly Flows the Don*, which was set in this region at the time of the Bolshevik revolution. It is a story of revolution, war, love and loss. To this land, I was now heading.

To get to Voronezh, we were bussed from Sheremyetovo airport down to one of the main train stations in Moscow in the south of the city, Paveletsky station, to catch an overnight train. It was after dark, so, unfortunately, we couldn't see as much as we would have liked in our first glimpse of the country from the bus that night, but I remember being surprised to see the streets so busy. The roads were packed with cars and buses trying to get somewhere, but it was monotone, with a distinct and apparent lack of advertising and colour. Most of the cars looked the same, as they were nearly all Ladas. I don't know if I had been expecting everybody to be hiding or standing around looking glum and grey, but this busyness caught me off guard for some reason.

We needed to take an overnight train with "couchette" cabins, consisting of two bench sofa seats facing each other and a pull-down bunk above those, so each couchette slept four people. Our guides from Moscow to Voronezh were two Russian university staff and an English student liaison person called Vicky. Vicky had been on the same residential course two years before in Voronezh and was there this year purely to hold our hands through it and help us orientate. It must have been her first job straight after graduating, and for her, it was a stint of work before going into the job market proper. The train was a very social experience as we all got to know each other better. It was an old-fashioned train, with a corridor along one side of the carriage, with the couchette compartments on the other side. A bit like the Orient Express, I imagined. A trolley-pushing attendant served hot sugary black tea from a very ornate traditional Russian silver samovar that was something to behold. I say silver, but it couldn't really have been actual silver - tin more likely - but silver in colour, reminiscent in design of the real silver ones of the past.

Although it was a public train with ordinary

Russians in the other parts of the train, we pretty much had the whole carriage to ourselves. It had been presumably reserved for us beforehand. We were green and new, so everything was a bit alien to us, except for Vicky and the Russian liaison staff. Within minutes our chaperones pulled out various bottles of alcohol which they shared, or sold to us for barely any money, it seemed. People were passing around bottles of Russian beer and, apparently, Russian champagne. I wasn't very familiar with champagne, prosecco or cava; not really a drink for my age demographic. But it was less than £1 a bottle, and it was pretty good - well, it was fizzy and alcoholic at any rate. The writing on the label I deciphered as "Sovietskoye Champanskoye" and it was something I would be seeing a lot more of over the coming months. The party train trundled through the night quite slowly as we merrily got to know each other, twenty or so students from different universities from around the UK, but now all thrown together for an experience of a lifetime in Russia.

We overfilled the cabins, eight or ten in each, using all the seats and bunks, chinking our glasses, and finding out who was who, and who was from where. The excitement about being away from our ordinary lives for a long while, but also now being in real Russia finally, I think, made us all drink fast and talk loudly, as the train clattered along the tracks through the night. The conversation wasn't very highbrow; just like at many student parties, we mostly talked about what fun might await us, and some shared stories some of us had heard from the group who took the course the year before.

"Apparently, there's just one good place to eat in town, Café Anna; that's what I was told by someone who went to Voronezh last year."

"I can't believe how cheap this champagne is... 50 roubles a bottle! I think I'll be drinking a lot of this."

"I don't think this Russian beer is any good, do you?"

"I heard last year's group got some good grass from Afghanistan or Uzbekistan, or somewhere; I'll be checking that out!"

Arriving the following day at 8am at Voronezh station, we were now in a much more provincial town than Moscow. Although still quite large by population, it was smaller and seemed like it would be easier to cope with. It was early September, and an unexpectedly warm summer still prevailed; the sun shone brightly in the blue sky accompanied with warm mid-twenties degrees centigrade air, even in the morning. We were led out of the station and across the square in front of it, which was more of a crescent-shaped car park, with lots more pastel coloured Ladas to see here. We headed a couple of hundred yards along quite a grand avenue, called Ulitsa Mira ("Peace Street" or "Street of the World"). I peered at the people walking in the opposite direction to us. There were quite a few moustaches, some dull-looking clothes, and some wizened looking older men and women. The women seemed to favour a headscarf around the top and back of their heads. These were the "babushkas", meaning grandmothers, who I would soon be coming to buy potatoes and other grocery items from off the street once I settled in. They may also be the babushkas Kate Bush successfully sang about in 1980. I wondered if these Russians would look at us, clearly western visitors, and was interested in knowing what they thought about us traipsing into their world, and if I could read anything into their expressions. But if anything, they looked oblivious, or they were deliberately ignoring us. Shortly we were led through a gap in the buildings, through an archway, and followed a path. We finally arrived at our new home. We were in a hostel, or "obshezhitye", number 4.

We had arrived at the hostel via the shortcut, through the archway and over some rough paths, approaching it from behind. But it fronted onto, for address purposes, a road called Friedreich Engels Street, named after the German philosopher and cofounder of original Marxist theories. It was set back about thirty metres from the road, with a few trees in a pleasant open area in front of it, along with two other hostel looking buildings close by, with crisscrossing paved footpaths between them. It was a rectangular, functional building of five floors with one long corridor running through each floor, communal toilets and shower rooms at one end near the main stairwell, and a shared kitchen in the middle of each one. There were around ten rooms on each side of the corridor, with two to three people sharing a room.

I had been assigned to share room number 33 on the third floor with Al, the Scot from the airport, which suited me well as we'd got on well on the train journey down. Our shared room had three single beds in it, one in each corner of the room, with the last corner being reserved for a row of narrow wardrobes, more like lockers really, which went from the floor almost to the ceiling. One big window in the room looked out to the trees and paths in front of the hostel, while the walls were lined with wallpaper of a nondescript pattern as busy as a paisley design, but nothing like it, more like a green, brown porridge effect. It was bad. All the British students had to share with a Russian roommate; this was ostensibly, we thought, to help us integrate and speak Russian.

As we entered room 33, we saw our new roommate sitting on his well-made bed (blankets and sheets - no duvets here). He got up to meet us, looking a bit shy but clean, neat and tidy, with light brown short hair, smaller and shorter than the pair of us.

"Zdrastvootie, minya zavoot Alastair," said Al, extending a handshake to our new roommate. I remember thinking it was good to hear Russian spoken with a Scottish accent, almost more suitable to the task than my English one.

"And my name is Nikolay," replied our new friend in real Russian, and I remember my first impression here was that he was the type of boy who would be well behaved; good to his Mum.

Nikolay explained a few bits of housekeeping to us; he explained that there was a wardrobe (locker) each, but as they were small, most people kept their things under the bed, where to find the kitchen, toilets, and so on. This was our first real Russian conversation for Al and me, and we took turns talking and sharing some personal information. Classic lines were used, such as "I have one brother and one sister…and you?" Al also explained where in the UK we were from and that we were from different universities. "Me, from Manchester…Henry, from Bristol", and Nikolay gamely played along. He told us that he was from Perm, a city over 1,400 kilometres to the East; he had one sister, and an uncle who lived in Voronezh, which sounded handy. It was all very friendly. But soon, it was time for us to gather in the foyer area by the main ground floor entrance to meet the adults in charge.

As the whole group of new UK arrivals assembled, I counted around twenty-five of us. We were met by a man who looked to be in his late forties, perhaps early fifties, greying hair, thinning on top, with an impressive bushy moustache, and blue, sparkling eyes, a bit like a Cossack, I thought, before also thinking that I didn't really know what a Cossack looks like anyway.

"My name is Vyacheslav," he began, "I work for the VGU, the Voronezh State University" . He seemed friendly.

"I will be the programme coordinator for your time here. Welcome to Voronezh!" he continued with a flourish, as a broad smile spread rapidly over his wide, Cossack face.

He went on to explain in very slow Russian, often simplifying it as much as he could, that he would be looking after us and how our stay would pan out.

"I would like...er... I very want, that you have a good time with us here in Russia," he continued in his easy to digest Russian.

Vyacheslav then explained that we could rest today, relax and get settled in, but that tomorrow morning, we would all be taking a trip, a sightseeing tour, to see some more of Russia. It was still two weeks before the academic term started, and he laid out the itinerary he had planned for us. We were to assemble in the foyer again the following day at 9.30 am, and we'd walk to the station to catch a 10.30 am train back up to Moscow. From there, we would be taking a boat trip up the river Volga from Moscow to St Petersburg and back; it would take one week in each direction with plenty to see along the way. It sounded great and we were all pleased by the sound of it. Although it did seem strangely organised that we had travelled a long way from Heathrow to Moscow, then from Moscow to Voronezh overnight, arriving on this day, only to be travelling back to Moscow tomorrow again.

We had each been provided with a small starter pack with basic food provisions, and our liaison, Vicky, had handed out information sheets pointing out the A-Z of how to survive in hostel number 4. It included where things were, such as the nearest food shop, and how to buy stuff in shops. When I eventually got around to going to the shops, I found out how hit and miss they were, often with empty shelves. Vicky's sheets did explain this and about the chit system.

The main food shop was called the *gastronom,* and there were many *gastronoms* in town. They were small, by no means a supermarket, or even a minimarket, just the size of a high street shop back home. No products were in the central area of the shop where you, the customer, were. Everything was kept behind the counters, whether fresh produce or packets of dried food or tins of food. You had to select what you wanted to buy by looking at it from at least six feet away, trying to work out what it was, and reading the price card below it. Then you went over to the cashier and explained which items you wanted to purchase, which she would tally up and take your money for. She (it was always a she) would hand you a chit (a receipt) for these items, and you had to go back to the first counter to exchange this bit of paper for your goods. It was the old Soviet system still in place and quite frustrating, especially if you hadn't correctly identified what it was you were trying to buy and ended up with something you didn't really want.

Vicky verbally explained that a better and easier way to pick supplies up was from the pavement street sellers on Ulitsa Mira and other streets close by. Here, babushkas would be lining the kerb selling potatoes, vegetables, and various foods produced from their own land. They would tip the stuff out of their canvas sacks or plastic bags onto their beaten-up metal scales and sell it by weight. There was also a proper big covered farmers market once a week, in the city's centre about half an hour's walk away, where season depending, you could buy from a larger selection of produce. However, as it was only day 1 and because we were leaving the next day, Vicky had organised a small group of four or five students to make a big communal stew with bread for everyone, so we didn't need to go foraging that day.

On the other hand, booze would be needed, and it was bring-your-own. Again, this could be bought from the gastronom shop with the chit system, but the choice would be limited and dependent on them having had a recent delivery. It would also be only one state-approved brand, and the price would be much higher than the street price for the same bottle. Vicky informed us about the more common, unofficial way to buy alcohol, which we did that first evening. You grab your rucksack and head for the train station, and in the crescent-shaped car park, you approach guys standing near parked cars with "looking for business" faces on. This we all did in small, apprehensive groups. I went with Al, Jim and Sam.

Jim was a straight character from Edinburgh University, but originally from Spalding in Lincolnshire, while Sam was a flame-red haired Londoner from Oxford University. We identified two leather-jacketed guys, stocky and dark-haired, perhaps from Armenia or another southern region, and asked them if they had any beer. We had no idea what we were doing, if this would work, or whether they would tell us to get lost. But we were acting on the advice we'd just been given in good faith here.

"Pivo?" we asked. (Beer).

That was all we needed to say, as up flipped car boots to reveal holdalls full of various bottles, much to our relief. The Armenians told us how much each drink was, and having estimated for how many friends back in the hostel we were buying, we came away with about 25 bottles of beer, 3 bottles of vodka and 15 bottles of Pepsi. There was no Coca Cola in Russia, we supposed. We'd been told beforehand that the local vodka, a wheat-based drink called Pshenichnaya, was an acquired taste and was best mixed with Pepsi at first. Our first night in hostel number 4 was like so many others repeated over the next few months - sociable, communal and aided by train station car park beverages.

That night, I discovered a little more about our home; the hostel really was quite disgusting. I hadn't really noticed before, having not really scrutinised the facilities when we first arrived. A communal kitchen was located near the centre of our third floor, a square room of about ten feet by ten feet. It had a metal sink and draining board near the window on the left, and on the right-hand wall were two free-standing white metal ovens with electric ring hobs and two big bins next to these. A tall fridge and a small, square, white table with two chairs were to the left. The floor was dirty from dozens of outside feet trudging through, and cockroaches were visible in the corners and shadows. I was to find out that these kitchens, one on each floor, got very busy as we had something like thirty people sharing each one.

After our meal, we gravitated to room 38 opposite mine and Al's, home to my friends Becky and Jane, my fellow course mates from Bristol University. On that first night it felt like at least two-thirds of the British students were packed into this room, which was much deeper than ours and on the other side of the corridor, so it had more space. Our new Russian roommates joined us, too, so in fact, maybe twenty-five or more people were in there, repeating the get-to-know-you conversations. Drinks were soon flowing, and even some guitars appeared, and songs were played. Russo-British relations were really getting off to a great start. Al and I talked more with our roommate Nikolay, our British student friends, and with some of the female Russian roommates, our first Russian girls. It was mildly flirtatious and generally just fun and new frontierish.

That first evening visit to the toilets, though, once the evening was in full swing, would not be easily forgotten. They were the very last door at the far end of the corridor, one door along from the shower room, which itself was an almost entirely tiled room with 3 shower cubicles on each side with swing doors for privacy on each. Upon entering the toilets with red-headed Sam, for a much-needed wee, , we saw the whole floor was not just muddy like the kitchen, but wet, too, and from the smell, it wasn't just water that was making it wet. The room had three cubicles on each side, but the light wasn't working and using the light emanating from the corridor, I could see across the glistening floor areas of higher flooring that were dry or dryish. We hopped across the darkened room from patch to patch like stepping stones and found a bowl to relieve ourselves in. It was awful, but I wasn't going to let it ruin my evening, presuming it was just an overflow problem that would be fixed, but there was undoubtedly the stench in there of both number ones and number twos. The toilets were the same bowl type as we had in the UK, only with no seats or lids, so it would be a case of hovering for a number two, but I fortunately only needed a wee this time around. While there, I also noticed a small bin next to each toilet, and although it was very gloomy with no lights working, these were evidently used for all used loo paper, not just as bins or for sanitary towels. My mind wasn't even wondering at that point why there would be sanitary towel bins in the men's loo, as I was more concerned by the excrement on the paper in the containers.

"Jesus, that was disgusting!" I said to Sam as we escaped back into the corridor, heading back to the party.

Two Russian girls appeared just as we were leaving the dim room, emerging into the light of the corridor. As we passed them, one of them called over her shoulder, "Hey, what do you think you're doing; these are the girls' toilets!"

When the words sunk in, we burst into giggles as we staggered away, realising with relief that we didn't have to go in there again (the male/female loos were on alternating floors) and seeing the irony in their possessiveness over the filthy room.

Back at the party, high spirits soon restored me to a good mood once again, and I began to get into more conversations. There was a smiley, friendly-looking guy I hadn't seen before, talking to Becky and Jane. His haircut was more stylish than most of the other Russians, medium brown with a fringe or even a quiff and short at the back and sides, a western-style, I thought. As I joined their conversation, he was entertaining them with tales of what happened last year with the British contingent. He was called Alexei.

I learned that there had been a guy called Doherty, who had become known as "Doc". Doc had been one of Alexei's best friends from the last group, and he'd heard he was planning to come back this Christmas. Alexei explained that he was a great guy, a party guy, and he hoped we were all going to be as much fun as Doc had been. The previous year wasn't the first placement of British students, he told us; the collapse of the Soviet Union was not what had kick-started the programme. It had been going on for years, and in fact, the well-known BBC Moscow correspondent Martin Bell himself had spent a year in hostel number 4 in Voronezh some years back. Alexei said if there was anything we needed, he would be our man. He also strongly advised us not to use the city's banks to change our hard currency dollars into roubles. They offered a poor official exchange rate, and if we changed it through him, he'd always offer a much better rate. He pulled out a massive wad of roubles and dollars from his pocket to demonstrate his point.

Although Alexei seemed like just a big show off at a party, he was so smiley and friendly that I couldn't help warming to him. And Becky, too, seemed not immune to his charms. I didn't know it yet, but Alexei was to become a close friend to both Becky and myself over the next few months. Alexei didn't live in the hostel but had a small rented apartment on Ulitsa Mira with some friends, and he said we must come over to party there some time.

Boosted by the party's high spirits and keen, perhaps, to big myself up, I remembered what I'd heard the night before about grass from Uzbekistan, so I decided to ask Alexei about it. Having been at university already for two years, I had enjoyed many a splendid session back in Bristol. But it had been just recreational, as they say, and I still preferred drinking in general as my first port of recreational call. I also steered clear of anything harder than cannabis; overall I was a bit too wary and risk-averse to go further than that. On late-night TV after a good evening out in Bristol, Prisoner Cell Block H just wasn't the same without a good accompaniment. So, I asked Alexei.

"I heard that it may be possible to buy grass here, Alexei, trava!?" I asked using the literal word for grass, as in the type you have on a lawn, hoping it would be the same. "You said you can help us find anything, so, do you think you can help with that?"

A huge smile spread across Alexei's face, like he'd been here before, and was now categorising me as someone in search of a good time, but it looked like he was also deciding that I could be someone to be friends with this year, maybe like Doc from the year before, to be in his gang.

"You heard about that? Sure, you can get that here, but not from me; you need to ask Sergei over there." He pointed towards a blond-haired bearded guy standing by one of the beds on the opposite side of the room with arms wide open, cigarette in hand, evidently in mid-story to a group of British students. "I'll go and get him," Alexei added.

Moments later, Sergei was over, and I was talking to him. He seemed pretty drunk; his face also looked drained, like he was used to being drunk quite a lot. His beard was a bit wispy and thin and reminded me of the Romanov royal family kind of look. He was also a little scary in the way that unpredictable drunk people can be. I asked if he could help me get some grass; he was all smiles and assured me that he could sort it out. Then I remembered that Vyacheslav had told us that our whole group was catching the morning train to Moscow. The two-week trip would commence via the 10.30am train. I began to think this deal could probably wait until I got back, as there was no rush on my part.

"How much do you want?" he prompted me out of thoughts. "Absolutely no problem, yes, tomorrow is fine, no problem, you come to my room at 9 am, I'll give it to you, sure, before you catch the train!"

Now that I had asked , and he was keen to do it, I felt

like it wasn't right to start putting it off until a later date. "OK, well, thanks," I said.

"How much you want?" he repeated.

Without any time to really think it through, I tried to guess what a small purchase would be, without wanting to say things like eights or 'teenths of ounces. I just suggested that I'd be happy with ten dollars' worth. Just a small something to slip into my pocket.

"Sure, no problem, you come to room 42 in hostel number 3 over the way, see you at 9 am."

CHAPTER 5

Awaking the following day with a bit of a hangover from the night before, as I was not really used to vodka and Russian beer, I remembered straight away that I needed to get going quite quickly to find hostel number 3 and the room where Sergei lived. I decided to take my bag for the train trip with me, just in case this took longer than expected, as I absolutely could not miss the student trip.

There was a four or five-step descent outside our hostel onto a path that led directly ahead, with trees on either side, with the main Friedreich Engels Street in front of me. Diagonally to the right beyond other randomly spaced trees, I saw what I guessed was hostel 3, recalling Sergei's directions, around thirty metres away. It was identical to ours, so I thought it would be easy enough to find my way around it to room 42. I guessed that this was probably just for Russian students rather than the cosmopolitan, multinational hostel number 4. As I entered the first-floor corridor, it was quiet and I supposed most people were still sleeping.

I knocked on the door to room 42. No reply. I knocked again, a little louder this time, and after a few seconds, I heard some mumblings from the other side.

The door opened, and the sleepy face of a guy I had not seen before peered out at me.

"Hi, is Sergei here?" I asked him.

"Uh-hum, come in," he replied and beckoned me to follow.

"Seriozh, English guy for you," he said as he found his resting place and lay down again.

I looked around, and there seemed to be more people in this room than in the ones we had in hostel 4. It was also double depth, a bit like Becky and Jane's room, and they had created partitions with sheets or blankets to create different areas. A couple were lying together on one bed, and sleepy faced guy retreated to a bed in the corner. As I looked to the back of the room by the window furthest from the door, I could see Sergei swinging to an upright position, grinning at me and rubbing his face and puffed-up eyes.

"Good morning. Come in; want a drink?" he said all at once. I presumed he meant a tea or a coffee and began to consider the question for a second when I saw he had produced a bottle of vodka and was hunting for small glasses.

"Er, no thanks…. my head!" I replied, hoping that would seem obvious and acceptable as an excuse.

He mumbled some reply I didn't really understand, as my Russian was still only that of a beginner, of course, but I guessed it to be something like "OK, suit yourself," as he found a glass, filled it to halfway and downed it in one. He offered me to sit on a tiny sofa next to a low table that was covered in drinks glasses, cups and full ashtrays, as he pulled some clothes on and explained he was just going to fetch my little purchase.

"Oh, so you don't have it?" I said, a little disappointed not to get this over with quickly, as there were three Russian strangers in this dark and smelly room, and he looked like he was going to leave me here.

"No, but don't worry, I won't be long. Have you got the money?" he asked before adding, "Hey, Vadim, look after Genry here," addressing the sleepy faced guy who had let me in and was now back in bed. I handed Sergei the ten dollars, and he left the room.

Once he had left, again calling me Genry before he did so, I was reminded of another thing that I had found out the night before about my name. On telling any Russian that my name was Henry, they instantly just called me Genry by return, without a second thought. They didn't have a letter that made the English "h" ha sound. The closest letter they had looked like our "x" and was pronounced "kha", a little like the "x" in Alexander, only a bit more from the back of the throat. To use the "x" would have made my name Xenry, but that was a bit harsh sounding, like spitting the word out like a hissing snake. So, they didn't do that. They just always changed H's to G's. So as Adolf would have had to probably

51

get used to being called Gitler if he had ever made any Russian friends that is, I was to get used to being known as Genry.

As he left, I looked at the table in front of my knees. It was a scene of carnage from the night before. I felt uncomfortable in a strange room with Russians I didn't know, but the guy and the girl on the other bed near me began to stir, stretch and yawn. The girl smiled at me, and I saw her dark mascara from the night before was giving her panda eyes and streaks on her face. She seemed only to be wearing a man's shirt, which covered her middle, but her legs were bare. She sat up, and then the man rose behind her, a bear of a man with longish dark hair, albeit still clearly of student age, pushing his arms out and sighing.

"Hello," he smiled, "How are you - drink?"

"Hello," I said back.

Then the girl said "Hi, I'm Kate" in perfect English. I was surprised to realise she really was English, but she wasn't one of our group, which confused me. "I was here last year; you're going to have a great time. I just came back for a couple of weeks, as Gennady's my boyfriend."

"Oh right, yes, we just all arrived yesterday," I added a bit lamely.

As Kate, Gennady and Vadim all carried on waking up and straightening out the room, I could see they'd enjoyed a party themselves the night before. It was awkward as I didn't know any of them, and I was here to buy grass, so I didn't know what small talk to start with. But I was relieved that Kate was there, as it helped me feel not entirely behind enemy lines. Soon, they gathered around the table and began arranging some biscuits, putting out some small glasses, and fishing out a bottle of vodka from a small fridge in the corner. Kate was speaking effortlessly away to Gennady and Vadim in Russian, which impressed me and momentarily made me excited to think that I may become as good as that by the end of this year.

"Try it," said Gennady, "drink with us, just one".

"OK then," I replied. Although I'd have preferred a strong coffee right then, I also felt I couldn't refuse now that I was stuck there. It was another local Russian brand, and as it came out of the fridge, it was moderately OK, the ice-cold fire water slipping nicely down my throat. We chinked glasses once or twice more while waiting for Sergei to return. Accompanied by a biscuit, this was the sum of my breakfast that day. Kate told me that she was missing the first week of her fourth year of study at Sheffield University by being here, but she would be home for the following Monday, so it wasn't that bad. I reckoned she had come to rekindle her romance with Gennady, but was unsure why now when we'd just had the whole summer off.

Soon, though, I was getting quite worried by the

time. First, it was 9.30 am, then 9.45 am, and I had to be at the train station by 10.15 am with the rest of the group. Finally, after nearly giving up on it at 9.55 am, Sergei barged back into the room. He said something again that I didn't understand and sounded frustrated and seemed a bit sweary. He was wearing a blue tracksuit top a little like a shell suit, zipped up and bulging underneath. He came to the table unzipping the top and produced a wrapped-up package of newspaper tied with string, about the size of a small brick. It reminded me of someone bringing back fish and chips wrapped in newspaper, only there was no warm salt and vinegary fish aroma, but an altogether more pungent aroma. It must be the grass, I thought, but quite a lot for ten dollars. He then produced another package, and another, and another. Four packages came out in total, and he then proceeded to open the packs and empty the grass from inside each onto one newspaper double spread in the middle of the table. Sergei looked quite intense, and I didn't feel I should interrupt. I thought maybe he had bought a job lot for me and other customers, so I waited, hoping that he would sort his whole stash out and then give me my pocket-sized aromatic takeaway. I surveyed the pile he had created; a herb mountain the size of a couple of shoeboxes and a few inches high in the centre.

Conscious of the ticking clock, I reckoned the station was about five minutes' walk away, and the train was due to leave in about fifteen minutes. I decided to push things along.

"I really have to go to the train right now, Sergei. Can I just have my bit?" I asked.

"What do you mean?" he asked with a quizzical look, but also a little smirk, "this is all yours!"

CHAPTER 6

Oh my god! I thought, what am I going to do with all that?! I knew I couldn't leave it there, so with no time to think, I quickly wrapped all four packages up as best as I could, stuffed them into my bag, and left Sergei's. I clocked the look on Kate's face as I left the room. Unless I was wrong, she, too, was quite shocked. My mind whirred. Why the hell had he even emptied them onto the table anyway if they were all mine? Have I got time to leave some in my room?

I marched through the trees and over towards hostel number 4, and as I approached, I saw Al trotting around the side of the building coming from the direction of the station. Al knew where I'd been as I told him beforehand, and he called out to me, "We're all there waiting for you; you have to come straight there".

"OK, fine, he just took forever. It was stressing me out!" I said, also now realising I wouldn't be able to leave any of my shopping behind, and it was all going to have to come with me. I joined Al, and we hot-footed it over the station where Vyacheslav was gathering everyone by the ticket desk, making sure we were all there. He issued us all with a ticket and led us onto the train.

I got into a carriage, and into one of the cabins, with Al, Connor, Becky and Jane, and let out a big sigh. This just all seemed a bit silly, but I was also pretty excited by what had just been achieved and told my friends about it. After the train got underway and people were more or less settled in their carriages or seats, I got the packages out, so I could repack them more securely after having rewrapped them hastily in Sergei's room earlier.

None of us could quite believe how much grass I had just acquired for ten US dollars. I wasn't really sure whether any of these guys were particularly into it or not, as before coming away together to Russia, I wasn't really in the same social circles as any of them.

"Holy shit, Henry!" said Connor, as he let out a whistle, "How much have you got there?!" he added with a big grin. I sensed he would be maybe more into it than I credited him for. Connor was Irish, an exceptionally bright student, and was studying Politics and Russian, like me. In fact, we were the only two people at Bristol doing that exact combination. He usually scored top marks in Politics assignments and approached Russian with a very methodical approach, which also brought him good grades. I had thought him a bit of a square really, before now, hardworking and destined for a first-class degree.

"I don't know how much it weighs, but I promise it's just ten dollars' worth."

"Can you spare me some?!" Connor asked with an ironic grin.

"I think I could part with a little bit, I suppose!" I replied sarcastically.

Everyone then turned their attention to guessing how much I had bought. Al produced an empty plastic carrier bag from his rucksack. "Here," he said, "will it all fit in here, do you think? We can try to estimate it."

"Yeah, but it's dry grass, so it hardly weighs anything, even if it is a lot," I said.

As we began to put the packages into the bag, though, I could sense it began to take on some weight, and when it was all done, I held it up with two fingers through the handles to get a sense of it.

"Dunno, no idea really," I admitted.

It was passed around for everyone to weigh it on their own personal hand scales. Jane then suggested we try to compare it to something we know the weight of, like a bag of sugar or a tin of beans.

"But I don't know how much they weigh," said Connor.

"A bag of sugar, I think, is 500 grams maybe, but I'm not exactly sure of that," said Becky, "and tins of tomatoes or beans are about 400 grams, I think. I use a lot of tinned tomatoes, and that sounds about right."

"No, a bag of sugar is one kilo, I use sugar a lot, and I can picture "1kg" on the side of the packets," said Jane.

The debate went on for a while, and in the end there was a consensus that it was more than one tin of beans, but perhaps not quite as much as the bag of sugar, which we agreed was one kilo. If it was that much, though, it meant that we could have as much as a kilo of grass. It covered the whole fold-down train table at any rate. As the train rumbled on, I carefully repacked all the newspaper bundles and moved them to the depths of my bag. I kept just a little bit out, about the size of my thumb, which we all wanted to try. The irony was that this amount was about the size I thought I'd be getting in the first place, for ten dollars.

Nobody had any cigarette papers yet, and I had no idea if they even sold things like Rizla or rolling tobacco in Russia. But we all had plenty of cigarettes, so I carefully emptied one out by squeezing and rolling it in between thumb and forefinger. You were allowed to smoke on the trains at that time; there were many smoke-filled carriages, so as long as we opened the window, we reckoned it would be OK. After making a tobacco and grass mix, it was a fiddly effort to manually repack the cigarette up again, stuffing it in with a pen lid. It wasn't a very good solution, but it was the best we could do for now. The outcome of this Uzbek grass joint was OK, but it wasn't too overpowering. This was, in fact, fine by me as I didn't have very good tolerance anyway. I felt that the others weren't regular smokers either, really, as I would maybe have picked up on that at some point over the last two years. So, it was a good thing, I reasoned, that it wasn't really strong, or else we'd have some white and green faces to deal with.

"You know... you normally do this stuff in ounces, right?" asked Connor, standing by the window, inhaling from the joint, and slowly exhaling out of the small window slot, as well as he could.

"Yes, you buy, like, an eighth of an ounce, or for me, a sixteenth is enough of a size usually," I replied

"So, I've just been working it out," he continued, "I think there are about 35 ounces in a kilo. I remember nerdy things like weights and measures. I did maths A level and advanced maths. Nearly did it for a degree, actually."

"What does that mean, then?" I asked.

"Well, let's say someone buys typically an eighth of an ounce then. It follows that a one-ounce purchase is eight times more than that typical purchase. If this is a kilo, it is 35 times more than that. So, 8 times 35 is...280. This means this is 280 times the size of a normal eighth of an ounce score! You've bought a few years' worth of grass!

"Jeez!" said Al, "what did you go and do that for, Henry?"

"I didn't mean to! It was an accident!" I joked back. "And anyway, I don't think it was much more than half a bag of sugar."

"Right you are then, pal, just 140 times bigger than a normal trip to your dealer!" said Al.

I had, of course, got way too much of the stuff, and contemplated that just chucking most of it away sometime might be a wise idea.

"What I was just thinking," said Jane, already looking a bit flushed, "is why do you have an empty plastic carrier bag in your rucksack, Al?"

"Ah, well, it's for my dirty socks, you know. I tend to get quite smelly feet, you see, and so, well, I can put all my dirty undies in the bag to keep the rest of *ma* stuff from smelling mingin'," Al replied.

We all processed what he said for a second or two… then burst out laughing.

The train was pretty slow, snaking through the countryside in its own good time. As I looked out of the window, I imagined someone riding a horse at a gentle canter (a Cossack perhaps?), or someone on a not particularly powerful moped, would have been able to keep up easily.

Arriving in Moscow that night, we crossed to the north of the city, where Vyacheslav had booked us into a bland student hostel for the night. The following morning, he transported us to a dock on the Moscow River where our cruise boat awaited us, sitting proudly in the water with its white hull shining and catching dancing reflections from the water below, with glorious blue skies and sunlight everywhere. We sat on some riverside stone steps for about an hour bathing in the warm sun, waiting for Vyacheslav to consult with various dockside officials, with twenty-five British passports held tightly in his fist. We had a boarding time of 9.30 am. When he was satisfied that he had achieved his aims, Vyacheslav gave out a small packed lunch to each of us containing hunks of bread and traditional Russian sausage, called *Kolbasa*. It had only been two hours since breakfast and certainly wasn't lunchtime. He said we had fifteen minutes more to wait, then I noticed he knocked the top of a bottle of Russian beer and practically downed it in one. Perhaps giving us the lunch at 9.15 am was to help him justify a lunchtime drink, I thought.

Throughout the next two weeks, he regularly refreshed himself in this way, no matter the hour. He seemed determined to enjoy it, too, as a holiday for himself, but I didn't blame him for that as he probably didn't get the opportunity to go on holiday otherwise. Russians on his pay grade probably couldn't afford them anyway. So I was happy that he would enjoy his expenses paid trip as much as his students, and good for him. I also discovered through conversations that a decent monthly wage in Russia at the time was between forty and fifty dollars per month at the upper limit. Teachers perhaps were earning only around ten or fifteen dollars per month, which puts it into perspective that the trip we were about to take was probably more than a year's wages for Russians like Vyacheslav; so no wonder he was going to enjoy it. Also, it became clearer still that my ten dollars outlay the day before was way more money than I had realised at the time.

CHAPTER 7

The boat trip we embarked upon in 1992 is still one that you can see on offer today, advertised as a luxury cruise for thousands of dollars.

I didn't realise this at the time; I thought we were just jumping aboard an old chugger for a nice bit of sightseeing. It was to be one week cruising upriver from Moscow to St Petersburg and then back again. It was primarily on the River Volga, the longest river in Europe, stretching from St Petersburg in the north to the Caspian Sea in the south. At times the river opened into lakes, such as Lake Onega, so vast you could barely see the shore, and you felt you could have been at sea, and other times it was narrower with countryside and fields either side. We had two nights scheduled in St Petersburg to see the city before the return trip back down to Moscow, the way we had come.

I shared a cabin with Al. It was small but comfortable with bunk beds and an ensuite WC and shower. I took the top bunk. As we left Moscow, the river expanded into a wide channel, and we stood on the deck and watched all sorts of commercial boats and barges going about their jobs in the crystal-clear air and bright sun, as well as a few leisure sailing boats that we waved to.

Meals were served three times a day in the cafeteria restaurant by bored-looking middle-aged women who hadn't heard about the western concepts of customers, or service.

The food was really quite terrible, too. Instructions were barked out to us, and food choices (not that there really were any) were slapped down onto our plates. Breakfast was limited to items such as hard brown bread, kacha (a buckwheat porridge), and very oily fried eggs on their own. This came with sweet black tea. At dinner time, you would see the mainstays of more hard bread and kolbasa – the hard sausage-like salami, a hard, tasteless cheese, and a thin, peppery cabbage soup with a great name – "shchtii", or a watery meat stew version, hopefully with potatoes. I am going to have to assume that these days the luxury cruises of similar itineraries you see advertised in the Sunday papers for thousands of pounds now have improved dining aboard.

The tour included several stop-offs on the way to St Petersburg, amongst often beautiful countryside and big landscapes. The settlement of Uglich was one of the first places we moored up for a wander around. It dates to the twelfth century and comprises churches, chapels and other old buildings spanning the centuries since. It is old Russia at its finest. Ivan the Terrible (1530-1584), the first tsar of all Russia, and a violent despot, exiled one of his wives here, Maria Nagaya. In one of the gardens, her 10-year-old son Prince Mikhail, heir to the throne, was murdered by Boris Gordunov, trying to clear his own path to the throne. Although it was unsuccessful, Gordunov eventually ruled Russia until 1605, but not until after Ivan's death. After Gordunov, Russia again descended into what history calls *dark years* of poor rule, with the good times not really restored until the reign of Peter the Great, nearly a century later. But from the early 1600s, the Romanovs retained their hold on power in Russia, which was to last until 1917. The whole settlement of Uglich felt very heavy with history, and I tried to imagine these characters walking through the very doorways I was standing in. It was largely unmodernised and was like stepping back in time.

The town of Goritsky is a tiny fairy tale settlement on the banks of the river, too, which we visited at another stop. We walked around it and took photographs, but also were shepherded around and fed information by a tour guide. Goritsky is home to monasteries and folklore. The Goritsky Nunnery is a ghostly white building nestling in the trees by the river, founded by Princess Efrosinya, the wife of one of Ivan the Terrible's sons, in 1554. Its aura of purity and religious calm was shattered when Ivan suspected her of treason and had her brutally drowned in the river. Worse still for the place, Ivan then turned the wholesome nunnery into his personal harem for abducted Russian beauties.

The journey up the peaceful river and lakes passed through settlements like this and stunning scenery along the way. On the third morning, I woke up very early at dawn and sat on the deck looking out at the sun rising over the misty dead calm water. It was beautiful. As the sun burned away the morning mist, it revealed hundreds of river birds racing over its surface in flight.

On the day before we reached St Petersburg, we moored up outside a town called Petrozavodsk. It was so far north that it had passed back and forth over the centuries between Russia and Finland. We weren't permitted to go into the town, as the captain was just killing a couple of hours to get our timing right for arriving in St Petersburg the following day with the port authorities. But we were allowed off the boat to stretch our legs in the grassy fields near the boat. As we roamed a short distance away, we saw some local lads playing football, and after putting a few glances and feelers their way, we managed to do our bit for Russo-British relations by having a little kickabout with them. It was UK vs Russia, and of course – jumpers for goalposts. It was a nice moment, and I can't actually remember the score, of course, but seeing as nobody can contradict me… I may as well say we ran out 5-3 winners, and I scored a hat trick.

CHAPTER 8

We weren't alone on this sightseeing river trip. The boat had four decks, dozens of cabins and probably nearly two hundred passengers overall. Built in Eastern Europe in the 1970s or '80s, the river cruiser was also designed for those on board to try and enjoy themselves, with two bars, a dance floor area, sun decks, and the restaurant. We were the only people from the UK, though; the other travellers were Russians, or from the former Soviet states, I assumed.

They were no doubt on a high-end trip themselves, people in a privileged position, a special job, or those with "new" money that was just starting to be made by those with quick wits in Russia in the early nineties.

On the first night aboard, we naturally took ourselves into the bar. Al and I were in a group that included the Bristol lot, namely Becky, Jane, Connor and Tom, plus Sam and Paul from Oxford. Although I had my newly purchased mountain of grass still safely tucked away in the depths of the bag, I decided it was best left as deep as possible in there for this trip across the Russian territories. So, we made good use of the bar, which had a good selection of drinks for Russia - some beer, vodka and Soviet champagne, the *Sovietskoye Champanskoye*. On the first night, there were plenty of people in there.

There was a Russian man with a guitar, in his thirties, who seemed like a bit of a cool dude, who played a few songs as the night unwound nicely. The traditional Russian songs he showcased were beautiful; they seemed so heavy with feeling and passion. Russian pop music had just begun to take off recently, but this Russian crooner was more into the classics, you could say, and cultured, too. He performed a romantic Russian accented version of "Summertime" by Ella Fitzgerald, which I liked. We could almost have been anywhere at that moment, a Paris bar or a café in Sicily. But on the back of a boat cruising up the Volga on a warm, Russian summer night seemed just as good.

Towards the end of that first night, I noticed a girl around my age arrive in the bar; she was a stunning Russian beauty: a classic Slavic look of light blonde hair, high cheekbones, piercing silvery-green eyes. Not being a very forward kind of guy, I didn't talk to her at all, but we did lock eyes for a moment or two, which my ego took to mean, "I see you; I notice you; I like what I see!" Well, that's what I thought of her, and I felt that she looked like she was thinking something similar. This country, I thought, just got more interesting.

Unfortunately, a couple of days passed after that, in which I didn't manage to see the Russian beauty again.

However, I had less opportunity to do so as Vyacheslav kept us pretty busy, including our sightseeing land walkabouts. We docked the next day in a beautiful bay surrounded by pine forests and hills, and we took a long walk through the fragrant fresh countryside. As we followed the undulating foot trails, we had great views now and then of wooded islands and birdlife in the lakes through which our boat was voyaging, but I kept a lookout for the girl.

After about five days of travelling through the rivers and lakes, we arrived in St Petersburg. We spent two days docked there, sightseeing by day, returning to the boat to sleep at night. It's an attractive and grand city in the northeast of Russia and was the old capital city of imperial Russia for two hundred years before Lenin decided to make Moscow the capital in 1918 to protect the government from potential anti-communist foreign aggressors. Peter the Great was quite comfortable with it as his window on the west and launched his navy from there in glorious battles against the Swedes. A great number of bridges over the city's waterways are reminiscent of Amsterdam, Paris, or other western European cities in a way. We went on two days of tourist day trips around the city. Its European and baroque architecture was very grand, especially the splendid Winter Palace, home to many Tsars and Tsarinas before it was famously stormed by the Bolsheviks in 1917. This led to the end of the longest monarchy Europe has ever seen, stretching back unbroken for nearly 600 years. It is an immense palace in the centre of St Petersburg with a vast square in front of it, all set off well in the bright sunlight and blue skies above.

I felt our timing was interesting, too. Reminders of the royal and aristocratic past, with the grandeur of this architecture similar to western capital cities, were everywhere. Contrasting this, I noted that the Soviet Union, which had replaced the Tsars 600-year rule, had itself only just been overthrown one year ago in 1991, after managing just 74 years. The political theories of communism and Marxism, which were embraced by Trotsky, Lenin and Stalin, were to give a voice, rights, and freedom back to the people of Russia, replace the inequalities of society, and make the country a fairer place. They overthrew the tyrants who oppressed and starved their people, but did they replace it with something better?

In their worst years, the Romanovs executed around 200 citizens in a year for being deemed enemies of the state. Within five years of the new Soviet Union, under Lenin, they were executing over 1000 people per month. Stalin, as we know, increased this to tens of thousands of murders once he really got going. Power, it would seem, had a dramatic effect on the Bolshevik leaders once they got it.

In the bar on the first night in the city, I was well lubricated and in high spirits and free of my usual inhibitions when I suddenly realised that the Russian beauty was next to me. She had entered the bar without me noticing and had taken up a seat at the table behind me. Although she was with a group of two other people, she smiled as our eyes connected. I leapt into action.

"Hello, how are you?" I offered, raising my glass as if to chink hers, and was delighted when she matched my opener and raised it with a gambit of her own "Hi, I am Katya. Are all Englishmen as handsome as you?!"

"No, I don't think so; I am one of the most handsome ones!" I was a natural at this, thanks to the Dutch courage.

The evening, which was already quite late, progressed quickly, and the flirtation continued. Katya joined our table, sitting with Al, Tom and Connor, but seemingly only with eyes for me. I surprised myself with my ability to flirt confidently, as this was usually not my strength. By default, I am shy and lamentably poor at flirting due to low self-confidence but catch me at the right time, with inhibitions removed, and I can do a reasonably good job, I suppose. Then again, many drunk people think they are funnier or more attractive than they really are. She explained that she worked for Radio Moscow, the official Russian state radio broadcaster, as a journalist - a music journalist no less. This seemed very impressive to me. As a student, I had yet to enter the employment world other than holiday jobs such as labouring or bar work. So being on a boat in St Petersburg, aged 21, flirting very successfully with a Russian beauty who also happened to be a music journalist for Radio Moscow gave me a surge of confidence.

As the evening wound down, I stayed out on the deck talking with Katya while most people turned in. She didn't seem quite as beautiful up close as I had taken her for when I spotted her across the room a few days earlier, and the pale eyes now seemed brown; she also seemed a bit taller than before. Nonetheless, she seemed super keen still, and we were leaning in on each other, shoulder to shoulder, and ultimately the leaning led to heads touching, and a kiss sealed the deal. She followed me, stumbling back to the cabin I shared with Al, and we clambered onto my bunk together, clawing at each other drunkenly.

I woke up the following morning in my bunk with bright daylight streaming in, and Katya squeezed in next to me. I felt awful; the cold light of day made the situation feel bad. I had a hangover, and neither of us looked very good in that way you do after you have drunk too much the night before. The fantasy of this beauty that had been in my mind for a few days was more distant now, the joyful feelings of triumph and achievement were lingering but mostly stale, and I felt a bit shameful. I didn't know what to say, but I was pleased to see we were both still wearing underwear, so I was pretty sure this backed up my recollections that we hadn't gone too far. She left, amicably so, and smilingly said we'd see each other later. She was interviewing some new band or other that day, and I had my own excursions planned with the group.

Over breakfast, Al was shaking his head, telling me we'd woken him up a little, but he wasn't that upset with me. I think he found it more amusing than anything else. I was more upset, as now I didn't know how to feel, and I already knew that I didn't want to see Katya later, as sobriety returned me to my usual shy self. It was just awkward now.

After breakfast, Vyacheslav explained that we had no group sightseeing tour in St Petersburg that day. We could go around by ourselves, but we had to be back on board by 3pm, as at 4pm on the dot, the boat would be leaving the city. Our time in St Petersburg would end, and we would be casting off, heading back to Moscow, which would take just four days due to fewer stops. "Don't be late!" he insisted, or we would be left behind, which sounded quite dramatic.

I nursed my headache around the city for that last day. We took photographs on Nevsky Prospect, one of the most famous streets in St Petersburg, and the Battleship Potemkin, a World War One Russian navy battleship from which shells were fired into the city to signal to the workers to join in the uprising of the Bolsheviks in

October 1917. As well as the grand Winter Palace, we saw more of the country's former glory evidenced around the city. There are also lots of canals from which the city gains the nickname of the Venice of the north. Peter the Great made this city his window into Europe, where he based his navy, and it was designed at great expense to stir awe and envy from overseas. Catherine the Great had also ensured the city continued to exude prestige, and it is by far the most beautiful city in Russia. Not that I have seen more than three or four, mind you.

Grand as the buildings and bridges are, however, the 74 years of communist rule had made a good stab at bringing the feeling of the place down. In contrast to the former glories, the once exclusive shops set within the facades of previous centuries' grand buildings had sobered into plain offices or cinemas. As this was just a few months into a new era for Russia, many of the shop fronts were still very drab and uninviting, which soured some of the splendour of the place. It seemed that every car was a Lada, and ramshackle vans or buses made up the rest of the traffic. I could see the lack of real wealth in most people and even some homelessness on pavements. On one occasion, two policemen were physically trying to move a homeless man on, perhaps under orders to avoid making this side of inequality visible to the general public.

On the previous day, our tour guide had pointed

down Nevsky Prospect with pride asking us to look at how beautiful the street was, although it seemed sad to have such excellent real estate housing such drab contents. She pointed out mansions or apartment blocks as we went, calling them by what they used to be, not what they were now. Here Gogol lived, and this was the place where Tchaikovsky died. Faberge's workshop used to be in this building, and Dostoyevsky drew his last breath in the building behind here. I loved the history of the place nonetheless. The rug had been pulled from beneath its feet for most of the 20th century. The enforced enslavement of the population to the state had left its mark. Still, a powerful country, of course, and a superpower if you score it in nuclear weapons, but the ordinary people were by no means enriched now.

For much of the day, I was also getting worried about seeing Katya again. In the first place, my beer goggles had led me to see things differently and act in a way I would not usually do and secondly, my evening with her in the cabin bunk bed was something I now felt bad about and didn't want to repeat. If she was still keen on me, how would I get through the next five days sharing a boat that I couldn't get off? Al unhelpfully told me not to worry, that things would work out, but if not, that I only had myself to blame. He was enjoying my suffering too much.

Back on board that afternoon, we were both leaning

on the upper deck railings looking over at the city just before 4 pm. We had got back in good time; in fact, we came back a little earlier as a few in our group had developed stomach cramps, which later turned into the runs that forced them to convalesce in their cabins for much of the next couple of days.

"I don't think my tummy is very well, Henry," said Al, "but not as bad as you're feeling, eh?" then he began singing "Katya and Henry... together on the Love Boat...!"

"Give it a rest, please!" in vain came my reply, knowing there'd be little sympathy from him.

Then the boat's horn blasted a final couple of times, engines chugged into life, and we began to slide away from the dock.

"Hang on, is that Katya? Yes, it is!" cried Al, pointing at the concrete steps on dry land now twenty metres away from the boat.

"I don't believe it," I said. Sure enough, as we looked over at the steps, it was unmistakably a panicked looking Katya, running down the steps and onto the dock, waving her arms, trying to get the attention of anyone on the boat. I couldn't believe it. We both waved back, for my part more in relief than anything else.

"Shall we get someone?" asked Al.

"It's too late," I said half in hope before adding, "They can't go back...." And indeed, they did not.

Of course, I feel awful for Katya, who missed her return boat, probably got in trouble at work, and probably had belongings on board. But only looking at it from my point of view, my predicament was sorted out in perfect dramatic fashion on the banks of the Volga.

I could say that nothing interesting happened on the return leg of the boat trip, but this would not be true. We enjoyed a couple of more restrained days after that; the food on the boat was still awful, and nearly half of our number were suffering upset stomachs with horrible diarrhoea, and kept low profiles in their cabins. We had a couple of bar evenings, but nothing crazy.

On day three of the southbound voyage, I pushed through the door of the bar and was stunned to see, sitting in the corner, none other than the Russian beauty I had first seen. Although I had assumed that Katya had been my Russian beauty, albeit more disappointing once I met her properly, now seeing this girl before me, I realised that they were two separate people! I was stunned, in a good way. Additionally, I could also see that this girl definitely was quite beautiful, just as I remembered her, and I was not wearing any goggles now, either.

We locked eyes once more as we had done over a week before. I could not believe that I had fallen into the arms of Katya, thinking it was this girl. I hadn't really been happy about the Katya "thing", trying to work out how to avoid her and then being saved by the bell literally when she missed the boat. Now, I was staring at this Russian girl right before me, again, and realising I had not even met her yet, and she was smiling back at me.

We introduced ourselves to each other, and she said her name was Oksana. Katya had been an imposter, although blameless, of course. We struck up a conversation and had a drink, but not too much. Oksana was one year younger than me and was on the trip with relatives. We talked properly that first night, and there was no drunken stumbling or fumbling.

We just talked and flirted mildly but respectfully. The next night, we met up again and sat out on the deck looking at the stars, not in the bar. We exchanged stories about our families, but in basic detail only as my Russian was still not very good for long conversations. Eventually, after what seemed like endless smiling and positive body language, we held hands, and kissed. It was much more wholesome, decent and respectful.

Oksana, or Ksusha as she told me her familiar or pet name was, was undoubtedly the beautiful girl of the boat for me. But she lived in Yaroslavl, some days' travel from Voronezh. I knew I couldn't control my own ability to travel around Russia, but we exchanged postal addresses and promised to write to each other.

Subsequently, we did write to each other once or twice. It was exciting to read her first *love* letter a few weeks later and respond to it, but we never saw each other again. It was a relationship that was destined to have no future, unfortunately. Now and then, I remember that night I spent sitting on the boat's open deck with Ksusha, looking at the bright stars twinkling in the black sky, in the warm September night on the river Volga. We kissed and looked at each other intently; for my part, this was because she was so beautiful to look at and quite mesmerising. Our conversation was limited, of course. However, I cannot really begin to understand what she may have seen in me.

For all its fairy tale memories that it holds for me, unfortunately, there is one other reason why I will never forget the memory of that second night. As we kissed, we were sitting on a pile of wooden planks on the ships deck, a bit like builders' planks. I have no idea their purpose, but we spent the whole night sitting on them. While it was a warm night to start with, it grew colder later on, and the planks themselves were cold even to begin with. For a few days afterwards, I suffered from haemorrhoids for the first time in my life. I put it down to sitting squarely upon these cold planks for a few hours with Ksusha, pressurising my posterior enough to induce the inflammation. I still suffer from piles every now and then, and every time, I still think of those Russian planks and the twinkling stars.

CHAPTER 9

A few days later, we were back in hostel number 4 after our Volga adventures, to begin our academic studies at Voronezh State University.

Late September was still warm, and our Russian friends revelled in pointing out that every year foreign students arrive with only one image of Russia in their minds, the cold and icy one. They told us our families would be surprised with our suntans. I suspected that any suntan would, of course, have faded by then, seeing as there would surely be a Russian winter to come along between now and when we saw our relatives again. Yet, it was as warm as a Greek island during the summer, which surprised us and was close to 30 degrees centigrade on the hottest days.

In the first week back, we were given more information about the university and how our classes would take shape. We visited the main university buildings in the centre of Voronezh. These were about a mile away from the hostel, half an hour's walk away. The direction would be to exit the hostel, cross the main road, Friedreich Engels Street, and cross straight through the pretty little Pervomaiski Park, crisscrossed as it was with footpaths. At the other side of the park was a crossroads, from which it would be one straight main drag all the way along Revolution Prospect. The crossroads at the head of Revolution Prospect was a significant traffic hub marshalled by police with the word "Militia" on their backs.

Militia sounds like a racket of some sort, but it really was just the official and actual title for these traffic police. Called *Militsiya*, pronouncing the "t", the traffic cops were just one department of the official internal affairs authorities, including regular police, firefighters, prison officers and maybe others. Later, I realised that corruption was, in fact, part of everyday life. The traffic cop *militsiya* also ran a reasonably strong racket, often stopping drivers for little reason other than to extract a bribe from them just for letting them on their way, or they would face a dreamt-up traffic offence. Throughout the 1990s, the militsiya was minimally funded, equipped and supported, and very poorly paid. So, bribery and corruption, combined with organised crime, led to almost no public trust in them.

From this crossroads, to get to the university's main buildings, students would need to travel up Revolution Prospect, the main street of this district, by foot, but there were also buses. Like many others, this street had large solid buildings on either side, forming blocks, and many contained official shops. As the economy moved much faster than the infrastructure, the road was also lined with dozens of kiosks in front of the actual shops, selling cheap and fast-moving retail goods, snacks, drinks, cigarettes and so on. About half a mile along, at the end of Revolution Prospect, it opened into a large square where there was a statue of Lenin in the middle, in the classic pose, with his right arm opening wide to the imaginary crowd. Around the sides of the square were several Voronezh State University buildings. The one we needed to know about the most was called the Deconat. It was the administrative centre where we reported, where our details and passport copies were held, and where our lives were to be run from. There was an office there, where we each signed in at the start of our stay at Voronezh university.

However, the university decided that rather than travel this short journey and mingle in the actual lecture halls with the rest of the Russian students, which I would have really liked, we would, in fact, take our lessons in hostel number 4, on the first floor. As we lived on the third floor, this meant all we had to do was get dressed and walk down two flights of stairs and into the classroom designated for us in the mornings. It wasn't a full day by any means, just three or four mornings a week. We were all taught together as a British group, so it was a little isolated. This year was for just the Russian language (and culture) part of our UK university course. It was a limited curriculum, mainly language development skills, listening and reading comprehension, and, curiously, traditional Russian folksongs. Really, though, just being in the country and socialising with Russians would be the learning. A few different teachers taught us for variation, but predominantly we were led by a fifty-something Anglophone called Sergey Belkin. He had a heavily pitted face and smoked deathly strong Russian filterless cigarettes, called *papirosa*. To me, that sounded a bit like a paper roll or something. The tobacco was wrapped in cigarette paper as was usual, but papirosas had a completely hollow cardboard tube attached to them for a filter, which also acted as a kind of disposable cigarette holder. These were the worst cigarettes I ever tasted, but they were helpful for making joints with, especially the built-in roach. We just emptied the existing tobacco and replaced it with the new mix.

Mr Belkin was a very genuine man, and as I mentioned, he loved all things English. He seemed very happy that he had been given the job as our principal teacher. His English was excellent, but he explained he had never visited Britain, or even left the Voronezh region, in all his life, except for about half a dozen trips to Moscow. His teacher's salary was, of course, meagre, which would have made foreign travel out of his reach but also until two years ago, leaving the Soviet Union for any citizen was very difficult, anyway.

He would sometimes spend the entire lesson just

talking to us, he was so interested in talking to us and learning about our country and daily life, but in this way, we also learned about him. Philosophical discussions often got carried away off-topic as we delved into areas such as democracy, freedom, capitalism and so on. Although you knew he yearned to see the west, he did also open our minds to realising the problems with excess, and the virtues of equality, at least as the original communists had intended.

As with most Russians I got to know, he was a very generous man, and he invited our class to the small apartment he shared with his wife one evening. They laid out biscuits and tea for us, using their best cups, and we listened and talked. In a way, Mr Belkin was a bit like the teacher, John Keating, in the 1989 film *Dead Poets Society*, played by Robin Williams. He was able to captivate his students and open our eyes to seeing the world a little bit differently from how we were viewing it ourselves, perhaps. He wanted to give us good Russian hospitality, which I found commonplace amongst many Russians I got to know, who had very little but shared what they had.

CHAPTER 10

Hostel number 4 was a cosmopolitan hall of residence unlike any other I could imagine. We Brits were spread over the 3rd and 4th floors, in rooms with one other Russian student most of the time. There were also groups of other foreign students sprinkled around. There were two East German girls, Hanna and Karla, who shared with their Russian host at the end of our floor, and at the farthest end near the stairs and toilets, there were a couple of rooms with Italian and Syrian students. The Edinburgh lot from our contingent were on the 4th floor, which was a mix of Russians, Georgians, and even two Uzbek students. Conor and the quiet girl, Gwyn, from Bristol were also up there. The 5th floor was home to predominantly African students. For some reason, this surprised me initially, to see Angolan, Nigerian and Malian students turning up here in Russia to learn Russian as part of their student course back home. But I suppose this was lazy prejudice on my part; Russia has strong trade links with Africa now, so maybe it was no different at that time, including cultural exchange programmes. This reminds me of a little-known fact I heard that the amount of international trade by value between Russia and the USA in the fifteen years after the Soviet Union collapsed was not very much different to the value over the previous twenty years during the Cold War days.

I got to know two of these students from Mali quite well: Issa and Mamadou. Mamadou was a quiet man with a small and striking face, sharp cheekbones contouring beneath smooth glassy skin. As a Muslim, he didn't drink at all.

He spoke to me in quite broken English at first, when we were making each other's acquaintance, but as it was a struggle for him, we tried Russian. I had only heard native Russian and English (or Scottish) accented Russian until now, so Mamadou's African style accent was a struggle for me. As my Russian was still a work in progress, we happily realised that French was an easier way for us to communicate, as it was one of the official languages of Mali thanks to (?!) its colonial past. Issa was a friend of Mamadou, although I didn't know if they were friends from Mali as Issa smoked and drank heavily and was generally inebriated most of the time as well as being promiscuous. Mamadou was none of these things. They were an unlikely pair, but I would continue to know them for a while as they both ended up back in Bristol a year later for various reasons. I even spent Christmas Day by myself in my student digs with Mamadou, where we enjoyed beans on toast together on the festive day;

festive for me only, of course. I had a couple of beers; he had orange squash.

Hostel life was very colourful, with the green painted corridors often crowded with people chatting, scrounging cigarettes, or carrying ingredients to and from the one kitchen per floor where you'd compete for space to make a meal. There would be drunk people, hungover people, and loved up couples trying doors in the hope of finding a room without any people in it so they could snatch some private time.

The kitchen on our floor, unfortunately, suffered from overuse. It was hard to find it empty, and you often had to compete for space on the hob. If you left a pan of something simmering for a moment and left the room briefly, it would not be unusual to find it relegated to the side upon your return.

As autumn turned to winter, the floor became filthy very early on in the day, too, as people would walk the outside in on their boots, and when those boots brought in the snow with them, the floor became puddles of melted snow and dirt. In early November, we had a problem that further strained the situation as one of the window panes became cracked and then fell out. It wasn't fixed for three or four weeks, so it was constantly freezing in the kitchen. I vividly remember snow blowing through the broken window and onto the edge of the hob or directly onto the food in the pan at times. Not the most hygienic of kitchens.

The toilets were also a horrible place to go, but we had to visit them. They, too, suffered the wet and puddling floors as the snow was walked in and melted, but it was mixed, not only with dirt, but human waste, too. From the smell, I felt sure some drunk people just pissed in the general vicinity of the toilets rather than going all the way in.

There were six regular toilets in the boys, no urinals, 3 on each side of the room. They were slightly elevated, which was a good thing, and you had to try to pick out a route through the wet floor to reach them. It would have been inconvenient enough if it was just water from snowy boots on the floor, but as I say, I was reasonably sure it wasn't just water on the floor, as the room nearly always stank. The toilets had no seats, so for a number two, it was a case of hovering above the porcelain, or just sitting on the cold rim, with the loo roll to hand which you had to bring yourself. It got worse that, unfortunately, as we were not allowed, or requested not to, dispose of used toilet paper down the toilet. There was a small lidless bin behind each loo for your used tissue paper. It was hideous, and not everyone's excrement laden tissue paper landed a direct hit in the bin. I think this was why some people didn't get too near the loos for their number ones, so they just went near to the toilet and took aim from afar, and hence the situation just got worse. I used to dread going but also made a journey up and down the hostel from floor to floor to find the least offensive loos to use. To this day, I still find really disgusting toilet conditions hard to handle; my stomach turns, and I wonder if I was mentally scarred by hostel number 4. In later weeks and months, one of the massive benefits of making friends with people outside of the hostel with digs of their own was the ability to use a proper bathroom.

A few months into our stay in Russia, on January 20th 1993, to be precise, an article appeared in an English language daily newspaper called the Moscow Times, entitled "Where have our fees gone?" It resulted from some of our student group venting their frustrations to journalists about the conditions. Each student who enrolled on the Voronezh study programme had paid a total of £1,900 for the pleasure of a year's stay. The article suggested financial mismanagement on some scale.

Felicity Cave, the executive director of RLUS, had even paid a visit just before we all arrived to inspect the facility for herself. She was said to be less than impressed but commented that the delays in a renovation programme which was to be partly funded with our fees, was not altogether unsurprising. The article contained a quote by Igor Zornikov, the university rector, as follows; "30 per cent of the sum received from students was spent on teacher's salaries, 30 per cent on maintenance and 40 per cent went into a university fund to pay taxes and other expenses". The Russia I had begun to discover begins to give you a hint as to what the "other expenses" may have been. The article ended with Cave saying that "corruption is endemic in Russia".

CHAPTER 11

Life did, however, settle into something of a routine. We attended our lessons downstairs in the mornings, steadily improving our Russian language, Russian literature, and even Russian folksongs. We would sing along to Mr Belkin's guitar – he was our very own Serge Gainsbourg. In the afternoon, before the snow arrived in mid-November, we sometimes trotted over to the park opposite to play five-a-side football. Or we'd go about Voronezh in groups exploring the town.

My increasingly regular group included Becky and Jane, my roommate Al, Tom, and Sam (the Oxford redhead). I had previously known Connor, from Bristol, of course, but I didn't really socialise with him back in the UK or here all that much since the train to Moscow with the grass. He was also on the floor above and mostly spent time with the students from Edinburgh, also upstairs. I was more friendly with Tom back in Bristol and kept his company more here. He got on well with Al as well, and joined most of the football kickabouts. You would put Tom more in the sporty camp than the academic camp, you could say. Later, he developed a close friendship with Paul, who was something of a brainbox.

There were hardly any restaurants, bars or cafes like you'd expect in most cities, as this was still just one year after the Soviet Union had ended. However, they would soon be exploding on the scene. One good restaurant, though, called Café Anna, was in a hotel near the centre of town. I remembered that it had been spoken about on the train into Voronezh on our first night in Russia. It wasn't great as we'd think of describing a restaurant today. It was popular because, firstly, it existed where we knew of almost no other restaurants. Secondly, it served chicken, lamb cutlets and good wine. Such luxuries were not ubiquitous in Voronezh in 1992. It was costly for Russians, so I expected most customers were senior state officials, favoured members of the new group of *biznismen* or other people of influence or wealth. Or, of course, groups of immature British student twenty-somethings with foreign cash.

A couple of months into our stay, we discovered a newly opened pizza place imaginatively called "Pizzeria Italia", which all the students, foreign and Russian, were excited about. It had opened near the city's circus arena (an actual concrete building, not a tent), about two miles across town. We went there one day drooling at the thoughts of margarita and pepperoni pizzas.

The end product was a disappointing doughy oval shape base about the size of a shoe. It had a nasty sweet red paste very approximate to the tomato base that it was hoping to pass itself off as, topped with foodstuffs you could not really name, but which almost definitely had come from a tin. It was a big let-down, but it gives you an idea of how food became one of our main preoccupations. It was just so hard to find anything nice in terms of takeaway or ready to eat. As young students, we wanted to buy stuff ready to go. However, over time, we resigned ourselves to the fact that the best option was to buy fresh food from the babushkas, the occasional chicken or cheese from the proper markets, and just cook everything from scratch.

The nearest McDonald's to us at the time had opened the year before, in the summer of 1991. Rumour had it that it was the largest McDonald's in the world. But it was on Pushkin square, in Moscow, 500km away. During the months we spent in Voronezh, someone would go up to Moscow every five or six weeks or so. On these occasions, they would ask if anyone wanted any shopping from Moscow's better-stocked shops, such as the Irlandski Dom, or the Irish House. They would take a list and come back with tea bags, Marmite, oranges, etc. But every time, without fail, there would be several orders for Big Macs from McDonald's. There was no problem whatsoever that the burger would be around 12 – 24 hours old by the time it arrived and stone-cold, no problem at all.

CHAPTER 12

For 74 years, the Soviet regime had told its citizens that Capitalism was the root of all problems for the western world; one of the fundamental causes of debauched societies and ruined minds. But it proved to be quite a popular pursuit in Russia in 1992. Although they had a million miles still to go in terms of infrastructure, law, regulation, fiscal framework and so on, the man on the street (and woman) (and babushka) was pretty interested in making a buck.

While the country was still trying to organise itself from the top-down, matters were also organising themselves from the bottom up. The train station car park, as mentioned before, was a thriving black market for alcohol sales. Along many streets, there popped up numerous kiosks and cabins. From these, young men and women, but mostly men, would sell western cigarettes like Marlboro, Camel and Pall Mall, and vodka, cognac, coffee, sweets, condoms, lighters, watches, shampoo, batteries, Chinese toys and other items. I supposed they'd be selling at twice the price they'd managed to buy them for the week before. Most of these kiosks were wooden beach hut type cabins with a glazed serving hatch and reinforced with metal bars for security. The best *biznismen* had also managed to get themselves into real shops on the ground floor of actual buildings with a good pavement frontage. Once there, you could go up in the world and buy and sell higher-priced luxury goods or foreign currency. This mostly illegal, unregulated trade made for some quite dramatic inflation.

The prices of these items for us rich kids were still affordable as two times very cheap, is still cheap.

Buying a kilo of potatoes from a babushka for 12 roubles one week, 20 roubles the next, and over 30 roubles the week after that made life feel a bit edgy. I realise this was a bit of a first-world problem for me. For the general Russian population at the time, struggling on wages that were probably not keeping up, this was no doubt scary and led to huge problems and desperation. Nobody really knew how much to price things. One babushka could sometimes be too slow to keep up with inflation, compared to another further up the pavement, and sell items too cheaply. In contrast, the one with the higher price may have been too hasty, so it paid to shop around. I often saw them changing the price tag; if you saw one getting their pen out, you either rushed to do a deal at the current price or skipped towards a dozier one. It was a bit like being a commodity trader. When we had landed at Sheremyetovo airport, one dollar was worth around 120 roubles, but by the time we had only just returned from the boat trip, it was already 160 roubles to the dollar. It was hard to keep up.

Changing money was also something we learned never to do in banks. The best way to exchange our dollars for roubles was to do it in the kiosks, which were much faster at moving than the official exchange rates at the bank. Or a few of our Russian friends would change our dollars for us, as Alexei had told us he was able to do in the first week we were there before the boat trip.

Alexei was often around in the evenings, and he had marked my group of friends out as the group he was going to become friends with.

"Whatever rate you see in the bank, you will always get 20% better than that if you change your money either in the kiosks, or to make it really easy you just change it with me, OK?" he would say with his huge grin. "I was terrific friends with the English group last year, and I hope with you, too?" he said. "I will always give you the best rate, or if you hear of a better rate, I will just match it!"

Having had just one year at getting used to a market economy, Alexei was remarkably up to speed on things like comparing the market and offering the best deals. It wasn't just dollars that he traded but also soviet military watches, Cossack swords and soviet war medals. You could say that he was thirty years ahead of Sergey, the meerkat, regarding best price comparisons.

We learned that he also used to fly to London a few times each year and sell these items by the suitcase load in Covent Garden or Camden Market. He said he made plenty of money from his entrepreneurial activities, earning way more than his parents and teachers. He hadn't been to lectures for nearly a year. In fact, when it came to the end of year exams, he just went to the examiner's office and paid for his grades.

"I don't ask for full marks or anything like that, but we talk about it. They ask what I am looking for, and we agree that an exam score of 70% or 75% would sound OK. I give them some dollars; everyone's happy!" Corruption was endemic at this time in Russia. If teachers were making as little as fifteen US dollars per month, you could understand how tempting it was for them to accept a few dollars in exchange for giving good grades. If you were making a few hundred dollars per month, as Alexei probably was, then it was easy to do.

Although I didn't know it yet, I would take a bunch of old Soviet military watches, sourced through Alexei, and sell them at a handy profit myself back in the UK.

I was comparatively rich in Voronezh, with my UK student grant money affording me almost anything I wanted. But back in England, that wasn't the case. I took the full government grant, and to make some extra cash, I took various temporary jobs, such as bar work and night shifts in the Parcel Force depot. Alexei's entrepreneurial skills definitely rubbed off on me, I would say.

As an example, one year later and back in the UK, I made a caviar trade. Unofficially that is. Back in Bristol the following winter, Alexei contacted me to ask if I was interested in making some money from a hundred tins of Russian Osetra caviar. Someone was flying in with it, looking for £7 per tin, hoping for a quick sale. After a bit of research and a few calls, I managed to strike an agreement with the owner of a delicatessen style small supermarket in Wimbledon who would buy it from me. On the appointed day, I had borrowed a red VW Polo from my flatmate. I drove two hours to Heathrow to meet a Russian twenty-something young woman who was flying in with it all inside her luggage. I can't remember her name now, but we met in the arrival hall quickly enough, having received descriptions of one another beforehand. She had a second female companion with her, perhaps for security, or maybe as they also had other plans; I didn't ask. I drove us all to a meeting point in an office further into London, in Hammersmith.

It was a small, ground floor office on a high street between estate agents and coffee shops and the like. As it was a weekend, it was out of hours and quiet. When we were buzzed in, I was greeted by the deli owner who had agreed previously to pay me £14 per tin. He was a well-spoken but scruffily dressed older gentleman called Anthony. He owned a small chain of four or five shops between Wimbledon and Richmond. He checked the produce with me while the Russian girls waited silently across the room and paid me £1400 for the lot. Thanking him for his business, I presented the Russian with £700, and the three of us left. They asked me if I could drop them at an address in Ealing, which I did before I jumped back onto the M4 and drove back to Bristol.

That was quite a day, and although it felt like a bit of a shady drug deal at the time, Anthony was so friendly and aristocratic almost that nothing really seemed that bad about it. At the time, my monthly spending budget was around £200 per month so making £700 in one day gave me a real buzz. I cranked up the stereo of that little Polo and sang my head off all the way down the motorway feeling like a dude.

CHAPTER 13

You may be wondering what became of that mini-mountain of grass; there certainly was quite a lot of it, after all. Most evenings in the hostel became a party somewhere in one of our rooms. We didn't manage to find cigarette papers in the town, maybe as the practice of smoking rolling tobacco wasn't something that happened, or maybe I just didn't know where to look. It wasn't in Vicky's manual, that's for sure. So, in order to smoke it, we had to use normal cigarettes and turn them into joints by squeezing out the tobacco, then repacking it with our mixture. It was a bit of a faff, but with time on my hands, I used to make a few at a time. The only advantage to this was that they handily went back into the normal cigarette box alongside the regular ones. The other way was to use papirosa cigarettes, which had the advantage of a ready-made big roach on them.

Back in Voronezh, the second time we tried it was one evening in mine and Al's room, with Sam from two doors along, and Becky and Jane from the room opposite. It was OK but nothing too special; not very strong, and not worth telling stories about it to the next year's students, I didn't think. We tried to keep it low key so as not to attract unwanted attention.

Over the next few weeks, we smoked our joints in one or other of our rooms, now and then. Our quiet Russian roommate Nikolay was around one night, quietly sipping a beer with us. He said he had never tried it and asked if he could give it a try, although, after just one drag, he signalled that it was not his favourite thing and passed it straight back. As Nikolay was a non-smoker anyway, it was hardly surprising. Alexei was around on one of the evenings and, being the party guy and being the general good-time host that he was starting to become, he also partook.

Already red-faced from the drink, he said, "You know this is OK, but in Russia, we don't do this as much as you do in the UK. But I am a party guy, so I am happy to join you!"

Alexei also made a point that while alcohol, and specifically vodka, was consumed in vast quantities in Russia by almost all the population, the taking of drugs, or "narcotiki", was quite frowned upon generally, and certainly illegal. In the UK, cannabis use was commonplace and popular among certain parts of the population of the population, and as students, we felt we caused far less offence and certainly less disruption or threat than rowdy drunken louts out on the streets at closing time.

"So," I said to Alexei, "Russia encourages, and almost

makes it compulsory from a cultural point of view, for its citizens to drink vodka every day, which causes huge health issues and widespread alcoholism, yet it sees cannabis as a more serious threat and a problem that it has to stamp out?!"

"Yes, and no. Officially we don't have a drug problem in Russia; it doesn't exist. But unofficially, I can tell you there is a bit of a problem, which is embarrassing for the authorities. They just don't admit it."

He continued, "By the way, there are also no homosexual people in Russia...officially. They don't exist, either."

"So, if something is undesirable, they just deny it exists, so there is then no problem?" I replied.

"Yes, that's it, more or less. For that matter, we probably have no vegetarians either." He smiled, primarily at Becky, who he knew was a vegetarian.

"Oi, that's not true, Alexei! I was speaking to a girl in the hostel yesterday, Sofia, is it? And she said she's also a vegetarian." Becky objected.

"I'm joking about the vegetarians! But seriously, there's a lot of things wrong with Russia. My advice if you want to keep smoking this is to be careful, or smoke it outside or where nobody can see you, as it could bring you trouble," Alexei concluded.

I had so much of it still stashed away, too much of it, that I was happy to dish bundles of it out to whoever wanted some. I didn't ask for any money, of course, as the whole consignment only cost ten dollars. I heeded Alexei's words, though, and began to be quite discreet, preferring to stand outside the hostel by myself or with a friend to smoke a joint rather than be in people's faces with it. Just a few weeks later, when winter came, so did the snow. One evening with the party in full swing upstairs, I was shivering outside for my non-loutish, relaxing purpose. The snow was falling, and the temperature was a few degrees below freezing as I hopped from one foot to the other. I listened to the guitars, the singing and cheers, and the warm camaraderie emanating from the windows above and realised I was getting nothing from this pursuit, and this wasn't where the fun was to be had, so I cast my butt into the snow, and went back into the warmth.

CHAPTER 14

Sergei, who I had bought the grass from originally, turned out to be one of those people with a certain strength of personality that slightly scared me. I saw him around quite a lot in our hostel, but never with a joint or seemingly interested in that sort of high; he preferred to get drunk. Very drunk.

One afternoon he appeared in our doorway and alerted me to his presence with a very slurry "Privyet, Genry, moi horoshi droog!! (Hello, Henry, my good friend).

"Oh, hello Sergei, how are you?" I replied.

"I am absolutely good, and absolutely druuunk," he replied, elongating the word, maybe because he was so drunk. "But I am a professional, you know?"

"OK, great," I continued, "and thank you, by the way, for the other thing…."

"No, don't mention the 'thing'. I mean it, please. You know that thing doesn't interest me; it's not so good anyway. I helped you as I wanted to show you that I am a guy who gets things done; I know people; I can do things. Do you have some vodka?"

"We have a bit here." I pointed to the third-full bottle

of Russian vodka, on the tabletop by the window.

"That's great that's all I need," said Sergei with an outstretched hand. I walked over and passed it to him, then watched with Al as he upended it and drained the whole thing straight into his mouth, with just a few dribbles of liquid running out and through his stringy, sandy beard. I thought again, as I did that first night I met him, how his moustache and beard were reminiscent of the last Russian Tsar, Nicolas II, and our own Prince Michael of Kent, who, of course, is related to Nicolas II (his grandparents' cousin).

I was snapped out of the thought quickly, though, as he passed me the back the empty bottle with a wink, and I saw his eyes were red and menacing. He leaned in overly close to me, in that off-putting way that drunks do. "Thanks, my friend. You know I like many of your girls. English girls are very nice, like a rose flower; you can introduce me to the nice ones?" As he spoke, I tried not to focus on the dribble still running out of the sides of his mouth.

"OK, tomorrow maybe, when you're a bit…more…." I struggled to find the right words.

"No, no, no! Not now! Fuck your mother! I am in the middle of my drinking month, haha!" he roared out loud.

"They won't like me now, but you know, I only drink for one month – every day, and I stop completely for one month; that is how I live. I can meet them next month when I am sober. I am a completely good guy then; it's only one week from now, in fact…I think, haha!"

"What do you mean; you drink for one month on and one month off?!"

"Absolutely right. What's so hard to understand? Are you stupid or something? Yes, I just love drinking, but I don't like to do it just a little and then have to be good tomorrow for my studies, and have a hangover. So, I drink every night, and every day, for a month. And I stop all my studies; I do no work, but I have a nice party all the time.

But I am disciplined, so when one month is finished, I stop - I stop completely. Then, I catch up with all studies and even work a bit ahead, and teachers are very happy. You will not recognise me; you will see such a good boy. You will not think it's the same Sergei."

"Wow! that's not something I've seen before. Does it…?" but before I could finish, he had pushed off from the door frame towards someone else he recognised shouting "Nicolai!! Droog! Haha! I'm absolutely druuunk!" so I hurried away myself into Becky and Jane's room, thankful for a getaway.

It was, in fact, still mid-afternoon, and as I looked into their room, they had steaming mugs in their hand.

"Hi, Henry," said Becky, "Do you want a cuppa?"

"And we have coffee?" said Jane, sipping from her cup, "…of a sort!"

I was surprised to see the coffee. Nobody had any

decent coffee, as it was hard to find in Voronezh.

"Ooh, any good, though?" I asked Jane.

"No, it's actually pretty horrible. It's Brazilian instant coffee from the kiosk in Pervomaiski Park," she said, directing my gaze to a silver tin on the table.

"Mmmn, no thanks. Tea, please!"

I went on to describe to them what I had just learned about Sergei, and they uttered their vague disapprovals. A Russian girl called Sofia was in the room, a sweet-looking girl, but with a slightly squeaky voice which grated a bit. She took great care of her appearance, wearing her best stonewashed jeans when she could, and was very rarely seen without carefully applied makeup.

"I advise you all to be very careful of Sergei, especially during his drinking months," Sofia warned, "He is a mean guy behind that smile of his and can cause you trouble. There was a story about him throwing two cats out of a window on the 4th floor, either just for fun or to teach someone a lesson somehow!"

"Jeez, that's horrible! said Jane, "were they killed?"

"Thankfully no - cats and their nine lives," Sofia chirped, "they landed OK, luckily in the snow, and survived, but try to keep away from Sergei!" she concluded.

CHAPTER 15

Although both Becky and Jane were my classmates from Bristol, I hadn't really socialised with them all that much back home. During my time in Russia, however, I was now getting much closer to them. There was a third girl, Gwyn, from Bristol, too, but she was upstairs from us, and I rarely spoke to her. In fact, Gwyn rarely spoke to anyone and was quite reclusive. Becky was near the top of the class and the best of our group at speaking Russian, seemingly getting it grammatically correct too, which was the hardest bit for me. You had to use all the right endings, not just for the verbs, but the nouns, too, and I found this quite tricky. Becky had a boyfriend back in Bristol, called Jake, who I didn't know as he was studying French, but I had a picture in my mind of a fairly cool guy with a ponytail, who was no doubt out in a French-speaking land currently as part of his course. She had a pretty face with big brown eyes and fine, straight hair, which was naturally light brown, but she had dyed it a maroon-red colour. She was a cool cat and tended to attract male attention.

Jane was also set to get far better grades than me, doing her Russian as joint honours with English. Jane had an English dad and a Chinese mum, so she, too, had a distinctive look, with big brown eyes, pale skin, short dark hair worn in a bob, and an infectious smile. Her sense of humour and quick wit made Jane impossible to dislike. She was such great company always. She was small in stature, and alcohol affected her very quickly, turning her face bright pink from the second glass. These two became my good friends, and either their room or our room would usually attract a crowd and become the centre of things.

Sitting around on beds in the hostel was a common pastime. It was predominantly our default activity, in fact, until we found something interesting to do. Proper sightseeing organised with Vyacheslav, such as the boat trip, were brilliant of course, but such wonderful diversions were quite rare as they were quite expensive for the always strapped for cash university to organise, as the state of the hostels could attest to.

In the evenings, when I wasn't doing fun social stuff, I would often lie on my bed reading, writing in a journal I had begun, or writing letters home. My relationship with Lucy had lasted a year and a half until about the spring of 1992, so by this time, it was already about six months since it had ended. But I hadn't been with anyone since, and in these hours of downtime in Russia, I felt the weight of being alone sometimes heavy, and I found myself missing her. I wasn't what you would call a particularly outgoing guy; I was comfortable with myself and happy enough with my own company, but I was generally a shy guy around women. I hated the fact that I was never bold enough to try to make a play for the people I fancied, assuming they wouldn't like me back. My usual practice was to detect when someone seemed to like me, then decide if I wanted to reciprocate. That was how I found myself with Lucy in the first place, at any rate. In the early weeks here in Voronezh, I found myself writing to Lucy again, as I missed the comfort of being in a relationship. Al was in a relationship with a girl back home, called Isabelle, and he talked about her a lot and wrote to her all the time. It seemed to keep him well sustained emotionally. I wanted to share my experiences of this interesting country with someone from back home, and so I wrote to Lucy about it. I had loved her even though our relationship had only lasted a short while, and out here I missed the feeling of being loved and cared for.

Our relationship had not only been short, but it had been quite intense and had also included a pregnancy and termination. This had both drawn us even closer together but somehow also forced us apart. Even though we both solidly agreed on the course of action we took, we'd probably internally had very different sets of feelings about it. I wrote in my letter that I missed her and would like to have her with me to share the experiences I was having. I was not so good at being single, I guess, and so in my letter, I extended a romantic SOS signal. I am not sure how much I genuinely really wanted or needed her, or whether I just wanted love in general. I think it was probably the latter. The letter was certainly aided and abetted by the alcohol I drank while writing. I did receive a reply, too, and although I could feel in her words that she cared for me and valued what we had together, it was obvious that there would not be any rekindling of the relationship in the real sense of it. She had moved on.

While writing letters in the evening or reading a book, I would often combine it with having a drink. Before coming to Russia, I had been a bit worried about not liking vodka but thinking this was predominantly all we'd have to drink. I liked beer mostly, and wine occasionally, but not really any hard liquor. On the few times I'd downed vodka before, it tasted of nail varnish to me, and I would gag at the taste. I recalled this thought a few weeks in as I sat on my bed reading one night. I had settled down with my book with a supply of Pepsi, a glass, and one of the pint bottles of Pshenichnaya vodka. As I refilled my glass, I was surprised to see that I'd already had half a pint or more of vodka without even noticing. How quickly you get used to things.

One afternoon Al and I were enjoying rather more sensible mugs of tea in Becky and Jane's room. Jane was reading, I was smoking while staring at the pages of a book, and I noticed Becky had a preoccupied expression, looking up into the corner of the ceiling, toying with some idea it seemed.

"What's up?" I asked.

"Alexei's invited us to go round to his place tonight," Becky said.

"For a change of scene, it could be fun," Jane added, looking up from her book, "but I think it's because he fancies the pants off Becky!"

Becky was blushing straight away, but I also knew it to be completely true as Alexei was not very subtle in his flirting with anyone, and I had seen it happening quite a lot towards Becky. She had been resistant to his charm and had been almost hostile to his advances, but two things were true about this situation; firstly, his charms had begun to work on her, and secondly, the lady had protested too much, and I think she fancied him back a little bit.

"Oh yes, well, he is a charmer, that's for sure, but he also loves himself so much it's untrue. He's such a chauvinist; it's ridiculous. He thinks women are just a prize to win or something," Becky protested too much.

"But do you want to go?" I asked.

"Well, yes, I don't think we should say no, but can you guys come with us?" Becky replied.

We agreed to go, to act as chaperones to our lady charges, but we knew, in any case, it would be fun. That evening, the four of us went together to Alexei's place. Alexei came over to the hostel at first with his friend Oleg, who I hadn't met before. Oleg was a big guy, with a bit of a gut on him, very much like the Russian bear of a man you read about in fiction, but he was all smiles, and I warmed to him.

"I am coming to the party of the main man, my friend Mr Alexei Kirpikov. I am Oleg Medvedev at your service," he said, extending his hand. We had a quick couple of drinks in the hostel first, and Alexei explained how close his place was. In fact, we'd all walked right past it many times already, he said, as the archway through which we walked to get to the Ulitsa Mira babushkas and the train station housed the entranceway to his apartment.

In the darkness we headed over the rough ground behind the hostel to join the pathway between the trees, in the direction of the archway and Ulitsa Mira. An occasional street lamp on the pathway enabled us to see well enough, though. Autumn temperatures were evident as I watched the steamy breath of those ahead of me rise through the cold night air into the arc of the yellow light of the lamps.

Soon enough, I supposed, winter would arrive and bring with it the Russian snow. As we arrived in the archway going through the building, we followed Alexei into a stairwell, up a couple of steps, then right angles up another few, and into his place, a ground floor apartment or *kvartira*, number 3. From the entrance hallway, there was a kitchen to the left, a separate bathroom to the right, then two main rooms directly in front of you as you entered, with windows that looked out onto the street. I didn't really think about it at the time, but kind of a prime location, I suppose. There were a few people in there already, all students we presumed, but all Russians - about three girls and two or three more guys. They had a small spread of nibbles on the table for us and could not have been more welcoming. I recognised slices of black bread, with Russian *kolbasa* (sausage), some cheese, and jars of pickled gherkins, cucumbers and onions.

I couldn't really work out who actually lived in the apartment, other than Alexei, of course. Oleg commanded the room and was the best English speaker. I think he must have watched a lot of American movies as he had a certain twang and flourish to his accent. He was also keen to show his English off to us. A small-framed chatty guy called Sacha arrived halfway through the evening.

He was full of energy, spoke very fast and seemed very interested in everyone, laughing a lot. There was a quiet guy called Vadim, who, by contrast, said very little. Vadim was of medium build and had very short dark hair like a crew cut, and spoke no English. As I got to know Alexei more over the coming weeks, Vadim seemed to be his sidekick; he had a car called a Moskvich, a small 5-door hatchback. It was a head-turner of a car at that time when practically every other car was a square, boxy Lada. Vadim drove Alexei wherever he wanted to go and us, too, occasionally.

There were two girls, Nadia and Tatiana, both with blonde hair. Nadia was super smiley, with bright lipstick, and I couldn't help noticing she also had an impressive bust. She had a sing-song voice and merrily got into the party mood. Nadia also seemed to mother the boys and did most of the food preparation. Tatiana, who they also called Tanya most of the time for short, was more restrained, cooler, and had that female assuredness that I had got to know since being in the country. I couldn't tell if this Tatiana/Tanya was confident or shy. I knew that my own shyness was sometimes mistaken for steely confidence, so I thought I perhaps recognised this in her. Either way, the two ladies got my attention, and I found myself thinking that here in Russia, men are men, and women are women.

What I mean by that is that the sexes in Russia seemed more defined, to me, than in the UK, where we had more fluidity and certainly more equality. Here, the men called all women "girl", regardless of their age, it seemed, and the women went along with the female stereotype. They waited on the men, did most of the domestic chores, and were the fairer sex. It probably felt outdated to us where we had long been narrowing the gaps between men and women. We had stay-at-home dads, women as main breadwinners, and women wore whatever style of clothes they liked, not just what they thought the men liked to see them wearing. We had gay men, gay women, and sexual equality had long been happening in the UK, although we were still a long way before the term LGBTQ became mainstream. But here in Russia, the distinctions were still more old fashioned, and of course, pretty sexist, you could say. Of course, homosexuality didn't officially exist, Alexei had told us before, that's how sexist and discriminatory it was. Being gay in Russia must have been a nightmare. The men would do the drinking and smoking, while the women would not, as it wasn't ladylike. Having said that, both Tanya and Nadia were from a younger and more liberated generation and were enjoying a drink, just as the female students in the hostel did. Things were, of course, going to slowly change in this respect.

They were even smoking too, shock horror! At this time, you would almost never see mature women smoking in the street; that was almost unheard of. The Russian girls I got to know in Voronezh, even if they smoked in their private life, would often feel just too uncomfortable to smoke in the street, in public, where they would be judged and disapproved of.

I must carefully choose my words here because I fully support sexual equality, choice, and gender self-identification and am against all forms of discrimination.

But I knew very little about some of that in 1992, at the age of twenty-one. But I do know that I was attracted to the *femininity* of some of the Russian girls. I had maybe lived a bit of a sheltered life up to this point, but at any rate, they turned my head. They had some aura about them.

The high cheekbones and piercing eyes helped, of course, or maybe their use of make-up contrasted impressionably on me versus my limited experience of how it was used in England. It was also more than just looks. Maybe their attitude or personalities were also different, their poise, or even just the way they walked. I was struck by Tanya's walk; the confident and unapologetic sway of the hips, she oozed confidence which I hadn't really encountered too much in England. Of course, it did exist, but I was naïve and thought I was seeing something for the first time anyway. It seemed to say, "I am a woman, look at me, you are a man, and we are different. We are opposites, not the same, and opposites attract". She wore a red cotton party top, which had long sleeves and a netting cuff, and a red skirt that nearly matched it with light tan-coloured tights that were slightly sparkly. I was attracted to her straight away.

The evening passed in much the same way as all the other parties usually did, and was fun - the self-made fun that Russians were brilliant at. Entertainment in Voronezh was quite limited; there were no pubs, bars or clubs like in England. This was the same for most parts of Russia outside Moscow. The city's hospitality was limited to a handful of restaurants, such as the Café Anna in the centre of town, the circus, and one or two theatres of stark soviet architectural design, which would put on traditional plays now and then, or even a puppet show. Puppetry was quite a big thing in Russia traditionally, - a critically acclaimed art form, nothing like Punch and Judy.

There was a cinema too, where in Soviet times, officially approved propaganda films would have been shown, but there were was still nothing of much quality there only one year after the end of communist party soviet rule. So, people used each other for entertainment. They crammed into small rooms much like this one, and talked, sang, and made merry.

In fact, this party was a good deal better than most of the ones in the hostel. The food had been thought about a bit more beforehand, it was served and shared around a bit better, and everyone was giving more attention to each other, making more effort than the standard level of party in the hostel. Alexei was certainly giving Becky a lot of attention, I noticed, but she seemed to be quite happy with it. Oleg played a traditional Russian song or two on the Spanish guitar - not really Spanish, of course. The vodka was drunk in Russian tradition too, which means in unison and neat. Glass beakers (*stakans*) were filled about a third of the way and passed around the whole group, and before drinking, a toast would be made, though before that the *zakuski* would be readied.

Zakuski was the word for tasters or nibbles. Vodka is an acquired taste, of course, but over the years, I imagine the quality was very wide-ranging, so some of it must also have tasted pretty bad, with varying levels of a nasty aftertaste. In Russia, it was therefore traditionally imperative to have zakuski to hand to immediately pop in your mouth to take away the rough taste after a vodka toast.

This ranged from the most desired options, such as a bite-sized piece of cooked meat, or pickled gherkin (nice strong taste), to the more commonplace options, which could be a chunk of black bread, a bit of cheese, or a slice of kolbasa. As Russians could spend most of the evening going through dozens of toasts, the table that evening was covered in many large plates of these appetisers.

"For the first toast," Alexei began holding his glass aloft, "I would like to welcome our English friends, Jane, Al, Genry, Tom and *Beckushka*, sorry I mean Becky!" he winked at Becky, "…to our small apartment, but also to our not so small country. You have been here a while, and I am happy that we have already become such good friends!" Cheers and chinks of glasses followed as we then drank our vodka – in one – as tradition demanded. Followed swiftly by the tasty morsels, of course.

Jane tried to drink her vodka in small sips. "No, no, no!" chided Alexei. "Jane, you must drink it all in one go!"

"I can't drink all that at once; it's too much!" she pleaded.

"OK, so let me ask you this: will you be drinking it *all*?" he asked. She nodded yes.

"Well then," he continued, "at the swimming pool, whether you step off the board with one foot or two, you still end up in the water! So *down the hatch*, as you English say!"

He smiled broadly, looking around the room as if expecting a round of applause.

"OK, but even if I sip it, I'll still be in the pool, won't I?" Jane replied but was met with blank expressions all around while people tried to follow the analogy.

"Oh, fuck it!" she followed up before we could work out whose line was the cleverest and downed the whole glass to a big cheer.

The evening continued in good spirits, with regular interruptions for more toasts. There was, of course, some beer and the cheap, ubiquitous soviet champagne brand, so we were able to sip "normal" drinks as we went along and not solely drink neat vodka all night.

"How do you like it?" someone asked me. I turned to see Tanya standing right by me and smiling at me after one of the toasts. "I'm Tatiana, but call me Tanya."

"Hello, I'm Henry, but you can call me…Genry?" I

replied. Then, remembering she had asked me a question, I continued, "Yes, very nice, I like it very much. But in England, I never drink vodka. I never liked the taste. But I am starting to like vodka since I have been here... in Russia, I mean, not in this apartment."

As I hashed my way through this sentence, I realised I was blushing, which annoyed me for three reasons.

Firstly, I thought this would make it look like I was a shy boy talking to someone he fancies, who is being betrayed by his cheeks. Secondly, because I hadn't decided whether I did fancy her or not, and if I should decide either way, this red face business was telling her that I did. Thirdly, I thought I was hopeless with girls when on the back foot and only good at flirting when I was being bold and confident and not blushing like a little boy, so should I be interested, my chances were now ruined anyway. And I thought all this in a quarter of a second.

"I don't really like it either," she replied, "I prefer champagne or juice," and she raised another glass with what looked like orange juice.

"What happens with the toasts when all the zakuski are finished?" I gestured towards the rapidly diminishing plates on the table.

"You just sniff the bread instead of eating it".

"What?!" I quizzed her

"You just sniff the bread. Even better to use hard, stale bread, a stronger smell. After you drink the vodka, you hold a piece of bread to your nose and... inhale", she simulated it holding a pretend piece. "It works just the same, and it doesn't run out," she said, educating me in new Russian ways.

"OK, strange, but when there is no more bread, what then?!"

"The boys just sniff their armpits!" she laughed.

CHAPTER 16

The next day I woke up in the hostel with a heavy head and blocked nose, as there had been quite a lot of toasts, and I was feeling the effects. Looking around the room, I saw that I was alone. I was used to Nikolay, our roommate being absent, as it happened frequently. We understood that his uncle lived in Voronezh, and he stayed there rather a lot. It was Understandable as the hostel was far from 5-star accommodation, or maybe Al and I had probably taken over the room a bit too much for his liking. We hadn't done this on purpose or to make Nikolay feel uncomfortable. It was just how the dynamic developed, I suppose. Combined with Becky and Jane's room directly opposite, these rooms down at our end of the corridor were often used by the UK collective for hanging out. As I looked at his empty bed, I hoped we had not unwittingly made Nikolay begin to feel as welcome as a turd in a swimming pool. Then again, maybe his uncle's place had a nice bathroom with a hot shower which would have got anyone running from the hostel, I suppose. Al also wasn't there, but no sooner had I given all this more than the faintest amount of processing the door opened than Al walked in, chuckling to himself.

"Henry, man, you'll never guess what; Jane said that Becky stayed over at Alexei's last night and hasn't come back yet!"

"Really, uh oh, well, we saw that coming a mile off," I replied.

The evening had gone well the night before overall. Alexei had been a good host and funny, too. He played to the gallery a lot but with a big smile and dancing eyes, and it was hard not to like him. He had been trying to talk to Becky most of the night, and without attempting to hide it or be subtle - he clearly fancied her. I recalled one part of their chat last night, where he was just not able to come to terms with Becky being a vegetarian.

"How can you survive without meat?" he had said, "I never get how come so many English girls are vegetarians. How do you even have the strength to stand up?"

"I can manage quite easily without meat." Becky had replied.

"But have you ever had any *Russian* meat!" the innuendo wasn't subtle, as more than a few groans bore witness.

I had liked talking to Tanya, though. After my initial awkwardness and blushing, I think we had got along well. I also recalled how she had sort of protected me when I had tried to get away with only drinking a sip of the vodka at the toasts and not downing it in one. Oleg and Vadim scolded me for it, but Tanya firmly told them where to go, making me feel good. Even so, not wanting them to think any less of me, I showed them I could down it anyway. So regardless of being well-defended, I still had a headache. By the end of the night, I nearly forgot we had been strangers at the start, or that she was Russian. I can't adequately explain it, but I hadn't felt that I was talking to a foreigner at all. I felt very comfortable, and it seemed we were of similar personalities. I knew I wanted to see her again soon, but then again, not really, as it made me feel a bit scared and sick just thinking about it.

I looked at the clock and saw it was late morning already. Al said we could find out about Becky later and then reminded me that we were going for a football kickabout in the park on the other side of Friedreich Engels Street. It was just a dusty bit of recreation ground, on the far side of the park, with some metal goalposts as the only bit of input to indicate football. Still, it was a great hangover cure and was good fun. With the lifestyle we had slipped into over the first few weeks in Voronezh, getting outside for a bit of exercise was very welcome. Besides, we were told that we'd no longer have the opportunity for this once the snow arrived in late October or early November.

Mamadou usually joined us for the football knockabouts, as he did on this occasion. Tom, Al and I were all bigger than him, but he out-skilled us easily.

He was a quiet and gentle person, with a soft voice and light frame. Mamadou was not the centre of attention in general, just a calm, smiling presence in most situations. However, on the football pitch, he dazzled with his silky skills learned back home in Mali. He took centre stage with the ball at his feet like never before. He also came alive, finding his voice, too, with fantastic put-downs, usually in French, for anyone he left on their arse. With stepovers, feints, and all sorts of nifty footwork, most of us were left for dust.

"Mamadou, you practically skinned us alive!" I said to him afterwards.

"Well, my friend", he replied, "I come in peace usually, but on the football pitch, it's a battle you have to win!"

When we got back to the hostel in the afternoon, I went into Becky and Jane's room and found them both there, drinking tea. Becky looked a bit sheepishly, having stayed over at Alexei's, and it was clear that the relationship had been taken up a level now, let's say. But she was keen to point out she was now very hungover and that last night was not altogether wholly her fault. I had a degree of sympathy for this viewpoint, as I knew she held him in a certain amount of disregard and liked to moan about him. If you asked her in the cold light of day if she wanted to sleep with him, I think she'd have officially said no. It would have appeared that Alexei did most of the seducing and not the other way around, using his clear skills in charm and persuasion. Looking at Becky, though, as embarrassed as she was trying to be, it does take two to tango. I sensed that she was not totally upset, and a wry smile escaped from the corners of her mouth now and then. My mind drifted to thoughts of Tanya and whether I would be giving my knees a hug of satisfaction any time soon, as I thought Becky was maybe doing with hers.

Hearing voices coming from the corridor outside, I thought I sensed some excitement, so I moved to get up to see what it was about.

"Yaasss!" the familiar sound of Al's voice told me that maybe something was going on.

When I opened the door, I could see straight into my and Al's room, where our group leader Vicky was sitting on my bed. I entered to see Al perched on his own bed holding the football, passing it from hand to hand, looking very happy. Tom was also in the room, looking like he'd enjoyed some good news too.

"You'll not believe it, Henry, man, guess what Vicky has just offered us?" Said Al.

I looked at Vicky, inviting her to spill the information.

"Well, the thing is, Henry," she said, "I have got a few tickets for a football match in Moscow next Thursday, and I wondered if you would like to come. Al and Tom already said yes."

"In Moscow?" I asked, thinking it was a long way to go for a football match, "Who is it between?"

"Spartak Moscow and Liverpool"

CHAPTER 17

Of course, I jumped at it, and we travelled up by train for the match the following week, which took place on a cold and rainy night in Moscow. I have since googled it; you can see grainy YouTube footage of the match, 22nd October 1992. In the European competition, now called the Champions League, it was named UEFA's Cup Winners' Cup in those days.

I was excited as Liverpool was the team I had supported as a boy, although I had been watching football much less since I left school. Tom was a Nottingham Forrest fan, and Al supported the Scottish team, Hibernian. But we were all excited about attending the match. It also sounded like a fun little trip, as Voronezh had relatively few attractions.

Vicky heard about the tickets on the day she told us about them. After working out the number she wanted for herself and her circle of friends, we were so pleased and grateful she'd also asked us. It had been handy that we'd traipsed by her room coming back from football that day, I think. There were about eight of us going. Al, Tom and I were probably the keenest on football, while in fairness, Vicky and her crowd were just up for enjoying the excursion overall, probably. Pleasingly, she told us Mamadou was also coming. I got on very well with Mamadou, but I didn't get too much chance to hang out with him, as he tended to avoid most of the parties, being a non-drinker. He was friends with Vicky, too, so a common denominator between us.

We enjoyed the usual fun of Moscow, such as visiting the rubbish-yet-much-desired McDonald's and the Irish Pub on the Arbat for a few drinks. Next door to the pub was an Irish mini supermarket that sold western goods like tea bags and Marmite. On the second night, following the match, which kicked off at 4 pm, we went to a Georgian restaurant recommended to us near the Metro station of Park Kulturi.

The restaurant lay just twenty minutes' walk from Spartak Moscow's stadium, a straight line down Komsomolsky Prospect, a big main drag of a road. It was adorned in Georgian traditional colours and textiles. It served grilled and barbequed meats on skewers, or shashliks as they were called in Russia. It is from the word "shashka", meaning sword, as soldiers in another era would cook meat over the fire on their swords. This was served with delicious Georgian red wine. The restaurant laid on entertainment in the shape of a small all-male troupe in traditional costume, taking to the floor in the middle of the meal and performing a Georgian dance to live music. They danced accompanied by guitars, with plenty of thigh squatting bouncing on their haunches. It was great fun and an excellent way to relax after the game, and I noted this place would be good to try to repeat on any return visits to Moscow.

As to the game itself, it was a miserably wet night as we jostled for position outside the Lenin Olympic stadium to approach the correct entrance. The rain soaked right through our clothes. Crowds of supporters outside were animated and excited. As our tickets were just regular ones, we knew we would be in with Russian supporters, not with the official away fans from the UK. The stream of supporters we were in was funnelled between a line of police mounted on horses. We felt a bit like livestock as we were herded by the authorities.

Mamadou was close to me, looking nervous, but like he was trying to hide it by also trying to look hard as nails. He had a woollen hat, which didn't really help as it was a bit oversized, but it did the job of hiding his head well. Racism was a big concern for him that day, as it was for us, too. Russia was not very racially diverse or multinational at the time. Although the Soviet Union stretched around the globe and contained many cultural and unique nationalities within it, there was still a pecking order. Being black would have made him a target, especially among a crowd of near 100% white Russian football fans. Tasteless jokes with black Africans as the butt were something I had heard a few times in Russia already.

So it's safe to say I was a bit concerned for Mamadou. I glanced over at him a few times, and he smiled back to reassure me not to worry and then resumed his hard man face. This seemed to consist of him mostly just narrowing his eyes. Maybe he'd watched a few too many westerns, I thought. While the Yul Brynner look worked now and then, it mostly came over like he had trapped wind. I thought I'd better not say anything, though, realising that this was no joking matter for Mamadou.

As we shuffled down the left-hand side of the funnel, one of the horses bobbed and jerked its head to the right. A trail of horse saliva rained towards me, followed by a clunk on my cheek as the horse's muzzle smashed into my face. It surprised me and really hurt, too - the first and last time I have been head-butted by a horse. Bruised but not broken, I found my way to our seats with everyone else, but now with a stinging face, that felt like it might turn into a bit of shiner. We took our places just to one side of the halfway line, halfway up in the stands. We had a good view of everything, in fact, including quite a lot of umbrellas going up in the exposed parts of the ground, many of which were red and white to match Spartak's colours. Liverpool, who traditionally wore red, were the away team and so on this occasion emerged in a predominantly green kit.

The eight of us were seated in two rows of four, above and below each other. It seemed better that way, compared to a long row of eight, as we were able to share the excitement, smiles and frisson all together. I took in the whole stadium. It was great to be there, that cold, dark October night, and the place was packed. Al was sitting next to me, with Tom on my other side. Mamadou was directly behind Al, while Vicky sat behind my shoulders. Al nudged me, "did you see what Mamadou's got in his sock!?" he said.

I looked over my shoulder, and Mamadou looked back down, past his knee, and gave me a wink and a hard man eye narrow, then lifted his trouser leg. He had a six-inch hunting knife in a leather holder strapped to his shin. Boy, he sure wasn't taking any chances. I had no idea about the knife before that moment, nor maybe had the rest of us. I supposed Mamadou hadn't wanted to burden any of us with the knowledge of it beforehand. Still, now we were in, I think he wanted to let us know that if things did end up getting out of hand, he had the means to protect himself, or us too, for that matter.

The match finally got underway. The Liverpool team was managed by Graeme Souness that night, with Ian Rush spearheading the attack, other names included teenagers Steve McManaman and Jamie Redknapp very early in their Liverpool careers in midfield, and Mark Wright in defence. The team had Bruce Grobbelaar in goal, already famous for his wobbly legs tactic to put opponents off when taking penalties. As it happened,

Bruce Grobbelaar had a shocking game. Liverpool were level at 1-1 when one of his clearances went straight towards a Spartak player who passed it into an empty net to put them 2-1 ahead. Later, Grobbelaar produced a bit of wobbly legs to put off an onrushing attacker. The Russian player wasn't fazed at all. He attempted to round him, and Grobbelaar ended up dragging the player down, conceding a penalty, and getting himself sent off. The Spartak fans in the Lenin Olympic stadium (now called the Luzhniki stadium) jeered Bruce Grobbelaar mercilessly. He stomped off in just a white t-shirt, and his shorts, having had to give his goalkeeper top to a Liverpool defender teammate who had to go in goal for the last ten minutes of the game. Spartak won 4-2 in the end. Liverpool did score through Steve McManaman, but that was just a consolation for the team who were utterly outplayed really.

Although there had been bag checks on the turnstiles, the Russians in front and all around us were merrily drinking vodka from bottles they had brought into the ground undetected. Luckily for Mamadou, his concealed weapon had not been detected either. That would have led to far worse consequences than being caught with bringing your own vodka into the ground. At one point, Vicky produced a Union Jack flag from her person and began to wave it about, but we collectively told her to put it away fast, telling her we didn't really want the attention. I looked at Mamadou, who imperceptibly rolled his eyes and shook his head. With the cat out of the bag, several nearby Russian supporters got wind of the group of *English* in their midst, though, and began to taunt and jeer us. I started to get more nervous. After a rare good bit of play by Liverpool, a Russian in front of me turned to us, jabbed his finger directly at me, and said in English, "Fuck your Liverpool! Fuck your Beatles!" It was intimidating, but we managed to appease them, probably by speaking Russian back and reacting with smiles. I think by showing clearly that we were not genuine travelling English football fans also helped.

Football hooliganism was still an ugly blight on the game at the time, so tensions were usually present at any match. In 1985, six years before this, there were some gruesome scenes at the Heysel stadium in Brussels in the European Cup final between Liverpool and Juventus. Fans rushed each other, and a part of the stadium collapsed, resulting in 39 deaths, mainly Italian ones, and hundreds more injured. It resulted in English clubs being banned from European competition for five years, and cemented the international opinion of English fans' bad behaviour and thuggery. The ban had only just been lifted the season before this, but I wasn't thinking about that. If I had been, and about the reputation that Russian 'Ultra' fans had, then I would have certainly been a lot more nervous about our Russian taunters. In retrospect, it was probably quite fortunate for us that the Russian team won, no doubt. Pleasingly, also nothing ugly developed on the race front either, well nothing that I was particularly aware of at any rate. Perhaps Mamadou was subjected to comments that night, but I don't recall an issue.

We returned to Voronezh the following day, all accounted for, having had an exciting visit to the capital. A short time later, Al and a few others revisited Moscow to see CSKA Moscow take on Barcelona, but I didn't manage to join that trip.

CHAPTER 18

When posting letters home from Russia in 1992, you had to expect to wait a little while before they got to their destination. It was a case of actually writing them; email was still not really around for another four or five years at that point. It was best not to write on just any paper either, but on the official light blue airmail letters, or aerograms. This was one gummed sheet of paper that you folded up after you had written it. The back of the page became the outside of the envelope. Only these letters would get to your recipient swiftly, by which I mean within a week to ten days. Some of my fellow students would choose to write pages and pages to loved ones and stick them in a regular envelope. Although these ones could still be posted, you had to accept that these heavier ones would take two to three weeks to arrive. The super lightweight ones weighed next to nothing and didn't weigh the plane down so much, I suppose, so they got preferential treatment.

A few days after getting back from Moscow, Jane decided we needed a self-identity boost by going to the post office to get some letters posted. So, Al, Becky and I gathered ourselves up and headed out. Jane told us about the bus, which I had not used yet, that stopped on Friedreich Engels Street right outside hostel number 3. It went all the way up Revolution Prospect towards the Deconat office in the main university area in the centre of town, and the central post office, or *pochta*, was one of the stops. We didn't need to pay for the bus as we had been issued with student identity cards, which gave us various benefits, including free travel on public transport.

Entirely in Russian, of course, I rather liked the student ID card, which I still have today. It was a flip-open hardback little booklet thing, about the size of a credit card, with a grey cloth-covered exterior, with "Student Card" embossed on the front. A black and white photo of me was glued inside with my name written in Cyrillic underneath. An authoritative inky stamp straddled the image and the paper.

It flipped shut with a satisfying *tock* sound. It was very soviet and cool, the sort of thing I felt like I would have to produce if a policeman from a wartime film had barked "*Your papers, please!*" at me. The free bus travel was good, too; it saved me the bus ticket price, which was about 2 pence a journey.

We jumped down off the bus and entered the post office, an old building with high ceilings and predominantly dark wood featuring inside. There were several short queues for the cashier clerks. One of us successfully bought the stamps we all needed for our letters after waiting their turn in one of the lines. There were also around six booths by the far wall of the post office, with some people seated outside them. Inside some of the booths, people were talking on telephones. The clerk barked out someone's name, and a woman in the waiting area shuffled into a booth, at which point the phone started to ring. She answered it and began her pre-booked conversation. There was a wooden sign above another clerk's window with the word *telegram* painted on it. At a counter just to the side of that was a box of forms.

Becky and Jane, the best Russian speakers, managed to ask the staff about all of this. They explained animatedly that we could write telegrams home, which would arrive in only a day or two. Or, we could even book time slots for placing national or international telephone calls: calls to the UK could be booked, but it would need to be done two weeks in advance. The telegrams sounded like something from a black and white film with Humphrey Bogart; and booking phone calls sounded fun. We wanted to try them both. The telegram was much quicker than a letter, as it didn't have to be posted to the UK. It would be tapped out like Morse code over the telegraph wire by the Russian post office and would be transposed in the UK counterpart office close to real-time. It would be typed out and posted at home, arriving quickly. The only downside was you had to limit yourself to a concise length, just one or two sentences, as there was a limit to the number of characters you could send. Full stops counted as a character, which is why when you heard people read them out, the "STOP" was sounded out. ("We are stuck in Russia. STOP. There is no milk. STOP. Send cows! STOP!")

We all really enjoyed the novelty of sending telegrams to our parents. The one I sent to my mum was uninteresting, but it was fun to send it. "Mum. I am sending you a telegram. A first for me. All is good here. Love Henry X".

Jane and Becky, possessing far sharper minds, also wrote to their parents to expect a phone call in a couple of weeks in their telegram. Afterwards, they booked a call with a surly clerk. They were given a bit of paper containing the relevant information about the time and date they would need to return and wait outside the phone booths for their call.

CHAPTER 19

When we got back to the hostel, it had already become
dark, and it was icy cold. A bitter chill was funnelling
down the big avenues of Voronezh. It felt like the snow
was imminent now, and we knew that once it arrived,
it would probably stay until March or even April,
apparently. Our football days in the park were numbered
for sure. As I walked by the kitchen on our floor, I could
see it was already busy with cooking representatives
creating evening meals for their collectives. I could see
the smashed window on the far side of the room doing
a great job of shovelling cool fresh air into the room and
acting as an extractor fan. Mitigating against the frying
and cooking smells was its only small redeeming factor.
As we approached our end of the corridor, I spotted
Sergei, in full drunk mode, leaning on the door frame to
my room. Bottle in hand, he was talking to a couple of
people I didn't wait to try and identify. I grabbed Al by
the elbow and swerved us both into the first door ahead
of us, which happened to be Tom and Paul's room.

"Hi guys," I said, "just avoiding Sergei; how're you
doing?"

In contrast to Tom's well-built, athletic and stocky

frame, his Oxford uni roommate, Paul, was slender and wore glasses, and was usually hunched over a book. Paul was a generally quiet and serious guy, and from what I heard, he was super clever, the type in line to graduate with a first-class degree. Tom wasn't a voracious reader type and was generally always game for a laugh and a drink.

They were not a natural pair of best buddies in my mind, but something clicked between them at least, and they appeared to really get on well and have each other's backs. They clearly connected on a spiritual level somewhere.

"We've just been talking about getting a place in town," said Tom. "Paul has found out that you can get a two-bedroom apartment for about $20 a month," he continued.

"Seriously, compared to this place that would be luxury; we could have our own setup and only be about fifteen minutes' walk from here at most. It's a no brainer." Paul confirmed, he'd done all his thinking, it seemed, and was summarising the results of his research. "Our own kitchen, living room, and we can bring girls back!" he grinned.

I hadn't had Paul down as a party guy, but I knew he liked to pack a few drinks away. I hadn't seen him being outgoing or talking to the girls either, so I was a bit surprised by the comment.

He was the strong, silent type when it came to girls, maybe.

"Well, that's cheap and tempting too," commented Al, "I'll think stop here, just now though, just I can't really be bothered with the hassle of all that."

At that moment, we heard loud voices rumble past the door, and I popped my head out and saw Sergei's back heading away from us down the corridor. "Well, he's gone, at least".

Tom and Paul then asked us about the party at Alexei's, and we lost no time in telling them about it and how Becky stayed the night. They were interested to hear that, and asked who else was there. We told them about Alexei's other friends, Oleg and Vadim. I mentioned Tanya and Nadia and that I'd got on pretty well with Tanya and quite liked her.

"There you go!" said Paul, "Stuck in this hostel, everyone living on top of each other, how are you going to take things to the next level? But if you get a little place of your own, you can do just about whatever you want!" he suggested.

"Well, yeah, maybe. Anyway, you do it if you like. I'll see how things go, I think," I replied.

Later that same night, we had a hearty potato, cabbage, and carrot stew with rice, courtesy of Jane and Abby and a few drinks as usual. Abby was one the Nottingham University lot and shared a room to the right of Becky and Jane, at the end of the corridor, diagonally opposite from ours. She was super smiley, with very straight, light brown hair, and although she also didn't tear the place up, she was friendly with everyone.

As I went to the toilets, I came across a very drunk Sergei near the stairwell, but I couldn't avoid him in time.

"Hello! He spluttered, how are you doing!?" he greeted me with a big smile and a slap on the back. I smiled back, and he clapped an arm around my shoulder. Now I was a bit tipsy, so I didn't mind returning the greetings too much.

"Have you had any sex yet?" he continued, and now I did mind that I'd greeted him.

"What, when?" I ventured.

"*What when*...? Here, in *Russia*, of course, you idiot. Have you tried a Russian girl yet? You know, I can set you up with someone if you need," he continued.

"Er, no, it's OK, I'm OK...I mean...maybe all will be good, thank you!"

"What are you talking about? Listen, you help me; I help you. That's how it works. You tell the English girls about my nice cock, yes?" he roared with laughter, "I will see you later. This is Georgi, by the way." He gestured towards two heavy set guys in the stairwell, who I had not noticed as I'd approached. "I've got to go," he added as he sloped off down the stairs.

I was very relieved when he left, as there is nothing

worse than an unpredictable drunk man teasing you. Especially when you have heard that he can also be dangerous. The two people looked well dressed, a bit shifty, and quite sober. They were smiling at me, and the nearest one, Georgi presumably, offered his hand to me.

"Hi," he said.

"Hi," I replied, unsure where to take a conversion with the Georgians. They didn't look like students, and I knew I hadn't seen them around before. They looked older, mid to late twenties, but their dark stubble maybe came quicker to Georgians than to fair-haired Englishmen like me.

"So, you know Sergei? He's a friend."

I was unsure whether they were asking me if he was my friend or telling me that he was their friend.

"Yeah, yeah, he's a good... he's good. He helps me sometimes." I was struggling already.

"I can help you too; you want to buy some hashish?" Georgi asked me.

"Thanks, but I am fine. Sergei already helped me," I wanted to not lose any face, but I didn't want to do any deals with these guys, either. I was reasonably sure he wasn't a student, and in fact, he seemed a bit like a nightclub bouncer now, in his black leather jacket and big barrel chest.

"You got an English passport?" came Georgi's next question.

"Of course, yes, I do." inwardly thinking that it was British but deciding against correcting him.

"You want to sell it?"

"No, not really."

"OK, well, you could sell it. I would pay you $100, … or $200," he added, "your friends' passports too. You just say you lost it; you will easily be given a new one. Easy money," Georgi continued.

"Ah, I see", I responded. This had taken me by surprise. There was no way I was going to get into anything like this. "OK, well, I don't think so, but… I will think about it."

"OK," came his deadpan reply, offering his hand again.

"Well, bye then!" and I was relieved to get away and head back to the party. In fact, I was so keen to walk *away* that I just headed forward and up the stairs away from Georgi and his friend.

A strange instinct told me not to walk back in the direction of my room, trying to not let them know where I was residing in this hostel. Some of the other English students lived on the floor above. I decided impulsively to visit them and use the loo upstairs rather than go towards my room.

I saw some of the Brits, and my fellow Bristolian, Connor. As I approached, I could see he was smoking, and I could smell that he was smoking some of the grass

I'd gifted him a while back from my monster purchase. He was leaning on the doorframe of one of the rooms, and inside I glimpsed Gus and John, two Scottish guys from Edinburgh university just chilling out with beers in hand.

"Alright?" I said.

"Hiya, Henry, man. How're you doing there?" they called back.

"There's a couple of Georgian guys on the stairwell who I think just offered to buy my passport for $200!" I told them.

"This place is getting weirder every day," said Connor

"By the way, you should be a *bit* discreet with that, maybe Connor," I gestured to his joint, "you can smell that right down the corridor."

"It's fine," he replied, "No one cares."

"Well, I don't know. Alexei said to me it can be a problem, that's all."

"I think you'll find I don't tend to pay attention to what Alexei says," Connor serenely objected.

"Well, could you tend to pay attention to it soon then? They could crack down on it if we're flagrant about it. And as I am the one who bought it in the first place, I just don't want this coming back to me!"

"OK, OK, sure. Relax. By the way, I heard about Alexei and Becky. Is that true?" he continued, maybe just wanting to change the subject.

"Yes. She isn't very proud of herself, though. But I have a feeling it's probably going to happen again," I replied. Then, thinking of Alexei's place, I added, "Did you also know Paul and Tom are maybe going to rent an apartment? Twenty dollars per month, apparently".

I spent a few more minutes chatting, hoping the Georgians would have moved off and then when I thought the coast was clear, I headed back down to my own floor.

CHAPTER 20

The snow finally arrived in Voronezh in late October, covering the whole city. Everything just looked a little better in the snow. The dirty, muddy, or dusty ground, for the most part, was covered entirely, and the trees looked pretty, laden with the white decoration. At first, the roads remained clear as the cars and buses kept the asphalt arteries of the city snow-free. Later, and throughout the winter, the smaller side roads and tracks became compact with snow and ice. They would have to wait until March or April to reveal themselves again. Naturally, we rushed outside to throw some snowballs around. But unlike the here-today-gone-tomorrow snow we sometimes see in England, this stuff was definitely staying around. So just like our Russian friends, we quickly got used to it.

I was pleased to finally wear my Russian furry hat now that it was cold enough. It was the traditional type with ear flaps tied up over the top that I had bought in the central market, souvenir-like, back in September when it was still warm outside. After a couple of weeks, the snow was already piling up and sitting in high drifts against some buildings. It was shovelled into big piles on the main roads to form hedgerow-like dividers forming a barrier between the cars and the pedestrians on the pavements.

One Friday night in November we organised a dinner party of sorts. We gathered some tables and borrowed a couple of desks from the classrooms on the first floor to make a long dinner table. Soviet champagne was on the table, and Russian beer, vodka and Pepsi, all bought from a car boot at the train station as usual. Becky and Jane's room was the venue, seeing as it was one of the deeper ones. We managed to get about fourteen people around the makeshift table. Included in the group was also Alexei, Nadia and Tanya.

I spent quite a bit of time talking to Tanya again. Although the drinks were flowing, naturally, she was undoubtedly intoxicating me in another way. We talked and smiled at each other a lot, and Tanya was in excellent form, full of confidence. I was becoming transfixed by the flicks of blonde hair curling up behind her ears, the sparkle of her light green eyes, and the hint of raspberry pink of her lipstick.

I stepped outside early in the evening with Al and Sam to smoke a joint, but I was hit by the bitter cold, well below freezing, while awaiting my turn. I looked up to the windows above with chattering teeth and listened to the fun being had up there, the sound of guitars playing. I realised the futility of what we were trying to do out there.

The irony was that I had bought that grass for fun reasons, but the real fun was going on inside. Coming outside for a toke on this joint was getting in the way of fun and inconvenient almost. I also wanted to get back to Tanya, much more alluring than shivering on the doorstep with two blokes, even if they were good friends. "I'm not doing this anymore. See you, lads; I'm going up," I said before my turn even came. Over the following couple of weeks, I decided to get rid of all the remaining grass that I had. It was still obviously a fair amount. After giving a lot away to those that wanted some, I just threw the rest away in the industrial-sized bins around the back of the hostel. It just didn't seem like a good idea to keep it stashed in my cupboard. Alexei's warnings that it wasn't viewed as lightly as in other countries also played a part in the decision. In any case, I knew I was not going to use it myself.

Back upstairs, the party was in full swing. Alexei was keeping people entertained at one end of the table. Others were having fun around someone playing the guitar. It had also spilt into the corridor and mixed in with other parties spilling out of other doors.

I was getting closer to Tanya all night. We were flirting, the signals going both ways were getting undeniably strong, and I was enjoying it. Being out in Russia was turning into a beautiful adventure, for sure. Everything was so different to any life I had led before. Living in this culture, not so far away from its recent Soviet past, its memories were still very evident and fascinating. I loved the old-fashioned student cards and even the system of chits and tickets for buying rationed food in the shops. Big Soviet-style architecture, snow everywhere, almost all the cars were old square Ladas, directed by the stern traffic police they called militia - I loved it all.

It was just so much fun, especially as it was just a couple of years since the population had acquired its freedom from the communist shackles. Revolutions had spread through Europe since the Czech purple revolution in 1988. The falling of the Berlin wall, which I had just about seen with my own eyes three years earlier, had left those countries with a sense of rebirth. Everyone was enjoying themselves, unsure of the rules, making things up as they went along.

The Russians I mixed with enjoyed getting intoxicated on this freedom and getting intoxicated in general. Everyone seemed to feel the release of pent-up pressure. However, some were still unsure of the authorities to a certain extent. For others, it was maybe like the swinging sixties that Britain had seen. They had political and financial freedom with which some (not all, of course) had managed to make money how they liked, like capitalists. Sexual freedom seemed to be another by-product.

I can't claim to know how free sexual relationships

were in the sixties and seventies; before my time, of course. Still, it felt to me that the break-up of the former regime certainly helped everyone let their hair down more than ever before.

I learned from Tanya that her parents lived in Penza, which was to the east, a similar distance away as Moscow was from Voronezh. She was an only child and had finished secondary school in Penza before coming to Voronezh University to study history. She was in her second year. I wondered what history they taught in post-soviet Russian universities. She had no pets liked music and spending time with friends. As you can tell, my classroom Russian was proving very useful, enabling me to find out all the important stuff! Naturally, I obliged by telling her I had an older brother, Rob, and an older sister, Anna, and that I liked going to the cinema. With a flourish, I also added that I enjoyed watching football and my favourite team was Liverpool Football Club. I stopped short of asking the equivalent of "*ou est la bibliotheque?*" but it was pretty much what we were doing, rolling out some classroom phrases.

It was getting dangerously dull, and I felt I was losing her, so I quickly turned it back to her. I needed to get away from pets and made-up hobbies. I learnt that she'd spent a few years of her childhood, from the age of about seven to thirteen, in the Czech city of Brno. Her father was stationed there in some army or civil government capacity, which I couldn't really take in. I told her that I had wanted to learn Czech, and she ran a few Czech phrases back at me to impress me, which it did. I was keen to get back to how we had been on the first night when we met at Alexei's, when the language barrier had seemed to melt away completely. As the evening wore on, it became less important what we were talking about, though, as we were just two people at a party having a few drinks, flirting and smiling. Body language became the most useful language. I enjoyed how she looked at me, which flattered and encouraged me.

Towards the end of the evening, the happy vibes and party atmosphere had well and truly swept Tanya and me both up. We'd been dancing and hand holding and were desperate to kiss each other. The evening was ending for everyone; many had already left. Perhaps by not wanting to stop talking and flirting with each other, we hadn't realised how late it was.

Finally, though, we were both on our way down the stairs. She was pulling me by the hand along the short distance through the trees and pathways to their apartment where I had been before, of course, on the night Becky ended up staying there. We entered the stairwell, giggling with arms around each other. She led me into a dark room on the right-hand side as we entered the apartment, which I didn't think was the main living room that we'd all been entertained in before, which had been on the left as you came in. We sort of sat, sort of fell, onto a bed, signalling to me that it must be her bedroom. Things moved on quite quickly; we were enjoying ourselves. We were, of course, a bit drunk but also with a strong appetite for one another. It was dark and hard to see, but the darkness helps when you're new to someone in these situations. I think it wasn't just the evening of small talk and flirting on this night, but also from the last time we talked to each other. All the time I had been thinking about her since then had also fed into this crescendo. Clothes flew off, contraception flew on. We made love on the bed, and then off the bed, and even on the floor in the middle of the room. Finally, we fell back into the bed in a state of happiness and exhaustion and, for my part at least, fell into a happy sleep.

Several hours later, I woke up, and we were still snuggled up to each other. I stared up at the ceiling, with my Russian beauty next to me, and almost straight away, the feelings of excitement returned. My hangover was relegated to second billing versus the thrill of the achievement of having consummated our relationship, and the immediate sense that this was no one-night stand. I felt sure this was the beginning of something, and as I looked sideways, I saw Tanya on her side, one eye looking at me, with a grin on her face, too. We lay there for a while in quiet contemplation before I levered myself up onto my elbows. I scanned the room lazily and was jolted bolt upright by what I saw.

Just a few feet away, I spotted that Nadia was sleeping on another single bed, possibly the other half of this divan/sofa bed type of thing we were on! She was no more than three metres from us. From the night before, I instantly had visions of myself and Tanya on the floor on our knees doing our very special conga. Had Nadia been there all that time, just a few feet away but politely keeping quiet, while we rode a love train around the room? They obviously shared a room; everything was instantly apparent, but I hadn't given it a single second's thought during our night of passion. Luckily, Nadia was still asleep or pretending to be and thankfully, she also had her back to us facing the wall. Tanya was looking up at me and watching me take it all in. My eyes were open as wide as saucers, probably looking mildly panicked. She gave a cheeky grin as if to say, "I know what you're thinking," but the look also calmed me a bit, as it also seemed to say, "but there's no need to worry, this is Russia, this is normal".

I knew that post-soviet Russia wasn't middle England, but I still felt awkward. People lived in small apartments, lived collectively, slept collectively, they shared things. I calmed myself down, but I felt like I didn't want to wait around for Nadia's appraisal of our performance. I got up and went to the loo, and it was a luxury to use a proper, clean bathroom. When I came out, Tanya was waiting for me in the kitchen area, with a small coffee each she'd made for us both, so I didn't have to go back to the bedroom.

The coffee smelled nicer than our Brazilian instant coffee. Maybe Alexei, with his connections and access, was to thank for that. I put my hands around her waist, and she did the same to me.

"Was she there all the time?!" I asked, but Tanya just shrugged and kissed me.

"I can't be sure," she said.

We agreed to see each other later, and I put on my coat and boots and left through the sunshine and snow back to Hostel number 4, just three minutes' walk away. As I swallowed in lungfuls of the crisp fresh air, I had a spring in my step and a happy head.

CHAPTER 21

When I got back, Al was happy to hear of me getting together with Tanya, which he said he'd seen coming. He was as shocked to hear about Nadia lying a few inches from my exposed bare backside as I had been to realise it, too. "No way! That's just about the funniest thing I've heard since we got here, Henry!" he chuckled.

As October progressed, my relationship with Tanya continued to develop. It was a bit awkward to see her the very next time, after our getting together, but I suppose that's normal. That awkwardness was more in anticipation of seeing one another, I think. When we met up the second time, all anxieties on my part instantly fell away, and we were quickly linking hands, arms and basking in mutual admiration. We began to spend time together in the daytime, going for walks around the town and in Pervomaiski park on the other side of Friedreich Engels Street, and I stayed at her place two or three times per week, which was quickly increasing. Alexei, Tanya and Nadia did some juggling, leaving us one of the two rooms to ourselves, as apparently English gentlemen like me require privacy and don't like an audience when we're in bed with our girlfriend. The other room, which was more often a living room, had furniture that doubled up as beds, so it was OK for the others. Al quite liked it, too, as it meant he had our room in the hostel mostly to himself, given that our roommate Nikolay was becoming a rare sighting, predominantly opting to stay away now, rather than live heel to toe with the British party animals that we were.

Becky was quite happy about it, as it meant that we now had a joint reason for developing the social circle with those guys. She had continued to see Alexei since her first night with him. She had felt a little awkward about that, I think, but now I was seeing his flatmate, it helped things in a few small ways. We sometimes crossed the ground to the apartment and back together, and when all four of us were hanging out, it felt like a bit of a double date gang. Poor Nadia sometimes had the short straw, though, and rather than staying around like on that first night, she sometimes went elsewhere to sleep, although I had no idea where that was, nor did I think to even ask.

On one of the trips back to the hostel with Becky one morning, she let me know that one of the girls from Nottingham university, the friendly Abby, was quite upset about me getting together with Tanya. Apparently, Abby had asked Becky why I had to get together with a Russian girl, who could obviously offer me nothing long-term, while she had been trying to flirt with me for ages. I had to admit that any flirting she had done had completely passed me by. It was nice to hear this, for my own confidence, but I couldn't see beyond Tanya's lure. I admit though that I hadn't been thinking long term about any of it.

By the third week of November, Tanya and I were properly boyfriend and girlfriend. We saw each other pretty much every day unless there was a good reason why we couldn't. We'd jumped into the relationship with both feet and were fairly and squarely in what you could call the honeymoon period. One awkward moment arrived at the start of our third week together when I met her ex-boyfriend, Vladimir. It happened on the ground floor of the hostel, where the building was managed from. Inside the front door in the main entrance area, there was a room on the right with an internal window and hatch into the corridor. The room was called the *Kabinet* and was staffed by a kind of administrator lady, who seemed to concern herself with whatever management the building needed.

As Tanya and I passed by it one afternoon, there was the figure of a man leaning on the window hatch talking to the lady inside. Finishing his chat with her, he turned around to face us as we came by.

"Oh, hi Tanya," he said, a surprised look on his face.

"Hi, Volodya," Tanya replied. I thought he was an older man at first with a full brown beard and light brown hair, but looking closer, he was pretty much a similar age to me, maybe a bit older, but still early twenties, the beard putting a few years on him, though.

They both seemed rather tense, and like they knew each other. "I was just checking to see if…well, doesn't matter really," he said.

"This is Genry," Tanya said, introducing me, still awkwardly.

"Vladimir," he said, extending his hand for me to shake, and smiling politely. I said hello back.

"Are you OK?" she asked.

"Yes, yes! Everything's good! And with you?" he replied.

"Yes, of course…well, anyway, see you."

"Yes, sure, bye," Vladimir replied, "and bye Genry," to me specifically.

"Bye," I said.

As soon as we were outside, Tanya explained that Vladimir, Volodya for short, was her boyfriend from last year, which made the whole exchange instantly make so much more sense. Although what made less sense was how the short version of his name hardly any shorter than the full version. She said they were both fine with it, and had seen each other around this year already, in fact, before today. Their relationship had ended before last summer, she led me to understand, and it was probably only a bit weird just then as she was with me, her new boyfriend. Vladimir helped the university in some administration role apparently, although he was still in the last year of his studies, too. I was fine with it, seeing the ex, and rather than feeling jealous, it just made me feel, if anything, slightly better about myself, like I was now the cat that got the cream.

CHAPTER 22

As the snow came down heavily one Monday morning in November, falling heavily onto the ground outside, in total muted silence, Vyacheslav called the British contingent together to announce that the university had made arrangements for another cultural trip for our group. It meant that Tanya and I would be parted, but it was OK as I was pleased to explore these opportunities, and Tanya said it was an excuse for her to catch up on her studies. Like all the trips we were offered, it was voluntary and would need to be paid for if we signed up for it, but the price was so reasonable that everyone did. It was to be a week's trip to Uzbekistan. It sounded fascinating to a travel lover like me; a train up to Moscow, flight to Samarkand in Uzbekistan where we'd spend two nights, then a coach trip west across the desert to Bukhara on the other side of the country. After a couple of nights there, we'd catch a flight back to Moscow and then back to Voronezh on the night train. This trip was maybe what led to the stories of the Uzbek grass from the previous year's students, but since I was no longer interested in that – I had alcohol plus, now, also a girlfriend – that was just a footnote. I was still excited about a trip to

Uzbekistan anyway; I knew it was part of the ancient silk route, land of spices, and minarets, but not much more. I couldn't wait to go. We packed for a week away and waited eagerly for the departure day to come around at the end of November.

Travelling around in this country was quite different from anywhere else I'd ever been, although, given my age, I wasn't exactly a seasoned traveller yet. There was just the six months spent in Paris in my year off from education, and the three summer months travelling around America with my friend, Steve, just before university.

That had been a low-cost trip, with the travel already paid for - we'd saved up for a rail pass on the Amtrak railways. - and our budget was just $11 per day each. Eleven dollars wasn't very much in the States, although I had already discovered it was quite a lot in Russia. You could get into a fair bit of trouble, potentially, for just $10 here. We saw a lot of the country from New York (including the World Trade Centre) to New Orleans, San Antonio to San Francisco, and lots of places in between. Although our accommodation was at times rather grimy, our Amtrak passes ensured we travelled in great comfort around at least half of the fifty-two states of the USA.

Travelling around Russia and the Commonwealth of Independent States was considerably less comfortable. I was growing to like the overnight train to Moscow, though. I liked the cosy couchette cabins, with the top bunk folded down, and the silver samovar with hot sweet black tea that the lady used to wheel up and down the train. From Moscow we caught our flight to Samarkand from Domedyedovo, the airport that was used primarily for internal flights, and not from Sheremyetovo Airport where we flew to from the UK. It was far less smoothly operated.

Our departure was supposed to be at 9.30 am, but it was already delayed by two hours as soon as we arrived. After sitting around for the morning on not very comfortable rows of seating, another two hours were added to the delay. In total, we spent around six uncomfortable hours sitting around in the waiting area.

Finally, we were called up in the afternoon, had our passports re-checked, and were led out of the terminal and onto the tarmac. A small bus drove us around the airfield towards our plane, but the route didn't seem that purposeful. The bus kept pausing and changing direction. At one point, we stopped near a plane that had some steps in place by its entry doors, and the airport official alighted from our bus, and trotted up the steps and into the plane. We watched, already somewhat irritated by our long wait, while she chatted for what seemed like an overly large number of minutes to someone inside the aircraft. Finally, she turned on her heels and came back down the steps gesturing to the driver that this seemed not to be the right plane and was pointing to another one off to the left. She jumped back in the bus and instructed the driver to go up to another plane waiting on the tarmac. It would have been quite funny had it not been annoying. At the next plane, she bounded up the steps again. I added my own script to the conversation we couldn't hear. "Are you going to Uzbekistan, mate?" I imagined her saying when she popped her head into the cockpit, "You got any room for twenty-five English students?"

While I mean British, Russians rarely used the correct term and called us all English, much to Al's annoyance. "I am not English; I am Scottish!" he would constantly remind people as if they'd just farted in a lift, and they'd just frown at him as if denying it.

On the second plane, again, she seemed to be talking for ages, and we didn't know why. Surely it was either the right plane or not. Why did it need five minutes discussion? She eventually emerged from the fuselage's entry point and gave the bus driver a big thumbs up, and we sarcastically cheered as she skipped down the steps. However, rather than us all getting out, she got in and began talking to Vyacheslav. What now? We thought. The following unbelievable thing then happened.

It was explained that although this was indeed the right aircraft and it was scheduled and prepared to fly us to Samarkand, there had been some issues that day over aircraft fuel and payments for it. I didn't understand some of the details about the airline's credit, airport authorities, and fuel authorisations. The upshot of it was that the plane would not be fully fuelled, and would be grounded until they paid another $1500 to the fuelling authority, we could not take off. They even asked Vyacheslav if he could organise a whip-round among the English students to find this money! He explained how embarrassed he was about the situation and about his country, and we thought there was probably something along the lines of bribes going on here. Vyacheslav suggested that with our permission, he could deduct some dollars from each of us from the float he held, and he assured us that Voronezh university would get it back to us the moment we returned there next week. Exasperated, tired and hungry, we eventually agreed to it after a quick consultation with our leader, Vicky, but on the understanding that the other passengers were also being persuaded to donate (to the corruption).

Five minutes later, we were aboard the aeroplane, buckling in. I can't tell you what model aircraft it was, but it looked like a normal plane with jet engines, a bit like an Airbus, although I think it was a Tupolev. As we taxied around to the far end of the airfield to find the start of the correct runway, things got even worse; I looked out of the window and saw an identical plane to the one we were in - only the one I was looking at didn't have wheels, was lying on its belly and was burnt out with black smoke marks covering the fuselage. All I could do was shut my eyes and take a deep breath.

The moment of truth arrived as the roar from the engines sounded out, and we charged down the runway. We were about to take off. Suddenly, a one-metre section of the plastic casing from the cabin ceiling lights became unclipped on the other side of the aisle, right by my seat. It swung open like a coffin opening and flapped away just a few inches from my head.

By instinct, I unbuckled myself, grabbed it and shoved it back up, clipping it into place as the plane was hurtling along the runway. I buckled myself back in straight away and a moment later felt the nose of the aircraft rising; we were getting airborne. Then, crash, the light casing came free again and swung open. A few metres further ahead of me, another light casing swung open, too. I wasn't putting it back now; we all firmly held into the armrests, and finally, we took to the skies. The light casings were swinging like washing on a line all the way down the aisle. The shaking stopped as we climbed in search of our cruising altitude. We all looked at each other with anger, fear and relief etched upon our faces. We were on our way, finally. The flight attendants moved through the cabin a few moments later, clipping the casings back in place. They were clearly quite used to it.

Thirty minutes into the flight, I had my first experience of in-flight meals, soviet style. They began by handing out trays which included small orange juice cartons. Next, they swept through and gave everyone a small plain cardboard box containing a bread roll, a wafer, a rectangle of cheese, and a pot of pickled cabbage. It was curious, but with expectations of this airline obvious now very low, it was somehow exciting to see what was coming next. Moments later, I watched as they began again at the front of the cabin with what looked to be cold cooked chicken drumsticks in clear plastic food bags. I was in row 15, but my mood was lifted by the sight of the chicken. Unfortunately, this good feeling was short-lived, as the chicken supply was quite limited, like the fuel. By the time they had reached row 7, they had announced there was no more chicken left. Moments after the main course, they began to serve out some chocolate biscuits, for dessert if you will, but alas, these didn't quite make it to row 15 either.

CHAPTER 23

Uzbekistan, together with Turkmenistan, Kyrgyzstan, Tajikistan and Kazakhstan, made up a group of countries newly independent from the former USSR, now known as the Central Asia republics. These stretched from the Caspian Sea and Europe in the west to Mongolia and China in the east. Uzbekistan to the south shares a border with Afghanistan, and below that lies Pakistan. The whole Central Asian cluster of countries are probably the same size as the whole of western Europe.

Tashkent was Uzbekistan's capital city, but we would not be seeing that at all. In fact, arriving in Samarkand at night, we saw very little in the dark at all. Still, the hotel was far more comfortable than our hostel, at any rate. It was a big grey blockbuster of a building in the middle of the city. The next day, after a good breakfast, we were ferried from one tourist attraction to the next.

The day began at a market where the hustle and bustle attacked our senses from all angles. For a start, the people were very different to the Russians. Central Asian in looks, the mainly Muslim inhabitants gathered in the markets to talk and smoke pipes together, the men in skilfully embroidered round skull caps and many women in brightly coloured cotton and linen clothes that wrapped their bodies. It was a fresh and misty morning, not much over 12 or 13 degrees, although much warmer than snowy Voronezh, of course. Steam from cooking food and smoke from open grills wafted across the marketplace. Baskets of foods were for sale, including mountains of coloured spices such as bright yellow turmeric and dazzling red paprika, and piles of fruit and vegetables. Although Samarkand seemed poorer than Voronezh, and certainly Moscow, in terms of food (thinking back to the sparsely stocked gastronoms and the babushkas), it was more developed and content.

In the afternoon, we visited the site of an ancient fortress settlement on high ground overlooking Samarkand. Our guides, as well as the signs, told us how Genghis Khan had ruled over these lands. We were transported via their stories into the dark reaches of history. We heard about the Kublai Khan, the Mongols, and of course, more about Genghis himself.

Many vendors were constantly trying to sell their wares to us, and quite a few of us bought souvenirs. I purchased two colourfully embroidered bed throws in the local style. They were decorated with swoops and curves in bright greens, reds and blacks that I thought would look good hanging on the wall back in Bristol, better than music posters at any rate. Obviously, I had to refuse the first price they were offered to me, as that would have been plain rude. I didn't want to insult the man, Life of Brian style, by not haggling. I didn't know where to begin, though. I thought that offering him half his price was maybe too flippant so rather than do that I offered him a bit more than full price but insisted on getting two. Buying two throws helped the suggestion of a deal come together. After a bit of haggling, not all of which I understood, even though we were both speaking Russian, I got both for just a little bit more than his original asking price. But his tanned leathery face with an extensive smile told me he was happy with the deal, which I was pleased about.

We were fed in the hotel that night rather than in the local restaurants, which was a little disappointing. The hotel was so characterless, so we thought it was a missed opportunity. But Vyacheslav remarked that with tourism still being relatively young, the best places to eat out were, in fact, official venues like hotels. He also assured us that the sanitation and food hygiene in the street stalls and eateries of Samarkand could not be guaranteed as well as that in the hotel. On reflection, we realised that we had not seen what we could have easily recognised as restaurants, not as we knew them, anyway. We did enjoy some delicious grilled meats, and I am sure that goat was one of the specialities, along with skewers of chicken and lamb with a spicy marinade. It was a fair reflection of the region's specialities. Due to the Russian influence, we also saw cabbage again, dumplings and soured cream on the menu and it was interesting to see Russian dominating the menu. Our waitress had light blond hair pulled into a bun and although I had no reason to think that she wasn't local to the area, she looked very different to most people I had seen in Samarkand by day. We were so close to the Indian subcontinent that my thoughts turned to Stalin's efforts to ensure the displacement of people around the Soviet Union. The result was that "white" Russians were installed in every corner of the Union of Soviet Socialist Republics.

We spent the following day in Samarkand looking around their bright turquoise mosques and mausoleums and their Registan which is a large public square dating back to ancient times where people would gather to hear royal proclamations, or witness justice that included public executions being handed down. It is surrounded on three sides by tall arches, and ornately decorated buildings, that are quite beautiful. On that last evening in the city we holed up in the hotel bar. . On the third day, we boarded a coach and drove for several hours across the horizontally arranged country, all the way west to the city of Bukhara. It took about six hours to travel the three hundred or so kilometres. I watched the desert landscape go by slowly out of the window, listening to music through my Walkman headphones. As I exchanged the cassettes, I tried to see which album matched the views from the window the best: Talking Heads, the Cure, Tracy Chapman or the Pixies - the answer is none of them, especially not the Pixies.

At one desert stop, we walked up and down the sand dunes for a bit to stretch our legs; the setting sun was warm on our faces. Someone spotted a scorpion in the sand, and we gathered around it and took photographs before it scurried off. It was a beautiful golden Sahara-like scene.

Bukhara was much browner and sandier than Samarkand, with mosques and Minarets' spires reaching into the sky over the cityscape. The soundtrack here was the sound of the call to prayer. I read about how the British had waged a campaign in these lands from around the 1830s and for most the rest of the century to protect its silk route and stop Russian influence going any further south, so that Britain did not lose their jewel in the crown – India.

Both sides commandeered local tribesmen over the years, and they were forced into many battles. Eventually, they got really fed up with these interloping bullies from abroad. Trap pits were set for putting captured foreign soldiers into - one tactic the Uzbeks would use to persuade them to clear out of these lands completely.

All too soon, we were headed to the airport in Bukhara to catch a flight back to Moscow. Bukhara was much smaller than Moscow, and the airport only had one runway and one main airport building. Once through the main hall, we found the waiting area.

It was just a tiny room with a few rows of hard chairs, but it had patio doors leading to an outside waiting area, so I was happy to wait in the open air with short sleeves in the sunshine. It was even warmer than Samarkand in the mid-teens of centigrade. The most unusual thing about the outside area was that it was already occupied by a massive long-haired orangey-brown yak. This big cow-like beast seemed unconcerned by us as we sat out there in the dusty garden smoking our cigarettes.

When our flight was announced as ready, it was a simple walk from the building across the dusty tarmac to the plane. Although it was much smaller than the last one we were on, thankfully, there were no dramas or pieces falling off.

CHAPTER 24

The snow had already made itself comfortable before we had left for Uzbekistan. Back in Voronezh a few days later, it had also turned significantly colder. The temperatures had dropped to below freezing both day and night, and the snow had compacted and hardened. Some of the less used back streets were topped with a hard white crust.

The Russian cars happily drove the new white roads rather than them being impassable, as would be the case in the UK. I suppose they all had winter tyres with very thick tread.

It was great to get back 'home' and see Tanya again, who met me off the train with a big hug. Unfortunately, a couple of people came back from Uzbekistan with an illness, which soon spread to almost all of us within twenty-four hours. I stayed in the hostel as I didn't want to even try to leave. It came on very quickly as an upset stomach, which rapidly got severe; it was a bout of dysentery for one and all. The diarrhoea was terrible. I couldn't drink so much as half a cup of water or tea without it just leaking straight out the bottom end. For all Vyacheslav's efforts in protecting us from whatever bacteria in Uzbekistan had made it into our systems, we had still succumbed. The toilets, which we would generally try to visit as rarely as possible, had to be frequented every 30 minutes or so for a couple of days. We self-medicated as best we could, and the university medical people handed out some powders and pills, which we took happily, thinking they couldn't make it any worse. A couple of students had to go and stay in the university sanitorium, primarily as they were so dehydrated it became dangerous. Fortunately, within a week, we were all just about better again.

Although Russia is prepared for winter, and the heating in all buildings worked brilliantly, by and large, it could be cold close to the windows, and our room had a wide window. So, Al and I decided we needed an electric heater to help take the edge off. We took a trip across town to a kind of department store called *Detski Mir*, which was literally translated as Children's World, but in reality, the shop sold many more practical items than just children's things. It was close by to another big shop called *Univermag*, or Everything shop, which was also going to be worth a visit, we thought. We set off with an open mind anyway as to if anything at either shop could be worth buying.

We saw a couple of heavily wrapped up old gents walking up the main road on the way out. It was an odd sight. They were encased in several layers, each carrying a bag, a bucket, what looked like a fold-up stool and a four-foot-long metal rod with a corkscrew drill over their shoulder. As we followed them towards the bus stop, we looked closer and realised they were heading in the direction of the river. We supposed they must be fishermen. The river in Voronezh, imaginatively named Voronezh River, was a substantial one as wide as London's Thames and with several car bridges crossing it. It wasn't as big as the mighty Don River, 12km downstream, but it had frozen over already. We guessed they were heading out onto the ice where they would drill a hole and drop their fishing line and hooks into the water to catch fish. They would be sitting out on the ice on the stools, staring down the hole, waiting for their dinner.

We didn't find what we wanted in *Detski Mir* - the advice to go there turned out to be dud - so we went to the *Univermag*. We successfully snagged a portable heater at the second shop and also couldn't resist a portable cooker, a Russian version of the Baby Belling cookers in the UK. It was a white metal box, the size of a small TV or mini microwave, and the front door opening looked just big enough to fit a whole chicken in if we managed to ever find one.

We figured we could occasionally use it for cooking stuff in our room and avoid the need to use the kitchen. We grabbed the bus back to the hostel. The temperature was so cold that the inside of the bus windows were opaque with condensation, frozen by the temperature on the other side of the glass. We had to scrub a little hole out on the window to see if our stop was coming. That, also, was hard as it was almost pitch-black outside at 4pm in the afternoon.

When we got off, we saw four fishermen again, no way to know for sure if two of them were the same ones we'd seen before, coming back in the opposite direction. They were all similarly kitted out at any rate, but what was amusing was how drunk they seemed. They were lurching from left to right, presumably having been drinking vodka all afternoon out on the ice to keep themselves warm inside while staring down the holes they had drilled. I hoped they'd also caught a few fish, at least.

Getting that bus that afternoon was probably the last time I used it, though, as now I was with Tanya, I was soon learning other ways to do things, including getting around the town. If we were heading into town, she would never take the bus, and from where I was looking, this was something akin to social positioning. I'd used it a few times happily, partly as it was a new experience, but also as it was dirt cheap. She maybe didn't use it as she didn't want this to mean she was dirt poor.

I sensed she was better than having to get the bus, and in fact, only if our destination was very close would she agree to even walk. For anything over 5 or 10 minutes, we just stopped a car, literally any car, and haggled a price for the driver to take us where we wanted to go. Anyone with a vehicle would use it as a taxi. Cars weren't cheap, and only people with some means could ever buy one, but having a car was a gateway to extra money in the newly burgeoning market economy. There were a few official taxis in the town at this time, but these were rendered almost useless by this basic precursor to Uber, a full 25 years before Uber even was a twinkle in Travis Kalanick's eye. We just walked to the edge of the road towards the oncoming cars, she put out her hand, and within a few seconds, a car would pull over. If not the first car, you can guarantee that no more than three or four would pass before one screeched over.

"Where are you wanting to go?" The driver would ask.

"Town centre, by Lenin square," might be Tanya's instruction.

"40 roubles," the driver would offer, "20," she'd reply, "30?" came the compromise return offer, "OK!" and in we'd get in.

Although the bus would have cost just a few roubles, or just a couple of pence, and even though our student ID gave us free bus rides, this private car system would still only have worked out at under a pound anyway. Actual taxis would have cost five times more, so nobody ever needed to use them with a stream of readily available cheaper alternatives.

For me, it became the only way I would get around after a while. It wasn't just in Voronezh, but if we took a trip up to Moscow, the same thing happened there. You could find yourself with some interesting drivers moonlighting for extra cash, too. In Moscow, I once found myself in a car driven by the head of astrophysics at the Moscow State University, an older gentleman with a bushy grey beard. His English was good, and he was keen to practice on his captive audience, but my Russian was relatively free-flowing and conversational by this time, too. I loved the novelty of stopping any car and bartering on the fee, even though I could easily afford their first offer. I tried to keep my haggling very monosyllabic, so they wouldn't realise I was a westerner and hike up the price. I'd give one-word answers where possible such as "station" or "central square", then I'd counter their first offer with a sharp "20" or "30" or such so that they couldn't pinpoint my accent quickly. Due to being 6ft 2ins and fair-haired, my accent was often mistaken for a Latvian or Lithuanian from "up north". I am sure many times after the car journey chat began and they realised I was English, some drivers must have wished they'd started the price higher.

Cars stopped without fail, and unlike on the street in England where you peered into the traffic with an arm half-raised hoping to spot a taxi soon, here you barely needed to raise an eyebrow.

I once played with this system by not even looking, almost looking the other way, and then briskly turning around and raising an arm to see how quickly it worked. It would be rare to get beyond twenty seconds before someone stopped if the traffic was flowing. Occasionally two or three cars would barrel over to you, competing for the fare.

There were wooden kiosks dotted around town, either in groups on some busy streets or standing alone in places like the parks. They would have a door around the back and a window and serving hatch at the front.

They offered a lot of Russian products such as cigarettes and strange-looking sweets, and near the front of their display, they tended to arrange their exotic or western goods if they had any. These were the highlights of the shop window to get people excited. You would sometimes see a can of 7-Up or a Mars Bar, and I once saw a can of Double Decker shandy in a window, which I got a little excited about. Pepsi seemed far more prevalent than Coke for some reason, although Coke did pop up now and then, and I reckoned neither came from the USA, but from somewhere with better economic ties with Russia, such as China or Turkey. To be desirable or attractive, a product didn't have to be from the geographical/ political West. I often saw the Brazilian instant coffee called Iguacu in a round silver tin taking pride of place in a kiosk. Or packets with Chinese writing on them, which you couldn't really identify unless there was a helpful picture on it, indications of whatever was inside. Having foreign goods and products was something to be proud of in Russian homes, no matter if they were rubbish.

At our teacher, Mr Belkin's house, there was a long since empty metal tin of Nescafe on his shelf gathering dust, and you could tell it wouldn't be taken down in a hurry.

CHAPTER 25

Tanya told me that one of the Russian crowd's friends, Alexander, or Sacha for short, had invited us for lunch one Saturday at his parents' place. Sacha was a diminutive guy with an angular face and he was full of nervous energy. I had met him the first night I went to Tanya and Alexei's place, and a couple of times since. He was friendly with everyone. He reminded me of the character Ratty in Wind in the Willows. He was constantly moving and chattering, and he ended almost every spoken sentence with "predstavlayesh?!" which means "do you follow me?"

He said his parents usually invited him to lunch most weekends, and having heard he now had English friends, they really wanted him to bring one around. Of course, Tanya and I were going - Sacha too, obviously, and big Oleg, as he was quite a pal of Sacha's. Like Vadim, Sacha also had a Moskvitch hatchback car. Perhaps it was the must-have car for their gang. The four of us would all go together in it.

"So, it will be an honour for my parents, you follow me? Dad and mum have always liked to have new people at the table, so having you there, Tanya, with the English boyfriend is just going to be too cool for them, do you follow me? There will probably be a few others; grandma, my niece and nephew too, so it will be really a bit squashed but, it won't matter to them, do you follow me? It will still make it a standout occasion for them, you know, with the Englishman and everything, do you follow me?"

So now I, in fact, became the shop window commodity. On the day we went here, it was fine and sunny, as we travelled in the car on the hard snow compacted roads. Sunglasses would have been helpful for the glare of the glistening white streets, but nobody seemed to have any. I thought again how, if the snow settled in England, driving cars became almost impossible. Here everyone was used to it, and Sacha drove confidently, chattering all the time. I suppose the winter tyres with thicker tread were doing their thing. As we drove up an inclined road or down a slope, occasionally, the car would slide or slip, but there was never any panic. Sacha let the car plane sideways for a while and then expertly caught it and pointed it back in the right direction. It certainly wasn't something anyone felt worth commenting on, as I guessed the snow laid around for six months, so they were all used to it - do you follow me?

At the outer city limits, the flat landscape became very dreary, and the roads widened to be big runways leading out into the nothingness, and presumably to go on for hours to distant towns or cities. Side roads appeared at right angles to carve their way into grids of identical-looking grey, or off-white, tower blocks, standing in groups of six at a time. In between these, there would be low-level blocks of buildings - shops perhaps. Although this all looked quite depressing on the face of it to me, the others got out of the car and approached Sacha's parents' apartment in one of the blocks in good spirits, so my mood was also positive. Their hospitality inside the compact home was fabulous. They had one main living room, and off this was a kitchenette, a bedroom and a bathroom.

There was absolutely no space in the living room left as the entire room had been taken over by a big table, or to be more accurate, three tables, covered with a large table cloth, which looked like it would seat about a dozen people.

There were the four of us who had arrived by car, Sacha's parents, who were in their fifties, and his grandmother. The grandmother sat and ate with us, but throughout the meal spoke very little, other than to accept or decline whatever dish was being passed. His older sister was there, but with no husband, but with her son and daughter around five and seven years old, respectively.

Making up the dozen was another couple in their fifties or sixties who I understood were next-door neighbours. I found out during the meal they had provided one of the tables. The parents had made every effort to bring out the best of everything, and Tanya explained that this was probably due to my presence. They used their best plates, best table cloth, and lots of food items were in their best jars or pots.

There was little agriculture traditionally through the snow-packed months, so the custom was for vegetables harvested the season before to be pickled in vinegar and stored in vast quantities, usually under beds where there was more space than in the cupboards or cabinets. On this day, plenty of pickled cucumber, carrot, courgette, and onions was provided and proudly served. I spotted a plastic carrier bag hanging on the door handle of the wall cabinet that housed their crockery. At first, I thought it was odd, with all the effort made, that they'd left a plastic bag hanging there, but with my second take, I realised it was a Harrods carrier bag and thus elevated to this position as a status symbol. It was so perfect, and straight they must have ironed it between towels or something. I didn't think that Sacha had been to England, but I knew that Alexei had visited a few times, so it was probably from one of his trips, I reasoned. There was also another plastic bag on the dresser surface which looked like Heathrow duty-free.

It was most definitely a feast. There was a thin broth with a few pieces of meat in it. The pickled vegetables, slices of bland tasting cheese, black bread, white bread, boiled eggs, coleslaw Waldorf-style with beetroot, and the ubiquitous hard Russian *kolbasa*. But of course, before even anyone ate anything, there was the vodka and the multiple toasts to each other. Even though I should have been used to it by now, I still got caught out by these toasts. I'd just taken my place between Tanya and Oleg and was eyeing up the plate with sliced sausage on it when the father of the house began to address us all.

I looked up to see he'd already filled most peoples' glasses a third full with vodka and was pushing the rest towards us three. Tanya quickly passed me some pickled cucumber and intimated I needed to quickly get a piece to hand as zakuski to follow the impending toast.

"…And so," began the dad, "with this finest of fine traditional Russian vodka, I would like to welcome you all to our humble abode today, and in honour of our special English friend," he tipped his glass towards me. "… it is with great pleasure that I welcome "England" to "Russia", and wish to you, Mr Genry, a great visit with us today in our home, but also a good time, and happiness in our country, as our respected guest".

"Cheers!" everyone clinked glasses, and as I knew they would, most heads tipped back as the drinks were despatched. The children were spared the vodka but still joined the toast as Sacha's sister had filled a couple of glasses with apple juice for them. As it was nearly half a small glass, the vodka ripped through my sinuses like a shot between the eyes that took my breath away. I popped the cucumber in, and the strength of the pickling on that was so tart it immediately counteracted the vodka like a magic antidote shot to a deadly vodka venom. It worked a treat. The vodka splutters that I was about to expel quashed straight away. Clever Russian tricks.

Glasses were banged down. I began once more to scan the table for what I might like to eat first. Sausage maybe, or some bread with the cheese could be a nice thing to start with. Then I realised Oleg was holding a plate near my eye line. Turning to look, I saw it was the gherkins again, and in his other hand, my glass refilled already an inch or two.

He had a cheeky grin. "Genry, come on, this is Russia. Everyone needs to make a toast, you know!" And so the process was repeated, this time the neighbour made a toast that I didn't really understand too well, but it seemed to be along the lines of complimenting Sacha's parents and how important it is to have good neighbours, so with the cry of "to good neighbours!" the second shot went down.

With a moment of apprehension, I began to fear that I would get completely hammered before really eating anything that day. But the concern was soon replaced with a comforting internal warmth as the vodka's buzz gave me the *what the hell* feeling that kicked all my worries into the long grass.

"Do you think I have to do one?" I whispered to Tanya. She squeezed the top of my thigh under that table, "Yes, but don't worry, it doesn't have to be a grand speech," she reassured me with a smile. Fortunately, not all the toasts would have to happen before the meal I saw with relief as then the plates were passed around, and we all began to dig into some lunch. But I'm not a natural public speaker; it was playing on my mind and preventing me from relaxing, so I wanted to get it over with. I had a sentence speedily created in my head and decided to go for it. I had no idea of the rules and didn't want to pick up the bottle and fill the glasses of these people who I had only just met, so I just raised my glass and stood up awkwardly. "Er, excuse me, please, I want to say...." I hoped they'd get my point and help me out, and the father instantly saved me and reached up and topped up all the glasses, including mine. "Thank you" I smiled into his eyes. He beamed back such a smile. He looked like he was my very own proud father.

"Er, thank you for me being here today..." my Russian was becoming a struggle, "...I am delighted to see you all...I am also happy for my country and Russia.... the relationship is good between Great Britain and Russia. So, I want to give a toast... to us!"

"To us!" they cried, *za nas*!! I sat down with a bit of a thumping chest. As I had been standing, nobody had passed the *zakuski* to me, so I hadn't actually had a refill, but it didn't matter. I'd ticked off my social and national responsibility. *God, that was really shit,* I thought to myself, but I didn't care too much - mostly just pleased it was done with. Tanya winked at me, leaned in and kissed me on the now even redder cheek. It became apparent that there were not going to be a dozen toasts, thankfully, as not only would the sister's children not be doing it, of course, but also none of the women did either. It was just the men's job, and as there were only five of us, I reasoned my initial panicking was going to be unfounded. I then remembered Sacha was driving, and strangely for a Russian, he didn't drink anyway (I like to be in control, do you follow me?), so there was only big Oleg's toast to go.

We enjoyed the fantastic hospitality of Sacha's parents that day and ate the generous food offerings they had brought out. In fact, after Oleg's eloquent toast, we refilled our glasses on other occasions during the meal too.

On the way back in the car, I said to Sacha that it was very nice of him to take me there as I sat in the back with Tanya snuggling against my shoulder. Maybe he thought I was just being polite, or he felt it was not the most exciting social highlight of my time in Russia, and so he said,

"The thing is, for my parents having an Englishman in their little apartment today was just so cool for them.

They will not have another for one year, five years, or maybe never! So *cool*!"

He overemphasised the Russian word for cool, *krootoi*. "They will enjoy speaking about it next week. The neighbours will tell the story of it another week. Do you follow me?"

"Yes, I get it. I saw the Harrods bag, too. So, are foreign things interesting because the place they are from is interesting, or just because they are not from Russia?" I asked.

"Absolutely certain. That's it. Russia is very closed. For 70 years, it's been closed to the outside world, distrustful even, and we shut our borders. Hardly anyone went out; hardly anyone came in. Our parents grew up thinking that all foreigners were from another solar system, and westerners were our capitalist aggressors and enemies. They would never have seen a foreigner. Only in the last year or so since the Party had to give up its power, and our country now wants to do business with the west, is it possible for ordinary Russians to see that you people are quite normal, do you follow me? Aiee!!", The car suddenly hit a rock of ice or a pothole or something, and we all yelped. Tanya and I were bumped off our seats and up into the car's roof and down again.

"Sorry about that, didn't see it!" Sacha continued, "We even want to become westerners ourselves. We want to do business, make money, and be - dare I say it –

capitalists, too! OK, so we aren't saying we are from the west; we are Russia which is not in the west, but in the east of… wherever the middle is. But we want to do the same things: drink Cognac, drive Mercedes Benz - and it will happen!"

"I agree," said Oleg, before continuing, "In ten or fifteen years, Moscow will be full of Mercedes Benz and Rolls Royces, you will see, maybe Voronezh, too, a bit later. Russia is now in a big hurry to catch up. We don't have all the laws, rules, economics or politics in place yet, but we have all the oil in the world. England has nearly none; you will buy it from us!"

"So that is why you see the Harrods bag in my parents' home, or packets of other foreign food in another home. It means "*I am on my way!*"" Sacha said.

"And so does having an English guest in your house!" roared Oleg, and he let out an enormous cackle of laughter.

"Actually, that reminds me - you are all invited to my place next Friday," Oleg said, "Genry, you can bring Becky, Jane, Al…whoever you want. Alexei, Nadia, Vadim and some others are coming, too. You too, obviously, Tanya."

"Yes, but Oleg," Tanya asked, "what western things do you have in your place to show that you are on your way?"

"Well, if I can get Genry and his friends in there, that's already more English things than Sacha's parents just had in their place!" Oleg chuckled again.

"We'll come, of course," I promised.

"Actually, I do have something else that's foreign at home. I just remembered. Do you know the drink Slimfast?" Oleg asked.

"Yes. It's a powder drink mix, I think, for... if you are on a diet?" I asked.

"Exactly, that's it. I have a friend who sent me four boxes of the stuff from England. Doc, from last year's group, if you have heard of him? You'll see it next week; it's my favourite drink, only, not with milk or water. I have it with gin. It's delicious. Gin and Slimfast. So, I get drunk, but also I can lose weight at the same time!"

I wasn't sure whether he was serious, but I decided against trying to correct Oleg. Also, I hadn't seen gin in the country yet, I noted inwardly.

When I got back to the hostel that night, I told Becky, Jane and Al about going to Oleg's in a few days, which they seemed keen to do. They seemed less keen on the idea of trying Gin and Slimfast, though. I wandered up to the floor above, as I was in the habit of trying to find the best alternative when needing to use the awful toilets and felt confident I could beat the filthy ones on our floor by trying upstairs.

As I began along the corridor, the aroma of marijuana snaked and filtered towards my nostrils. I was reminded of the Bisto gravy TV advert back home with Lynda Bellingham. "Hey everyone, it's ready!" she called in my mind, only it was not a *roast beef* joint that was aromatising this corridor. As I came to the door it emanated from, I heard English voices and peered in. I saw Connor and a few Edinburgh and Nottingham university guys enjoying their downtime, lolling on the beds and listening to music. I knew it was still some of the old stock that I had given away to them from nearly three months before.

"This stuff's still not run out then? You should keep the door closed at least, or open the window. I can smell it all the way down the corridor. You know, don't make it so obvious. You could go outside, or at least hang it out the window a bit?" I still felt a bit of the weight of responsibility having bought the *massive* ten-dollar consignment in the first place.

"Ah. It's alright, Henry, man," assured Gus. "Even Vladimir joined us earlier. I don't think they mind as much as you think they do." I didn't know which Vladimir he meant; it was a common name; could have been Tanya's ex-boyfriend, I supposed, though I didn't know Gus knew him. But I got the intended point that I was fussing too much.

When I got to the toilets on their floor, I was pleased to score them higher than the 1 out of 10 ones on my floor. These ones, I'd give at least a 3 out of 10.

I went back to Tanya's apartment that night as I was

beginning to do more and more, as everything was better about staying there. She always prepared a meal which was usually better than anything we would manage in the hostel for a start. It was warm and cosy, too, without any broken windows, and of course, it had a good bathroom, with a toilet, basin, and a bath with a shower over it. Although it only had two rooms, having one bedroom just to ourselves was the crowning benefit for me. It was generous of the others too. It provided us with the privacy to enjoy our new relationship.

The relationship developed me in some ways, that's for sure. I realised that Tanya was more experienced than me early on, so I was happy to be led and try new things that I hadn't done before. Once underway, though, surges of confidence, and lust, would overtake me, and I surprised even myself in the bedroom. As I said already, Tanya had femininity, which had a knock-on effect on me. I think I became more commanding, but it could have been down to her, of course.

It was as if it helped me to develop a level of masculinity that I hadn't really felt in myself before then. Or, that could just all be a load of old hog's wash. Probably in all relationships, if they are good, they make you feel good about yourself; pheromones and hormones are flying about everywhere. Either way, I liked it, and I couldn't get enough of it.

CHAPTER 26

Everyone's Russian language was getting better by living among Russians and going to our daily classes on the first floor of hostel number 4. I felt mine was getting especially good, as I was spending more time with Tanya, with whom I only spoke in Russian. Although she was taught English at school, I don't think she paid much attention, as she had little confidence in trying it out on me. I must admit that my discipline did slip towards my own studies; now and then, I missed the first class of the day, and occasionally I missed the whole morning of classes. The Russian sing-song lessons were a bit bizarre, too, where we had to listen to and then sing along out loud with traditional Russian folk songs. They just didn't seem too important, as my Russian language was coming on quite rapidly, including slang and pet names for things.

I did quite like the songs like "Kalinka Maya", "Ach, Odessa", and the crowd favourite "Happy Birthday" (nothing like our melody, by the way), which ends with a melodic "unfortunately… a birthday… is only once… per… year!"

A week after I visited Sacha's parents, Al, Becky, Jane and I went out to try the Pizzeria Italia place again.

It was the only pizza place in the whole city, and it deserved another try. It was located on the ground floor of a big building block, and we were crammed inside, standing around circular tables, a bit like breakfast bar counters, and the windows were steamed up. I think it probably had outside tables in the summer, as there was a sizeable paving area out there, although right now in winter, the snow was piled up outside.

"This is not a good pizza," Al sadly acknowledged.

We all lamented. The cheese and tomato base, which in Becky's case was all she had as she was vegetarian, was just about ruined by the fact that the standard Russian cheese they had as a base ingredient was just not good at melting; indeed, it was neither cheddar nor mozzarella. It was married with a somewhat bitter tomato puree paste, and it was not a happy marriage, and would probably end in an annulment rather than just a plain divorce. Our versions had Russian sausage slices on top to make them into pepperoni pizzas. They had tried to make it more melty and oozy by underlining it with mayonnaise, but the mayonnaise seemed to have curdled and gone a bit weepy.

"This is just disgusting," Becky said, "it's almost sour. It's like mayonnaise mixed with sour cream under here!"

"Oh look, they're even doing takeaway," I added with mock enthusiasm as a small group of Russians walked out with cardboard *Pizzeria Italiana* boxes in their hands.

"Er, let me see…no thank you, spasibo, very much!" said Jane pushing hers around the plate. "Maxim said he actually likes this pizza; can you believe that?" she added.

"Who's Maxim?" I asked.

Jane didn't answer straight away, as if she was considering how to. I looked at Becky to see if it made more sense to her. She raised her eyebrows and winked at me, and looked to Jane.

"He's a friend of mine," Jane said. "Sofia introduced us. He's from hostel number 3."

"He's more than a friend really, though, isn't he Jane, wouldn't you say?" suggested Becky. "…more of a boyfriend?"

"OK, OK!! Yes, well, we do see each other now and then," she added, "but we're not, like, *married* or anything. We just hook up when we can. His family own a farm outside of the city."

"Wow, that's great. So, what's Maxim like, then?" I asked.

"Well, he's quite outdoorsy, and he said he will show us the forests and where to go mushroom picking, whenever the season is for that. Oh, and… he's absolutely gorgeous!!" Jane said excitedly, beaming finally.

Outside the pizza place, there was a big open square which surrounded a very tall and wide building which had the word 'Circus' written upon it. It was a brick and concrete building, and I supposed it was a multi-purpose building also used for other things as well as circuses which inhabited it only periodically during the year. Tanya had told me the TV game show *Wheel of Fortune* was coming to Voronezh. It was called Polye Chudess in Russian, literal meaning "Field of Wonders". It was quite an exciting event seeing as the entertainment industry was still in its green shoots of infancy, and this was one of the only shows that seemed to be nearly always on TV. Oleg was apparently going to be getting us tickets.

I had seen it on TV at Tanya's, and the game show's host, Leonid Yakubovich, was slick and had probably honed his delivery watching American TV shows somewhere. He would be hosting the Voronezh show in this circus building, and the signs around the doorway I spotted for *Polye Chudess* attested to it. To take our minds off the pizzas I explained to the guys that Oleg hoped to be getting tickets to it.

"It'll be fun if we go. That Yakubovich guy could even call us down. They spin the wheel to get a number, and if that's the seat you're on, you *Come on Down!* and become one of the contestants. He's a bit like a Russian Lesley Crowther, I guess."

"Come on Down!" chorused Al, "and you could win this fabulous Mercedes Benz!" Indeed, the star prize did seem to be an eighties Mercedes saloon every time I had seen the programme.

"Is it definitely happening?" asked Becky.

"Let's ask Oleg later. We're going to his place tonight," I reminded her.

That night the four of us made our way to Oleg's, along with Tom and Jim, too. Jim rarely joined us for socials, but he played football a lot, came along with Tom to things now and then, and bored us with his tales of life in Pinchbeck, near Spalding, Lincolnshire. (He reeled off the full address most times.) He fascinated us one time, relaying the story about how he'd bought his whole family matching dressing gowns one Christmas.

Tanya didn't go in the end. Apparently, she had some studies to do, which was a rare occurrence, as I'd barely seen her with as much as a textbook with her.

As well as us six *Britanskis*, the Russian guests were; *do-you-follow-me* Sacha, Oleg of course, Alexei, and Vadim, the guy who didn't speak much but seemed to drive Alexei everywhere. We also met two new people that night, Mikhail and Alina, a brother and sister. Mikhail seemed very serious, with dark hair and thick rectangular glasses and a sense of humour shortage, but Alina was fun and full of energy. She was quite different to most Russian girls in that she had cropped brown hair, short as a boy's at the back but a bit longer on top. She had a striking face with a prominent nose. It was a combination of Sheena Easton and Barbra Streisand. She talked at a hundred miles an hour, and a bit like Sacha, she also said *predstavlayesh* (do you follow me?) at the end of most of her sentences. Alina told me that she was a good friend of Tanya, so I did my best to make a good impression, in case it was true, but in truth, I found it hard to understand her, as she talked so fast.

Oleg's residence was on the far side of town on the other side of the river, and I didn't think in the few months I had been there, I had yet been over any of the four or five bridges that went over to the Eastern side of Voronezh. He had a decent main room where we spent the whole evening, with a galley kitchenette off the side of this. The view from the apartment was excellent. It was on the tenth floor of quite a big block. We got there after dark, but I could still see the cityscape, including the winding river denoted by the lit bridges crossing it, and some big wide main roads with heaped snow in piles at the sides glistening under the street lights. There were, of course, the ubiquitous blocks of flats by the dozen, too.

"So, Genry, this is what I am talking about!" Oleg shouted proudly, holding up a big plastic glass in one hand and a tub of Slimfast in the other. "*Gins' Slimfast-om!*" he announced proudly in Russian. He even correctly grammatically declined the word Slimfast as if it was a Russian word, ending the noun with the instrumental case ending of "om", which made it sound even more of a ridiculous invention.

He was standing in the kitchen area of the main room, and I walked over, shaking my head and smiling at his strange concoction.

"You begin with two measures of gin," he announced as he poured a random amount of gin into the bottom of the tall plastic beaker, which I thought maybe came with the Slimfast as part of the product. "Then you mix in 4 spoons of Slimfast powder; here it goes…" he continued the commentary while I watched him create the drink. "Then some tonic," in it went, "but if you don't have tonic, just water will also be absolutely OK". I hadn't seen either tonic or gin before this night, so Oleg was clearly well connected. "You add lemon if you have some." At this point, he squeezed half a lemon into the beaker. "And, then, you can add an ice cube or two, or…" he stepped over to the window, opened the balcony door with one hand scooped a handful of snow off the railing, "… a lovely bit of Russian snow!" He dumped the snow into the drink and shut the door, and clipped a plastic lid into the top. "Then you give it a big shake…" and he did so, "… you take off the lid, and there you have *Gins' Slimfast-om*! A better drink there isn't, and it's good for you, too!"

Oleg then chinked his glass against mine with a proud flourish, and said, "Here, try it!"

The first thing I tasted was cold snow, then gin. Next I discovered the lemon and sweet taste of the weird fruity drink that this powder had been made from topped off with the taste of the tonic. It was like no other slush puppy I had seen or tasted before, and I had tasted many better drinks than this, but I wasn't going to spoil his fun.

"Oleg, this is OK…in fact, it's good!" I lied.

We had a good evening at Oleg's place, and it was interesting to be not in the hostel or Tanya's apartment for a change. Later, though, the chat amongst the Russians was becoming a little intense. They seemed to be talking about something quite serious, and I asked Alexei how he was doing when I got the chance. Alexei wasn't carrying his face in a permanent grin for once.

"Everything is perfect, Genry," Alexei said, trying to reassure me.

"It doesn't look like it to me; you seem much more serious than usual, Alexei," I replied.

He beckoned me to sit down and join him and Vadim on the sofa. He explained that his elder brother Anton had been arrested the day before, and he was worried. I'd already known that Anton was a bit of a rogue. He wasn't at the university, but he lived in the city and was in trouble with the authorities on and off, as he lived on the shadier side of Russian society. To be honest, in Russia in 1992, many people lived on the murkier side of life.

Wages were so low that almost everyone did something a bit dodgy, be that moonlighting as a taxi driver even though you could be an upstanding university professor or traffic cop taking a small bribe from the motorist. Alexei himself was just one of the newly created breeds of *biznismen* in Russia, exchanging our dollars for several percentage points better than the banks would, knowing super inflation would very soon ensure him a profit. He even had Vadim as a driver, who you could also say was his henchman if you wanted it to seem more sinister. If you were a completely law-abiding citizen and as pure as the driven Russian snow, you were probably living close to the poverty line in Russia.

Anton, however, I think was much shadier still. From buying and selling contraband alcohol and cigarettes, he had strayed into drugs. As I had heard already, the Russian authorities had little patience for drugs, something they blamed western society for.

"They've been trying to get something to pin on Anton for ages, but he's always been one step ahead of them," Alexei began.

"Hitri kak lis!" chimed in Vadim, meaning *cunning as a fox*.

He then explained that Anton had been well and truly set up. "Police followed him on the street." Alexei began, "They chose their moment. They approached my brother from different directions; the first guy in plain clothes bumped into him and planted drugs on him, and without him noticing, he planted drugs on him, I guess and then disappeared very quickly. But then, two more police approached quickly from the opposite direction, stopped him, and searched him. They found heroin in a small bag in his coat pocket... the first police guy had just put it there!" Alexei angrily explained.

"My god, that's bad!" was all I could say. "So, what's happening?"

Alexei said that heroin (*geroin,* of course) was something his brother had nothing to do with and put him in a really bad place. "They've arrested him now, and I just don't know what he can do. They've got him. If they find him guilty, they'll keep him in prison for a very long time."

"But this is what I have been saying to you about drugs, by the way, Genry." Alexei continued, "It's just not worth it. It can be so much trouble, even if you haven't been using drugs, if they want to make you guilty of it, as you see with Anton, it's the way they can get you. Stick to as much vodka as you like with your English friends. Don't give them an invitation."

"I know, I know. I don't have any now anyway. I only bought that grass in the first week, but now I don't have anything to do with it. I'm sorry about Anton, though. That's unbelievable!" I tried to take my concern and attention back to where the serious trouble was.

"Does he get a lawyer or something like that? Will he be able to defend himself about this?"

"Ha! Lawyers?! No, I honestly don't know. There will be a hearing, but probably the judge will be paid, the lawyer will be paid, and Anton will get locked up for a long time. Maybe we need to see who we can try to pay…?" said Alexei, glancing at Vadim, who was looking at the floor, nodding and taking a drag on his Marlboro.

This shocking news was a bit of a sobering moment, reminding me that I was in a harsh country with a murky recent past and secret police still going strong. It was not too long ago that people regularly went missing, never to be seen again, I supposed. We enjoyed ourselves, having parties, and living a bit of a charmed life as VIPs in Russia almost. But we were actually living in a bubble, quite removed from the reality of our surroundings. The news about Anton didn't dominate the evening, though. In fact, Alexei didn't even mention it to anyone else that night, so the group were mostly unaware and continued to have fun. Someone played the guitar, shots were downed, *zakuski* were eaten. Around midnight I have the image, in my head still, of Oleg serenading Becky on the icy balcony, to the tune of a Russian folksong, but swapping in made-up English lyrics, calling her his beautiful *Cornflake Girl*.

The evening carried on deep into the night, and soon it was somewhere around 2 a.m., and Becky, Jane, Al and I realised we needed to probably head back to the hostel. With Tom and Jim also with us, it meant that somewhere near 2.30 a.m., the six of us stumbled out into the bitter cold to try to look for a car. We were going to have to look for two cars, of course, and as it was unlikely that we'd see two at once, we reckoned we'd split into two groups of two guys/one girl each to improve the security, for our separate journeys.

However, this part of the city was a bit quieter than the parts where we usually hailed cars in, and we walked for five or ten minutes in almost eerie silence with no traffic passing at all.

It was a wide road lit by streetlamps, with thick snow covering underfoot, and snow beginning to fall out of the pitch-black sky. We were all quite drunk, talking loudly, hearing our own voices echoing back to us out of the darkness.

Finally, we sensed the light of a car behind us, and moments later, the engine sound could also be heard. We stood to one side and got ready to turn around for our first group to get a lift. As the car approached, Al put his hand out. It grumbled over the snow up the road towards us. It didn't appear to slow, but as it came by, the pale blue Lada was lit up well by the street lamp close by to us. We looked into the car as it passed to see who was driving, still hoping that they would stop. Two men in the car looked back at us, and it sent a shiver right through me. They were both dressed in dark clothing, while the driver wore a hat, and under the glare of the lamp, I could see dark stubble on his face. He seemed youngish and maybe the type to make money other than from taxi moonlighting. On the far side, the other one seemed to be leaning forwards as if to get a better look at us across and in front of the driver. I couldn't make him out, but I knew I didn't want anyone to get in that car.

"No thanks! Drive on!" I blurted out under my breath, to nobody in particular, looking away from the car.

"Oh god, I don't want to get in there," added Becky.

"Go, go!" said Al.

The car didn't seem to lose pace and continued on into the snowy scenery ahead. We all continued to watch its rear-view lights, willing it to keep going. As it did so, we began to walk once again, a little relieved. Then, brake lights ahead. Had the car stopped!? The right indicator came on. Oh no!

"Al?!" I said, asking him I wasn't sure what.

Then the car turned off to the right and rounded the corner and out of sight. Relief again. But now we just really needed a car, two cars in fact, to take us home. It became a pressing need as we realised that we were potentially in a precarious and dangerous situation. The snow, if anything, fell harder, and it was freezing cold. It was close to 2.30 a.m., and probably about minus 10 degrees, our alcohol happiness was about to desert us.

A few minutes later, another light, another sound of an engine. We looked around now, really wanting to be rescued from the situation we had put ourselves in. As it got closer, we could see it was bigger than a car, perhaps a small van. Then a second or two later, Tom called out, "It's an ambulance! Can we stop an ambulance?!" None of us knew what the etiquette was for this, but sure enough, it was a proper ambulance with stripes and lights. But we put our hands out anyway.

It didn't appear to be on duty, but we could see that the rear was illuminated through the driver's cab. As it approached us, it began to slow, and then it stopped when it got to us. The window came down, and the uniformed driver spoke to us. He appeared to be driving alone. Hopefully, that gave us a better chance. We were still not sure if he would tell us off for being out so late in such conditions, or if he would tell us to get lost.

"Where are you going?" he asked me.

"Friedreich Engels street, near the train station," I said.

"Well, OK, 80 roubles?" he replied.

"How about 60?" I don't know why I was even haggling; we just wanted so badly to get in.

"OK, get in!" He jumped down and opened the back doors, much to our relief, and we clambered in.

Indicating that four people were enough in the back, he motioned Tom and Jim to sit in the front. He shut the doors behind the rest of us; we couldn't believe our luck and stared at each other in disbelief. We had hitched a lift with an ambulance. Our relief was complete, and our spirits instantly were lifted. Driving through Voronezh back to the hostel in the dead of night in the back of an ambulance because we wanted to get home, and it was the only vehicle around to get home in, was just nuts, but in a very good way.

Al lay on the gurney and pretended to be the patient. "Shall we play doctors and nurses?"

"Do you want gas and air?" I asked him, holding a face mask aloft that I had found on the shelf.

It was a surreal end to another day in this Russian adventure, as we drove through the freezing cold night in the back of the ambulance, back to hostel number 4 and to bed.

CHAPTER 27

I hadn't been to Moscow since going up for the Spartak
Moscow vs Liverpool football match in late October, but
my next trip came around a couple of months later, with
Tanya for the first time. My dad and step-mum were on
their way to Hong Kong and engineered a one-night
stopover in Moscow to meet with me. I was excited to
see them as this was such a wild place, and to see them in
this scenario would be an experience anyway, and I was
keen to show off Tanya to them. I was proud of myself,
not only to be holding my own beyond the recently iron
curtain, at the tender age of just twenty-one on arrival,
but now twenty-two, but also as I had a genuine native
girlfriend to boot.

Our family unit in Buckinghamshire suburbia
unravelled in 1980. My family was scattered and
certainly not much of a team at this time. My parents
had divorced a decade earlier when I was around ten
years old. The marriage had been breaking down ever
since I was born. Don't worry; I don't feel responsible
for it, if you were wondering. My mother suffered from
post-natal depression, apparently, and then succumbed
to alcoholism. She had coped with it up to a point, but it

took its toll on the marriage, and they eventually divorced. She ended up in a hospital, followed by a series of clinics and membership to Alcoholics Anonymous. Things were quite bad near the end, with constant parental fights and the occasional visit by the police.

After the split, I lived with my then sober mum, brother and sister, in a functional new-build house, bought with the proceeds from her divorce settlement, while my dad went to live with his new woman, a German divorcee, in London, with her two children. He played his part too in the disintegration of the marriage and family, having various affairs before the eventual split. Things did settle down eventually, and my mum got the support she needed to turn things around. To her credit, she never drank a drop of alcohol again after hitting rock bottom and losing everything. She had the fortitude needed to turn things around. Us five children, separated by only six years of age, got along very well when we all spent time together at my dad and new step-mum's house, while the parents were quite civil and cooperated. By the time I was about fifteen, though, my brother and sister, Rob and Anna, who were three and five years older than me, had moved to college digs to study for their degrees. Now that we weren't living together, I gradually saw them less and less. They spent the holidays in their student digs or had the luxury of a buy to let house my dad and step-mum had bought. It was made available to their combined four children (if you exclude yours truly, still living with my mum) for periods at favourable rates. My mum then downgraded to a two-bedroom apartment, into which she moved with me and her new partner, who she'd met at AA, and who soon became her second husband.

A few years later, by the time I went off to begin my university years, my siblings were backpacking around the other side of the world (Philippines, Malaysia, Thailand, Australia, Hong Kong, etc.). I thought it seemed as if they couldn't get away fast enough, and maybe I was right as they never lived in England again after this. By the winter of 1992, my mum had divorced for the second time. She had also embarked on a relationship with someone who would become her third husband. Rob and Anna were both living and working in bar and restaurant jobs in Hong Kong, and it was thither that my dad and step-mum were flying for a week's visit to see them.

It had taken some organising without mobile phones back then, but we somehow managed it with airmail letters. I was happy with having Tanya, and I suppose I thought that my dad would be impressed that I had a pretty Russian girlfriend. As she didn't speak very much English, a bit of me knew I'd be showing off by talking Russian to her during dinner in front of my parents. Tanya and I would be staying with the sibling of a friend she knew in Moscow who had space for us. My dad and step-mum were staying at pretty much the only place foreign tourist visitors could stay in Moscow at the time, the Intourist Hotel on Tverskaya street, which was a stone's throw from Red Square.

It was a flying visit; we were meeting them on the same day they landed in Moscow, and they would stay one night in the hotel before heading back to the airport the following day. They would do no sightseeing at all, but they had, unusually, visited Moscow a couple of years before anyway, and done sightseeing soviet style. My dad was a classic car enthusiast in the 1980s, and they'd taken part in car events in the UK and around Europe. They had both taken part in one called the Milan to Moscow rally, where they'd taken a 1950s Alvis along with a procession of other enthusiasts in bestickered cars all the way from Italy to Russia.

The night before, as we lay in bed, Tanya was understandably nervous. From her point of view, she had bagged an English boyfriend whose parents were coming to check her out and pass a verdict. "What if they think I am just with you for the wrong reasons? Will they think I am just looking for an English passport?" she asked.

"They won't think that, don't worry," I assured her.

"But, how do you know that?"

"Because there is no such thing as an English passport. It's a British passport!" I joked.

"Oh, stop it, Genry-chik! (a pet name she used), you

know what I mean."

I wasn't giving it too much thought, her feelings, I mean, as I was mainly keen to show her off along with my achievements in both the language and my adaptability to the surroundings and culture. It was shallow of me. I was sure my dad would think something along the lines of "that's my boy" rather than genuinely contemplating a future Russian daughter-in-law at this stage.

In the first two years at university, I had put him through the mill a bit with my first university girlfriend, Lucy. We had got very serious and emotionally bonded for various reasons, including the pregnancy. For a while, he must have thought I might end up being married and a father myself before I even graduated. With that in the past, but still relatively recent, I guess I thought that he'd be pleased I was now moving on and lightening up, even.

As we travelled across Moscow on the underground from the central Paveletskaya station, I thought that Tanya looked great. She was always stylish and had a great way of walking, or working it, as some would say. I began to wonder, and I hoped my dad wouldn't start flirting with her, as I knew he could do that with women of any age.

On cue, as we walked across the concourse of one of the train stations, I noticed admiring glances and even the occasional comment from Russian men towards Tanya, which I didn't understand.

"Ignore it, as I do," she said to me.

But then one man turned as she passed. He reached out, and almost in a lunge, he pinched her bum. It wasn't something I'd seen happen before. For starters, it was so cliché and crass, and I was pretty shocked a man would do that in broad daylight in a public place. He literally grabbed a piece of her arse between his thumb and forefingers, about two metres in front of me. However, Tanya didn't break stride, carried on towards the down escalator, and I just followed. I wasn't about to start an international debate with the guy.

It was just another illustration of how the attitudes between sexes were quite different in Russia compared to the UK. A British woman, quite rightly and justifiably, would have been far more likely to swing around and give the man a piece of her mind in this situation. We have sexual equality and are intolerant of sexist behaviour, generally speaking, of course. In Russia, the genders did seem to conform to a high degree to poor stereotyping at that time. The men were somewhat chauvinistic and expected the women to be there for their needs to some large degree. Not all of them, obviously, but in general. This was matched by many of the women seemingly being quite happy to, or was it more resigned to, taking on that role, looking after the men, cooking for them, and complementing the whole stereotype.

What is the opposite of feminism? It's not

masculinism. Chauvinism and misogynism are not something to aspire to, though I realise that it misses the point of feminism, which is more about promoting equality between both sexes, only with its origins of advocating women's rights. It just seemed wrong anyway to see that man treat Tanya as fair game in such a crude way, as if the men felt they had some control over women.

We collected my dad and step-mum from the Intourist Hotel. It was stiff as far as introductions went. Tanya surprised me by wearing a stern face full of nerves, and with the loss of cheek muscle control, she lost some of her natural effervescence at first.

I wasn't used to hearing her speak English, and I wouldn't say I liked her stilted pained English contributions to my parents' conversation. It wasn't the Tanya I knew and I felt a tender pang of sympathy towards her that she was unable to present to them the Tanya that I wanted her to be. Gone was the confident, cheerful, and funny person, and here was someone with stage fright, a different voice and defensive expression.

I was happier, though, when we got to the Georgian restaurant, the same one I had been to after the Liverpool match. Tanya was able to talk rapidly and fluidly with the restaurant staff in Russian, doing all the ordering for us. Although they would not have understood her, I felt her shackles fall off and hoped they'd be able to glimpse a little bit more of her relaxed personality. It was good to catch up with them over the meal, and the food and drink were delicious as it had been the time before. Once the traditional Georgian dancing got underway, we were all relaxed, and the international language of pointing, clapping and smiling made everything better.

As we parted, I got a big squeeze of a hug from my dad, and he whispered in my ear that he was very proud of me. Tanya, for her part, also said she had a good time, but we were both still flushed with relief when it was finally over, and we left them at their hotel. As we walked up the street, we dived in our bags for cigarettes and a lighter, lit up, and smoked with relief – something neither of us did in the presence of our parents.

CHAPTER 28

When Christmas and New Year came around, the university took a short study break. Some students went away to visit their families, although many stayed in Voronezh. Over half of the British students returned home to the UK to their parents for the holidays. I remained in Russia, however. My family was not a very nuclear one at the time, and there was no family home to go to as such. My dad would be working in London and never had a lot of time, as he was always so busy working. He shared a mansion block apartment with my step-mum where I had never lived, so I had no bedroom or things there. It wasn't my home. My mum was soon to marrying husband number three, ten years her junior, and moving into his house in Maidenhead, in fact, so visiting either of them would have felt more like intruding than going home. Neither of my siblings would be around, having already completed their studies and currently living in Hong Kong as part of their current globe-trotting status. I had just seen my dad in Moscow a few weeks before, so I had ticked a family box of sorts.

Staying in Voronezh for Christmas was no hardship, though it was a nice break with no lessons to go to it. I spent the whole week with Tanya and rarely came back to the hostel as Al wasn't there, and neither were many others. Although in Russia they knew it was Christmas day in the western world, it was still not a date in the calendar they notably celebrated. I don't even think that businesses closed that day. It was a normal day for them.

Russia half followed the Julian calendar, which meant their Christmas day was about a week to ten days into January. Nevertheless, a group of us, including Sam, Becky, Tanya, Nadia and myself, managed to get two big chickens from the market and potatoes and other bits of vegetables, and had a Christmas lunch of a style in the apartment altogether. We filled our bellies and clinked our glasses to the Christmas of 1992.

A few days after Christmas, we were graced by a visit from James Doherty, aka Doc, who Alexei had said right at the start of our time in Russia was his best mate from the previous year's student group. Doc arrived at the door to the apartment early one morning, having disembarked from the overnight train from Moscow, with arms full of Soviet champagne and a beaming smile. Alexei was delighted to see Doc, and the back-slapping and hugging attested to the fact that the feeling was mutual. Doc had a freckly face, dark brown hair, a big smile, and an incredibly infectious laugh, frequently employed. He reminded me of the actor Tim Rice, most famously from the Rocky Horror Picture Show. Even though it was early in the morning, with absolutely nothing on the agenda, we cleared the table and set the bottles down to celebrate the arrival of an old friend visiting town. I got on well with Doc straight away.

Tanya, Nadia, Alexei, Doc and I enjoyed an impromptu session that morning with Tanya quickly rustling up some food, so it became a fizzy brunch.

"Wow, it's so nice to be back," Doc exclaimed, "and everything's just the same, too; I was worried it would have changed. How do you like it, Henry?" he asked.

"It's great. I love it!" I replied.

Conversation flowed very easily between us all. While it was like an old friends' reunion for everyone else, he and I had never met before this moment, and yet, somehow, it was like we already knew each other. Maybe because of the *any friend of yours is also a friend of mine* effect. We almost immediately began to joke with each other, like old friends. Doc said he had just spent Christmas away with his family in northern Italy, and when his family returned home, he took a flight to Moscow to seize a few days here before the new term started in January.

"Hold on," I interrupted him, "when you said you've been away with the family in the Dolomites, I thought you were talking about cars!" I said, tongue in cheek.

"No, we've not just spent Christmas in some old Triumph cars; Henry, we had a lovely villa in the Italian mountains, thank you!"

Later, after Alexei had filled him in a bit more about things around here, he jibed back at me. "Listen, I can see you're probably a bit worried about Tanya and me, from last year? So, for full transparency, and so you don't waste your time wondering, I did not sleep with her."

"Well, that's full transparency, alright; I appreciate that," I replied.

"OK. I'm just joking, obviously," Doc continued, "I may have fancied her a little bit; who wouldn't? But she was having absolutely none of it. Tanya is much more discerning than that, and I am *way* too unworthy for her! You're a lucky man, and she's saved herself for you."

"Oh, Doc! You're such an idiot!" chided Tanya, throwing a bit of bread at him, as he let out his deep chortle of a laugh again. "Don't listen to anything this man says, Genry!" she added.

Doc and Alexei spent most of his few days in Voronezh galivanting around, indulging Doc in revisiting some other of his old friends, too, and we hooked up with him most evenings. In the daytime, I mostly spent my hours with Tanya and Becky and Sam, the only other Brits from my circle not to have gone back home. Sam was also, by this time, getting quite serious with Hanna, one of the East German girls from the other end of our floor. There had been a bit of a 'musical rooms' in the hostel by this point already; some room swapping had allowed Sam to move into Hanna's room, and her old roommate, Karla, had found other friends to bunk up with. The pair of them would often be locked away for hours on end - getting to know each other really well, one assumed.

On a fine but freezing, sunny day between Christmas and New Year, a few of us visited a forest nearby just for something to do. Russian woods are often a feature of many a literary masterpiece for some reason, and I can see why when I think back to this place. The trees stretched as far as you could see as we walked through just a fraction of it, sometimes across clearings, but also in-between the trees with the canopy above. It was freezing, probably minus ten degrees centigrade, but the blue sky and sun helped make everything feel so fresh and quite beautiful. Blowing away the cobwebs would be what my mum would have called it. I walked with my arm wrapped around Tanya's furry coated arm as we leaned and pressed on each other.

"This is great out here. Why don't we come out more?" I asked.

"I like it too, but we do it more in the summer. We'll probably only manage about thirty minutes at this temperature."

I don't know if Tanya had mentioned that on purpose, but I realised that I would probably not be in Russia by the summer. Our *non-exchange* exchange would take me until the end of May or early June. We walked on, and

I realised neither of us was talking. I wondered if we were both thinking about our relationship. What would happen when this academic year ended?

"Genry-chik, do you like me?"

"Of course, I like you. I like you a lot," and I squeezed her to me extra tightly.

She stopped walking, and we turned to face each other.

"You know…you must know, that I love you, don't you?"

I smiled very broadly. I guess that I already knew it, and for my part, I knew I was very into Tanya, too. I had never felt as intensely about anyone as I did about her. I held both her hands in both of mine, and we looked each other directly in the face.

I had a momentary thought inside my head about whether it was the right thing to say or not. I looked at her face, surrounded by her red scarf with bits of blonde hair escaping from under it. I took in her silvery grey furry coat (I don't know if it was real fur or not, reader, and it was not something that concerned me at the time) coming right up to and caressing her face and chin, her sparkling green eyes, and lightly painted lips. I felt it, too.

"I love you. I love you as well!" I said and pulled her close and enveloped her in a big hug.

As we parted, we exchanged small, quick kisses and had big smiles on each of our faces.

"I was also thinking," she continued, "that we should look into getting a place of our own. It is not easy as it is now. I don't want to come to the hostel to sleep, and in Ulitsa Mira, we always have Nadia or Alexei, or someone else, on top of us."

I thought back to the first night. While not literally on top of us, I cringed at the thought that Nadia may have been awake while we energetically acquainted ourselves that first time in the middle of the room. Then the next thought that came to me was what Tanya had suggested. A place just for us, a love nest, where we could go home to at the end of the day. We could do many more things together, anywhere in the apartment, and she had just said she loved me, and we would not have to be trying to keep it quiet or discreet because of flatmates. It sounded like a brilliant idea.

"Yes, but where? How do we do that?"

She explained that a one-bedroom apartment in the centre of town near Lenin Square, which was at the end of Revolution Prospect near the university Deconat building, would be possible for around $20 per month. I pictured the buildings that I thought were around there.

They were grand blocks in the late 18th and early 19th century neo-romantic European style. The love nest idea was growing on me straight away, literally. $20 per month seemed affordable too. Tom and Paul had got a place for themselves already, so I knew this was going to be a reality, not just a fantasy idea. We agreed we would start making plans as soon as possible.

Presently, New Year's Eve rolled around and was celebrated with several parties around the hostels, and I went to more than one of them, ending up at a big party in hostel number 3 with Tanya. It was the same hostel where I went all that time ago in my first week in Russia to the bedroom with sleeping bodies to buy grass from Sergei. He was usually very drunk, every other month anyway, and always quite intimidating with it, unlike a funny drunk. I had seen Sergei in November a couple of times, in a non-drinking month. He had been completely sober and was quite different; cleaner looking for a start, with smarter clothes. I walked past him while he was talking to some other students. He appeared every bit a proper student, with neatly parted hair and a more kempt beard. He said hello to me, but there was still something unsettling about the sober Sergei, almost like he had a split personality. Those were just fleeting encounters, though; it was December now, and he was back in drunk mode somewhere, and I would try to avoid him at all costs - a nasty bastard who threw cats out of windows for fun. I don't think I had been back to the building since that visit, and although it seemed like a long time ago now, in fact it had probably only been about three and half months. But much had happened since then.

I could now speak Russian much better than back

then. I had a girlfriend, a bit of routine, and I planned to get an apartment in town. Also, I had long since given up trying to smoke crafty joints here and there, and was a fully-fledged vodka drinking semi-naturalised inhabitant of Russia.

I have a New Year's Eve memory of standing in the middle of a big common room in hostel number 3, dancing and thrusting my hands in the air to the beats of the music. I was a boy from Buckinghamshire in England, just twenty-two years old, and dancing away on a deep, midwinter's night in the middle of Russia. I was not just far away from home, but I was in a nondescript concrete student hostel function room, dancing for joy, cigarette in hand one hand, drink in another, in a city I am pretty sure most people in England had never heard of. I was surrounded by Russians, Africans, Germans and other nationalities, too, and felt exhilarated by these bizarre circumstances that brought me to this point. Snow was falling out of a pitch-black sky outside to add to the half a metre deep snow drifts that were piled up permanently. I don't even think I was with any of my English friends by midnight. A vague sense of the forests in the dark outside the city came to me and of the characters in literary novels like Dr Zhivago and Anna Karenina being pulled along in horse-drawn sleds.

And then, as with every party, I woke up the next day. It was now 1993.

CHAPTER 29

In mid-January, Vyacheslav, our friendly, moustachioed, beer-drinking programme coordinator, gathered the British group in one of the downstairs classrooms after our morning lessons. He told us that another trip was coming up and he was looking for a show of hands. It was a coach trip for the following weekend to Yasnaya Polyana, the family estate and home of the great author, Leo Tolstoy. Lying about 200 kilometres south of Moscow near the town of Tula, it was a good 300 kilometres and a whole day's coach drive north of us. There was a small cost associated with it, but everyone agreed to go; we all loved the trips.

Our departure duly arrived the following Friday. After an early start, we endured a mostly uneventful plodding drive up long straight main roads with more than a few coniferous pine forests to look at along the way. I was interested in the destination as I had read a lot of Tolstoy's books as part of my studies. I also watched a few film versions, which was cheating, but I like a good shortcut. Unfortunately, the coach driver didn't know any shortcuts, and it took nearly seven hours to get there.

We arrived late at night and bunked up in a sort of

campus of buildings in a countryside setting around a landscaped area of lawns and connecting pathways. A group of functional looking accommodation buildings, with names like Korpus 1, Korpus 2 and Korpus 3, were our digs for the night, with three people to each room. It felt a bit like workers' accommodation for a nearby factory, or company, or even government facility whose existence I was entirely imagining.

On Saturday morning, the coach took us on a ten-minute drive around to the entrance car park of Tolstoy's country pile. Having been used to more modern Russian architecture and town planning, which was generally light on beauty, Yasnaya Polyana was a welcome change. We walked up a long tree-lined drive with the sunshine glistening off the snow on either side and took in orchards and other acres given over for vegetable growing and living off the land. The Tolstoy estate included various farm-use buildings such as stores and stable blocks. Into view came a fantastic country house with verandas and terraces around it, of European mid-1800s country estate style. A solid looking, very wide, white stone house with chunky corners and a green roof. The first impression was that Tolstoy was no pauper, writing from deprivation and hardship. This was the house of a country gent.

He was "Count" Leo Tolstoy and was born into an aristocratic Russian family in 1828, but he was well placed to comment on society's issues. His novels were not about promoting the poor or the disenfranchised, as later Soviet dissident writers did. His works dealt with love, relationships, the futility of war, and societal and philosophical issues. He travelled around Europe, too, where he even met Victor Hugo in 1860, author of Les Miserables.

It was a fascinating visit around the house. The estate was turned into a museum to commemorate his life and work after his death in 1910. Some of his many children ran it initially, and some descendants are still involved today. Many rooms where he worked have been turned into exhibits and preserved, complete with his writing table and ink pots. I could keenly imagine Tolstoy sitting at *that* desk and looking out of *that* window at *that* tree over *that* lake. It was a beautiful home, almost a mansion, complete with outbuildings, horses, orchards, vegetable gardens and a lake full of fish. It sat in an idyllic position surrounded by rolling countryside. We wandered from room to room, many of which were set up to recreate precisely how they looked when Tolstoy was living and writing here. There are even photos of the man himself sitting on the very furniture I was looking at in many rooms. Even the bed had the same patterned counterpane as in one of the photos, where the bushy-bearded Tolstoy was perching on it. One room was a mini-exhibit of his novel War and Peace. The original manuscript was on display, in his handwriting, the printed book, and audio recording through headphones.

It was a superb link directly back to my Russian literature essays back in Bristol and a pause for thought for me in the middle of my Russian immersion. If you're ever in the area, I recommend it as a visit.

Getting back to Voronezh the next day was good for two reasons. Firstly, I was becoming increasingly eager to be with Tanya anyway as our relationship was getting stronger all the time. Secondly, we were keen to get an apartment sorted out, and Tanya had started to look at some in January already. I was looking forward to having a place of our own that was not her flat-share and not the dirty hostel, either. For her part, I guessed that getting a pad with her English boyfriend maybe came with social currency, also, but I wasn't worried about whether she was using it for any social climbing. I just focussed on what seemed to me like a genuinely blossoming relationship, and besides, I was twenty-two years old, and things really couldn't be going any better. I had a beautiful Russian girlfriend, who I saw quite a lot, and with whom I was feeling a bit like a king. We managed to sleep together already very creatively in and around the schedules of the other roommates. My mind was getting a bit excited about coming home to our very own *pied a terre* in the evenings and finding Tanya there.

In contrast to the rich literary and cultural diversion that the visit to Yasnaya Polyana had been, Oleg had managed to get us tickets to see the show *Polye Chudess,* the Russian version of Wheel of Fortune, which was coming to town. It was for the following weekend, the last one in January. We'd been watching it on Russian TV for a while – there wasn't a lot of joy on TV, and far less actual entertainment in Voronezh, so we got a bit excited about it. It was in the old round, circus building near the disgusting pizza place. As we took our seats, arranged in steep banks around the main performance area, I noticed the familiar shiny red Mercedes Benz I had seen on the weekly TV show. The car was tonight's, and every night's, star prize. Soon TV's Leonid Yakubovich waltzed onto the stage, and the effect was complete. If you don't know, the format is a game show where contestants must guess the letters of a blanked-out word or phrase, a bit like the game hangman. If you guess correctly, you get to spin the wheel hoping to land on monetary prizes and not on the hazards which did not pay you anything. You could win through the rounds by having the higher score, or by guessing the whole word or phrase to get to the final game and the chance to win the 80s' Mercedes.

Firstly, however, they needed contestants. This was the exciting bit where they'd pull lucky people from the audience to make up the first panel. Think of Lesley Crowther in the 1980s/90s and "Come on Down!" They didn't know the names of anyone in the audience in Voronezh, so they were selected by calling out seat numbers at random. Yakobovich began to call out the numbers, and people jumped up in excitement if they were the lucky ones, as if their seat had given them an electric shock. After the first few, they called a seat number, and someone near me suggested it was my seat. My first reaction was disbelief and then a strong wish not to go down on stage in a Russian game show where I knew I wouldn't understand half of what was going on. I stood to check the badge on the seat, though, and sure enough, they had called my number. I nearly froze, but the audience was cheering encouragingly. Should I go down? I couldn't believe it. I looked at Oleg and instantly realised I should ask him to go. He was beaming at me.

"You have to go for me!" I blurted out, "I won't understand anything!"

In hindsight, if I had gone, then I'd have a better story to tell about the time I was an Englishman on a Russian game show with an actual TV celebrity presenter. It would probably have made for interesting viewing for the Russians, too, but this is a real story here and what happened was Oleg replied, in a flash, "OK, yes, I'll go!", and he skipped off down the steps to take the contestant spot that should have been mine.

"Hello, young man, and welcome! What's your name, and what do you do?" Asked presenter Leonid.

"Erm, hello, my name is Oleg, and I am a student here at the university," confirmed Oleg into his microphone a little nervously.

I was so excited it was Oleg. I was aware it could have been me, and I felt that he was in my shoes down there. Leonid Yakobovich skipped on without missing a beat to call out the next number.

I do wonder if he would have been taken aback if he'd have found himself with a young English captive instead, or skipped on just as professionally.

Unfortunately, Oleg didn't last beyond the first round. It was a real shame; he didn't guess a correct letter and didn't spin the wheel, and the round was won by a lady who worked in the children's shop *Detski Mir* (Children's World). Oleg was soon sitting back beside us, nevertheless glowing from his experience.

It was a fun night, and it is still the only game show I have ever attended.

CHAPTER 30

The search for an apartment was at the forefront of my mind at this time. Tanya had seen a couple already that she hadn't liked, but I was getting a bit worried about the timing of everything as our study year in Russia was going to run until June, so that only left four to five months.

Tanya had said it was possible to get six-month leases. The private sector was still unregulated, and there were no standards or rules about any of it. Alexei had said that in reality, you could say precisely how many months you wanted the place for, and most property owners were happy to entertain that proposal. Especially when they see the tenant is English, or to put it another way, a rich foreigner. I didn't go with Tanya to view them. She said it would be better to keep me away from the process because of the likelihood that the owner would grossly inflate the price if they knew they were renting it out to me.

This made good sense to me, so she went with Nadia, or Alina, the other friend that I had met at Oleg's, on the night of the ambulance ride.

But one Monday night, right after the weekend of

the Polye Chudess show, I saw her after classes, and she was very excited. It was the 1st of February now, and I hoped it was good news.

She said she'd found the perfect place that afternoon and that the owner was looking for $25 per month in rent.

It was more than we'd been thinking about spending, but it was on the 4th and top floor of a handsome block in the centre of town, and for me, the price was still OK. Of course, it was.

We agreed to go back, for me to have a look, too. Around 2 pm the next day, we found ourselves outside looking up at the building. It was on a side street close to Lenin Square, leading off Revolution Prospect. The building was chunky-looking with columns on its facade. It was old but good; I estimated it predated the Soviet Union, as it had that mid-19th century classical European style to it.

We walked to the 4th floor up the stairs holding hands and smiling like kids, but I was still a bit nervous for some reason, like it still wouldn't happen, maybe. What if they wouldn't rent it to an Englishman? What if they needed all sorts of documents that I couldn't provide?

A woman of about forty-five years of age opened the door and introduced herself as Lyudmila. I was relieved it was a woman for some reason. If it had been a man, I would have somehow felt more worried or even under judgement by him for setting up a home with one of Russia's daughters. Even though Lyudmila could have been just as outraged, I maybe thought a part of her would be pleased that a *wealthy* Englishman was looking to care for Tanya. She certainly didn't appear upset, which was a relief.

She was full of smiles and spoke enthusiastically to Tanya, and I felt like she was pleased to have me considering her property, like I was an esteemed visitor. She had prepared some sweet black tea for us in the main living area. Maybe she could use me for social climbing, like having a Harrods carrier bag in your house.

The apartment had a tiny windowless bathroom immediately on the right as we entered, which was perfectly suitable, if a little basic. Then a kitchen was next on the right with a window on its far side allowing natural light in and seemed to have everything a kitchen needed in it, but I didn't even really pay much attention to it. A few paces further along this entrance corridor ,was quite a large, living area with a rectangular table by the far window, with four chairs around it, on which the tea had been laid out. There was also a small sofa with a low table and a wooden wall cabinet opposite that housed shelves, a sideboard section and cupboards. Lyudmila explained with great pride that the property had everything we would need and belonged to a relative who no longer needed it, but she lived nearby with her own family. Perhaps the relative no longer needed it because they were no longer with us on this earth.

I peered out of the window and saw the Voronezh municipal theatre diagonally opposite. It was quite a grand theatre that had put on its fair share of plays and shows over the years, I imagined. But the main attraction inside the apartment had still not revealed itself to me yet. It didn't seem to have a bedroom. I eyed the sofa once again, this time with a little more disappointment. It didn't instantly look like a sofa bed, and I tried to imagine if this bit of furniture could double up as a bed.

Then Lyudmila walked towards what I had thought was the back wall of the room, neighbouring the kitchen, with her arm outstretched. Without really looking at it, what I had taken as some horrible fabric wallpaper, it became evident was bead curtains the width of the room, which she parted to reveal a bedroom area.

I now realised that the walk along the corridor from the kitchen had been the depth of this section. The room wrapped back around to the right. Lyudmila had used curtain fabric and hanging beads to divide this area from the living space. As she parted the beads with her hand and allowed us to follow her, I could see a double bed and a small window on the same wall as the kitchen window.

This was going to be just perfect as far as I was concerned!

As she talked to Tanya about various details and admin

about the maintenance, I found that I wasn't listening or following what was going on. All I knew was that I had what seemed to be a great little bolt hole for us. It was in a good area, and it had a spic and span bathroom with a clean functioning toilet – very important by the hostel context - and a bedroom with a very chintzy curtain. In other words, this *was* a love nest, and I couldn't wait for it to become my reality and routine.

"...the rent is $25 per month, and I would like to receive two months deposit, with each one month paid in advance.

What do you think, my dear young things?" I zoned in to hear Lyudmila saying to Tanya, as they both looked at me for confirmation.

"Yes, yes, of course. It's all good!" I confirmed.

They discussed it together further, and from the gist, I understood copies of the rental agreement had to be lodged with some local government office. As it turned out, the paperwork would take 1 or 2 weeks. Details, *schmeetails*, I didn't really care now, as long as it was all going to happen.

I had a feeling that my first spring in Russia was going to be very, very enjoyable.

We left the building and walked back towards Ulitsa Mira, sharing a feeling of excitement. We wouldn't have to put i[with too much more of sharing that place with Nadia and Alexei, and Becky too when she stayed over,

253

and a whole bunch of visitors on any given day. No matter whether I slept in the hostel in the room I shared with Al (and our mostly absent Russian roommate Nicolay) or if I slept in the apartment, as I did most nights, we never really had any privacy.

Even though by now Nadia was in the habit of giving us the room and bunking up in the next room with Alexei (except when Becky was there), we still had five or more people in what was a very small place most nights, right up until sleep time.

"Let's celebrate. Let's get something from the kiosk on the way back." I said.

"But, *Genchik*, we haven't moved in yet," Tanya protested meekly.

"It doesn't matter, and we can celebrate again, then. It's to celebrate *finding* the place." I knew she'd agree, and her smile told me she did.

We walked a bit beyond the apartment, about one hundred yards further to where Ulitsa Mira fanned out into a crescent shape in front of the central Voronezh train station. Next door to the big, usually empty, state *gastronom* shop was a permanent kiosk inside the building. The kiosk front wasn't much bigger than a doorway with a glass window. The man behind the window was smoking and counting out wads of banknotes. As one pound was worth hundreds of roubles by now, and the twenty-rouble note was maybe the third largest note, behind the hundred and five hundred, wads of cash didn't always mean it was of great value. He still looked like someone not to mess with. With his muscular, stocky build and beanie wool hat, he looked like a gangster, but then that's pretty much how most of the kiosk owners, and money changers, came across.

"Let's get two bottles of champagne, shall we?" she asked of me, and then before waiting for a reply to the man, she said, "Give me two bottles." (No *please* or *thank you* in usual spoken Russian).

"No, get four!" I suggested to her, "why not? There are always lots of people to share with." She upped the order, and with a cigarette hanging from his mouth, the man smiled back and gave her a wink, too. I was used to the way Russian men flirted with Russian women, but it still made me feel slightly inadequate for a moment. He produced two bottles from the shelves behind him, but he saw no more, it seemed.

"Hey, Vlad!" he shouted over his shoulder, "Bring another box of *Sovietskoye*." Turning back to Tanya, he said, "You celebrating?" Tanya just nodded but offered no reply. "Tell Alexei that I have something for him. He needs to come to see me. You can all come and celebrate here with us sometime if you want. We have a party room upstairs, you know."

I could see another guy, presumably Vlad, squeezing down steep steps behind him with the box of champagne.

This kiosk benefitted from being within a building by having a room upstairs. We took the four bottles and retraced our way back up the short distance to the apartment.

"He does some business with Alexei then?" I asked.

"Yes, currency, or military watches, or who knows what," came the reply, "I don't know him, though. He's called Ivan."

There was nobody home yet when we got in a few minutes later. It was late afternoon, and the last afternoon lessons were still going on at the university, not that Alexei went to his anyway. My compatriots would not be at class either as we had no afternoon classes, so they'd be relaxing one way or another, either in the hostel or out and about in the snow-covered streets somewhere.

"We'll soon be using our own fridge!" I chimed out as I put the bottles in the fridge, "and we'll soon be using our own kitchen, and …and bedroom with funny curtain things," I added, outlining the bead and fabric netting with my hands in the air as I had no idea of the Russian words for it. She walked to me, and we embraced each other with a kiss.

"I hope it doesn't take too long to get all the papers done so we can have the keys," she added as we squeezed each other tightly and kissed again.

That evening we did indeed get a few people over to the apartment, even though it was a Tuesday. Mind you, days of the week didn't make much difference whether it was OK or not OK to have a bit of a social. Becky and Jane came, Alexei and Nadia, of course, and Issa. Issa was the drinking Mali guy, as opposed to the non-drinking Mamadou. Issa was a bit of a party magnet, by which I don't mean he attracted parties, but wherever there was a party, he found himself drawn into it. I had noticed Alexei and Issa had started to hang out together more lately. They seemed to both like a good time as far as chasing women was concerned, almost acting as each other's wingman.

I had even heard from Alexei how he and Issa had recently enjoyed a drunken group situation with some Russian girls. I felt terrible for Becky that Alexei wasn't faithful to her, but then again, she did have a boyfriend back home, so there was no exclusivity on either side. Besides, Becky knew what she was in for and was fine taking what she got out of this.

This night, Issa brought Gwyn along, a Welsh student in our group. Gwyn gave the impression that she and Issa were an item, which completely surprised me, as she was timid and sensible. Although Gwyn had a dry sense of humour, she was the opposite of a party person, always buttoned up, never showing even an inch of bare skin, and I barely ever saw her drinking. She was quite the opposite of the smoking, drinking, putting it about a bit Issa. So, seeing her with her arm around him confused me. I was unsure whether I was being naïve to what she was really like, or she didn't care and was a dark horse herself.

Nadia, Oleg, and Vadim made up the rest of the crowd that night. Nadia and Oleg had brought in some pork and beef meat skewers, or shashliks, and some other zakuski. We ate the delicious foods and quickly finished the champagne, which was chased with vodka and beer, as per usual.

I shared the news with Becky and Jane about the place that Tanya and I had agreed to rent. I wasn't sure if they were genuinely pleased for me or not, but they did seem to think it would work out well. Jane was still seeing her Russian boyfriend, Maxim, the friendly outdoorsy guy. But it just seemed to be isolated dates rather more at arm's length than a relationship, as far as I could tell. Becky was sleeping with Alexei, but this seemed more about having a good time together when they saw each other rather than being a couple. At any rate, our move out would mean that Becky could stay over as often as she liked, and Nadia would still get to keep a room for herself, at least. I felt that what I had with Tanya was more than Becky and Alexei's relationship; we only had eyes for each other, like a regular boyfriend and girlfriend.

I did recognise this relationship had limitations, but I wanted to ignore that for now. I knew it wasn't entirely normal; there was the language barrier to start with, but

I didn't notice that too much anymore; such was my improvement on that front, thanks to total immersion therapy. There was also the big unspoken topic of the future, but we didn't need to think about it yet. I still viewed this romance idealistically, and if it was love, we would find a way to carry it on beyond the confines of this academic year. Putting that to one side, though, I felt that moving into this apartment together would be a logical, comfortable step, and I hoped my friends thought it wasn't completely insane.

The evening continued until quite late, with the last people leaving around 1.30 am. As I went to sleep that night, I was thinking back to the place we had seen earlier that day. I was hopeful that it wouldn't take too long for all the tenancy paperwork to be done, as I was excited about what lay ahead.

Unfortunately, things were about to turn in a very different and unexpected direction.

CHAPTER 31

A loud knocking on the door woke me. I thought at first that it was still the middle of the night. I heard someone in the other room stirring. Perhaps it was someone coming back to the party, desperate to get in from the cold. Maybe they couldn't get to where they wanted to go and returned to our place for a patch of floor to sleep on. It wouldn't be the first time something like that had happened.

"I'm coming. I'm coming," I heard Nadia mutter. I didn't hear all the words, but there was a short conversation between her and the visitor, but I distinctly heard the visitor say, "Genry Pettit, is he here?"

A couple of seconds later, Nadia's bedraggled face appeared around the door. "Genry, it's someone from the university for you."

I felt a strange pang, as the voice had sounded quite abrupt, and I couldn't think of any reason why anyone would want me, apparently so urgently. Someone was here to tell me a relative had been killed in a tragic event, perhaps. Maybe there had been an accident.

I momentarily, illogically cursed its timing, so early, and after a bit of a late night. What's wrong with finding me in the afternoon, anyway? My head was spinning from being woken so quickly, and a bit of hangover was germinating.

I sat up and rubbed my eyes. Tanya was still sleeping and moved only to get deeper under the covers. I stumbled upright and walked over to the door in boxer shorts and a T-shirt to find out who it was. Nadia had already gone back to bed. Two men were at the door, one about thirty years old, the other nearer forty, both with thin moustaches, an uninteresting double act.

"Hello, are you Henry Pettit?" the younger one asked, not going for the friendly *Genry*, but the more technical *Xch...enry*, to be more accurate to my name. I confirmed that I was. "We are from the Deconat office. Please, come with us. It's imperative."

I was not in any shape to do much other than agree. A minute before, I had been fast asleep, and now I was going to go with them to find out what it was all about. If it was an accident or some important news from England, I assumed these guys were not the ones to tell me. Their job was to find me, which they had done, and when I got to the Deconat office, somebody more senior would tell me whatever the news was. I felt a bit like a rabbit in the headlights; these guys were so awake and lucid while I was dishevelled in my boxers, complete with bed head and sleepy face.

"OK." I said, "But, can I have a quick wash? Is that

OK?" I asked. I had a feeling something quite important was going to happen, or else they wouldn't be here at such an unearthly time of the morning, and so definitely needed a few moments in the bathroom to straighten out. I didn't want to do whatever this was, looking like the wreck I felt I was.

"Of course," said the older man with a smile, "take your time. We'll wait here."

I pushed the door closed not to let the cold in, leaving them on the doorstep outside. His smile relaxed me a little, and my initial confusion, and mild sense of guilt and panic, subsided slightly, as I had now bought myself a few minutes to compose myself in the bathroom. The small white plastic clock by the bathroom basin said it was a few minutes past six in the morning. I wondered why they had to come so early; half annoyed at their choice of such an ungodly time. I didn't like the state of my reflection at all, with a creased face and red eyes.

If someone is going to tell this face some important, or even tragic, news, I'd better not look so ridiculous. So, I turned on the shower over the bath and stepped in for a quick three-minute attempt at turning into my usual looking self. They did tell me to take my time after all, and a shower was a bit of a miracle cure for hangovers. I threw some shampoo over my hair, but it stung my eyes as I neglected to close them properly, staring at the tiles, wondering what this could all be about. I rinsed it through swiftly, and after about five minutes, I was dressed and went to join my two chaperones who were still on the doorstep. We slipped out of the building and onto the snowy footpath.

We walked over towards hostel number 4, as the first embers of daylight were filtering into the sky from the bottom up. None of us spoke, so the only sound was the crunch of our boots on the top crust of snow. We entered the back of the hostel and made our way through to the main lobby on the ground floor. I spotted our group head honcho Vyacheslav, standing by the main stairs chatting to another man in an oversized coat with hands thrust deep in his pockets. He turned at the sound of us coming in and looked directly at me, looking just as freshly showered as I was.

"Ah, Genry! How are you? Oh, are you OK? Your eyes. Been having a party?" Vyacheslav enquired. I felt as if he was trying to make a subtle point, but I didn't know what.

"It's the shampoo," I said, "I got shampoo in my eyes, in the shower," I instinctively responded, feeling a need to pin the reason for red eyes on the shampoo rather than the party of the night before.

The hands-in-pocket man had a short conversation that I couldn't hear with the older of my moustachioed chaperones, and then he shook hands with Vyacheslav and strode off out of the hostel front door. "Please come this way," the chaperones said to me, and we followed on after hands-in-pocket-man. We headed towards another building, descending the front steps along the main pathway between the sparse trees. I was getting more uncomfortable now as this strange situation continued to play out. Seeing Vyacheslav for a start was unusual at such an early time of day, and neither of these guys was talking to me. I had thought there might be some bad news from England, to begin with, but I was doubting this theory now.

"Where are we going?" I asked the younger one who was nearest to me.

"Excuse me. It is just in here. They will explain to you," came the reply. We were entering another building with the same layout as the other hostels. It was only two minutes from hostel number 4 and was standing on the front of the plot, fronting directly onto the main road, Friedreich Engels Street, not set back like our one. As we entered, I took in a sign by the entrance denoting it was hostel number 1 with loads of words underneath that I couldn't take in on the go. I thought I deciphered the word *office* a few times in the blurb, an easy one to pick out as it's a transliteration of the English word for office and pronounced the same, therefore. We ascended the main stairs, leading me along a first-floor corridor. Whereas in our building you would see the kitchen and some accommodation rooms, this one seemed to be an administration block where the rooms here mainly were offices.

The man ahead had disappeared, and *Pinky and Perky* finally led me into one of the rooms at the end of the corridor. However, there was nothing in the room except for a desk and a chair. We stood there in silence momentarily, then in the opposite corner of the room, I saw another door open, and a man came through it with a file in his hands. This man was also around forty years old, and wearing a shirt and jacket, rather like an academic, I thought; sandy blond hair, and he too had a moustache. He fixed my eyes with his as he approached and asked, "Henry Pettit?"

"Yes," I replied.

"This way, please," he motioned with an outstretched palm towards the door he'd just come through.

Things were getting plain weird now, I thought, and as I went through the door in the corner, there was another door no more than thirty centimetres from the first one. It was open halfway, so I walked through this double door arrangement into a second office. This room had more furniture than the first. There were a couple of filing cabinets along the right-hand wall. A man was standing behind a desk with paperwork on it and two chairs in front of it. I noticed a jug of water and some glasses on the desk, and I suddenly felt very thirsty.

I recognised behind the desk hands-in-pocket man.

He had arrived just moments ago, presumably, and had removed his coat. He looked past my right shoulder towards the double doors I had come in through and raised his hand, a bit like someone motioning to a waiter in a restaurant. I spun my head around to see the sandy-haired man had followed me in and was now closing both the outer and the inner door.

"Please excuse me, Mr Pettit, for waking you so early today. Please, you can put your coat on the chair. Would you like some water?" he began.

"Thank you, yes please." My mouth was parched, I was unsettled, and I needed it. I took the water and sipped some, then held it on my lap, waiting for him to speak again. I noticed that my hand rapidly shook the glass, trembling from my nervous energy.

My name is Ivan Stepanov," he began. He then explained that he was from a Militsiya (police) department and a Russian Internal Affairs police department, I think. I didn't correctly understand what type of policeman he was, for as soon as I heard the first mention of "police", my mind froze and just thought "authorities". I began to look more closely. His shirt now seemed crisper, with double breast pockets, small details and finishes, and a pen in his top pocket. My mind began to race about what sort of trouble I could be in.

"So, are you having a good stay with us in Russia?" he continued.

"Yes. Thank you," I stammered.

"Good. We can see that you are. We came to collect you from Ulitsa Mira today. It's where your friends live, is it?" he continued.

I nodded, then added "Yes".

The blond man was still standing behind me, in the corner by the door, which was unnerving. They had certainly not brought me here to tell me some important news from England. I knew that for sure now.

"You have made many new friends, in the hostel, outside the hostel: English friends, Russian friends, a Russian *girlfriend,* too?" he emphasised the word girlfriend. I wondered if I was in trouble for that. Was he going to call me out about bagging one of their women? Was it an insult to Russian men that I had done this? Nobody had led me to believe that my relationship with Tanya was controversial. Besides, some British girls had romantic relationships with Russian guys, so it was silly even to think I had crossed a line, let alone broken any law. Yet, I was quickly feeling like I was somehow in trouble with the police here.

"You like to have a good time, I think. Your eyes look a little bit red today. Did you have a bit of a party yesterday?" Stepanov continued.

"No," I lied, "I just had a shower, and shampoo went in my eyes." I had no idea why I felt the need to lie about having a party; it wasn't illegal, but I *did* just have the quick shower.

"Ah yes. Nicolai?" he asked the man in the corner, "What do we keep hearing from the British groups about the water in Russia?"

"Yes, Ivan Mikhailovich. We keep hearing that our water is much softer here in Voronezh than in Great Britain generally. The English students like how their hair is much softer, but it takes longer to rinse the soap out of their hair. I think our comrade took a quick shower today, and the shampoo did not come out, probably. So, you see, red eyes," the man behind me, Nicolai apparently, said with gobsmackingly bizarre detail.

I wondered what the hell was he talking about; things were getting a bit surreal—what the hell had soft water got to do with anything? I wasn't sure that I was getting his point, either, if there was one, or that I fully understood his words, seeing as it was also entirely in Russian. Stepanov was looking directly at me while I was trying to take things in, and I thought this must be a random preamble designed to ease in gently to whatever was the purpose of this meeting. However, it wasn't putting me at any ease at all.

"Yes, we have very soft water in Russia, but in our country, our rules are not so soft, we take the rule of law very seriously," he began, "and we expect our guests to this country to conduct themselves in a way that is lawful and respectful".

He had started at least, I thought, now he's going to reveal what this is all about. Am I somehow in trouble for having too many parties, getting too drunk, or is it for Tanya? I knew that her ex-boyfriend, Vladimir, who I'd met around the hostel once or twice, had done a year or two of military service and had completed a spell in Afghanistan a year ago. Was he disgruntled and using his connections to give me a hard time here? Had I offended them somehow with my debauched western and loose morals? Was it because I was taking things too far by trying to rent an apartment and live in sin? It was pretty speedy of them even to find out, actually; I'd only seen the place yesterday. I didn't have a clue what to say.

"So, we are very concerned to hear stories about the use of drugs and narcotics in our country. Narcotics have no place and are not welcome in this city or country. We believe that you have been using these drugs here in Voronezh," Stepanov stated dryly.

Although my Russian was of a reasonable standard, it was by no means perfect. Stepanov and Nicolai were only speaking in Russian, and my responses to them were in Russian. I understood what they were saying to me, but not every single word. I got by OK in Russia, and Russians usually spoke to me in a way and at a pace that made it easier for us foreigners to keep up. When they talked amongst themselves, I could quickly lose the thread. But I knew what he was saying, although the bit about soft water had mostly flummoxed me.

At the mention of the words *drugs* and *narcotics*, however, I felt the blood rush up my neck instantly, and the room shrink in size so that I was the focal point of the room. I was already feeling like a naughty pupil summoned to the headmaster's office, but now I felt like the target of a much more serious agenda. Of course, I realised that I had bought that grass all those months ago, in September, but it seemed so long ago, and besides, I had turned my back on it all anyway. In a fraction of a second, I decided I would play dumb about it—usually, the best default starting position whenever someone accuses you of something. I frowned, gave my best quizzical look, and shook my head. I have never been a good actor, and I didn't know if this trio of expressions would win any Oscars.

"Well?" he continued, "Let me ask you directly, have you been using drugs, yes, or no?"

"No, I… I did not. I do not… no."

I was losing the ability to string words together at this point.

He pressed on, "OK, so, we have a report that states you are very much at the centre of this drugs situation. What do you say to that?"

"That report is a lie," I lied. Things were not looking good for me right now.

At this point, Stepanov moved back from the desk on

which he had been leaning, and leaned right back in his chair instead. He didn't seem too perturbed, almost as if my words were of no consequence to him. He motioned again to the standing Nicolai, still in the corner of the room, circled his fingers in the air like a conductor, giving a sign for Nicolai to proceed. "OK, Genry, listen to this then," Stepanov added.

I half turned in my chair towards the doorman. He took the file he had been holding from under his arm, opened it, and began to read out from it.

"On Saturday, 26th September, Mr Pettit, along with Becky Daniels, Alastair Stone, Sam Quick and Jane Barker, was witnessed to be using narcotics classified as illegal in the Russian Federation, in room number 38 of hostel number 4, between the hours of 9.30 pm and 11.30 pm.

On Thursday, 1st October, Mr Pettit, along with Becky Daniels, Alastair Stone, Tom Thomson and Jim Bentley, was witnessed to be using narcotics classified as illegal in the Russian Federation, in room number 33 of hostel number 4, between the hours of 10 pm and midnight.

On Friday, 30th October, Mr Pettit once again was seen to be present on the 4th floor of hostel number 4 in rooms 45 and 47, at around 8.30 pm, where witnesses have said he delivered a bag of narcotics to British students Connor Thorne and Paul Fisher...."

I sat in silence in my chair as he continued to read out a list of times, dates, and locations where I was apparently witnessed sharing joints in the hostel with my fellow students. My head began to whirl. Of course, I hadn't kept any mental note of all the days and times myself, but as soon as the guy was reading off the list, I was reasonably sure he had probably got his facts correct. The dates sounded all about right, back at the very start of my time in Voronezh when I had first bought the stuff, and the people I would have been with at the time sounded right on the money, also. We had most definitely been spied and informed upon, it seemed, with many of our group assigned Russian roommates. We did smoke inside at the start, for sure, before I took it outside instead.

After the first flurry of excitement of having the grass back in September, I thought I had been careful with it, albeit we perhaps weren't watching our backs that much. Later, we became more cautious about who was in the room or walking the corridors. What added insult to this injury for me was that I had given it up now; I threw the last butt into the snow one night, months ago, when I realised it was not where the fun was at anyway. What came to mind immediately was Alexei telling me way back to be discreet, but laid on top of that memory was visions of the guys on the 4th floor, like Connor and Gus, who carried on smoking the stuff, far less discreetly. OK, so maybe I had passed it on to them, but it was their fault I was now the one being questioned.

"OK, that's enough." Stepanov signalled to Blondie, then looked back at me. "So, you see, there is much evidence in our file. Are you sure you don't know anything about this? We have a lot of witnesses. I think you must agree that our file holds the correct story, yes?"

I didn't know what to say. I didn't know how much trouble this could mean for me. I stared at the floor in front of the desk, realising it would be useless to deny it. Their version of events was based mainly around the truth anyway. I had a dry mouth again and drank some more water. This time my trembling hands caused some water to almost spill from the glass. Faces of the Russians featuring on a few occasions back in the autumn months filled my mind. Even Tanya's ex-boyfriend Vladimir was maybe at one or two of the larger gatherings, but whether we smoked joints then or not, I couldn't recall. It would be easy for him to say we did, though. Maybe he was so offended and incensed that she'd moved on from him, and was now carrying on with an English guy with low morals and weak principles, that he had shopped me to the authorities to hit back at her and punish us both.

"Let me tell you what the law says on this in Russia," Stepanov began, "if a person is found guilty of buying narcotics and selling narcotics to others in the Russian Federation, they can face a prison term of seven years in prison". He paused and stared at me for a few seconds, a deadpan expression on his face. "We think that we have more than enough evidence against you here, and I am talking about seven years in a Russian prison, not an English prison."

I felt as if he had punched me in the chest.

"Having said that, it may be possible that Russia lets you serve your sentence in Britain...but I don't want to think that far today. We don't want it to come to that, and nor do you, I suspect."

My mind was going into overdrive now. Seven years in prison, especially in Russia, was just not something I could even begin to consider. But I was considering it, like a hole in the head. Surely this conversation was going to go further. A thought then occurred to me that he had just said that I sold it, but I did not sell it, I *gave* it away!

"No, I don't want prison..." was all I could say. I was shaking now. I was losing control of my face. I felt like I was going to cry. I probably looked defeated, and Stepanov had me beaten at this point, quite easily from his point of view. He'd only needed a couple of minutes. I was quite a useless criminal.

"Listen. We know that you are a nice guy," he carried on, "you are having a lovely time and enjoying yourself. You have friends and a great girlfriend. You know. We don't want to charge you with any crime if we don't have to."

He was changing tack. Was this going to be OK after all, I wondered? My face control was returning now. I kept listening to what he was saying.

"We know you have not started this. You just got mixed up in it, for sure. But if we arrest you, what do we achieve? What does this mean? The university must contact your university to tell them what's going on. Your parents, what will they say? We will have to contact the British government, and it becomes an international affair. Lots and lots of problems, and for you, it is not good especially."

He was starting to repaint a negative picture; I didn't know where this was going. One hundred per cent I did not want to get in any trouble; Russian prison most definitely not. Furthermore, I was desperate for my parents not to know about any of this. They were anti-smoking and didn't even know I smoked in the first place. A memory came to me just then of a time in the last term when my dad and step-mum had visited me at university. I was a daily smoker at the time but was in the habit of not smoking all day if I knew I would see my mum or dad, so the smell wasn't noticeable. I could happily put off smoking all day, anyway, and if I went to visit them for a weekend, I could go without it entirely, just about. We had arranged to go to the Clifton Gorge Hotel in Bristol to have a meal on its fantastic outside terrace overlooking the Isambard Brunel designed suspension bridge. A memory that returned to me just then was of getting into their car half a mile away so that I could navigate them to the hotel, and the first thing dad had said was, "You smell of cigarettes. You don't smoke, do you?" as I climbed into the back of the car. I realised I must have had clothes that just smelt of my bad habit, but made the excuse that I'd just got off a bus which had lots of smokers on it (in those days you could still smoke on buses, in cinemas, and restaurants, etc.). Back in the room now with these policemen, I was starting to think; if I was scared for my parents to know that I just smoked, how much should I turn up the dial of worry for them to think of me as some sort of international drug dealer?!

The Russian man of authority brought me back from my thoughts. "…But we are more interested in stopping the drugs coming here in the first place, OK? We know that you bought them from somebody, and whoever this somebody is, is of more interest to us than just arresting you. If you help us, then we can help you, and we can forget all about the seven years; you can finish your nice stay here as normal and go back to England, and all will be just fine for you. Does that sound OK? Will you help us do that?" Stepanov said.

"Yes, I will!" I said, feeling the first stirrings of relief. Are they just scaring me with threats, but actually, this bad dream could be over quickly if I comply?

All I thought at that moment was that if I told them

who I bought the drugs from, then as I understood it, they'd let me go. It was, literally, a get-out-of-jail-free card. They wanted to get to the suppliers, the proper criminals. Of course, I was just the end-user, but they had bigger targets in mind.

"Good!" he continued, "What we want to know is where you got it from, which people are bringing drugs into our city and selling it to our students. Getting to these people is far more interesting to us. These are the people we want to stop."

CHAPTER 32

Now that it looked like maybe a bargaining part of the "interrogation" was to begin, I was slightly more comfortable if shitting yourself slowly while seeing some tiny flicker of light at the end of the tunnel could pass for comfortable, that is. All I had to do was to tell the police who I had bought the grass from so they could crack the supply chain. Even as I sat there before them, the one problem I saw was that this meant snitching on the madman, Sergei. If they went directly to him based on my tip-off, he'd surely just come straight to me. The man threw cats out of windows for light relief. Yes, he was blind drunk for a month at a time, but he was stone-cold sober for a month, too, and was a scary fucker. I measured up very quickly in my mind that I didn't want to find out what he did to people who he judged to have put him in serious trouble. So, I decided, at that moment, that I was not going to dob him in.

"So, tell us, who did you buy it from?"

I made a hasty, but what I thought was also a superb, decision. It had been around three months since the only time that I encountered those two Georgian guys in the hostel who had asked to buy my passport. They also had,

I remembered now, offered me some hash. Even so, they were as dodgy as anything, with criminal tendencies nailed on. I had never seen them again since that night, and as far as I was concerned, they were not even residents of Voronezh, and maybe very far away now. I made up my mind that I was going to say that it was them who I had bought the grass from, and I liked the fact that I could pin it on real people so that I could have some credible detail in my story while knowing that there was no chance of this coming back to bite me. Much better than snitching on dangerous and unpredictable Sergei anyway.

"It was in October, I think. Two Georgian guys came to the hostel. It was them," I said.

"Georgians? How do you know they were Georgians; do you know their names?"

"I don't know their names. I think they were Georgian. Maybe they said they were from Georgia." Because I could recreate the memory of meeting them, I hoped this would help me give a plausible account.

"I can't remember much of our conversation. Oh, I think one of them said his name was Georgi," I added.

"OK, what else?" Stepanov encouraged me on.

"They came to the hostel; I had never seen them before...."

"Who introduced them to you to?" he ventured.

"Nobody. They just came by themselves." Although I

nearly tripped up, this was smart, as I just remembered it was Sergei who had introduced me to them on the stairwell. "They just approached me; at first, they asked if they could buy my passport!" I hoped to get across how shocked I was at such a terrible suggestion by adding this authentic detail.

Stepanov raised his eyebrows and looked at me, and I took this as a sign that I was feeding him some good *intel* here. So, I continued.

"Of course, I didn't sell my passport," I went on, "but then he asked if I wanted to buy some grass. It's not so bad to buy grass in England as it is here...."

"It is very serious," he reminded me, looking serious.

"Yes, I know this now," I admitted, also trying to look serious.

"Then what?"

"It was just ten dollars' worth, as in England this is a small amount." I considered whether to tell them this furnished me with four newspaper bundles full, the most enormous grass mountain I had ever seen, but then I thought better of that, so I remained quiet and waited for him again.

Stepanov seemed to be contemplating what I had said, but he didn't say anything. He folded his arms. It made me want to speak more. I suppose the art of a good questioner was to say little yourself and let the other person do lots of talking.

"So yes, that's it," I said. He raised a finger, which I took as a sign to stop talking, and was happy to leave it there. I was tempted to add that I was surprised about how much ten dollars gets you in Russia and that it covered a whole table so that he could see my honest mistake. I wanted to say that the other people I gave it to had puffed away on it for weeks afterwards, not me, but I resisted that too.

I hoped that what I said had sounded believable. There was enough of the truth in there, I hoped, for it to sound credible.

"OK. This is very good. We have known about these two gentlemen for some time. We have been keeping our eye on them, too," Stepanov surprisingly asserted.

Bringing two people into the story, who I was convinced were absent from Voronezh by now, had somehow been the part of the account they were most interested in. I was taken aback by that.

But for them to say they were looking for these two people also made me feel like I had said something they wanted to hear. Hopefully, by some stroke of luck, I had pleased them.

"Do you think you would recognise them if you saw them again?" he went on.

"Yes, I think so." But even saying this made me nervous once more.

"An identification of these gentlemen as the ones who

sold you the drugs could be helpful for us. And beneficial for you. I would like to suggest the following: you meet with us again, and we look through some photographs. You tell us if you see these two gentlemen in the pictures we show you.

We can sit, you look through our book of photographs, and tell us if you see them. If you like, this can be somewhere else, somewhere comfortable, the Café Anna restaurant in town, perhaps? You can have a beer; I think you like a beer, yes? Does that sound OK? It's straightforward, don't you think?" Stepanov was behaving so politely to me now that I felt less like a wanted man and more like a guest of honour. But it wasn't a comfortable feeling.

"OK. Yes, that sounds OK". I puffed out my cheeks, flushed red with the pressure I'd been under, and tried to smile back.

"Good! So let us say this coming Saturday, at 2 o'clock, in the Café Anna. Today is Wednesday, so that is three days from now, OK? You will meet us there."

"Yes, OK," I replied. I don't know what I expected the protocol to be, for I had never been in such a situation before. Also, I didn't know why this could not take place *down at the station* like on TV, but I was grateful that it wasn't for some reason. Still, beers in a hotel and getting all chummy was a bit of a turnaround from being threatened with seven years in a Russian prison half an hour ago.

Stepanov stood up, and Nicolai by the door began to tidy and straighten his files into the shelving unit on the wall.

The meeting, it seemed, was nearly over, as we had agreed on a plan. Stepanov walked towards me as if to shake my hand, I thought, but he stopped before he got to me and patted himself down looking for cigarettes, which he duly found and extracted.

"One other thing, Genry," he went on (the friendly *Genry* was wheeled out now), "and this is the most important thing of all. Our Georgian friends mustn't suspect anything, so I don't want you to talk about our meeting today to anyone, do you understand? You are not to tell your student rep, is it Vicky Brown? Don't tell your friends about this either, and don't even your girlfriend, OK? This must stay between us. We can only help you if you help us. Remember that. See you on Saturday," as he then finally extended a hand and shook mine.

I walked away down the corridor accompanied by the sandy-haired Nicolai, feeling OK at that point, but he left me to exit the building alone while he went back inside. I walked across the space between the hostels along the snowy footpath in my own company, at a brisk pace at first, perhaps to get away from them. When I sensed I was alone, I slowed to barely moving, exhaled deep plumes breath into the cold morning air, and let out a stuttered shudder of released tension as tears ran down both of my cheeks. I realised I had to decide whether I would keep this a secret or not, and this decision was going to have to be made in the next few minutes.

CHAPTER 33

My interrogation, for that was what it was, left me considerably shaken. As I trudged back to the apartment, I wondered how I could keep this matter a secret from Tanya.

She would surely ask where I had had to go with my morning visitors. Furthermore, I was unsure how I could keep something this big from my other friends. I got in, removed my boots, went into the bathroom and sat down on the toilet lid.

With my head in my hands, I began to consider whether I really could carry out this bit of police work, undercover, as it were. Could I carry on as normal? It was only looking at photos, after all. Presumably, I wouldn't see the Georgians' mugshots anyway, so that would be that. But then, how did Stepanov seem to know about the Georgians? I thought I had been putting random characters in the frame there, but he claimed to know them, which was not a good feeling. I saw those guys only once, over three months ago, and never again since. I genuinely thought they were merely visiting Voronezh that day and were by now elsewhere, in Moscow, or even Georgia perhaps.

I heard a tap on the door, "Genry?" came Tanya's voice.

"Yes, it's me. I'm OK." My shaky voice surprised me. I stood up, ran the taps and waved my hands under the water and rubbed my face to freshen up.

I went into the bedroom, and one look at Tanya's concerned-looking face made me sit down with defeat written all over mine.

"What happened?" she asked.

I burst into a monologue and told her everything that had happened. It was a relief to offload it. Alexei joined us, too, but I didn't mind at all; he would probably know, better than most, what to do. I summarised as best I could how they had taken me to the other hostel, questioned me, landed incriminating dates on me and threatened me with seven years in prison. I told them that it would all be OK if I looked at photos to identify the people I had bought the grass from. I added that it was Sergei, but that I'd said it was the two random Georgians, and they surprisingly had said they'd been looking for two Georgians. I mentioned the proposed meeting in Café Anna and that I was not supposed to tell anyone about any of this.

As I relayed that morning's turn of events, Tanya and Alexei listened with interest, but I could also see increasing agitation. When I finished, Tanya was the first to speak.

"Was the whole thing done in Russian? Did you not have any interpreters?" she asked, and I confirmed yes, then no.

"This was in hostel number 1, you say, not the police building in town?" Alexei added.

To Alexei and Tanya, things seemed far more apparent than they did to me. Their irritation was now evident. They shook their heads and exchanged glances. Alexei stood up, walked to the window to look out, and paced the room while talking.

He looked very frustrated.

"OK, Genry, so listen. If they were real police, they would have brought you to the official police station, they would have had interpreters, and they would have had someone else there for you as an official representative, or witness..." he began.

Real police? I didn't get it; what was he saying?

"Now you have admitted it, too," Tanya added. "You should have just denied everything. Deny, deny, deny. They cannot prove any of it. Their only proof is, in fact, your confirmation that you did any of this."

"But they had dates and rooms and times, and everything?" I contested.

"That is just because someone said you were in those rooms at those times. Russian students have told them that. Being there doesn't prove anything. I don't think they have any proof of you buying this shit," Tanya continued, quite upset now. She was also frustrated, I supposed, that this could be ruining things between us. Calling it *this shit* showed her anger with the grass situation. She never did any drugs, and I think it was maybe the only thing she didn't like about me, or rather, my *past behaviours*, I should say.

"They only really have you present in the rooms, don't they?" Alexei said. "But that is no reason to admit to the rest; you were far too quick to admit to that. One thing doesn't prove the other thing! Not at all!"

I was now getting embarrassed that I had been so naïve. My friends were right. All Nicolai did was read out the dates and times we were in a room sharing a joint, and I just crumbled instantly. They had no proof of me buying anything. I had not needed to go that far at all with my confession. I felt green with foolishness, but I was under quite a bit of pressure earlier in my defence. Thinking back, I realised I hadn't even been told what Nicolai's full name was - another sign of their dodginess, probably. I racked my brain to remember what I did admit.

I remembered that I did resist, on instinct, adding too much detail about the purchase. Did I perhaps not admit buying it? Maybe they just inferred it. I tried to recall the words I used. I certainly resisted saying it was a ton of the stuff and that I gave it away. Then I remembered saying it was ten dollars' worth. They said I supplied it to others, but I had not commented on that, just ignored it. I suppose I admitted enough, perhaps. I tried to remember, but I couldn't be 100% sure what I'd said. And this I also explained to Tanya and Alexei.

"Listen, it is not important now what you did or didn't say. The important thing is this; these were not the police! They did not follow any official or correct procedures. These were probably KGB, or ex-KGB to be correct, as KGB does not officially exist anymore. These people are secret police at best, but scum anyway. Once they get you hooked around their finger, with something pinned on you like this, they get you to do one thing for them, then another, and another and so on. You will be forever having to do things for them, as they'll have the threat of seven years in prison on you!"

"This is true, Genry, and Alexei knows this; remember his brother?" Tanya reminded us about Alexei's brother Anton who was currently in the police system somewhere. I felt I should probably ask Alexei about the latest on Anton right then, but I was more concerned about myself to ask.

"So, what shall I do then!?" I pleaded.

"You do nothing. You do not go to this meeting in Café Anna. You pretend this morning never happened," Alexei advised. "If this questioning or arrest is valid, they need to do it properly, again, with interpreters, in the proper place."

"And if that happens, you deny everything this time, of course." Tanya chipped in.

"OK," I said. "But when I don't go to the meeting on Saturday, won't they come to find me?"

"Maybe not, not these KGB bastards," said Alexei. "They can't pull the same trick twice because if they catch up with you, you will ask for a translator, you will pull it over to be official, but they can't operate that way. They're like a mafia. Just be a very good boy for a while. Go to all your classes, don't skip any."

"You refuse to play their game, and you force it to go down the proper route only. But there is no proof, so you will be OK." Tanya held both my hands in hers, reassuring me.

I made coffee and had some black bread toast for a delayed breakfast when I realised how hungry I was, and of course, we talked of little else. Generally, though, I felt heartened by the support I was receiving. I saw new light, which I now believed could exist, at the end of the tunnel.

However, I was still filled with adrenalin to think that the KGB had just questioned me; the KGB from John Le Carré novels, and that now I was going to be trying to take the KGB on, or rather, ex-KGB. Even though the old regime had ceased, tens of thousands of former KGB operatives were still operating in very similar ways, without official backing or authority but still on the payroll. Old habits die hard, so this level of people still existed like the ones I had spoken to, who did not know how to operate, still using the old techniques as they hadn't yet adapted to the new ways. There were not officially in the police, but they were still drawing their wages from the state and having to do a police-type job. The lines were not yet adequately redrawn. It felt perilous, but Alexei advised it meant they could not officially bring charges. I was still worried, though.

CHAPTER 34

It wasn't until the afternoon that I sloped back into the hostel. I had to share the morning's events with my friends, knowing it would make for exciting storytelling. However, I was not exactly excited, of course. I went first into the room I shared with Al. He was alone writing a letter to his girlfriend back in Edinburgh. I was always impressed by his dedication and evident love of Isabelle; nothing would have caused Al to miss sending his regular letters home, and nobody here would have caused his head to turn, either. They were, as the saying goes, tight.

"Alright there, Genry (everyone had started using the G version of my name now), how're you doin'? Emma is up from Krasnodar, by the way, arrived last this morning. She's in with Becky and Jane."

Emma was one of my fellow Bristol classmates from back home, but she wasn't staying in Voronezh like us but in Krasnodar in the far south of Russia, near the Black Sea and the Crimean Peninsula. It was an odd choice of places to go. Nobody from our university or any other in the UK had chosen to go there. It was on the list of options, however. Emma chose it as she was finding Russian hard and thought that going somewhere without any other international students would mean her Russian would have no alternative but to improve via total immersion therapy. Her father had written to the Bristol tutors asking them not to send her there, without any support network or friends, but he was told it was Emma's choice, and they couldn't force her to choose another option.

As it turned out, Emma hated it in Krasnodar, where she found herself one of only two English speaking foreigners on the programme. The other was a married American lady whose husband also wasn't happy with her choice and insisted that his wife and Emma go everywhere together. Hence, they were each other's babysitters effectively. Indeed, Emma found life miserable in Krasnodar in the end and told us she felt isolated and a bit lonely there. Since the end of December, she had taken to coming up to Voronezh on the overnight train as frequently as she could for a few days to hang out with Becky and Jane, and to use the spare bed they had in their room. She was fun to have around, enjoyed a touch of Thai dye in her wardrobe, and hung out and had a good time with everyone. I completely understood why she got out of Krasnodar as often as possible to come and see us. I assumed this just led the American lady to be even more isolated, but then again, maybe it gave her the freedom to enjoy herself more, but I never found out either way.

"Is she? OK, well, I have a bit of a story to share," I said.

"Yes, I know! Very sweet, Genry! Becky told me earlier. So, you and Tanya have got yourselves a little nookie pad then, eh? I guess more room here suits me just fine, mate. What's it like then? Is the bed going to be able to withstand the activities you have in mind?" Al said with a smile.

"Oh, god, the apartment. Yes, it's great. But that's not what I was going to tell you. Something bad happened this morning," I said, my face probably showing signs of worry across it, I felt.

"What happened? Are you OK?"

"I'm fine, but I need to tell you about it, but probably I should tell the others at the same time to save having to say it all over again to them."

We went to the girls' room across the corridor, and I sat everyone down to reveal what had happened.

"Bloody hell, Genners, this is crazy!" Jane uttered a short while later after I had delivered my recap of the morning's events to Al, Becky, Jane and Emma.

"It's *so* much more interesting here than in Krasnodar!" Emma added.

"So, you're definitely *not* going to show up on Saturday at Café Anna and look at the mug shots, then?" Al asked.

"No. As Tanya said, I need to call their bluff. Turn up to all my classes, keep to my normal timetable, and, I don't know, maybe they'll just give up or leave me alone!" Even as I said this, it sounded unlikely that I'd not see or hear from them again, but that was the way I had to play it.

"But what are you going to do at the time you're supposed to be seeing them?" Becky asked.

"Yeah, 2 pm...I don't know!"

"I've got an idea," said Al, "How about I organise a kick about on Saturday? Say 1 pm or something, and then at 2 pm, we'll all be playing football over in the park, and at least you'll be busy doing something?"

"Yeah, OK, let's do that," I replied, looking out of the window at the snow that was covering everything.

"Don't worry about the snow," Al added as if following my thoughts. "There's still a good enough cleared area over there; it's hard, but we can easily play on it, and if we can't, it doesn't really matter, it's just something for you to be doing, isn't it?"

"When a friend is in need, we'll all do what we can to help our Genchik!" Jane said with a flourish.

As out of my depth as I was, it did feel good to have my friends there for me. It was all quite a surreal day. Just yesterday, I sorted out the apartment in town with Tanya, and now that felt like a long time ago. I was not even sure it was worth moving into that place now. Perhaps the security of staying in my UK group in the hostel was a better option than being isolated and more easily approached again in town. But I wasn't going to concern myself thinking about that for now.

The next twenty-four hours passed by mostly uneventfully. I chilled out in the hostel with the girls, drinking tea and smoking cigarettes in their room for much of the day, and walked over to Tanya's place that night. I dutifully went to all my morning classes as per the advice to not put a step wrong. On Friday afternoon, one day before my scheduled date with the secret police in Café Anna, I noticed that across the street from our ground floor rooms, one car with two people inside it had been there rather a long time. It was a black Lada, rather like every other car on the streets of Voronezh those days, of course, but just a slightly bigger and better model. The two figures inside were men, but we couldn't see them clearly; the car windows were opaque with condensation produced by the occupants.

"The thing is, I think they were there yesterday afternoon, too, after you returned here, after your questioning," said Tanya. "Alexei pointed them out to me, but we didn't say anything to you about it. You were already upset enough as it was, Genry".

"Really?! So, they're following me. Is that what you mean?" I asked, moving back over to the window to have another look.

"Just watching to see what you do, probably. Get back from the window. It's good not to let them know you know they are there!"

"Jesus," I said, sitting back down on the sofa again, "I'm not really cut out for this sort of thing".

"Do you want to go out for a walk in the park or something?" Tanya suggested.

"Out there? No thanks! What if they follow or approach me or something?" I objected. "I prefer just to stay inside, I think."

"I don't think those guys will. Their job is just to watch and report back. You don't need to worry about them," she said in a surprisingly reassuring and matter of fact tone.

As weird as it seems, I was quite reassured. Ordinarily, I should have been freaking about two men in a car stationed outside the apartment and clearly watching me. It was straight out of a spy novel. But as I was not in my normal life, or country even, none of it seemed real, and the fact that Tanya seemed so relaxed put me at ease. I didn't understand it, but I was happy to follow her lead.

Saturday morning was a beautiful day with clear blue skies and hard white snow lining the streets. As per the plan, I had no intention of going into town to meet the KGB, hell no, and so after midday, I began to get ready to go and play football in the park across the street. My immediate close friends group had well chewed over my unfolding drama, but the broader group of my UK companions were mainly unaware, as far as I knew. Maybe rumours were already sliding out by then, although unbeknownst to me.

Dressed in training gear, gloves, scarf, and coat, of course, I walked down the corridor at 12.45 pm, feeling a bit weird still and bumped down the stairs. Everyone else was ahead of me; my feet seemed reluctant players in this plan. I pushed open the hostel door and burst into the sunlight. Ahead of me, the footpaths crisscrossed the short tree specked area between the hostel and the main road. I took a refreshing lungful of ice-cold air as I prepared to jog down the hostel steps, but then something happened. Two figures who had been standing outside of the side of the door turned to me, cigarette in hand, and addressed me.

"Genry! Well, hello again, how are things?" one said, smiling broadly. I was confused for a moment. Not expecting this, it took me a couple of seconds to register the fact that standing here before me, outstretching their hands to shake mine, were the very same two Georgians who I'd talked about to my questioners. Out of autopilot response, I took a hand, shook it, but suddenly felt a bit sick. This was crazy. I was supposed to be going to Café Anna right at this moment, to meet the KGB, or whoever they were, to look through photographs to identify these very two people. So many things went through my mind in a fraction of a second. It was such a massive coincidence, was my first thought. Followed instantly by, this is not a coincidence at all, but a set-up. Of course, it could not be a coincidence that these two guys, who I had not seen for over three months, and who I had, in fact, only met once in my life that night back then, were now standing in front of me.

I hadn't bought the drugs off them anyway, of course, but on the spur of the moment a few days ago, I had named them as the drug dealers who supplied me. Guessing or hoping that they didn't even live in Voronezh and were now hundreds of miles away in a different city somewhere, or even in Georgia, I had named them precisely as I thought they effectively didn't exist. I thought I'd never see them again. I also named them because I thought they'd not be able to get revenge on me for informing on them and because I thought nobody would know who they were. I'd already been surprised when Stepanov had said he'd heard of them, but I'd got over that. But this was just insane.

"Are you interested in doing a little business?" said one of them, still smiling. I snapped my hand back in fright. I sensed all the trees out in front of me. If this was a set-up, I imagined someone out there behind a tree. They could have a camera to photograph the handshakes of the conspirators and the accused.

"I…I…No!…I'm not…I don't do that, not interested, excuse me!" I was in a total muddle. It all took place over the space of only a few seconds, but this moment has stood still in my mind for a long time. After withdrawing my hand, I managed to say goodbye and muttered that I had somewhere I was running late for, and stumbled down the steps and headed up the path towards the main road.

"OK, see you another time!" Georgi called after me.

After just a few minutes, I managed to catch up with the other guys over in the park as we arrived at the clearing to play football.

"Al, I just saw the two Georgian guys. They were right outside the door!" I confided.

"What, aren't they the ones you're supposed to be dobbing in?"

"Yes! They shook my hand, right there. It's all completely fucking mad! I haven't seen them for ages, three months or something, and suddenly I see them *right now*; this is not a coincidence, I'm sure of it."

"Well, just stay here. We'll play for as long as we can, and, we'll just keep you inside the group as much as possible so nobody can get to you from now on."

We played football for at least an hour, running fast to keep warm, but so cold whenever we stopped. We eventually couldn't keep it up, so we had to finish. I had wanted to be out and unfindable at the time of the rendezvous. At least I had managed that. As shaken as I was, it felt good to have the physical exercise; it helped purge my anxieties and stress. As we walked back to the hostel, I kept my eyes peeled. I also had Al enter the foyer first and then the upstairs corridor first, just to tell me if he saw anyone there who looked in anyway connected to the game I seemed to now be playing. I felt I now needed to have minders.

I spent the next day with Tanya and Alexei in the apartment, and Oleg and Vadim came around in the afternoon. Fortunately, there didn't seem to be any immediate results for my no-show at Café Anna, so I was able to enjoy a relatively relaxed Sunday.

CHAPTER 35

The following week began as normal, and I relaxed even more. Maybe these people had tried their luck, but it hadn't worked, as I wasn't playing ball. If this were official, then they'd have done something else; Tanya and Alexei must have been right. Whoever they were, maybe these people realised I now had advice from Russians who knew all about the rules of these games. They failed to isolate me before I got advice to ignore them completely, so now I hoped they'd just disappear. The car also seemed to give up on watching me, but I remained vigilant.

The wonderful and weird life in this strange place kept on playing itself out in its rather hedonistic fashion.

On Wednesday afternoon, I wandered over to the apartment and knocked. I heard a few voices and movement inside while waiting for the door to open. Presently the door opened, and out came a Russian girl who I had never seen before. She looked somewhat flushed and red-faced. At first, I thought I had the wrong door as she looked me in the eye. But catching sight of the familiar entranceway wallpaper behind her, I knew it was the right place a millisecond later. She exited the premises and skipped past, clutching a coat that she hadn't managed to put on properly. I went in and saw a grinning Alexei at first. "Ah Genry, come in!" he said.

Issa was pouring himself a vodka in the main room, cigarette on the go. There were several glasses on the table and a few bottles of drink. Alexei and Issa looked messy themselves and exchanged glances which told me they were rather pleased with themselves, and I could guess why.

"I love this life, Genry!" Alexei said with a big grin, coming back into the room. "Issa brought her over from this morning's class. She said she was curious about... well, she just gave us...you know, at the same time!"

I looked at Issa again; he was grinning while pouring himself some more vodka into a glass. I immediately thought of Gwyn from our group. I couldn't believe that she thought of him as her actual boyfriend, even before today, but she'd be hurt to know that he took part in events like this. I couldn't even really see Gwyn and Issa together like that anyway, and cynically I thought that what Issa saw in Gwyn was someone to hoodwink so that she could get himself to the UK one day soon. Well, it wasn't my place to judge what others were doing, though, so I was not going to get involved. As Tanya wasn't at home anyway, I stayed for no longer than a short while and then went back over to the hostel.

However, the next day, things began again for me on my agenda. We had no lessons until 11 am that day, and having spent a rare night in my bed in the hostel, I was still dozing when, at around 9 am, Jane knocked on the door and came in.

«Henry, some people are coming upstairs,» she said breathlessly, «I think they may be looking for you! They just looked different, and I heard them asking in the kabinet office hatch about room numbers, and I›m not sure, but I think I heard them say ‹*Pettit*›.»

I jumped out of bed and thanked her. Jane left as quickly as she'd arrived. Al was already up and dressed, on his bed, writing a letter.

"OK, you hide. I'll speak to them if they come in here," Al said, getting up quickly. Dressed in only a T-shirt and boxer shorts, I looked around the small room for somewhere to hide and thought maybe I'd skip over to Jane and Becky's room. I cracked the door open and looked down the corridor. I saw two people in full outdoor coats walking up the hall. I closed the door quickly, too late to leave the room, I thought.

The biggest space was probably under the beds, but I quickly realised we'd both stored rucksacks and all other sorts of things under there, so there wouldn't be space for me.

"I'll make your bed. Try the cupboard, quick!" Al barked at me.

Against the wall behind the door swing, opposite my bed, stood our three cupboards. They were floor to ceiling built-in wooden ones and thankfully reasonably solid, but they were also relatively narrow, a bit like lockers you get in schools. As quickly as I could, I flung mine open and saw that fortunately, there wasn't a lot of stuff in there; I grabbed my coat and a couple of bulky hanging clothing items and flung them towards the floor by my bed. Al was straightening my bed covers, and as my clothes missiles landed, he kicked them under my bed. I squeezed into the narrow coffin and pulled the inside edges of the door to make it close, but I couldn't shut it properly as a sock on the floor was preventing it. Footsteps stopped outside the door now, so I just held the door as best as possible. Through the tiny crack in the cupboard door, I managed to see Al resume his position on his bed just as the sound of knuckles came rapping upon the door.

"Yes?" Al was trying to sound nonchalant, which I appreciated. It was quite a good "Da", but I wasn't sure if he was a born actor. For my part, I was trying to stop breathing so fast and was struggling to stand comfortably with my shoulders at an uncomfortable three-quarters angle constricted by the narrowness of the space.

"We are looking for *Xchenry* Pettit. Is this his room?» barked a male voice, massacring my first name.

"Yes, this is his room," Al answered matter-of-factly.

"Where is he? We need to speak with him," came the voice.

"I don't know. He's not here," said Al.

"OK, we'll look for him at his girlfriend's place, but tell him we need to speak to him."

"Who shall I say is looking for him?" Al asked after them, but there was no reply, they had already left, and I heard retreating footsteps in the corridor.

After a few seconds, I opened the door and stared at Al, who stared straight back. I stepped out of the cupboard. "Fucking hell!" I said.

"I was just thinking the same thing!" Al replied.

"They're not going to find me at Tanya's either," I reasoned, then added, "They didn't answer when you asked who they were? Just as Tanya said. They can't say who they are if they're not totally official. Maybe this will be OK. I'll just keep going to class and keeping myself busy and ride it out. Not that this is any fun, though."

The rest of the day passed without any further development, and I went over to Ulitsa Mira in the afternoon to tell Tanya about hiding in the cupboard. She said I did the right thing and reassured me that because they didn't tell Al their identity, it was probably a good sign. She also confirmed that she hadn't seen them at the apartment either.

This strange game of cat and mouse resumed a holding pattern over the next couple of days. Most of the other British students learned about my story and thankfully assumed an unofficial lookout for me. Now and then, I'd be walking to or from somewhere, and a friend coming in the other direction would tip me off about any suspicious-looking types they had seen nearby or thought they had seen, and I'd go a long way around to avoid them, just in case.

At the start of the subsequent week, something happened that I took as an excellent sign. Vyacheslav came to the door at the end of class one day and signalled to Mr Belkin that he wanted to address us all. Of course, naturally, my first instinct was a sinking feeling that something official concerning me was now going to happen. But the feeling was short-lived, as Vyacheslav wanted to tell us about another trip coming up to Pyatigorsk. Pyatigorsk is an old spa resort in Russia's southern, eastern tip, overlooked by the Caucasus mountains. It was a cultural trip, which was supposed to appeal to us for various reasons. The city was famous for being the home town of the writer Lermontov, who died in a duel there, commemorated by a monument. Peter the Great had also made the mineral springs in the area well known since around 1700 by paying a royal visit and conferring his favour upon them. People have visited it as a holiday destination ever since. The trip wasn't for six weeks but needed to be booked and would cost us the usual small surcharge each to sign up. But more relevant to me was Vyacheslav asking who wished to go, and he included me in the question. So, it seemed that things were carrying on as usual as far as my stay in Russia was concerned.

I signed up, as did practically everyone else. It would be good to get away from the city for another trip, and I was looking forward to seeing the place. Vyacheslav described cable cars going up the mountain, and a small ski resort too, which I hoped we'd be visiting; if I got there, that is. A small group of my compatriots from Bristol university were down in Pyatigorsk too, who had chosen a few months there and the rest in Moscow, so it looked set to be a good social trip.

Vyacheslav also told us that we would be increasing our numbers in the hostel a week or two before the Pyatigorsk trip, as more students would join us. Fifteen more English students who had spent the first half of their Russian experience in St Petersburg were coming to spend the second part in Voronezh with us.

Becky, Jane and I were excited by this as a few of them were our UK classmates from Bristol, and it would be good to see them. I certainly had a few things to bring them up to speed on in my personal life, I thought.

Just over a week after we'd viewed the apartment and agreed to take it, I asked Tanya what she thought we should do about it, given everything that had since happened. I wanted to know if she thought things would be OK now, and whether we should think again about pursuing the lease. Her view wasn't as enthusiastic. She maintained that it was too early to be confident that my troubles had gone away and not to take being included in Vyacheslav's Pyatigorsk trip as a sign that we were out of the woods completely. The people who were pursuing me were still not very official, as we knew, so all the proper management of our group would naturally continue very much as usual, she said. She added that Vyacheslav wouldn't have a clue about my interrogation or the other shenanigans. Naturally, she didn't use the word *shenanigans*, of course; nor do I even know if they have such a word in Russian. I suggested that maybe Vyacheslav had some idea, though; why else would he have been up at dawn on the day they took me through the hostel for the interrogation? As to the apartment, she held the view that it wasn't a very good move for us to move in there right now, where I could more easily be isolated and targeted. We thought it could antagonise them further if I set up shop in a city centre apartment. She said the lady wasn't hurrying her anyway, and she'd not rush it for the time being, either.

After another few days, another incident took place, punctuating the calm again. It was a Saturday afternoon, a week and a half since my questioning, and a week to the day since my missed appointment at Café Anna to look at mugshots. I was in the apartment with Tanya and Nadia.

"I'm a bit bored," I said. "Shall we get pizza?"

When you were not being questioned or chased by

the KGB, playing football, drinking, smoking, visiting the forest, or looking for food in the empty shops, there wasn't much else to do in a provincial Russian city in 1993. There was nothing on TV worth watching in the daytime; shopping malls didn't exist, and no cool bars or cafes existed yet, either. But there was the rubbish pizza place over by the circus building. As horrible as it was, it was something to do and different, and I was getting a bit more tolerant of it now.

"Oh yes, good idea," said Tanya. "I was just thinking about cleaning up the place a bit and washing the floor. Look how dirty it is."

"Is it? It doesn't look too bad to me," I replied.

"Oh Genry, you're just like all the other men!" chimed Nadia, "Why don't you get us all pizza then? You can hunt and gather it while us silly women mop the floor and tidy the home, OK?"

"It sounds a bit sexist, to be honest, but OK, I'll go and get it. See you in about an hour," I replied.

It was about fifteen minutes' walk to the pizza place, and it was a bitterly cold day, as usual. I was wearing my Russian hat with the flaps on top, which I didn't always wear, but I needed to on this February day. There was an unwritten law about these hats in Russian society that it had to be super cold before you pull the flaps over your ears - something like minus 20 degrees Celsius.

I wasn't sure if it was real or a joke, but apparently,

only wimps, or foreigners, put the flaps down. All I knew was that it was freezing for me, and I wanted to put the flaps down. I looked around, and sure enough, most people I saw with one of the hats had the flaps up. I'd always played to the rule, but on this occasion, it was too cold for me, so I put the flaps down.

After a short while, I started wondering if this made me stand out as an obvious a foreigner, which might not be such a good thing, given my situation. I slowed and looked around. My attention was immediately drawn to two figures thirty or even forty metres away behind me. It seemed as if they stopped when I stopped. They were talking to each other but too far away for me to see much. Then they fully turned their backs on me.

I began walking again, and after a few seconds, I looked back over my shoulder. They were now walking again, too, in my direction but with heads down and hands in their coat pockets. I stopped and looked directly back, this time in their direction, and they stopped. My tummy somersaulted; they appeared to be following me! I resumed the pace once again, and sure enough, they stayed with me. I walked faster, and they walked faster. My instinct was to try to stop this happening rather than to let this happen, even though I ought to have reasoned that they only wanted to follow me, not catch me.

But I was not feeling reasonable and had no experience at this sort of thing. My pace flipped between a fast walk and an intermittent trot. They kept up. I had a strong urge that I wanted to shake them off. I didn't like being followed. I rounded a corner with them still some thirty metres back and saw an archway entrance leading to the interior of a block. As they couldn't see me at this point, I sprinted down the archway into an open-air interior garden courtyard. Directly ahead was a bench, cleared of snow, with what appeared to be a bank or a big snowdrift running behind it. Without giving it a second thought, I ran towards the bench, planted my leading foot on the seat and vaulted over it, landing, as I hoped I would, in a few feet of soft concealing snow the other side. The snow caught me perfectly, like a big white armchair, and held me still. It was very comfortable. I stayed motionless for a moment but then slowly tipped my head to the left to ensure it wasn't poking up too high over the top of the bench. I stayed as still as I could, breathing heavily but into my gloves and the ear flaps of my hat to try to stop my steaming breath from giving me away.

I stayed there for a full five minutes or more to ensure they were gone, or no longer interested at any rate.

As I eased myself forward and upright, a piece of metal, and then another, revealed themselves in the snow just in front of me and to the left. These prongs were pointing skywards at a 45-degree angle, and as I brushed more snow away from them, it appeared to be an old rusty agricultural plough or harvesting tool of some sort.

Many more bits of metal accompanied the first two, making up a nasty collection of discarded metal hazards. I winced, and my bum-hole contracted at the thought of what could have happened if I had have landed on that.

I left the courtyard, all in one piece thankfully, and peered down the street in both directions. With the coast clear, as much as I felt like scurrying directly home, I decided to go ahead to the pizza place anyway, as I was nearly there. I waited about 15 minutes for them to make three pizzas, and once I had the three little boxes, I headed back out, across town again. It was not great pizza, but it would do the job of offering us all some comfort.

Approaching the apartment finally, I rounded the final street corner and began to head up towards Ulitsa Mira. I looked ahead to see two men walking directly towards me. They looked different to the other two, and I was momentarily comforted by that. But then we locked eyes, and I realised that one of them was Nicolai, the man who had stood by the door during my questioning. I didn't recognise the other.

"Ah, hello Genry!" began Nicolai. My first impression was that he seemed surprised to see me, but then my second more suspicious impression was that this was not a surprise for him at all.

"Why did you not come to see us last Saturday? We were waiting for you," he continued.

Caught out in the open, with nobody to help me, I

had to say something.

"I, er… yes, I'm sorry, I… couldn't make it. I was really busy and couldn't come," I stammered.

"OK, don't worry," he replied. "So why don't we just go now? Our office is close to here," Nicolai said.

I wasn't going to do that; I knew I had to get away quickly. I looked down at the pizzas.

"I can't come now; I've got these pizzas, and they're for my girlfriend and a friend. And I also said that I'd help clean the floor today."

I inwardly frowned at myself; the pizza part of my excuse was lame as it was, but why I added the part about washing the floor, God only knew. I was just so rubbish at this fugitive from the law stuff! Nicolai gave me a strange smile and cocked his head on one side as if to check if he heard me correctly.

"So, I have to go," I added and made as if to walk away.

To my huge relief, it seemed as if he wasn't about to arrest or detain me. Maybe he really didn't have the power to do anything without my agreement.

"OK, Genry, but we do need to see you. Come to the Deconat as soon as you can. Monday is good, OK?" he said.

"OK, bye," I said, and made off with the pizza.

"Oh, and Genry?" Nicolai called after me, and I glanced back to him. "You shouldn't put the flaps down when it's as warm as this. It makes you too easy to find!" he added, grinning.

Back at base, while eating the pizza, Tanya said that it looked both good and bad at the same time. It was good; she said because Nicolai couldn't do anything, reasoning that they would be doing this far more officially if they were serious or genuine. It was a good sign that they didn't seem to have authoritative powers to do anything after I refused to go with them. But it was still bad that they stopped me in the street and tried to get me to go with them.

In response to my account of the first incident, I got far more sympathy concerning how I could have ended up seriously injured by the metal poles and the heart racing nature of the chase. But ultimately, they said the positive aspect of it was that they hadn't tried that hard to catch me, or want to even. It didn't make me feel that much better, to be honest.

"You did very well, Genchik, even though your excuses were rubbish, darling!" she said, pushing me over on the sofa bed.

"Now, when are you going to clean the floor!?" laughed Nadia.

CHAPTER 36

Somewhat relieved, by their curious inability to do anything to me on the street, and that I had faced them off successfully a few times now, I began to believe that all I had to do was stand firm and all this would soon be over. It played out once more during the next week but in a different setting. I was in the morning lessons, as I now did much more than before. Mr Belkin was teaching us a challenging aspect of the Russian future conditional tense when there came a knock on the door. I was sitting right at the back, with as many people between me and the door as I probably could have had. Through the glass panel in the door, I could see two men who I hadn't seen before. Maybe they had a limitless supply of henchmen. Belkin bade them enter.

"Good day to you, Gospodin Belkin." One of them said. A couple of years earlier it would have been *tovarish* Belkin, meaning comrade Belkin.

But now it was *gospodin* meaning *Mister* Belkin instead. More politically correct, now that the communists had been overthrown.

"Good day. How can I help you?" Belkin replied.

We would like to speak with Henry Pettit. Is he in

this class?" the visitor asked.

"Yes, he's there at the back," the teacher signalled towards me with his hand.

"Thank you," the man said, then continued, "Mister Pettit, please come with us. We would like to see you."

The room felt achingly quiet; if a pin had dropped, it would have made everyone jump. My heart thumped in my chest, but my autopilot kicked in. "What is it concerning?" I asked the man from my seat.

"We would like to speak with you in private," he pressed.

"Yes, but what about?" I said, bluffing him.

"You've been missing too many classes, which is not good, and we need to speak about this," he said.

"Well, I can't come now because I am *in* a class, as you can see," I countered.

The man paused looked at his *comrade* as if trying to work out what to say next. After a moment's contemplation, he responded with, "When does this class finish?"

"I think there is one more hour." It seemed like the longest I could get away with saying.

Frustrated, he said, "OK, but you must come to the Deconat office when the class is over".

An audible sigh of relief came from the whole room as they disappeared down the corridor. I felt like I had won again, but that was a very tense and public stand-off.

When the class ended, Becky and Al came over to me.

"What are you going to do, Henry?"

"Well, I know what I am *not* going to do; I'm not going to the Deconat. Did you see how they just couldn't answer the question?" I smiled.

"It was priceless!" agreed Al, "but still a bit worrying, though, surely?"

He was right. What happened that day was significant, although I may not have realised it immediately. Before then, they'd kept their approaches to me mostly off the radar, mostly one on one and out of sight. Coming to the class in full view and calling me out signalled that they didn't mind everyone knowing that they were looking for me, that I was a person of interest. I didn't realise it, but this could have been a point of no return for them. If they dropped it now, they would lose face.

Becky asked me if I had spoken to Vicky yet, which I hadn't. She said that I should probably go to Vicky first to tell her that I was being targeted or harassed or something, at least. It could be better that way, being upfront and not hiding anything, rather than her hearing something from the official channels first. It wasn't a bad idea, so I made a mental note to discuss things with Vicky soon to paint the picture to her exactly how I wanted it to sound. I hadn't done anything that bad after all, I was certainly not a drug dealer or anything, so this was all a bit out of proportion, as far as I was concerned.

That afternoon, the four of us walked down Ulitsa Mira to get some food for dinner from the babushkas. A big potato-based vegetarian stew the most likely outcome, with some pickled veg to accompany it, hopefully. The snow was piled high on the edge of the wide pavements as usual, but there were also long lines of orange plastic tape which were cordoning off large parts of the pavement itself, and I wasn't sure why.

It meant the usable area was now much reduced, although the cordons did often turn in at shop doorways allowing access.

"Look up," Al said, realising I was trying to work the cordons out. The buildings on Ulitsa Mira were about five storeys high, and they had a roof which overhung the pavement, from which hung giant, thick icicles, as much as three metres long in some cases. The word icicle does not do it justice, though; they were more like stalagmites. Massive lumps of ice, weighing over a hundred kilos perhaps, formed into pointed arrows hanging directly over the pavement.

"Somebody said that as it gets near to spring and they start to thaw, they can fall, but even before then, sometimes they break off if they get too heavy, and there is a warmer day."

"Nasty," I said.

"And every year without fail, they kill at least one

or two people – a huge pointy shard of ice right on the head!" Al followed up dramatically. I began to feel these icy shards hanging above us were a metaphor for the Russian daggers that seemed to be out for me right now.

"What a way to go, and what bad timing too!" I said, thinking of the unfortunates who happen to be passing exactly when one of these lethal icicles falls. I reviewed all the roof lines on the road ahead and other side streets. Sure enough, nearly all buildings had big ice daggers pointing menacingly at the citizens below. It reminded me of how Trotsky met his demise. Shortly after Lenin's death, he was sent into exile in the power struggles that eventually led to Stalin grabbing the reins. After ending up in Mexico, he was ultimately killed there in 1940 on Stalin's orders by an NKVD (precursor to the KGB) operative swinging an ice pick into his head.

As we walked up Ulitsa Mira, I noticed the black car on the side of the road near to Tanya's apartment once again, looking like it had my special watchers sitting in it. The situation I found myself in just didn't seem real anymore.

People had questioned me, then people were following me, and people were also sitting in cars, generally monitoring my comings and goings. It was, of course, bizarre but also so foreign that I almost felt a bit anaesthetised as if it was a bit of a game that I was just participating in. At some point, it would end surely, and then everything would go back to normal, hopefully. I was just allowing it to play out, not sure what else I could do anyway. At least I was carrying out the instructions Tanya and Alexei gave me, trying to keep ahead of my pursuers.

CHAPTER 37

"I don't think we should take the apartment," Tanya said. We were lying in bed around midnight on that same day that my class had been interrupted. I had sensed she was in a bit of sombre mood when I'd come over in the evening. Her reaction to the news that I'd had classroom visitors had not been good when I told her.

"Why not? It'll be OK, won't it?" I asked, half in denial about the changing situation.

"It's beginning to feel different," she added. She was more worried, more so than before, because they were seeking me publicly now - not secretly. She said they could be trying another angle. "I don't know what's going to happen," and she began to cry silently. I felt the tears moisten my chest in the dark.

"Didn't you say I can pay three months in advance? Or six months? It's fine. I can pay that!" I said. "They can't do anything to me, can they? You said they can't. It'll be great in that place, just to the two of us!" I said into the darkness, considering the excitement of the idyllic living arrangement.

"It's not about the cost." Tanya sniffed.

"What then?"

"I'm worried about us, of course."

"I love you; it'll be OK."

"I don't know what's going to happen. And I don't want an apartment just for myself."

"Of course. It's for me, too, though. Isn't it?"

"I don't know."

I didn't want to push it; I couldn't see her face as we lay there in the dark. Since the start of this, Tanya had been coaching and reassuring me. But she was losing confidence in it now, though, and I hadn't got anything to say. I stared into nothingness. I squeezed her shoulders and kissed her hair. I didn't have any words.

As I thought about it more, I had to admit that it would be against all logical expectations for them to lose interest in me and finally drop the whole thing. An optimistic mini strand of thought tried to suggest itself in my brain. If they weren't who they said they were and were trying to recruit me into their network to do secret work for them, then maybe they would have to give up if they realised that I wasn't going to play ball. If they saw that I was receiving good coaching from my Russian friends, and wasn't going to fall into their trap, then maybe they'd admit defeat. If so, things would go back to normal, and I could get on with my Russian studies and carry out a normal year abroad as planned.

On top of that, we could move into the apartment in town, and life would be perfect for us. But then what?

This was not exactly a long-term life plan anyway, was it? The scheduled time in Russia was due to end in June. One way or another, some decisions about our relationship were looming. I didn't want to think about that. It wasn't something I had the emotional maturity to process either, if I'm honest. As I lay there in the dark, thinking about them coming for me in lessons and increasing their pursuit, it seemed unlikely they were about to lie down or go away. I had a sense that things were coming to a head, and this feeling proved totally founded just a few days later.

CHAPTER 38

One day followed the next, and I felt like everything was on pause with all that was happening. I continued with the vigilance policy, ready to give my pursuers the slip or send their messengers packing. I found myself often waiting for their next move. I hadn't seen the Georgians again, but it was just so fishy that they'd been there to greet me at the door at the time I was supposed to be picking their faces out of a photo parade. With the people in the car also watching me, the whole thing just felt like an elaborate set-up. While I liked to think that maybe I was playing them, I began to acknowledge that I was powerless and couldn't control the situation. I suppose Tanya had also started to see the helplessness of the problem.

While I could hide in cupboards, not show up to rendezvous, and refuse to play their game, what I couldn't do, was control what these people were doing or would do next.

So, while I wouldn't say it came as a relief, one early Tuesday morning at the beginning of March, a knock at the door once again woke me up in Tanya's place, and I felt this time my fate was going to be decided.

It was the same pair who had collected me from the apartment at the crack of dawn the first time. For a moment, I wondered if the stance of refusing to go unless they gave me a good reason would work.

Standing there in front of them at that time of day, I didn't think it would work to say I was busy. I couldn't exactly say I was in class at 7 am in my boxer shorts. And even if I was doing a thousand-piece jigsaw, then that was going to have a wait, too.

Fortunately, or unfortunately, my visitors broke the tension. They helped me yield by telling me they were taking me to the Deconat, rather than asking me to go there myself, *and* that our student rep Vicky was going to come with us. Bringing Vicky meant that it felt much more official. It wasn't just me, with no witnesses.

Unfortunately, as soon as they said that, I also felt a sledgehammer blow to my chest as the reality struck me was that they would have to play their cards. What was going to happen to me? Would they be locking me up for seven years? Would I be given a severe reprimand? I didn't know how it was going to play.

"So, you must come with us now," the older man said. I didn't see any point in arguing.

I quickly got dressed, and as I was about to leave, I noticed Tanya was standing against the bedroom's doorframe. I turned to look at her.

"I have to go with them. They said they are bringing

Vicky too; we're going to the Deconat. I can't really say no this time, can I?" I said as I began to get dressed.

She didn't say anything at first but just looked back at me as if in pain, and then closed her eyes and very slowly shook her head. "No, you must go, lapochka," she said finally, then added, "but you will be OK; it is official now - and you are English, so you'll be safe. It won't be like with Anton".

I hadn't heard much about Alexei's brother, Anton, since he had been arrested; there was still not much information coming back on him, but I knew he was still in custody. As unsettling as it was to be reminded about someone else who'd been fitted up for a drug-related offence, I felt reassured that my British passport should act in some way to help to a good outcome. I went to Tanya and held her to me.

"I love you," I said.

"I love you, too," came the reply before she added, "remember, just deny everything this time".

I pulled myself away, pulled on my coat, and without looking back, I went out of the door. I followed the two nameless ones over the rough ground towards the hostel. It was a cold and gloomy morning; it was light but had not been for long, and the sky felt heavy with unreleased snow. We arrived through the rear door again and into the ground floor foyer area. Vyacheslav was there once again as we arrived, surveying me over his huge brown moustache.

"Good morning, Genry. What have you been up to so very early this morning that you need these two people for?" he said.

I instantly felt like he was teasing me, and he knew more than he was letting on. I recalled the last time he asked me about my red eyes. I decided to ignore him completely. At the same time, I saw Vicky in the foyer with a concerned look on her face, surrounded by her frizzy brown curls. She was standing next to Vyacheslav, and from the way it looked, I guessed it was he who had fetched her down here himself. She was looking at me without speaking, but I assumed she also wanted to ask me what was happening. I wanted to fill her in somehow and immediately regretted not getting around to talking to her. It would have looked a lot better if I had, as then she could have worn an expression akin to some injustice going on, rather than the present solemn one she was using. Of course, I had no idea what she'd been told when she was awoken a few minutes ago.

We weren't kept long in the hostel as another man, moustachioed and dressed mostly in black and brown, duly arrived trotting up the front steps.

"OK, let's go," he said, looking only at my two escorts, and then he turned on his heels back out of the door.

"Let's go," repeated the elder one to me, signalling to Vicky with a hooking action with his finger.

Vyacheslav remained where he was, which I was glad about. Maybe his role had just been to get Vicky, as he and she were the official contact points between the Russians and the British students. Perhaps he also had to witness my summons. As we followed, Vicky was starting to look more confused now, scanning me with her eyes for more information. I fell in step with her a little and managed to say, "I'll tell you in a minute!" with a look which I intended to reassure her with as we went back out into the dull morning. Out on the main Friedreich Engels Street, as close to the hostel as it could have been, was a pale blue university bus, and our now three babysitters indicated to us to get on it. The one who came up the steps a moment before got into the driver's seat, and the other two sat in the first row but on different sides and sat sideways on so they could survey all around them. It wasn't a big bus, although it was far too big for the four passengers. I was undoubtedly relieved it wasn't a regular Lada, and I led Vicky a couple of rows beyond Pinky and Perky so that we could get a tiny bit of privacy.

"What the hell is going on?" she asked me as soon as we sat down.

I liked Vicky a lot. As I said before, she'd been in Voronezh before when it was her third year at university and had loved her time here so much that she put herself forward for the student liaison job to start after she'd graduated. She'd stayed in touch with the Russian friends she'd made and hooked back up with some of them that were still around. She helped us get settled, and she gave us the inside tips about buying alcohol and how using ration tickets for sugar, milk, and other essentials worked. She enjoyed a party, too, like everyone, and drank heartily on many an evening with us.

She was all in, but I never told her about the grass purchase in the first week. And I had not compromised her by telling her about it since, either.

"OK, so, I'm sorry. I meant to tell you about this before. For the last few weeks, these police people have been chasing me around the place," I began, talking in little more than a whisper. Although I didn't think my custodians in the front spoke English, I didn't have any way of knowing.

"What?!"

"Alexei and Tanya said I should ignore them. They told me they were probably not who they said they were but were like *KGB*!" I mouthed KGB rather than say that bit out loud.

"Sorry, whaaatt?!"

I then tried to summarise the whole thing as best I could in what I thought would probably be not much more than a five-minute journey to the Deconat. Even though I knew that Vicky would be fine as a friend knowing the whole truth, I decided to protect her a little bit by simply saying that in the first week Sergei had given us some grass, and how, for some reason, they'd got furious about it, and decided I was the fall guy for it. I recounted how they'd questioned me a month ago, but secretly, not involving Vicky or a translator. I said they were also maybe annoyed that I had a Russian girlfriend, were hitting back at the Moscow Times article, or that too many students were indiscreet in the hostel with the smoking. I briefly whispered to her about how they tried to get me to meet in hotels and stuff, and that they followed me around town. And ultimately why Alexei and Tanya said that these were very suspect methods.

"You should have told me! I could have done something; not sure what mind you…" she said.

"It was just crazy; I didn't know what to do," was about the sum of my reply. We were now approaching Lenin Square and the Deconat.

"OK, let's just see what they say now, and we can talk to the British Embassy after this, but try to not say very much in here if you can," she advised.

They led us inside the building, down a series of brownish-greenish corridors, the *go-to* colour scheme around here, it seemed. Over the previous few weeks, I had been gamely trying to master my circumstances rather than be mastered by them, but I felt that the tables were turning firmly now. Helplessly I followed my masters into a bright office. As the door opened, I first glimpsed a desk at the far end of the room with shelves stacked with various books behind it as well as some certificates in frames, and behind the desk a small side table with an ornate metal samovar at least two feet high upon it. The room smelled of stale cigarettes, which, combined with my nerves, made me feel slightly sick. But my eyes more immediately were drawn to the middle part of the room where there was a table big enough for 6 or 8 people to sit around, where two gentlemen were seated. Our escorts retreated and closed the door behind them quietly, as the two seated figures rose to a standing position. I had seen neither of them before. The more centrally positioned man looked around fifty years old and beckoned us in to take seats opposite him. He bore the look of someone who looked after himself well; clean-shaven with a healthy complexion that was not something to be taken for granted in Voronezh in 1993.

He wore a uniform of some sort, but I didn't know whether it was police or military. The second man was a shorter, stocky man, wearing a suit he had been acquainted with a long time and a tie whose knot was trying to hide under his double chin. Nevertheless, he still managed to exude an aura of some distinction.

"My name is Mikhail Gerasimov. I am with the Russian Federation Department of Internal Affairs, responsible for the Voronezh oblast", said the uniformed man, "and this is Mr Konstantin Timochenko, the deputy rector of the Voronezh State University."

At that point, I noticed a third person away to my left at the end of the table, who I hadn't seen at first as they were obscured by the door when we had entered the room, which I began to suspect belonged to the deputy rector. The third person was a thin younger man who sat over a file and a writing pad. As I looked in his general direction, it was as if Gerasimov was reading my mind. "He'll be taking notes," he snapped, the chap deemed not important enough for a proper introduction.

They both had some sheets of paper in front of them, and some of these I noticed had inky stamps on them, and Gerasimov was straightening his pile.

"You are Henry Pettit and Victoria Brown?" he asked, looking each of us in the eye, in turn, while enunciating each of the proper nouns. Although the question seemed rhetorical, we confirmed that we were.

"Good," he replied; I think for the notes - he was setting this off on an official footing. "So, on Wednesday, February 3rd of this year, Mister Henry Pettit, you were interviewed by Mr Ivan Stepanov and Mr Nicolai Pakrovsky of the Voronezh police."

My heart sank even lower with these introductory words from its already low starting point. So, it had come to this, I thought. The days of running a few steps ahead of these people were now looking to be concluded by whatever Gerasimov was going to say next. It was official. My first thoughts veered towards the prospect of seven years in a Russian prison, for that was what Stepanov had first threatened me with, and it was that meeting which Gerasimov referenced straight away. My second thought was to acknowledge the first meeting, which I'd increasingly believed was carried out either by ex KGB or corrupt militsiya men looking to entrap me into some form of dirty work for them. It was now being repurposed as an official meeting to suit the new narrative that I was about to hear.

"During the interview, dated February 3rd", he continued, "you did admit to buying and selling amounts of illegal narcotics. You have admitted to using these narcotics yourself on numerous occasions, and you have distributed them amongst students at Voronezh State University. This is a serious offence, and one which has caused a challenging situation for the university, the state justice department, and the Russian Federation in general."

At this point, the deputy rector, who had said nothing thus far and was perhaps feeling a bit left out, sighed and added, "Very challenging," shaking his head and looking at me. I bit my lip and said nothing.

Gerasimov resumed his monologue once again. "At this time, Russia, as you know, is trying to build good relations with Great Britain, and your actions have placed a big problem before us. So, therefore, we have come to the following decision. In the best interests of international relations between Russia and Great Britain, we have decided that, rather than taking other more serious courses of action, which we could do, you will instead be repatriated at the earliest opportunity back to Great Britain. We will arrange for you to be on the next flight to London, and after you have taken this flight, all charges against you will be dropped and the case closed. It is, I hope you will agree, a good way to end this matter."

With that, he turned over the piece of paper in front of him and sat back. There was silence in the room as we were all letting what he had said sink in. I looked at Vicky, who returned my gaze with a degree of shock on her face.

My inner mind told me from instinct that I should probably object at this point and begin my denial in earnest. Maybe say something about how I'd thought the two men on February 3rd were not policemen, that I was scared, and... but Gerasimov interrupted my thoughts by speaking again.

"Now," he went on, "can I confirm that you have understood everything I have said? We have with us, Ms Brown. Miss Brown, can I please ask you if everything was clear? The deputy rector here also speaks perfect English if we wish for anything that was not clear to be explained again, in English."

Vicky looked at me and began to ask if I understood it, and at the same time, Gerasimov pushed two pieces of paper over towards me.

"Everything I have just said is here in this letter, and as you can see, one version is in Russian and the other in English. Please, take your time to read it," he continued with a flourish. I glanced at the letters with official inky stamps and signatures on them and recognised the words which had just filled the room; he mainly had read it word for word, I realised, as I read the pages and scanned the English version.

"Do you have anything you want to say? If not, then this meeting is now over, and you will be contacted in your hostel by tomorrow morning at the latest to inform you of your travel details."

I looked at Vicky plaintively to suggest I wanted to object or complain somehow. She gave me a look, motioning her head to outside the room, letting me know there was no point and that we should talk outside. As we all stood up, the door opened behind us and the two men who had brought us appeared and we knew to go with them to be taken away and back to the hostel. Stunned by Gerasimov's verbal volley, we walked out into the sunshine and onto the bus. As I took my seat, I looked across the main square and took in the vision of the colossal statue of Vladimir Ilyich Lenin, in black metal, atop a stone plinth with his one outstretched arm.

"Look, Lenin is showing me the way," I said to Vicky, "Go home. It's that way!" I said dejectedly, mimicking his arm pointing, to Great Britain, for my *best interests*.

"OK, so I'm going to call the embassy in Moscow as soon as we get back", she said in an urgent voice. They need to know what's just happened, and they can also advise us."

"Well, I think it's stupid, and I never sold anything to anyone. And as for that first meeting on February 3rd, I had no clue who they were, I didn't understand them half the time, and I am not sure what they think I admitted to anyway. I didn't even believe they were the police," I offered. Vicky didn't respond, and so I continued, "So, anything this person just said I admitted to is rubbish. They certainly can't prove I sold it to anyone, as I didn't, and proving I bought it is not something anyone's done yet, either. I've been scammed here, haven't I? They're embarrassed that the whole hostel is partying the whole time. And they're embarrassed about the bad press they're getting about us paying thousands of pounds for this, getting a kitchen with broken windows, muddy floors, and toilets that are permanently swimming in shit! They're hitting back, and I'm the fall guy!"

We got to the hostel, and Vicky said she'd make a call that afternoon to the British Embassy in Moscow and would come to me later. I dumped myself on my bed upstairs. I felt thoroughly shattered, and it could not yet have been much later than 9 am. Al was still asleep in his bed on the other side of the room.

I stared at the ceiling and the cracked white paint that was less white in some areas, maybe from people cooking in their rooms over the years. We had a baby belling cooker, and I found myself thinking about the time Al tried to roast a whole chicken in it a few weeks earlier. I wondered how it had come to this. Like the ceiling, I was certainly not whiter than white by any stretch, but I didn't think of myself as that bad.

How was it that I now found myself about to be deported from Russia at twenty-two years old? Well *repatriated* at any rate, whatever the difference was.

I began to wonder how I would explain any of this to my parents. Maybe I wouldn't have to; perhaps I could go back to Bristol or stay with friends until the time came for the rest of the group to return, and then I could turn back up at that time. But then, Tanya, what was to become of our relationship? All sorts of feelings flashed through my mind at once. I wanted our relationship to continue because I loved her, and she loved me, and I had never had a relationship quite like this. I felt so good with her, and I loved how she made me feel.

Could I just *up sticks* and leave? Thanks for the great times, darling, but my ship sails in the morning! I didn't think so; I wasn't that kind of man, and it didn't feel honourable either.

I would have to see how we could continue the relationship. One moment we were going to be moving into our own pad together and all the wonderous personal pursuits that offered, and now I was facing being sent home to England in the best interests of the diplomatic relations between the Russian Federation and the United Kingdom. This is bullshit. It didn't bear thinking about. I was just about to have my cake and eat it, for god's sake. Tanya would have to come to England, that was for sure, and I would be proud to have her there, too. *Normal* English girlfriends were fine, but I wanted to keep my beautiful Russian one. I wasn't ready to give that up. Not yet. I was kicking myself up into a big stew, lying on the bed, in full tantrum mode now.

This whole situation still seemed so ridiculous that I half thought that the authorities would sort it all out. But I was getting ahead of myself, and there was still so much to consider. I had to see what the British Embassy said for one thing. Once Vicky made the call to the embassy, maybe a senior British diplomat would speak to a Russian counterpart, and they would spit their cornflakes out laughing so much. Not that you could get cornflakes in Russia, of course. With all the real adult problems in the world and the critical international affairs they need to deal with, they'd surely look at my issue here down in Voronezh and agree to cancel the whole thing as an irritation they could do without. Surely Perestroika or Glasnost was more deserving of their attention than some student who bought ten dollars' worth of grass six months ago?

Al awoke after a few minutes of my ceiling gazing and greeted me with his usual cheery and upbeat tone. Straight away I filled him in on the morning's events, and, as expected, his reaction was of shock and disbelief as he sat up in bed. He said he couldn't believe this was happening. Until now, it had been weird enough, he said, but the hiding in cupboards and being followed by people who wanted me to talk to them about drug dealers had seemed to be a local issue really, not something for our national governments to care about. "The British Embassy in Moscow is right now talking about you, Henry!" he exclaimed, before adding, "this shit is real now".

I realised that Tanya was probably waiting to hear what happened, and I needed to let her know as she was perhaps worrying herself silly. I also wanted to know what Vicky would learn from her call with the embassy. I wondered where she was even going to call them from; the only calls I had ever made were booked days in advance at the post office. Then again, those were international calls. I decided to go over to the apartment anyway to see Tanya. I asked Al to let the others know the latest, as I didn't feel like conducting a speaking tour now. I slowly moped down the corridor and found myself taking the stairs at a snail's pace of two feet per step, rather like an invalid walking to the doctor to have their colon checked. A feeling overcame me that every hour for the next day or so would bring worse news and a more horrible situation each time to deal with. I was shaking my head and feeling sorrier for myself than, perhaps, I ever had done. As I shuffled off the final step, with a downturned mouth the shape of an upside-down letter U, I was surprised to see Vicky already in the lobby returning from somewhere.

CHAPTER 39

"I just got off the phone to the Embassy," she said breathlessly.

"That was quick. How did you do it so fast?" I asked, almost like my brain was stalling her from delivering the verdict.

"There's a university administration phone I can use in hostel number 1," she added, the same hostel with the offices in it, I noted, that I had been questioned in initially by the two so-called policemen in early February.

She suggested going somewhere quiet to talk about it. After considering indoors, we decided to go onto the open ground area in front of the hostel and stand by one of the trees - one of the trees I suspected I was photographed from the day I was door-stepped by the Georgians.

I investigated Vicky's face trying to see if I could find a trace of hope in her expression. I was trying to detect something along the lines of, "Listen, the Embassy is outraged, this whole thing is a waste of their time and yours, they said, and they're going to make sure it all goes away. I heard them spit out their cornflakes. Our foreign secretary Douglas Hurd is speaking to Kozyrev and Yeltsin this afternoon!"

Unfortunately, she didn't say anything quite like that. She explained that the call had gone quite well, and the Embassy was prepared to stand by me, as a British National, and do everything they could to support me at this time. They sounded as if they were on my side, which gave me an excited feeling of hope in some way. They had told Vicky that they were highly disappointed that I had initially been detained and questioned in Russian alone, with no interpreter or other representative present. This was against all the rules. This was a good start! Vicky explained that the Embassy's position was that if all these allegations were false and there was no proof to support any of the claims against me, they would help me. If I was 100% sure, they wanted to make it clear that they would stand by me and challenge this course of action to repatriate me with all their resources. It sounded like they were indignant at how the Russian authorities treated me, which was very heartening to hear. They were going to save the day and stand up to Russians for me.

But then it got less good. Vicky went on to relay to me that they also wanted me to think carefully about it and consider if there is any way that I thought they could come up with any evidence. If I had even a minor involvement or had any part in what they were saying I have done, I should think twice about a challenge. If there were any doubts, they seemed to suggest the

Russian authorities would know how to exploit that and that I might like to consider the easier option of simply taking the early flight home and putting it all behind me.

"OK," I said. The initial feeling of encouragement I had had while listening to Vicky had been swiftly replaced by the realisation that my only real option was to leave after all.

"Don't know if you know Alexei's brother at all, but they had been trying to catch him on some pretty serious charges for a while but were unable to find evidence. Eventually, they just walked up to him on the street, and one police guy pretended to bump into him by accident, while another one planted drugs in his pocket. Then, a minute later, another police unit stopped and searched him, found it, and he's been in prison since then, I think."

"Really? My god, that's terrible!" Vicky said.

"I know. Even though I don't think anyone can prove I bought anything, and certainly not that I sold it because I didn't, I don't trust some Russians. Some would happily make up what they saw me doing to please Stepanov and Gerasimov, and condemn me at the same time. Even if that wasn't to happen, the police are not going to lose this, and they'd do something like they did to Anton."

Resigning myself to that choice, -the easy way out - I told Vicky that I would go and see Tanya now, to see what she thought. Vicky said she'd speak with the Embassy again when I was sure of my decision later that day.

It was a sombre atmosphere over at the apartment, but Alexei was in no two minds about what I should do. He could not have been clearer. His brother was still in prison, even though they had fabricated the evidence against him. He said they would not let me win this one and throw it back in their face. They would find all the evidence they needed to support their claims and make an example of me. I needed to take the flight, he said. Tanya was sitting with me on the sofa all the time, holding my hand but saying very little.

Tears were falling down her face.

"Yes, Genry-chik," she said finally, "you don't have a choice". She buried her face in my shoulder.

I squeezed her tight and experienced a feeling that I was not me, but I was looking at me. The sensation was perhaps a defensive or self-preservation instinct, enabling me to detach myself from feeling the raw emotion subjectively, and consider objectively, at least, a tiny bit at any rate, what the best course of action should be. The detached and objective me knew this was the end of the road. I'd be stuffing everything into a bag, catching a train to Moscow, a plane to Heathrow, trundling along the Piccadilly tube line and peering into the suburban back gardens of Hounslow on the way into London, in just a few days. It seemed safe, predictable, and almost a million miles away from where I was right now. Is that how it was to end? I would finish the chapter and close the book, just like that, as if none of this mattered?

I tried to guess what Tanya was thinking. She was quiet now. I didn't want her to feel that I was just one of those guys, who came, who seduced her, but now his train was leaving, and he's hopping on it with no feelings left for her, only for himself. I admit that there was a feeling of just wanting to get out without any further trouble, without looking back, in some corner of my being. But I didn't want anyone to see that corner of my mind. I cared what people thought of me, which itself is in some way a selfish motivation, perhaps. But I hated for anyone to think that I was heartless or selfish.

Then, a massive pang of loss hit me in the sternum. It surged through me like I imagine a heart attack perhaps feels like right at the beginning. A thump to the heart caused me to want to jump up suddenly. I didn't want today or tomorrow to be the last day ever for Tanya and me. A voice inside told me that she was the best girlfriend I had ever had (cynical me, or objective me, replied that you probably always think like that about your current girlfriend), I'd never felt so alive, or so desired, as she made me feel.

"Come on!" I said, "Let's go for a walk".

Outside we walked down Ulitsa Mira towards the train station, looped around the crescent shape set down and pick-up road in front of it, up the other side, and passed the babushkas selling their potatoes and vegetables.

"What does this mean for us? After you leave, will I ever see you again?" she asked, putting it in my court and not giving away her feelings on the topic, except the heavily nuanced way she asked it with a tentative voice. Perhaps self-preservation on her part, not wanting to lay herself bare for me to embarrass her.

"I love you so much. You know that."

"I love you too," she replied.

I didn't know if the relationship could continue, though, as clearly a long-distance one at three thousand miles apart was not practical. I was selfish enough to know, also, that I was unlikely to drop out of university and come and live in Russia. So, there was only one thing I could say.

"If I send you the money for a ticket, or if I have enough to leave behind, will you come to England and stay with me there?" The words came without really thinking.

"Oh yes! Genry, yes!! Absolutely yes!" she threw her whole body around mine and hugged me so tightly that I felt proud that the words that had come tumbling from me had been the right words.

It felt good, and I felt happy.

As quickly as the hug had started, though, it stopped, as big shows of affection were also something you did not see too much on the street. My mind raced forward to imagining Tanya waiting for me back in whatever place I would be living in Bristol in the next academic year. Was this even going to be possible? What would she do for money? Live off me? I barely had that much even for myself. What about visas and her right to even stay? There was quite a lot to think about there. We didn't talk about any of the details there and then. We just headed back to the apartment with at least a promise that things were not over between us. This appeased our minds. I knew, though, that what I had quickly promised was an easier thing to say than it was to do, which troubled me slightly. Even though I felt I had said the right thing, I could sense we both also felt that although we both wanted it to be so, was this, practically, going to happen? I hoped so at that moment, with every ounce of good-willing I could muster.

I headed over to the hostel towards the end of the afternoon to find Vicky in her room. I told her that I'd take the option to leave the country and asked her to communicate that to the official people. I didn't want to speak to them, but they had said earlier they'd be in touch the following day, a Wednesday, to tell me about the travel. There weren't many flights between Moscow and London at that time, I thought it was only one or two per week, but I wasn't sure which days. I felt that even if there was a flight in the next couple of days, that would surely be too soon to arrange to get me bundled onto it, so I could be waiting for up to a week, maybe.

In any case, how soon did they really need to remove my sorry soul from Russia entirely? Was it necessary to do it as quickly as possible, as the man had said, or would it be OK to do it at a more relaxed pace? Vicky said she was sure there was a London to Moscow flight on Mondays with British Airways, which returned to London the same day, but she also said there was also an Aeroflot flight on another day. We'd have to wait to see which one was to be my transport home.

I went up to my room in the hostel after seeing Vicky. Nobody was there, so I looked in on Becky and Jane's room. Al was in there with them, along with Sam and Hanna. Seeing me enter, Jane, ever the cheerful and chirpy soul, jumped up off her bed.

"Hi Genchik, a cup of tea, darling?" she said.

"Thanks, *Janushka*, yes, please," I replied.

"So, er… just wanted to say…." I began tentatively. "It's happened…" I began, looking around the room face to face. "I've been to the Deconat. They came and got me this morning from the apartment. We then got Vicky…" my heart was strongly beating as I tried to get the words out, "…we went in some special bus across town, escorted by a couple of their heavies. It was a bit scary. I felt like an outlaw. Anyway, they took us into a room with a police chief or government official, with some uniform on, and the university deputy rector. They said following my "crimes", which I admitted to the police last month, in the best interest of good relations between Russia and the UK, I have to leave the country.

I'm being sent back to England. *Repatriated* was the word they used. They're chucking me out." Saying this out loud to my friends made me a bit emotional, and my voice cracked and wobbled as I said the last words, my bottom lip taking on a mind of its own, contorting into a mini shake. It was a bit embarrassing as I thought I felt OK.

Becky came over and put her arms around my neck for a hug. "Aw, Henry!" was all she said. It was all I needed. I felt tears running down my cheeks as I closed my eyes tightly. Jane immediately joined us for a three-way hug as she added, "Genchik, that's ridiculous." The others present all exclaimed various words of protest to display their outrage and solidarity for my cause.

"Keep the faith, Henry man," Al said, then added, "listen, as terrible as this is, you do get to go home, and you can have a nice comfortable bed again and a proper wee pint in a proper pub and all the rest of it. Also, you want to be as far away as possible from seven years in a stinking Russian prison cell. D'you know what I mean?"

"Yeah, yeah. You're right." I sniffed as I wiped my face with my hands.

"Did they really say your "crimes"?" asked Hanna. Her

East Germany viewpoint was probably mainly interested in the language used and the charges against me.

"No, sorry, that was just my word," I replied, "They didn't say crimes exactly. There hasn't even been a trial, has there? I guess they are just saying that to avoid getting into all that, if I just go quietly, they will forget all about it."

Hanna sat back down with Sam, taking his hand in hers, "Well, you definitely don't want any of this to go further," she said, "just get out of this fucking country while you can, without any trouble".

"Arseholes!" said Becky.

"What about you and Tanya?" asked Sam, and I could tell from what perspective he was thinking about this.

Since he got together with Hanna, we saw him less and less. Other than her physical attractiveness, Hanna was also a sharp wit, principled and a little bit fearsome. The pair of them were often locked away in their room at the end of the corridor, where I presumed she had him for breakfast, lunch and dinner.

"Well, we just talked about it, and I'm going to try to get her to come over to England. She wants to, and I'll look into tickets or money for a ticket or something." I replied.

"When do you go?" asked Jane.

"Not sure," I replied. "Vicky is going to talk to them and find all that out".

"We're going to have to organise a big send-off party, then, as soon as possible. 'Cos if they think you're going to go quietly, they've got another think coming," said Jane, to universal approval.

"Yasss! That's what I'm talking about!" agreed Al.

Everyone thought it would be good to have a party that Friday in the hostel. According to most people's view, flights were Mondays and Tuesdays so I ought to have one more weekend here. I would leave it all to them, and in case I had to travel up to Moscow that weekend, Friday seemed the absolute latest for a leaving party.

CHAPTER 40

The next couple of days were strange ones. I was like a condemned man. Vicky confirmed that I would be on a flight the following Tuesday, which meant we could have a leaving party on Friday. She also said that the British Embassy in Moscow wanted me to visit them on Monday for a debrief, where I was to tell them everything that had happened. It sounded a bit daunting, and I had to decide which version, or how much detail, to say to them between now and then. Vicky reassured me it was their job to look after me and ensure my safe passage home, not hinder or judge me.

Tanya said that she would come to Moscow with me, and her friend Alina would come, too, as we could stay at Alina's brother's place in Moscow. I had met her brother, Mikhail, at Oleg's place, though I could not recall speaking to him. But I was grateful for their hospitality. Then when we parted for the final time, they would return to Voronezh together, Alina giving Tanya company for the return trip. It was not a good idea for single females to travel alone on the sleeper trains in Russia, but Alina would be helpful moral support for Tanya.

The word had spread about my news, and I felt like

I was a bit of a minor celebrity. People who passed me in the corridors would either high five me or give me a thumbs up of sorts. It was not just the British students, either, but the African and other groups, too. Only the Russians were a little bit harder to tell with.

My friends amongst them were smiley and supportive, but I also knew that it was from amongst the Russians that the initial informing must have come. Those who were not my friends would just blank me or remain inscrutable, so I wouldn't know if they even knew me, or of me. As for Sergei, I didn't see him around these days, and, I was grateful for that, as I would not have wanted to speak to him about the situation at all.

Sofia, who had warned me to be careful of the cat-throwing-Sergei many months before, seemed to tease me with her comment.

"So, Genry, I hear you are leaving us already? Are you going back to your mama and papa?" she said in passing, somewhat patronisingly.

Over the months in Voronezh, I had developed a bit of a spikey relationship with Sofia for some reason. In my mind, I think it could have been because she was offended that I didn't fancy her as I felt she expected most men to. Everything about her was disagreeable, from her apparent obsession with trying to be the prettiest girl in school to the way she wore her East European jeans too tight so you could make out her personality downstairs a bit too easily. If Sofia were in an American movie, she'd be the pretty popular one, but also the bitchy one. There was a gym of sorts in the hostel's basement, with some benches and a few free weights, which I went to about three times in the early weeks before I gave up, as I was not much of a sportsman anyway. On seeing me heading there one day, Sofia had asked if I could show her my big muscles sometime. It was in front of a group of her friends, so I felt embarrassed and a bit humiliated by the comment as she giggled at me. Defensively I had retaliated by replying that I'd be happy to, as long as she'd show me her nipples. The funny thing was I had wanted to say tits, but I hadn't yet learned the word, so all I could bring to mind was the rather anatomical word *nipples*. She blushed instantly and looked ten times more embarrassed by this than I had been by her comment, perhaps. We never really hit it off after that.

"No, Sofia," I replied. "I haven't talked to my parents for some time. But you're right; I'm leaving next week. I've not decided where to go, though. I think perhaps Paris or Rome, maybe Madrid even. I spent six months in Paris last year. It's great. Have you ever been?"

That shut her up. I know it was mean of me as she was highly unlikely to go there ever, I thought.

The ex-boyfriend, Vladimir, popped up, too, in the hostel the day after my "arrest". All the times I'd seen him previously, which wasn't many, he seemed generally relaxed to see me. He was a gentle person; I never saw him drunk or partying. He knew who I was, and he'd been polite when we met. I thought me being with Tanya wasn't issue for him. But seeing him here now at the end of the corridor in conversation with a couple of other people gave me a sense of unease. They murmured together, and I saw him look over in my direction a couple of times. I had a feeling that he may have been more involved with the situation I now found myself in than I had previously credited him for. It was a society that for two generations had informed on one another routinely as part of life, so a natural habit for many, especially so for those who had recently served in the army, in service of the motherland.

Alexei was another person who buttonholed me quite purposefully in my last few days. He wanted to offer me, and him by default, the opportunity to make some money. As I already knew, Alexei took regular trips to London to flog his goods and come back with cash or other western goods to sell here. Items he took to England were usually old soviet military paraphernalia, such as army watches and medals, and he brought back things like jeans, condoms, and aftershave.

Each country at the time lacked a supply of these things and had a desire to buy them. Alexei laid out a few watches for me back in the apartment. They were pretty good looking, with curious sting faces of green, blue and dark grey.

These watches, Alexei explained, were issued to the higher echelon of the soviet army, so think colonels and generals, and were of the highest soviet precision and quality. They were chunky, a bit like some Rolexes I could recall, with metal surrounds, but they looked distinctly Russian with the Cyrillic writing in the centre of the dial. I wasn't too interested in the piece of metal and glass all that much, and I wasn't too concerned with his patter. But what I did believe, due to my trust in him, was that they would sell for a profit back in England.

In the end, he convinced me to take around thirty, and I paid him the equivalent of about five pounds each. He must have made a quid or two on each from me, but he explained he was not going to England for a while, so he was happy for me to have the opportunity. He said I could sell them for at least twenty pounds in London.

"Help you buy a plane ticket for Tanya, even!" he winked. I smiled back.

I ended up taking them back with me, and he was right. I sold the first few in Camden Market and the rest at a summer festival in Bristol.

However, Alexei took my breath away when he jumped down to the floor to pull something from under the bed.

"Now this, Genry," he said with obvious pleasure and his huge cheeky boisterous grin, "is going to take your breath away!"

Alexei pulled out a long ruby red velvety bag wrapped around something. He fished inside and pulled out an antique sword, complete with a hard leather scabbard.

The handle was straight but curved over at the end. It was ornately detailed in the metal with a jewel of some sort in the centre. I could also see that the scabbard or sheath was decorated with the same metal and bejewelled detail at intervals going down it, and the whole thing was slightly curved too, as was the sword.

"An imperial Russian Cossack shashka!" he said of the sword, "genuine item from around 1900-1905".

"No way!" I said, "I am not taking that through Heathrow Airport".

"For five hundred dollars, I would sell this to you, and you could easily make your money back three or four times over," he explained.

It was an impressive thing, and I was surprised he'd never shown it to me before. I wondered if it had been there under the bed for a long time without me knowing, or if Alexei had recently swaggered along Ulitsa Mira waving this about in the air with his mischievous grin. Either way, it would not fit in my suitcase, nor could I even contemplate smuggling this through the airport, and finally, I did not have a spare five hundred dollars, so that was the end of it. It would have to be just the watches stuffed into socks and shoes and so on in my bag, and I would end up wearing three of them, too.

As the countdown had now begun for me to leave the country, I struggled to hold back time. It was as if someone had pressed fast forward, and I couldn't slow it down. The day of the party arrived very quickly, and Al and Tom, with Vicky's help, had secured the use of a room on the ground floor for a party.

The room was just along from the main foyer and was usually used for functions, meetings, or classes. It was large enough to fit fifty people quite easily. The official reason given to our hosts for the party was nothing to do with my departure, but that it would just be nice to have a party. As we had just welcomed the new influx of UK students to Voronezh a fortnight earlier, we also mentioned that as the excuse for a party. But we most certainly did not say it was my leaving party.

However, it was exactly what it ended up being, in some measure at least.

CHAPTER 41

I thought a lot about my imminent return to England. I hadn't told my parents about any of this. *Dear parents, I am coming back next week, following a Russian government decision to repatriate me in the best interests of our two countries following charges brought against me for buying and supplying drugs to my fellow students in Voronezh.* That, I reasoned, was just not a conversation, or a letter, that I could even begin to contemplate.

Every time I began to think about how to communicate this, I ended up just moving it out of my mind and into the "too difficult" pile. I was, therefore, most likely going to arrive at Heathrow unannounced and would make my way from there by myself. I could go to Bristol straight away, where I could easily stay on other student friends' sofas, or I had also begun formulating a plan to stay in London. My sister Anna had several friends in London, and a couple of these I knew well enough to visit and who would put me up.

It all seemed so far away and unreal right now. It had been around seven months since I was in England, and while that is not a very long time, my weird and wonderful ride in Russia had been a different experience for me, far removed from my comfort zone. I tried to imagine walking through Heathrow, catching the tube to London, walking up ordinary streets with no snow on them. It all seemed alien. All I could think to do was plan one move at a time. I'd probably go to London first, stay with my sister's friend, Emma, who lived in Brixton and then decide.

I didn't have any party clothes for the Friday send-off, so I put on my cleanest jeans, a fresh t-shirt and a dark blue long-sleeved shirt. It had a slight sheen that said "party" more than any of my other shirts. As we were staying in the building, I didn't need a jumper or coat, although I did put on my usual sturdy boots rather than trainers, which I habitually shunned as they were useless if they happened to get beyond the front door.

There was what felt like 100% attendance by the British group, and at least a couple of dozen again came from other groups. Issa, Mamadou, and a handful of the African contingent came. Hanna came as well, as did her roommate with a couple of her other friends. Of course, Tanya, Nadia, and Alexei came, and even Oleg "the bear" Medvedev, and Vadim, were there, which was nice. Tanya looked gorgeous in a pale green blouse with intricately embroidered stitching running vertically down each side, her silvery grey high line jacket, and black skirt and tights down to black shin-high boots. Even though we were only going downstairs and not even leaving the building,

I noted with internal appreciation on my part the effort people had made as if they were going *out* out. Nadia sported her black dress and tights and her silky blue and black blouse, which was her definite going out top, which both clung to, and showed off, her impressive bust. Overall, I think there were more than fifty people, but numbers seemed to increase as the music drew people down the stairs from the floors above as the evening progressed. It was no nightclub, of course, and with chairs pushed to the sides and *Bring Your Own* drinks on tables or under chairs in private stashes, it had a bit of a corny school disco vibe about it.

However, that was not detrimental to the enjoyment and lent it a feeling of innocence. I liked that feeling. It was like a tonic to me, knowing that I would be deported within a few days. Someone had set up music in the shape of a dual-cassette super woofer ghetto blaster by the drinks table, and Scottish Gus had taken it upon himself to be the DJ, or at least the caretaker of the cassette changes when needed. I don't recall if one of the students had brought that lump of a thing with them as carry-on luggage or whether it was now a permanent Russian resident, but either way, it was not indigenous to the region.

It was a random mix, from Beats International and Soul 2 Soul to the Fine Young Cannibals. Bands like Depeche Mode and Spandau Ballet were popular in

Central and Eastern Europe, so Tony Hadley crooning *Gold* made an entry. Dexys Midnight Runners, already overplayed even in 1993, made an outing to a rolling of the eyes by many. Gus circled back to the Proclaimers now and then, their songs being well known to everyone, so we all screamed along, holding our drinks aloft. *I'm Gonna Be,* and *Letter from America* seemed to be talking to my situation, and I held both of Tanya's hands and told her that I would walk 500 miles just to be the man that ends up next to her. As her spoken English was poor, I was unsure if she was even familiar with the song, but she got the gist. "But it's more like 5000 miles, Genry, not 500!" she said in my ear.

As the evening wore on and spirits were elevated, more and more people came to me to slap me on the back and wish me well with a hug. Even the newly arrived British students who hadn't known me for long were clinking glasses with me, wishing me luck. The evening was becoming a farewell party in my honour.

Through conversations with people from the recently arrived St Petersburg group, I had found out that my story had been retold to them up there before their departure.

The organisers had gathered all the British overseas students together, not just the ones about to come to Voronezh, but students in St Petersburg, Moscow and other cities to tell my tale as a warning to others. I found it bizarre to hear that perhaps more than a hundred

British students, almost none of whom I knew, had been gathered into rooms around Russia to be told about my case, to warn them against dabbling on the wrong side of the law. My deportation, or repatriation, was to remind them to behave themselves.

My evening of celebration reached a crescendo quickly as I found more eyes looking to me for their focus. I clambered onto a chair and looked down on all the faces, holding my arms and my drink aloft. Everyone toasted me back as the music blared, and they chanted my name. Someone put on *Should I Stay or Should I Go* by the Clash, which was perhaps an attempt to be funny, but I knew that the trouble I could be in might easily be double if I had stayed. It felt like a perfect send-off, and to me, it felt like everyone was getting swept up in the mood, jumping up and down, and the celebrations were a significant release of the tension of recent weeks.

I spotted Vladimir, the ex, sitting on the far side near the door from my vantage point. I had not seen him before then, and I knew he was not there as my friend but more likely to have come to observe for a bit. I came down off the chair. Tanya looked a bit glum by now and stood with Nadia and Becky. Maybe she was not enjoying this as much as I was. I skirted the room aiming for the door to visit the loos, and passed directly in front of Vladimir, who caught my eye and beckoned me in close to talk. I leaned towards him, and he moved his head to the side of mine to speak into my ear. He was smiling, so what he said came as a jolt to me.

As I faced the wall behind his head, I heard him say in my ear, in good English, "time to fuck off, now, my friend!" I stood back up straight. He smiled, raised his glass of beer, downed it, placed it on the table, and left the room.

I turned back to the room, puffing out some air from my lungs. I didn't feel like I wanted to be a celebrity anymore. It felt like Vladimir was not only pleased to see me leaving but that he was pleased with himself, too, that he had helped achieve it. My mind raced about, had he been there when we were smoking joints? Was he the one who had informed on me? I didn't remember seeing him. I hadn't seen him more than about three times in six months. A memory came to my mind of seeing Connor, Gus and the Edinburgh lot some time ago and me telling them off for not being very discreet smoking in the hostel. Gus had replied that Vladimir had just been there and had not seemed to mind and that I had no need to worry. But now I considered that perhaps Vladimir had been researching us and gathering observations on our group for the whole time.

We were made to feel welcome; it was certainly fair to say that, but certain people amongst our hosts had also probably been noting what we were doing and reporting back to the authorities of the Deconat throughout our time. Force of habit.

Don't Leave Me This Way by the Communards blasted into the room. I looked over to Tanya, she was still with the others but was looking around for me, and her eyes found mine. This track was as ironic as the Clash song had been before. As I looked at Tanya, I felt that she was saying these words to me now. A sudden and tremendous sadness swept over me now. I felt guilt at leaving her next week. I cut through the dance floor, and as I did so, I passed Jane, who was dancing with her man Maxim. He looked awkward and completely without rhythm, like someone who never usually danced and didn't want to be doing so now. She grabbed both my hands. She was drunk, but I didn't mind that – we all were. She sang out *Don't Leave Me This Way* in time with the music, throwing her head back in a playful way and then pulling me in for a hug.

As I got to Tanya; she and Nadia told me they wanted to return home, and I was ready to do the same anyway.

We had already been there nearly two hours by then, and Vladimir had soured the hostel party for me. Alexei, Oleg, Vadim and Nadia were ready to go. Becky, Al, Tom, Sam and Hanna said they would come too. We made our way out of there and on to the after-party.

We left the hostel gig in full swing, but it seemed like a good idea to remove myself from it. I didn't want the whole evening to be about me. I am sure it wasn't anyway. Of course, human beings are social animals and need little excuse to throw a party. For some reason, I sympathised with the Russian authorities in a fleeting moment. I knew my situation was their choice, but also, I didn't want it any more awkward for any of us.

CHAPTER 42

It was only a short walk to the apartment, across the rough ground behind the hostel, and rather than go up to the third floor for my coat, I decided to make do with what I was wearing, crossing the fifty metres arms linked with Tanya and Nadia. I was hot from the party and rosy-cheeked, and as we hit the freezing air, the refreshment it brought was temporarily welcome but that didn't last long.

"Ooh, it's so cold!" I said, pulling their elbows to my sides.

We laughed and stumbled, and I pulled them closer. Tanya and Nadia squeezed into me, and I felt the softness of their coats as well as some of their body heat making it through my shirt, which was welcome. Feeling both of their bodies pushing into me from either side was a nice distraction from the frigid air, too.

"Keep me warm, girls, please!" I implored of them. As well as the cold, it had started to snow again, and the wind blustered in flurries. It pushed the cold right through my torso.

"Genry, why didn't you bring your coat? It's at least minus 15 degrees right now!" chided Tanya.

"I don't know. I was hot in the hostel. We're here now anyway." We entered the archway that housed the entrance to the steps that led to the apartment's front door.

Once inside the warmth, we set about enjoying ourselves once again. Nadia and Tanya arranged a few bits of food for the table; drinks appeared from cupboards, and vodka was extracted from the freezer. The party resumed with chatter and laughter. Alexei held people's attention with his usual wit and charm and stories of his latest entrepreneurial conquests. At the same time, Al and Tom had decided to educate big Oleg about how Scotland was not a place in England but a country within the British Isles. I am sure Oleg knew this anyway, and I think he must have just been enjoying winding Al up by claiming ignorance.

After we'd been there for some fifteen or twenty minutes, the door opened and closed, and Jane arrived in a swirl of energy. She put her coat in the corner and sought Becky and me out. She was upset. A few drinks often got the better of her quite quickly, which could also explain a flustered appearance with Jane, but this looked different.

"I'm done with that bastard!" she exclaimed. "He's only told me that he's going back to his girlfriend, hasn't he?!" her red face was full of emotion, suggesting she had just been arguing with Maxim.

"What do you mean?" I said, "what girlfriend?"

Jane hadn't mentioned anything before about him having any other girlfriend. However, from the looks I noticed between Becky and Jane at that moment, I guessed the existence of a prior, or other, girlfriend was something that they both had talked about before. Becky extended her arms to Jane, and they embraced each other with a big squeezy hug.

"I'm so sorry, Janushka, honey!" said Becky "these Russian men..." she said, shaking her head. Becky had had her fair share of man trouble with Alexei, but she was philosophical about it.

She and he slept together reasonably frequently, but there was no pretence that it was anything more than what it was. I knew he slept around quite a bit, and she knew it, too. She didn't like that he was such a shitbag in that sense, but she was at peace with it, and besides that, she also had someone back in England, so whatever they had seemed to suit them.

"Well, he can go fuck himself, then. Not much more to say than that is there? I need a drink!" Maybe Jane was more philosophical about this than I had taken her to be. "It wouldn't have lasted anyway," she added.

Alexei himself came to join us at this point, holding a drink out for Jane, his timing impeccable.

"Thanks," she said.

"Up your bottom!" Alexei said, in his accented

English, looking from face to face for our approval extending his glass to us.

Jane giggled, "Er, it's *'bottoms up'* if you want to be completely correct about it, but, sure 'up your bottom!'"

We all clinked our lasses. I think Alexei knew he had said it wrong, but I also think he took pleasure in saying it incorrectly for comic effect. Writing this now, I am reminded of a time when I was visiting Mumbai for work, years later. I was in a group of people travelling in two cars around the city. Setting off on one of the short zips about town, the driver of the second car indicated that my group should go ahead in the first car, and he would follow us in the second car. To my great amusement, he phrased it thus: "You go ahead, and I will come behind you, in your backside".

"I just wanted to say," continued Alexei, "that you are a great guy, Genry. It is not every year that we get good English guys coming; maybe one or two, we hope at least. But you are a good one, as Doc was last year, and I will miss you when you are gone. I hope you will not forget us, and that we will see you again. To our continued acquaintance and friendship!"

"Yes! To that!" I said as we clinked our glasses along with Becky and Jane. I had been thinking over the last few days of not much other than the wrench of leaving and flying back to England next week. I was devastated about being ejected from Russia and unsure how to tell my parents or my university back home. I hadn't done anything about it yet. I was also valiantly trying to compartmentalise the heartbreak I started to feel when I contemplated being apart from Tanya. I loved her and did not want this to simply stop. I had already envisaged her back in Bristol with me, being home in my student digs when I got home, coming out with me everywhere I went. We would impress everyone by chatting away in Russian together, and I would be proud to have such a girlfriend in boring old grey and dull England, however shallow that may seem.

I noticed Nadia and Tanya at that moment getting their coats on.

"We're going to get some more drinks," Nadia said as I walked over.

"Shall I come with you?" I asked Tanya, grabbing her hand.

"No, it's OK, you stay and enjoy your party," she replied, and I thought it made sense for me to stay as, in a way, I was still feeling like the guest of honour, fresh from the toasts and the party earlier in the night. I pressed a few notes into her hand from the money I had in my jeans pocket to contribute.

"OK, see you in a bit," I said and kissed her. She turned away quickly, or so it felt, and they disappeared out of the door.

When I returned to the room, the conversation

moved on to the Pyatigorsk trip, which all my UK friends would be going on quite soon. It was a shame I would miss that, for I really liked the trips we had taken so far. I loved to travel, and exploring more of this great country would have been really interesting. The journey right at the start by boat from Moscow to St Petersburg and back had been a great way to see the country and people. St Petersburg was a beautiful city, different from Voronezh, and linked to European history. I remembered Katya, my first Russian romantic encounter, and my great relief when she had failed to get back to the boat on time.

Then there was the beautiful Oksana, whom I mixed up with Katya in my ignorance, and our night kissing under the stars and on uncomfortable planks. Before meeting Tanya, I even exchanged a couple of letters with Oksana in the weeks afterwards.

In November, the trip to Uzbekistan was also a highlight, with the exotic herbs and spices of the markets of Samarkand, the minarets and sandstone centre of Bukhara, and the presence of Genghis Khan still in the faces of the local people. The dysentery we all caught on that trip was not a fantastic experience, of course.

Buying alcohol should have been a quick trip, either from the kiosk close by, or the station approach direct from peoples' car boots. Either option would have taken no more than ten minutes, really, so after fifteen minutes, I was thinking Tanya and Nadia would be back any moment. I noticed after half an hour that they were still not back and remarked upon this to Oleg, who did not seem to share my concern and told me not to worry. After forty minutes, I was getting worried; after 11 pm, two females out on their own could be vulnerable, and it was absolutely freezing out there, too. After three-quarters of an hour, my brain told me I needed to react. Alcohol was perhaps overdramatizing the situation, but I didn't really appreciate that. I thought that something must have happened, and I decided I needed to go out to find them. They had now been gone for easily half an hour longer than necessary. Yet, I was the only person to have noticed this.

As I got more fretful, I recalled feeling that there had been something odd about Tanya tonight as if she was distracted, but I couldn't put my finger on anything. Going towards the coats, I remembered that I didn't bring mine, but I knew I needed one, and looked through the ones by the door.

Oleg approached. "I'm worried about Tanya; I'm going to look for her," I told him, still sorting through the coats.

"Here, take this then," he said, offering me what looked like a padded puffer type of coat, navy blue. I grabbed it and stepped into my boots and laced them up, and then stumbled out of the door.

As I left the darkness of the stairwell, I began to

feed my arms into the coat, stepping into the archway heading for the main street. Hitting the main drag of Ulitsa Mira, the cold really hit me. It was also snowing again now with a whip of a wind coming directly up the street. Having got my arms into the coat, I realised it was too small. My hands and wrists protruded far beyond the cuffs. I struggled to get the zippers to meet each other around my front, and when I did finally manage, I could only zip it partway up my chest.

This could not be Oleg's, I cursed to myself. It was more of a summer coat. The cold was really biting at me. If it was Oleg's, I reasoned he probably bought it for its value as a fashionable western design, and definitely not for a Russian winter, or because it fitted him, which it couldn't possibly do. I trudged on. Although there were streetlights, I couldn't see much as the snow was now driving into my face. I forced my bare hands into my jeans and tried to continue on the same side of the road I had begun on, the same side as the apartment. This would ultimately lead to the road intersection across from the train station. Tanya and Nadia couldn't possibly be standing outside the station in this weather, I reasoned, if they had even bought any drinks there.

My resolve was rapidly waning, it was painfully cold, and the ridiculous trendy jacket was doing nothing for me. My knuckles were stinging even inside my pockets, and my head was hurting. The snow stabbed at my face like hard, metal nails. If it was minus 15 degrees earlier in the evening, and was undoubtedly lower than that now. My breathing was so quick I felt like hyperventilation would be next, like when you jump into a freezing lake.

I had no choice but to turn back to the safety of the apartment. They had to be inside somewhere; I reasoned that being outside wasn't an option, so I wouldn't find the girls out here.

Upon returning, I saw Alexei nearest the door. Getting my breath back gradually, I explained a little about my mission to find the girls to him.

"Don't worry, Genry, they are grown-ups. And they're used to Russian weather, unlike you," he explained, taking my excuse for a coat, glancing at it quizzically. "They must have taken shelter inside somewhere. We'll find out when they return."

Oleg appeared and took the jacket from Alexei, almost sheepishly. "That wasn't very useful, Oleg, and it's very small!" I said. "It was impossible to stay outside for more than a few minutes in it. Is it yours?"

"Sorry, yes, I just got it. Excellent brand - look," he said by way of explanation, showing me the logo of a cockerel, "Le Coq Sportif! Many football teams in Europe use this brand, some national teams, too," he added by way of explanation.

"It's too cold for a football kit," I replied scathingly.

Ten minutes later, I had warmed up again in the

main room, but was no more reassured about Tanya's well-being when the door opened and closed. I caught sight of the bathroom door closing, heard it being locked, and hoped it was Tanya. I went to the hallway and was relieved to see Nadia hanging up her coat, holding a bag of drinks. I looked to Nadia for reassurance.

"We're back!" she said, which confirmed to me that it was Tanya in the bathroom. "It's so cold out there, though!

A funny thing happened. We were at the station, and we saw Tanya's aunt there. She and Tanya's uncle are in Voronezh to see some friends, so we got in their car with them to keep warm, and they had a bit of a chat."

As Nadia explained it all to me, I was pleased to find something that made sense of it all. I had been worried that they'd had an accident, or they'd been attacked, or I don't know what else. Nadia's face looked a bit odd, though. Gone was her usual near-permanent grin. Her face looked flushed and serious, and her hair slightly ruffled. It was odd, but I processed this to being inconvenienced at having to sit in the car for ages while her friend had a catch up with her relatives, right in the middle of a fun night, which can't have been much fun for Nadia.

I went to the bathroom door and knocked. "Tanya, it's me. Are you there?" I called through the door.

"Yes, Genry. I'll be out soon. We saw my aunt! Had

a chat with her!"

"OK," I said back. I heard the running of taps, and she sounded busy and distracted in there, so I left her to it and went back to the main room.

After five minutes, she was still not out, so I returned to the bathroom door. It was quiet on the other side. "Tanya... are you OK?" I spoke softly to the door frame.

"Yes," came the immediate reply, followed by some movement noises, then what sounded like the shower being turned on.

"What are you doing in there?"

"I... I fell... I slipped in the street. I got dirt and slush all over me. I have to take a shower. I'll be out soon."

This seemed a bit strange to me, so I went to Nadia in the main room. She'd not mentioned anything about falling over in the street, and I didn't know why falling over should mean you had to take a shower. I told her what Tanya had said as her face processed my words. "Yes, she slipped right on the ice by the kiosk and went into the dirty snow. I think she wants to clean herself up," she said.

Something didn't add up to me. But it was late, and I was now too tired to get my head around this. My head was still whirring from the whole evening, the party in the hostel, with drinks both there and here.

The party was slowing now a little bit. Tanya was still in the bathroom when Vadim said he would make a move. Oleg asked to go with him, so he could get a lift. Oleg asked me if Tanya was OK, and I told him she was, but that she'd fallen in the street and got a bit messed up.

After what seemed like ages, but perhaps around fifteen minutes, Tanya came out of the bathroom. Her hair was still wet, and she was wearing jeans and a jumper top, contrasting to the tights, skirt, and blouse she had been wearing before. I went to give her a hug and kissed her on the lips. She was shaken up. That much was clear.

"I tore my tights when I fell in the street, and my skirt is messed up. So, I just thought the easiest thing was to shower and change," she explained.

"Sure, I understand," I said. "I came to look for you, as you were gone so long. But I didn't see you, and it was so cold that I had to turn back quite quickly."

"Sorry I was gone so long; we were walking past some cars at the station, and someone called me. It was my aunt; I couldn't believe it! My uncle is in Voronezh this week for something to do with his work, so they both came. I had not seen her in so long, so I had a good catch up with them in their car. I used to be quite close to her. And then, on top of that, I fell over on the way back here." It all sounded a bit, well... made up, but I couldn't see what for. But I didn't want to get into it with people all around.

Not long after this, more people began to leave, and eventually, the party was over. We settled down quickly and tidied most of the mess into a single mess to deal with in the morning on the table in the living room. Alexei and Nadia took the living room day bed and floor mattress, while Tanya and I took the bedroom. We lay in the dark next to each other, but I sensed she wasn't sleeping. Although I was drowsy, I rolled towards her and reached my arm around her as she lay facing away from me. I heard her sniff in what sounded like a blocked nose and felt her body shake slightly. Something else had happened earlier this evening. I was sure of it.

"Tanya?" I asked and swallowed hard.

"Yes."

"What happened today? You've never mentioned your aunt before…." I waited for a few seconds, but there was no reply.

"Nadia said your aunt was here visiting relatives. But you said it is because your uncle is here for work."

Still no reply.

"You both said you fell in the slush, but everything is frozen solid."

"I didn't see my aunt, Genry," she replied finally, "I'm sorry".

"OK…?"

"You're going back to England next week, and I'm going to be back on my own again. I don't know. I don't know what I'm thinking. Without you, I am just me, again." She said.

"What are you talking about?" I leaned up on my elbow, looking at the dark form, which I think was her, still looking away from me.

"I'm sorry, Genry, I wasn't with my aunt. I was with someone else," she began sobbing. "I was with a guy. I was with someone; I had sex. When we went to get the drinks."

My mind did a complete somersault. I was utterly stunned. My mouth went dry, and my hands began to tremble.

I didn't know what to say.

"How...? What...?" was all I could manage.

"I don't know what I was thinking," she continued, "but all I know is, over the last few days, I have been scared about what's going to happen to me after you leave. Nadia and I went to the kiosk, the one nearby, where we bought champagne to celebrate after seeing the apartment.

"Yes. So?" I remembered the kiosk very well. Not only had I bought cigarettes there myself a few times, but I also now remembered the guy who ran it quite clearly, Ivan, with the cigarette hanging out of his mouth, winking at Tanya when we were last there together. I felt sick.

"We asked for some drinks, but it was freezing outside. Ivan invited us inside to wait." She continued. "Then he... he and his friend...Vlad... they invited us upstairs. I don't know why, but we went up. He gave us vodka - too much. We slept with them." She let out another sob.

"You and Nadia, both?" I asked. All I could now see in my mind was how great they looked earlier in the evening, when I first saw them in the hostel wearing their going out sexy clothes. I couldn't stop my mind wandering and imagining those two gangster Russian *biznessmen* who probably treated women as mere conquests, with their hands all over Tanya and Nadia. I couldn't bear to listen, yet I wanted to know.

"What's upstairs? I asked, "Is it an office or...?"

"They have, like, an apartment with TV, music, sofa... and bed," she continued.

No, this was too much. They had beds up there, too! I couldn't contain all the thoughts in my mind. I was no longer tired but fully awake, fired up and angry. All I could imagine was these two bastards, who flirted with their female customers daily, and who no doubt screwed their girlfriends and whichever other girls succumb to their winks and brutish charms. They didn't exactly have to work hard tonight; two girls came around, dressed up nicely, knocked on their window, came inside and gave themselves to them. I was beyond hurt. I felt crushed and paralysed by what I was hearing.

"I'm sorry, Genry, it wasn't planned. It just happened," was all she said next.

For some reason, I wanted to know more details. I

almost wanted to hear if they were pressured into it or trapped. Did they do this willingly? I didn't know what to think.

"Did they force you?" was all I could say.

"No. As I said, I was confused about you leaving. I wanted to take back control of my own future…" was all I could hear. Tanya was still talking, but all I heard was that she did this willingly. She chose to. She wanted to. I couldn't help now but begin to wonder if she just lay back and let it happen, or if she instigated it even; did she come onto him, voluntarily, and enjoy it?!

I stood up. I located my clothes and quickly put them on. I had to get out of there. I didn't want to be there anymore.

"Genry, I'm sorry, believe me, it was an accident!" she was crying and sitting up in bed now.

"It doesn't sound like an accident," I replied.

With that, I headed for the door and put on my boots. I was going back to the hostel tonight. I needed to be on my own. In a moment of clarity, I spotted and took an oversized coat which I saw on the peg now although I hadn't seen it there earlier. If it was Alexei's, I was sure he wouldn't mind me borrowing it. I left the apartment and shut the door behind me, breathing hard, shaking slightly. As I exited the stairwell and into the night, I noticed the snow had stopped, and the wind had subsided. Everything was deadly quiet. It was that particular silence that only a fresh fall of snow can achieve by muffling everything. I was looking in the direction of the hostel, but in the eerie calm, I abruptly turned to the right, through the archway towards Ulitsa Mira. I was headed for the kiosk. Without really thinking it through, I headed straight out into the middle of the road, crossing to the other side.

There was nobody around. By now, it was well after 2 am, perhaps nearer to 3 am. The streetlamps lit up the pavements, blanketed in a fresh white carpet.

Upon reaching the end of the street, the road gave way to the wide arched crescent upon which the kiosk was located, only about five shops along to the left. I slowed to amble around the corner, and still, there was nobody around. I had tears in my eyes as I tried to make sense of what I had heard.

Without the wind and snow, it didn't feel as cold as it had earlier, and the coat must have helped, but I was also fuelled predominantly by adrenalin. I found some gloves inside the coat pockets and gratefully put them on as I walked past the kiosk without breaking stride. It was dark, all closed now. Their glass window carried the sign "Hard Currency Changed Here". It was protected by metal bars that fanned out like sun rays from the bottom to the top corners with 6-inch gaps between the bars and a small rectangular opening below for Ivan and Vlad to carry out their transactions through. I tried to imagine Tanya and Nadia standing there hours before and wondered if Ivan had fancied Tanya or Nadia first. Nadia was single and could do what she wanted, of course, and maybe one of these lecherous bastards had noticed her boobs, which started the flirtation. But then Tanya herself had seemingly just told me that she was trying to assert control over her destiny, so maybe she chose to go inside this grubby little place and initiated the whole thing?

I continued with my internal dialogue; whatever had made this happen, these guys did not deserve either my girlfriend or my friend. I was angry at how happy and smug they must be feeling right now, sleeping in their beds, after Tanya and Nadia had come around earlier, invited themselves in, fucked them, and left. As I got to the end of the crescent, I turned back around to make a return pass. At that moment, I spotted a shape on the ground. It appeared to be a stick of some sort, but it looked like a metal pole as I leaned close. I picked it up. It was a thin piece of metal about 50cm long with a 1-2 cm diameter. It felt weighty, like a bit of steel bar to reinforce concrete in construction.

I knew what I was going to do. I looked around me, and still, there was not a soul around, so I strode the few metres along towards the kiosk, faced the window and whacked the pole into the glass, in between the metal sunrays. The first strike smashed the glass on the left-hand side, as did the second on the right-hand side. I heard a delayed clap thudding around the crescent as the sound echoed back. My heart was racing. As I struck it for the third time, there was no glass left as the whole pane had fallen in by now, and the pole cartwheeled out of my hand into the shop, hitting the back wall with a crash.

Realising this would probably have woken them inside, I instantly went into flight mode. I was certainly not going to fight or confront these guys.

Fact is, they were was as hard as nails, from what I could tell. I wanted to teach them a lesson with my metal pole, but I didn't want to do this face to face. I ran just as fast as I could without falling on the slippery surface, back towards Ulitsa Mira. I heard a shout behind me as I reached the corner, that sounded like it came from inside the building. One of them, I reckoned. I rounded the corner taking tiny, almost balletic steps so as not to slip, but an ungainly dancer for sure, and headed up the street. I didn't want them to get as far as looking around the corner to see me crossing into the archway, so I continued my escape as fast as possible. As I crossed the road ahead, I saw a car approaching from the top. A thought occurred to me that if the militsiya stopped me for this, what would they do? This was another crime to add to my rap sheet, but I was already being deported, so it couldn't get any worse. I sprinted over the road into the archway and rested on the edge of the building to look back, just in time to see the car passing down the road. I noticed that it wasn't a police car. It didn't slow and just cruised on by, and I was convinced the driver couldn't see me anyway where I was, in the dark shadows, chest heaving. I jogged on through the waste ground and headed back to the hostel.

Al was asleep in our room when I got there, so I just piled my clothes at the end of my bed and got in quietly so as not to wake him. I slowly calmed down from my excursions, staring up at the ceiling, but still felt stunned by Tanya's confession of cheating. I had dozens of conversations in my head with her about how wronged I felt. I also remembered Jane's words from earlier about how she didn't care about Maxim anymore, now that he'd betrayed her love. She was just going to turn her back on him and be in England soon. I was going to be in England even sooner than Jane, yet I felt I loved Tanya or wanted for our love to still exist, and I wasn't sure that I could just close the door and throw away the key. My feelings for her went deep, and I couldn't just flick them off like a light switch. However, I could not see past images in my mind of her with Ivan right now, nor how I would be able to get over this. I lay in a foetal position in bed, shaking my head, tossing and turning, and until eventually, probably close to dawn, I finally dropped off.

CHAPTER 43

I awoke mid-morning. Al had already left. It was Saturday, and I remembered he had plans to go out in town with some of the new St Petersburg lot to show them the sights, but I was still surprised he had gone this early. He would probably be out most of the day. It was a bright sunny day with a blue sky, and I could see the fresh snow layer from my window, sparkling like diamonds. It was a beautiful sight, and I nearly started to enjoy it before I remembered my personal pain. I felt miserable quite quickly. I made some tea and found something to eat.

I knew that tomorrow I had to be on the train to Moscow with my bags packed, ahead of visiting the British Embassy on Monday, and then catching the London flight the following day. I also realised that Tanya was coming to Moscow with me, as we were supposed to be staying at Alina's brother's place. It was too awkward now. From a practical point of view, I also didn't know if I could do it alone. I'd have to speak with Tanya today to sort this all out one way or another.

Presently, I heard voices in the corridor and I recognised Jane's voice chirpily calling back to someone. I opened the door a few inches, enough to peek at the back of Jane, walking away, and caught sight of Becky standing inside their room opposite through the still open door.

"Hiya," she said, "you alright?"

My eyes were probably red and gave me away, I thought, although she would have been within her rights to think me hungover.

I shook my head and closed and opened my eyes, "No, not really." I said. "Can I talk to you?"

A few minutes later, I was in my bed, back under the covers but sitting up, back to the wall. Becky had settled on the spare bed, belonging to our now completely absent Russian roommate. She had brought us both a cup of tea. I wanted to tell her what happened; I needed to share my pain but found it hard to begin. I felt like telling her what had happened would be like somehow admitting some failure on my part; that I hadn't been magnetic enough to prevent this from happening; that somehow, I wasn't a good enough boyfriend to Tanya, and that if I had been, she would not have even blinked at another man.

I found myself circling the key fact at first but not saying it. I began by asking Becky if she remembered the part of the evening last night when Tanya and Nadia had gone for drinks. She said she did. I asked her if she remembered that they had taken a long time to return. She said she thought she noticed that. I asked if she knew that Tanya had said she had run into her aunt at the station, and got chatting in her car for a while, which was why she was so long. She said she didn't know about that bit. I didn't know why I wasn't just coming out with what I wanted to tell her, but I felt rising nerves in my chest in admitting it. I felt sick. I asked if she remembered that Tanya had a shower when she got back. She said she did notice that. I badly wanted to tell Becky to get her support and sympathy, but also, at the same time, I didn't want to tell her. It was getting to the moment now, and I felt a loss of control over my face. My right cheek felt like it was made of wax.

"Well, she didn't see her aunt. She made that up." I finally began to spew out the story. It felt like I was sicking up the facts.

"She went to the kiosk; you know the one on the crescent opposite the station…" my voice was quivering a lot now. I even felt embarrassed about that, too. It was proving so hard to tell Becky what I wanted to say to her.

It was like I had to admit to an embarrassing crime, and I was in front of the headteacher for judgement. But Becky was not judgemental, she was my friend, and her face looked supportive of me, so I finally managed to get it out.

"…the one that's run by those two guys…and she went in…and had sex with them." I blinked tears down my cheek.

"…with Nadia," I added the last bit quickly, as I

realised that without it, I had unintentionally maybe made it sound like Tanya had sex with both Vlad and Ivan by herself.

Becky did the right thing and just came over to me, sat on the edge of my bed and gave me a hug. We held each other for a few seconds, and it felt good, almost a relief to finally get it out, but I still felt pathetic. Becky said she was sorry and how horrible that must be for me, but didn't try to explain it all away. She just let the facts be the facts.

I pulled myself together fairly quickly after that, exhaling deeply. We talked about the matter a little more, and I relayed how Tanya said how sorry she was. I then explained that I didn't know what to do now about today, and travelling up to Moscow tomorrow, and so on. Once it was out, it was no longer a burden, at least.

After a while considering it all, Becky then went on to explain there was maybe something in the viewpoint that Tanya may have felt as if she was losing me, and it could have been a rebound type of action on her part, and that it certainly wasn't planned in any way.

I tried to tell Becky that I hadn't planned on dumping her, on flying away and forgetting about her, that I had some money, I planned to leave behind with Tanya, as we talked about her getting a flight to England to come and join me there. Just on a tourist visa, of course. We hadn't planned anything too far ahead.

"Is that what you want to do?"

"That's what I *thought* I wanted to do."

"Let me go and talk to her now," she said. "You can't just do nothing, especially with your leaving tomorrow."

A couple of hours later, I had cleaned myself up a bit and had also done half of my packing. We agreed that Becky would go and see Tanya to act as the mediator. I began to feel that Tanya had probably not acted to spite me or hurt me, but that maybe she was the one at the short end of the luck stick. She hadn't been herself over the previous few days. In retrospect, I could see that a little. Despite the pain I kept feeling when I imagined her with that big oaf of a contraband dealer, getting his rocks off.

There was a knock on the door, and Tanya appeared. She looked like she'd been crying as she entered the room. She was still wearing the jeans from last night, but as she removed her grey woollen coat, I noticed that she was wearing her red cotton shirt, which she knew I quite liked, and not last night's jumper. She looked embarrassed but earnestly towards me. I jumped up on Nikolay's bed which was furthest from the door and sat with my back to the wall. It was subconsciously probably quite defensive, but ignoring any signals, she came directly over and sat right next to me.

"Genry, I love you. I'm sorry. I love you so much, lapochka," she said straight away, which broke the ice and gave me reassurance. I could now decide to permit this to play out the easy way or the hard way. To say I was in two minds would be a massive understatement. I felt hugely let down, betrayed, and deceived. I would be on a plane in three days, and if I wanted it so, all this could be behind me forever. I also loved Tanya. Until about 2am last night, that is, when my commitment to that feeling was tested to the limit. She still loved me, she said, so did I still love her? Could I still love her?

We talked for an hour, and I explained how hurt I was. I'm not sure if I really explained it well, as I was monosyllabic, picking at the stray threads of the bedding and not meeting her gaze. This was in Russian, don't forget, although I had much improved over the last six months, it was a tough conversation all the same. I felt that I certainly made it clear that I was devastated by her actions of the night before. She articulated her feelings much better than me, as firstly, it was her mother tongue, and secondly, women are from Venus and men are from Mars. She remade the case that Becky had led to me open up to, that she was also the victim of our situation. It was a relationship that stood in a very precarious place. I was leaving. She was being left behind. I was going back to my easy life in the west - of supermarkets, restaurants, with flowers on roundabouts, stability and comfort. I could easily forget her. For most of my time in Russia, we were here together, properly together. She was my girlfriend. I would be gone by next week, and I could become my old self.

But she would *still be here*, she said. Who would she be? She could not be Genry's girlfriend anymore if Genry wasn't here. Would she be Tanya, the girlfriend, or ex-girlfriend, of the guy who isn't here anymore? She said that over the last few days and weeks, she had begun to realise that she was going to be just her again, having to stand on her own two feet, to look after her own happiness, as I would just be a memory. She had been scared by that. She hadn't planned or intended to do what she did last night, she said, but she was hurting inside. She said throughout that she loved me, and I felt that I believed her and her pain and impending loss.

"I don't want to lose you either," I said, tears in my eyes. "I want you to come to England and be with me, " I heard myself saying.

I began to process everything as she had been talking. The next few days would be easier if we were together in practical terms. If I could just park this soul searching. While that may sound shallow and insensitive, I genuinely needed time to think about things. I needed to adequately examine the depth of my feelings.

But I didn't have time. I had to pack today. Ideally, I had to travel tomorrow with Tanya to her friend's place in Moscow, then visit the embassy, and then get on a plane. My brain began to kick into the practical and logical mode.

I also genuinely really felt strong love, attraction, and desire for her now, right at this moment. She was laying herself bare, imploring me to love her back.

"If you want to come to England, that is?" I asked, "I can leave enough money for you to get a ticket. I won't need the rest of the money I brought. It should easily be enough. When this term finishes, you can come and be with me in England. This was chapter 1. Shall we do for chapter 2?"

"Yes, yes, please, Genry!" she said as she lunged up the bed and threw her arms around me, kissed me, and lay her head on my chest. I bristled, involuntarily, at the thought of her with the meathead from last night. She sensed it.

"But... I am not happy, still... with what you did," I said. "How can I believe that you love me after that?"

I couldn't believe myself, sinking so low as to think about taking advantage of her guilty conscience for some *make up* sex. But I knew I was going to. I genuinely believed her remorse now and did not question her love, nor my own for that matter. I felt an emotional and physical need for her to trump or cancel out what had happened. She was vulnerable, I knew that, but I, too, needed my confidence bolstered.

"I think we had better make sure the door is locked," I said.

CHAPTER 44

The next day, Sunday, at 10 am, I finally boarded a train one last time leaving Voronezh. I had only ever taken the overnight sleeper to Moscow before, but there was also a daytime train on Sundays, which was a bit more expensive and a little faster, arriving before 6 pm.

Having now patched things up with Tanya, parking my feelings temporarily, I travelled with her and Alina, carrying out our plan to stay together in Moscow for my final two nights in this country. We were joined on the train by Vicky and her friend Maggie. Somewhere between a strawberry blonde and a redhead, and with a black greatcoat of almost a military-style, Maggie had been in the same student group as Vicky two years before. She'd been visiting Vicky (and Russian friends she'd made) for the past few days and was now on her way home.

I had only met Maggie that morning for the first time, but she came across as a straight-talking practical person, and I was, in fact, quite pleased with my travelling entourage. Vicky needed to visit the Embassy to record the details of my situation in her capacity as a group representative. If I'd been alone, I'd have been absorbed by introspection. If just with Tanya, it could have been an emotional test. But with two Russian girls and two English girls travelling with me, I felt well looked after, nicely balanced, and protected from my worries about my situation. Maggie was suitably impressed by my tale.

The previous afternoon had been a demonstration of Tanya's commitment to me. I was still pushing aside my feelings of doubt for our future even now. There was so much going on. I couldn't fully understand my feelings, so I had pulled the shutters down halfway on them as a coping mechanism, no doubt. She had spent the time in my room demonstrating her devotion to me, and I half guiltily just accepted it. It was hard to resist. We rearticulated our love for one another and agreed that she would come and join me in Bristol after the academic year finished for her here. This was her last year of studies in Voronezh, although I still had one more year to complete. She would spend the next three months concentrating on finishing her course with as decent a result as she could and would then get an open return ticket on a six-month tourist visa, which we could repeat after that, we assumed, but those details were for the future. Alexei could help her do all of that, she said, with his ever-increasing number of return trips to London that he was somehow making, he'd become the expert.

She had left my room mid-afternoon to get herself packed for the short stay in Moscow, and for my part, it hadn't taken too long to finish packing; I arrived with only what I could carry in a big rucksack and a smaller holdall, and that was the way I was departing. All the things I had bought over the last few months, such as the fan heater and some kitchen stuff, I naturally left behind, as well as the few English novels I had now read. On the subject of books, however, I did manage to get a few Russian language copies of some literary classics in my bag; some Chekhov plays, Bulgakov's *The Master and Margarita*, and my favourite, *Crime and Punishment*, by Dostoyevsky. I thought these hardbacks would look good back on my bookshelf at home, wherever home was next going to be.

I still hadn't written to anyone back home to say that I was returning, not my parents or the university. Neither expected me for at least seven more weeks or so, and I wanted to land back there before deciding how to broach this. I would aim for my sister's friend, Emma's place in Brixton, south London, first. I had been there a couple of times, as my sister used to share the apartment with Emma. Emma was one of my sister's best friends from college, and they'd come to London together to seek their fortune. This began with a series of temp jobs before they got an entry-level position in the same department at the Press Association. Although my sister, Anna, had left to go travelling across Asia, Emma was still there with a new flatmate, and I am sure she would make some temporary sofa space for me.

I spent part of early Saturday evening having a final meal with Becky, Jane, Al and Tom. As all these people were from my Bristol course, and I would see them all back home soon enough, it was good to have the familiarity of home faces around me for my last supper. It was a chilled-out affair, no party or dramas this time. I also went around our floor, and the floor above, saying my goodbyes to a few other people; Gus, Jim, and the guys from Edinburgh; Gwyn, who I'd found with some of the new St Petersburg arrivals; and Abby, Claire and the Nottingham crowd.

Abby surprised me by crying and giving me a big hug, squeezing me very tight for a full-frontal body clasp, which for a second felt so intimate that it should perhaps have to remain as our little secret. When I approached Connor, he extended his hand to shake mine, and the other he wrapped around my shoulder for a partial embrace. My situation had been maybe exacerbated by Connor and the upstairs guys continuing to smoke the grass in the hostel without trying to hide it. Ironically, I had given it up a long time back, while he had scented the whole place with weed aroma, and it may have been that which had prompted the Deconat to act in the first place. Seeing him now, still smiling to himself, was mildly offending me, to be honest.

"See you back in England then!" he said, before

adding, "Where are you going to go when you first get back, I mean?"

"Let me bring you up to speed on that; I haven't got a clue; you are now up to speed!" I replied, slightly getting my knickers in a twist. He just raised his eyes at my ever so subtle tantrum.

"Oh, well, good luck. See you in September, anyway." I detected a tiny bit more humility from him that time.

Issa and Mamadou said they hoped to see me in Bristol, which surprised me. Issa told me with a straight face that he would come over to visit Gwyn next term, and I was genuinely surprised by that. My first thought was to wonder if Gwyn even knew about this. It seemed that Issa was taking advantage of her generous nature, but I didn't give anything away to him. Mamadou said he was already trying to find out about any postgraduate courses he could take in Bristol, as he wanted to come too. I embraced both, as they were friends in any case, and said I'd look forward to seeing them if they came, not believing it at the time. Fast forward six months, and they somehow did turn up in Bristol. I did not know this at the time, but I would spend the following Christmas day with Mamadou in Bristol, waiting tables - serving Christmas dinners in a Trust House Forte restaurant on the motorway services of the M32, as a temp job.

I left the hostel with the minimal ceremony the following day. Becky, Jane and Al came down to the ground floor with me, Becky linking arms with me down the steps asking me to give my best to England, while Al carried my backpack like a gentleman. We were met in the foyer by Vicky and Maggie and waited a few minutes for Alina and Tanya to join us. Vyacheslav was in the office room by the front door, the "kabinet", busying himself with something on the desk. To my mind, it also looked like he was just pretending to work as if his real purpose was simply to be around to see that I left. He didn't look at or speak to me, but Vicky popped in there for a moment. I didn't know whether they talked about me or other group administration subjects. After final hugs with my friends, I joined my four travelling companions and walked out of the front door, down the steps, around the building to the right, towards Ulitsa Mira.

The front of the train station was bustling when we got there a few minutes later. People were filing in and out of the main front door going about their lives, and others were standing on the wide-open front paved area. Some were smoking in small groups of people waiting for their train or fellow comrades to arrive, while even those who weren't smoking looked as if they could be as their exhaled breath evaporated into steamy clouds just the same. I entered the inner hall with my backpack over my shoulder and holdall in my left hand with my right hand free and began to feel for my wallet approaching the ticket window. People crisscrossed the room in front of me when suddenly, the unmistakable figures of the two Georgians were right before me, hands in pockets, seemingly on their way out. My blood rushed around my chest again in an instinctive panic. Drawn to Georgi, the only one I had really spoken to before anyway, he smiled at me and held out his hand. I took it in mine without thinking and exchanged the physical greeting.

"Genry!" he smiled, almost warmly. I relaxed. My fraction of a second inner reaction was to think that he did not appear surprised to see me. But then I realised that I was going home now, and nothing could change this.

"Georgi," was all I said in reply.

"Have a good trip!" he said, releasing my hand, and just walked on past me. I didn't even have a chance to say anything back. I stopped and turned to watch the two thickset Georgians with their dark leather jackets continue towards the exit and out through the doors without looking back.

I resumed collecting the tickets with the others, without saying anything just then. I was stunned, perhaps. Had they, like with Vyacheslav earlier, specifically been there to witness and confirm I was on my way out of the country? I had previously wondered if it was a coincidence that they had turned up on the hostel steps precisely when I was supposed to be identifying them in mugshots or if it was a set-up. Now I was surer than ever it wasn't a coincidence. This was only the third time I had seen them, and as before, coincided precisely with significant moments towards either my recruitment to whatever purpose they had in mind or my deportation as it now felt like. I just wanted to get on that train now. I needed to leave.

On the train, I had to go through the whole story from the beginning again for Maggie's benefit, about how we thought the entire thing was dodgy from the start with the meetings in secret to start with. Hiding in cupboards and refusing to come out from class particularly amused Maggie. Alina was intrigued, for she had not heard the full details before and was getting a translated version of my account to Maggie from Tanya as we went along. Alina's English was virtually non-existent, and although Tanya's was not great either, she was so familiar with the events that she could work out which bit I was talking about.

"O, bozhe moi, kakoi koshmar!" was Alina's frequent contribution ("Oh my goodness, what a nightmare").

Finally, I told everyone about Georgi at the train station, by which time we were already over an hour away from Voronezh. It seemed to confirm the conspiracy theory of this whole thing to everyone, including Alina. "O bozhe moi, kaki ooblyudiki!" ("Oh, my goodness, what bastards!")

It was good to talk it through with the girls on the train, as I would have to relate the events of the previous weeks and months to the British Embassy the next day anyway. It also helped Vicky check her story against mine, too.

While I was open and honest with her about buying the grass in the first place, I would downplay that part. I'd just be saying something along the lines of *I was at a party/ it was there/ some of us managed to get hold of some.* The group obtained it, and it was used around the hostel. I could relate the rest of my story exactly as it happened. The main point was that it seemed this caused an issue for the authorities, and I was made a scapegoat, for whatever reason.

That night, we all went to the Moscow apartment of Alina's brother, Mikhail. Vicky and Maggie had a cheap grey student hostel booked for the night (the one everyone always used on their trips up from Voronezh), but as it turned out to be very close to Mikhail's anyway, they came to his place for dinner and drinks with us. We'd enjoyed each other's company on the train, and they had nothing else in particular to do.

Mikhail was in his late twenties. He sported big square glasses and a terrible brown moustache. Impressively, he was already a *bizness* man. I had met Mikhail at Oleg's apartment on the night of the ambulance ride but hadn't talked to him back then. He owned a metals company in Moscow which seemed to export metal kitchenware to the UK. When he heard that I was taking thirty of Alexei's watches back with me to London, it flickered an interest in him. He knew Alexei, having met him in both Moscow and Voronezh, and went on to explain a bit more about his business. It felt like he was keen to show me, and Tanya, that he could be just as impressive, if not more so, than Alexei.

He spoke directly to us, ignoring the two English girls and his sister, who presumably had heard it all before. Mikhail explained that he exported saucepans, frying pans and other pots and stuff for cooking. His price beat the competition, he went on, meaning he made a good living. He drew some of his designs on scrap paper for us, which looked rubbish and not exceptional, but then he revealed the unique selling proposition. While I was privately frowning at the basic frying pan outline that didn't even have a proper handle, he made his big reveal. The designs were basic on purpose with nothing intricate about them as the buyers were only buying them to smelt down for their metal value. Mikhail's business just traded metal disguised as pots and pans. Russia has enormous amounts of ferrous and non-ferrous metals, precious metals, too, for that matter. Mikhail wanted to export it to buyers in Europe, but the London Metal Exchange, for example, had official prices for each metal, which you couldn't fall below. As well as the regulations and other competition, he described how he overcame the challenges by calling his tin, copper or aluminium - a saucepan, frying pan or a tray. In this way, he could set his own prices and beat the per tonne official price. That's how I understood his business at any rate. He had a well-developed business mind for someone only a few years older than us, which was quite impressive.

Given he ran a successful international business, you may think his apartment would also be grand or expensive, but it wasn't. Simply put, property was not yet a developed market, residential blocks were all similar, and his two-bedroom place was the same as most others in layout. It was as plain and functional as most of the ones I had been in before.

The money that people like Mikhail had begun to make was still so new that all he could do with it was buy things like the flashy wristwatch I spotted. It was too soon for things like Maseratis or Manhattan-style lofts, as neither could be purchased in Moscow yet.

He also seemed keen on Tanya; he kept looking at her to see if she was impressed. With his curly, brown hair and flat and monotone voice finishing off his unattractive appearance, though, I didn't feel threatened concerning her. I still felt that my trump cards (being English, plans to bring her to the UK, and, in my view, being better looking than him) made me the winner. Well, I had my fingers crossed that it did, anyway. Nonetheless, I still liked Mikhail and thought I should probably keep his contact details for potential business opportunities in the future.

It turned out that this meeting did transpire into a future commercial relationship, by the way, and I ended up opening a UK limited company for him about a year later, as well as helping him get banking and other administrative services in London. I would have been amazed that night if someone had told me that in a year from then, I would be withdrawing not exactly small sums of cash from Mikhail's UK bank account, on his behalf, ahead of one of his business trips.

A few years later, I would also become the UK managing director of Interfax News Agency, the largest independent news agency for Russia and the CIS. I would have been even more surprised if a messenger from the future had told me that, although it is exactly what ended up happening.

The six of us enjoyed the evening; it was certainly no party, though, more of a meal and a chat. I didn't want to discuss my case all night with them or start with Mikhail again, so we listened to Maggie and Vicky's stories instead. But it was on my mind that I would have to report to the British Embassy to give my version of events for their records the next day. Vicky took some photos of us that night around the dinner table, clinking our glasses. One shows Tanya giving me a possessive all arm cuddle from behind, her head nuzzled into my shoulder, and her head tilted towards the camera. It almost says, "he's mine, and I won't let go".

CHAPTER 45

The next day my plan was to visit the embassy in the morning for my appointment and then buy a few last things in Moscow to take home. Then, after one more night at Mikhail's, I'd be on the early morning flight on Tuesday. I was planning to stuff as many blocks of 200 cigarettes in my luggage as possible, as they were cheap compared to the UK.

The British embassy in Moscow was situated in a prominent position on the Smolenskaya embankment looking out over the Moskva River. It was in an old and traditional part of the city with several nearby embassies. The new Arbat avenue was close by, a street I was familiar with as it led to some lanes I had been to as a tourist on my Moscow visits, including the Irlandski Dom. This was the *Irish House*, which we visited for two main reasons; it had a UK style mini supermarket where you could pick up things like PG tips tea bags, Bovril and other products that reminded you of home. It also had an Irish Bar, which was the closest feeling you could get in Russia to going to the pub. Here, you were guaranteed to find English speakers enjoying a pint (including Guinness on draught), such as British or American students, young professionals working for the few western companies setting up representation, or embassy workers. It also attracted what I assumed to be high-class Russian prostitutes. I don't really know if they were *high class* or not, nor do I really know what *high class* means, technically speaking, but they were very well turned out at any rate.

I approached the embassy walking along the river embankment, the pavement separated from the road by large banks of snow at the sides of the road. Dirty buses trundled past, filled with passenger's faces staring out through the steamed-up windows, Muscovites going about their lives. Lada cars zipped about in front and behind them. This city scene was played out all over the city and in cities all over Russia, no doubt.

Such a vast country but everywhere conforming to the same format. It was a format that I loved, for although it was living almost in a straight-jacket, the country was beginning to burst the seams of this jacket, desperate for new threads, and was therefore highly unpredictable, too.

It had excited me, even though I was now being removed. On the day I had arrived, one dollar was worth something like one hundred and twenty roubles, and six months later, it was over six hundred roubles to the dollar. Four years after this, it was nearly six thousand roubles to the dollar. Such fast inflation created a seat of the pants style economy and society. It fuelled the so-called wild west years in Russia and laid the conditions for the new breed of oligarchs who became billionaires overnight. In its simplest explanation, they borrowed money, often from the government, to buy national utilities at knock-down valuations, then had them valued at ten times that amount the following week. Crime and corruption ripped through the place. Three or four years later, I would be back in Moscow, having lunch with the CEO of Interfax News Agency in a quiet restaurant, while his armed bodyguard enjoyed his soup at the table next to us, pistol in his holster.

The embassy was an imposing 18th-century Neo-Gothic building with burnt umber yellow exterior walls and big windows arranged symmetrically on either side of the grand entrance. As I walked up the entrance steps, I stood on the central door step platform with six columns around its edges, holding up a veranda above my head, accessed from one of the presumably important first floor rooms. I entered the darkness of the doorway and paused so my eyes could adjust to the dark interior. Immediately inside to the right was a reception window with an office behind, with a pleasantly smiling woman in her forties looking to greet me. Ahead was a main inner foyer, the route guarded by two uniformed security men. I gave my name to the woman but realised as I did so that I didn't know the name of the person I was here to see. Vicky had merely told me to come at this time and that I was expected.

"Yes, Mr Pettit, I have you here," she said in a surprisingly reassuring English home counties accent, which wrapped me up like a blanket. It was as if by crossing the threshold into the building, I had almost flown the few thousand miles to London already.

She asked me to pass through the hallway and the security men and wait for someone to collect me from the main inner hallway shortly. There was a grand stairway in the double-height interior and dark wood panelling on most walls and alongside the staircase, which wrapped its way, left to right, around the walls and up to a first-floor landing. I found a selection of chairs and picked one to wait on. A man in his early forties carrying paperwork emerged from the far dark corner of the ground floor and traversed the hallway's hard floor towards me. I made to get up to greet him, but as I did so, he looked down and continued his angle diagonally across the space and carried on straight past me.

He was on another mission clearly, so I relaxed back into my seat feeling slightly foolish. Another noise signalled the entrance of another human being onto the scene, but this time I didn't move, keen to give off a more carefree vibe. I looked up more casually this time to see that it was a cleaner with one of those plug-in floor buffers, which whizzed around in circular fashion, polishing the floor as he held onto its handlebars. Watching him, I was contemplating that it would be quite fun to have a go. I realised how ridiculous it would be to ask for a try when I heard another "Mr Pettit?" from behind my left shoulder, as out of nowhere a youngish English woman had appeared to collect me.

"Yes," I stammered nervously, slowly rising to greet this person. I felt stupid to have initially mistaken the first person for my host and then been so focused on the cleaner to have even noticed my real chaperone approach me.

"Hello, I'm Liz Ruscombe," she said, extending her hand with a smile, "I'm assistant to the First Secretary here in Russia. Please come with me."

I followed her across the hall and up the impressive stairway to the first floor. At the midway turning point halfway between the floors, there hung a large portrait of Queen Elizabeth II in full Queen attire, complete with sash and crown.

I wasn't sure whether bow or curtsey and was about to make a joke to my own "Liz" in front of me before a sense of decency got the better of me, thankfully, and we just walked on past. We entered an office a short way along the first-floor corridor, and Liz introduced me to a man called Richard Lightfoot, who she informed me, was the First Secretary of the British Embassy.

As we entered the room, Lightfoot stood up from behind his desk in front of the window and came to greet me with a handshake and friendly smile. I sat down at a chair in front of his desk while he resumed his place behind it. He was a tall, slim man of around fifty years old, dressed in what I would call office worker clothes, or maybe I should more accurately say civil servant attire: a crisp white shirt, buttoned-down collar, navy-blue tie, dark trousers and shoes. Hanging on a coat stand near the desk, I noticed a matching dark jacket with a collection of other coats and hats. I wondered if Mr Lightfoot knew about the unwritten rule that you were not to put the flaps of these hats down unless it was cripplingly cold. Along one wall was a bookcase with a few books and ornaments, including a silver teapot, which looked like it was part of a samovar set but also merely ornamental. There were two desks in the room, and Liz took her place behind the other one on the right.

He offered tea or coffee to me, and I was happy to accept coffee which Liz then went to fetch and returned remarkably quickly with coffee and water for all of us, including biscuits. Even biscuits such as these I had not seen in a long time, so I felt yet another step closer to home. It must have been prepared before she came down to collect me, just in time to stop me asking to have a go on the floor polisher.

I spent the next hour in Richard Lightfoot's office speaking with him and Liz Ruscombe about my ordeal in Voronezh. Lightfoot explained that they were going to provide me with my "emergency" British Airways ticket and other necessary exit documents, but that he also wanted to go over events with me and sign a statement that we were now going to write up together before I left. He explained that this statement would serve as a record of my version of events, remaining on file.

I felt a bit of trepidation in having to do this, but Lightfoot was sympathetic in the end and had a slightly tired look about him that made me feel more relaxed. A relatively big life event to me, he managed to make it look routine to him, although I could not imagine he was dealing with repatriations and deportations every week; maybe he was, for all I really knew.

"Henry, try not to worry," he said. "It may not be used for any other purpose than the file, but if for any reason your repatriation, or events leading up to it, need to be discussed again in future, by the Russians here or in the Home Office back in the UK, then we'll have this record."

"OK, thanks," I said, taking a sip of my coffee.

"We'll also help and make sure you don't put anything down that you shouldn't," he added.

I explained everything all over again, but I didn't include anything about where the grass came from in the beginning. It had appeared from somewhere, as these things do, and I was at a party or two where most people were partaking. People smoked joints at parties the world over, so I knew that this shouldn't be a real shock to anyone in a position of authority.

I confirmed that it happened, and I was also there. Almost a year ago to the day at a press conference on March 29th, 1992, during his ultimately successful presidential campaign, Bill Clinton admitted to trying marijuana. It was at a party during his student years (in England as it happens), but he "did not inhale" and did not enjoy it. I reckoned, was a generally non-scandalous thing to be admitting to. If it was alright for him to admit to being about it, then it was no scandal for me, either. Later, when Clinton did become President of the United States, he told another press conference, in 1998, that he didn't have sex with a particular woman, Ms Lewinsky, when in fact he most definitely did. He also introduced her to cigars, I read somewhere. I would wager that he inhaled and enjoyed the marijuana too, but was economical with the truth.

I reminded Lightfoot that the conditions in the hostel were poor, the hygiene standards in the toilets and bathrooms awful, mentioned the broken kitchen windows that allowed snow to blow directly onto the cooker hobs. This was the background, with possible corruption, that I thought it worth painting that led to the newspaper article in the Moscow Times. The article entitled "where has all our money gone?" had no doubt caused much embarrassment to the Russians and maybe had contributed to their need to hit back at the British students.

I asserted that I didn't think I had done anything particularly wrong except to be present at certain parties. The fact that some students had been smoking marijuana in the hostel had maybe irritated and frustrated the administration in Voronezh, who saw it as a stick to hit us back with. I wasn't sure why I was personally selected for their revenge. Maybe it was because I had a Russian girlfriend, I offered, or because I had plans to rent an apartment in town and leave the hostel altogether. Related to this, I told them that two of our group, Tom and Paul, had already rented property in the city early on. Renting places was not a crime, albeit maybe another embarrassment for them, so the illicit substances was perhaps something they wanted to latch onto.

As I told them about Tom and Paul's place, I recalled to my mind the house warming party they'd had and how a group of exuberant attendees, not myself, had dared each other to run around the block naked, in nothing but boots. I didn't tell Lightfoot about this, though, inwardly shaking my head at why my mind always brings up inappropriate things at the wrong time.

I told them about my early morning questioning in February by people I took to be police, but who my Russian friends later suggested were more likely to be ex KGB than real police.

"They told me they had witnesses and records, and of dates and times, of the parties when marijuana was smoked." I explained, "It was all in Russian and was quite hard to keep up. They also said that I had bought it and had sold it to some of the other students, which is *completely* untrue!"

I insisted upon this with genuine feeling as I had not sold it to anyone, in fact.

"But they just kept going at me and were very intimidating, and then went on to tell me that I was looking at seven years in a Russian prison. I was scared, as the dates of parties all sounded roughly right. They said if I helped them find the drug dealers by telling them who they were, and identifying them in a book of mugshots, then they wouldn't arrest me, or detain me, or whatever."

"OK, Henry, that doesn't sound very nice for you," said Lightfoot. "As you say, all in Russian, too, with no interpreter or other official accompaniment? What happened next?"

I went on, "Yes. I just didn't know what was happening to me. It was unreal. But as it happens, I was once offered some grass by two Georgian guys around two or three months earlier, in our hostel one night. These guys I had never seen before, or since. I said "no" to them, of course, but I told them about the Georgian drug dealers under the pressure of the questioning and the prison threat. But I never, in fact, bought any from them, or anyone! The police, KGB, whoever they were, seemed pleased to hear this and even said they'd been tracking those guys for a while, so asked me if I could meet them again to look at some photos."

"OK, this does sound like a bit of typical tactic, I am sorry to say, Henry, where someone can be frightened and threatened into doing something, under the threat of prison if they don't," said Lightfoot.

I agreed that I, too, thought this to be true, adding my Russian friends had also told me this afterwards.

"Well, after I agreed to meet them in a hotel that weekend to look at mugshots, they agreed to let me go and insisted that I was not to talk to anyone about it at all, neither my English nor my Russian friends." I continued, "I went back to my Russian friends' apartment and hid for a bit, but I couldn't stop myself from telling them!"

"They then told me straight away that this was typical KGB, and they couldn't have any evidence for something that I didn't do. They basically told me not to meet them and not go along with any of it. If this was official, they would have made it official, but as they were doing it in secret, it was completely dodgy, they said," I added.

I described a few of the other sequences of events; the hiding in my room, the car outside the apartment, the bumping into me in the street, their attempts to get me from class, and of course, how the two Georgians magically appeared on the hostel doorstep, and yesterday at the train station.

"OK, I think from what you have described today and what we have already managed to put together," Lightfoot concluded, "everything is clear. Old habits and all that. These seem to be tactics similar to those used by the KGB, who officially are no longer in existence, but whose personnel still do exist. I think anyone would have had concerns about how you were approached, and you were rightly very confused by it all."

"We could either fight this or, as explained already to you via your rep, you can take the flight back home, which may be an easier option all around."

I thought about what he said for a moment and about Alexei's brother.

"Thank you, but even though I don't think I have done anything wrong, especially not what they said I have done, I am more than happy to go home. I don't really trust their justice system or how this will play out, even with your offer of support," I replied.

After spending just over two hours at the embassy, I was all done by mid-afternoon.

Liz Ruscombe gave me a copy of the typed-up account of my ordeal, which she had been typing up throughout, for me to review and sign. Entitled "Events Leading to the Repatriation of Henry Pettit, March 22nd, 1993." It was seven pages long. There was a copy for me to take away and one for the embassy to retain.

I read through it, shuddering at some memories, and signed both documents.

They passed me an A4 size envelope with my exit visa and a British Airways ticket for a flight the following day from Moscow's Sheremetyevo airport.

I was emotional by the time I stepped down the front doorsteps of the embassy and began to walk out along the bank of the river Moskva towards the Novy Arbat.

I was pleased to be leaving the threat of prison and the ridiculous harassment I'd had in Voronezh behind me, but I also had to admit I had never felt as alive as I did right then. This country was enormous, historical and unforgettable. My experiences in the last several months, having studied Russia through the literature of Tolstoy and Dostoyevsky, almost felt like some dramatic novel, including, of course, the romance with Tanya.

I was going to meet her in the Irish house bar at 4 pm, and I had a bit of time to kill, so I was happy to walk and be alone with my thoughts. She said I had to get there before her, as she didn't want to be a Russian girl waiting by herself in that place, of course, due to how it could be misinterpreted. That in itself was weird compared to my previous life. My girlfriend of the year before in Bristol, Lucy, would never have had to tell me to get to a venue first to avoid any risk that she'd be mistaken for a prostitute. I'd have just had to get there first as it was simply polite to not keep a girl waiting.

Russia was just such a different place to England. Russia was stimulating, and I felt that this had been the best year of my life. I'd gone from a boy to a man. The romance had been intense and real. Tanya had made me feel so good about myself, and I am sure I had made her feel good about herself, too. But it wasn't over, for she would come over and live with me in England, and she would be with me, back in Bristol.

For sure, her infidelity had hurt me a great deal, but I still wanted to enjoy being with her, and I wanted to have her in England. I wanted to transport the new me, with her, back home. I felt that it would make me more of a person. My insecurities were quickly bolstered by the thought. I sympathised with the reasons for her actions somehow and felt sorry for her despairing soul that night, even though I was angry about it. I wasn't ready to stop enjoying the fantastic highs and satisfaction that she brought. I could tell that she loved me, and that she wanted to prove this to me. Even though some part of me, perhaps subconsciously, had begun to realise our future was possibly destined to not be forever, I wanted it to continue some more anyway. My vanity and selfishness wanted her still on my arm, improving me, making me look good. I could also see how much it meant to her for it to continue, and she'd set her sights on more time with me in England, and I didn't want to deny her that. I still loved her and wanted to give her that next stage, too, with no promises to myself or my own heart, yet, about the long term.

I walked past the entrance to a metro station and, strung along the pavement outside, were kiosks selling the usual cigarettes, vodka and other unrecognisable alcohol brands. It seemed that I might have some joy here for the last purchases I wanted. I didn't really want to buy them from a kiosk with high upkeep and higher costs, but something like the boots of cars back in Voronezh where the prices would be lower. Sure enough, as the line of kiosks dwindled, some street traders had stuff on blankets and upturned boxes on the pavements. I spied their wares with one eye so as not to look like a potential customer until I was ready. I spotted one person offering coffee tins from Brazil and boxes with Chinese writing that I had no idea what they could even be. He also had several blocks of cigarettes; L&M, Dunhill, Marlboro red and Marlboro lights. I bought five blocks of Marlboro Lights, 1000 cigarettes in all, at a fraction of UK prices. Just what I was looking for.

I handed the unshaven salesman the money, and he squirrelled the notes into his pocket as I watched, wondering if the ash from his own cigarette hanging from his mouth would fall into his pocket, too. I would keep one block for myself and sell the rest in England.

I would get maybe twice what I paid for them, but the customer would still be getting a good bargain. Russia had made me more entrepreneurial than I had already been. If I couldn't fit them all into my luggage, back at Mikhail's place, I would leave the remainder with Tanya.

"Electric shaver? You need one?" the hawker asked me, producing a couple of boxes of Chinese electric shavers from behind the cigarettes and holding them up to me expectantly. "750 roubles," he added.

"No thanks."

"500 then?" he added, quickly.

"No…thanks."

"Suit yourself," he said without looking back at me and resumed rearranging his cigarettes on the blanket.

CHAPTER 46

It was like we had been anaesthetised or prescribed some anti-depressant at least, on the final evening in Moscow. Our impending separation created an eerie atmosphere, and the last hours were uneventful, ponderous. I met Tanya in the Irish House bar, and we had a drink and some dinner - steak and chips, quite a treat by local standards - before heading back for one last sleep before the *offski*. We'd been dealt the hammer blow of our enforced separation, and we were in something like a state of shock, going through the motions. I had committed events to paper in the Embassy. It was government knowledge now and no longer my private experience. Our fate was sealed, and I was forced from the country, even though it was partly my choice. We held hands, we looped arms, we kissed.

But we also disappeared into our thoughts as I drifted ahead to landing in Heathrow and the practicalities of my next steps. For her part, I guessed that Tanya was thinking forward to travelling back to Voronezh, empty-handed as it were, without me. Alina and Mikhail had made themselves scarce, so we had the apartment to ourselves, which was kind of them, but maybe the company would have helped distract us. We only had ourselves and our relationship to look at. Although it was not the end, it felt like the end of something. It was the end of this part of the adventure. We didn't frolic around with high energy or anything like that; there was no reason to celebrate our last night. It was solemn but loving. Tanya kept fixing me with sad eyes as if trying to read what was in mine. As we lay in bed, we held each other tight and entwined together, not wanting to let go.

"We'll see each other soon, OK?" I assured her, "it's just a few weeks".

She wiped tears from her eyes, and I kissed her wet cheeks. "Yes, OK."

In the morning, I passed her one of the blocks of Marlboro lights that wouldn't fit in the case to take back to Voronezh. I also handed over a decent amount of my remaining dollars. She and I knew it was more than enough for her flight to London, and I think this cheered us both up. That little folded wad of notes was proof we'd be with each other again.

"We'll be together again soon," I said.

"For the next step of our adventures?" she smiled.

"For Chapter 2," I replied, "and I'll write all the time until then".

###

The British Airways flight took off for Heathrow from Moscow's Sheremetyevo airport the following day. And yes, I was on it, of course.

As the plane made its descent through the cloud canopy, I was welcomed back to England by the unexciting sight of rows and rows of semi-detached houses of west London's suburbs. Orderly roads, well-behaved traffic streaming logically around the main roads, flyovers, and manicured roundabouts. All bathed in overcast English spring weather. Bump. As I landed back to earth, with a mildly painful jolt, already Russia seemed a million miles away.

I hadn't told my parents I was coming home, and if possible, I wasn't going to, either. If I could get away with it, I'd wait until the intended return date about seven more weeks away, then somehow get them (whoever was going to meet me) to meet me somewhere other than Heathrow; then I'd pretend I came home along with everyone else. In fact, this plan was doomed to failure, as I couldn't communicate any of this from Russia. I ended up calling my dad about a week later and giving him the Embassy version of events, more or less. *Flabbergasted* was the word he used to summarise his reaction once I had told him everything, but he was supportive rather than outraged. He showed some sympathy with how I got mixed up in events out of my control. He insisted we speak to the organisers to ensure the Home Office knew our version of the truth. It was better if I volunteered it to them rather than it coming out in the future when a passport control flagged an issue one day. When I called Felicity Cave at the RLUS programme, she was surprisingly cheerful and told me flatly that the Home Office were well aware, and nothing more needed to be done.

As I filed off the plane, though, I mainly thought of putting one foot in front of the other and the practical steps. Firstly, to Brixton for a night or two at Emma's place, then I'd be making my way to Bristol by train where I'd stay with some of my friends, back in my old stomping ground. I hadn't contacted them; it would be a case of turning up on the doorstep and surprising someone.

Then, it occurred to me that I'd have some explaining to do and would have to tell them the whole story. I resolved there and then, in the baggage reclaim hall, that I simply had to ensure that Tanya fulfilled our plan and got herself over here. I needed her with me, by my side, as I did love her. I didn't want to just slip back into my old life, and for this to just become a story I told about the time I had in Russia. I gathered my rucksack, loaded it onto the trolley, and headed for passport control.

When I got to my turn at the window, I looked at the customs official.

"Hello," I said.

"Good afternoon," he said back and waved me through.

There was nobody in the arrivals hall to meet me, of course, so I followed the signs for the London Underground. As the tube train clattered along the tracks, I observed the other passengers. Some looked bored, others were reading books with concentrated faces. It was just another normal day for them. My mind wandered to what my university teachers would say to me. I suspected they would think there was no smoke without fire, but they couldn't punish me further as the official documents confirmed that I was a victim of a horrible series of events. As for Tanya, she would come to England, I was sure of it. But how it would be when she was here, I had no way of knowing. This place already seemed so different to Russia. Would it work out? I would have to wait and see.

ABOUT THE AUTHOR

Henry Pettit graduated from Bristol University in 1994 with a degree in Russian and Politics. He moved into a career in the news publishing industry and spent fifteen years as the Managing Director of the London office of Interfax Russian News Agency. He has also worked in the UK newspaper and magazine sector in collective copyright licensing, and founded his own consulting business that serves news publishers around the world. He lives in Kent in England, with his wife and three children.

References:

The Moscow Times article, Jan 20th 1993: <ins>https://www.themoscowtimes.com/archive/british-students-ask-where-have-fees-gone</ins>

Printed in Great Britain
by Amazon

15758791R00255